THE WOUNDED WARRIOR'S Wife

A Novel

by

Hannah Conway

Published by

Olivia Kimbrell Press™

Olivia Kimbrell Press™

The Wounded Warrior's Wife, a Novel

PUBLISHED BY: Olivia Kimbrell Press™*, P.O. Box 4393, Winchester, KY 40392-4393.

The Olivia Kimbrell Press™ colophon and open book logo are trademarks of Olivia Kimbrell Press™.

*Olivia Kimbrell Press™ is a publisher offering true to life, meaningful fiction from a Christian worldview intended to uplift the heart and engage the mind.

Some scripture quotations courtesy of the King James Version of the Holy Bible.

Some scripture quotations courtesy of the New King James Version of the Holy Bible, Copyright© 1979, 1980, 1982 by Thomas-Nelson, Inc. Used by permission. All rights reserved.

Library Cataloging Data

Conway, Hannah (Hannah Conway) 1983
 Wounded Warrior's Wife, The / Hannah Conway
 275 p. 20cm x 12.5cm (8in x 5in.)
Summary: Newlywed Collier unexpectedly deploys again leaving military wife Whitleigh hundreds of miles from family and friends. She struggles with loneliness and faith counting the days until he returns. Unfortunately, his homecoming makes things much worse than she could have imagined.

ISBN: 978-1-939603-53-1 (perfect bound) ISBN: 978-1-939603-58-6 (trade paperback)
ISBN: 978-1-939603-52-4 (ebook)

U.S. Library of Congress Control Number (PCN): 2014949656

1. Christian fiction 2. man-woman relationships 3. military romance 4. love stories 5. family relationships 6. Christian romance

PS3568.H656 0922 2014
[Fic.] 813.6 (DDC 23)

THE WOUNDED WARRIOR'S Wife

A Novel

by

Hannah Conway

I want to thank God for granting me an opportunity to write and for giving me a story to tell. I'm thankful He makes beauty from ashes, gives hope to the hopeless, and is in the business of restoration.

A huge thank you to my husband who has served our country valiantly. I admire your courage and willingness to sacrifice for our country and for our family. You do it because that's who you are. Thank you for all the late night coffee shop runs to help keep me going — best husband ever. I love you always and forever.

Thank you to my kiddos who endured way too many chicken nugget suppers while I completed this manuscript. I couldn't have finished without the love, support and motivation of my family.

Mom, Dad, Luke — thank you for being who you are, for always knowing I could do anything I set my mind to.

I want to thank the ACFW, MBT, and all my writer friends for your encouragement, guidance, and instruction.

To Olivia Kimbrell Press, thank you for bringing me on board your company. To Heather McCurdy, my amazing editor, and Debi Warford, my talented cover artist. I'm honored to even be associated with you.

To Stephanie Reeder, you're truly a talented photographer and I'm grateful that you equipped me with professional photos for my author pages and propaganda.

There are so many of you from my past and present who are dear to me. Those I love, listened to, laughed, and cried with. I've sat at your tables, shared meals, and swapped recipes. We've done life together — the good and the bad. We've prayed with one another. I've prayed for you and I know you've prayed for me. You've loved me at my worst and with all my quirks. I acknowledge and appreciate you! You're a gift from God.

To those who critiqued my manuscript before it was released, God bless you for your time and effort. All of you supporting the book launch, wow, thank you! I wish I could hug all of you.

One more big thank you doesn't seem enough, but it's all I can offer on this page. Thank you and God bless each one of you!

Dedication

This book is dedicated to my husband.

Look at us go!

Romans 8:28

THE last hints of sunlight poured through the modest bathroom window. The tub water, now lukewarm, retreated in slow waves across Whitleigh Cromwell's neck. Mellow tunes, defending the house from silence, drifted through the tiny tiled room. No matter the soft, easy nature of the melody, there was nothing relaxing or distracting about her *Elements of Education* textbook.

She crossed her eyes and tapped a pencil on her bottom lip before circling a long, drawn out explanation of differentiation. How many more definitions did she have to underline? Senior-itis was kicking in two semesters too early.

Whitleigh sank lower in the tub. Studying would've been much more enjoyable with Collier home. Life in general was better with him around.

She huffed. With a wet finger, she turned the page. Waiting was the worst. Worse than reading a bound book of boredom, but that's Army life — hurry up and wait.

She couldn't complain too much though. Whitleigh closed her eyes for a moment. Her lips curved into a smile. In a manner of weeks it would be over soon. All of it. The wait, army life — all done. Life with her husband could resume as normal. She sighed, her breath creating ripples in the water. Weeks would be no problem to pass compared to the year they'd nearly conquered, but studying seemed to be an inadequate way to pass time.

The words in the text blurred. She squinted through the wire frames sliding to the tip of her nose, unable to make much more sense of the paragraph.

It had been a long day. A long year.

Whitleigh snapped the book shut with a clap. Scarce patches of bubbles from the bath threatened to ruin her note page where it was balanced on the edge of the tub. She pushed the papers to safety on a footstool turned bath-time desk. An angry buzzing rang out. Whitleigh lunged from the sudsy waters, clambering for the clattering cellphone perched atop the toilet seat. A stack of textbooks fell prey to her flailing limbs.

"Whit." The line cracked and popped. "Can you hear me?"

"Sorta." She squealed and groused as soapy shampoo suds seeped into her eyes.

"Whit?"

"I'm here." She swatted the volume on the MP3 player stand and felt around for a towel. A shirt would do the trick. Shampoo seemed as effective as pepper spray.

"Hold on." Grumbles echoed from the other end of the line. The static stopped. Whatever he did worked. "Better?"

"Loads." She laughed, her eyes still stinging as she twisted her soaking hair into a towel. "Collier, oh my gosh. I've missed you. How are you?"

The line crackled. Whitleigh threw on a robe before walking down the hall and into their bedroom. Even their phone conversation required patience with the interference and delay. She skirted around their bedroom, mindful of the books and folded laundry ready to be put away.

"I'm good, Sweets." She could almost hear the smile in his tired voice. "Just missing you."

"You counting down?" Her stomach knotted. Things were looking up.

"Yeah."

"Don't sound too excited." Whitleigh plopped on the bed and gathered a few pillows underneath her arms.

"I'm excited. Just some things, you know, going on."

Whitleigh frowned. Though Korea hadn't been a war zone in fifty years, Collier and the other soldiers spent a lot of time drilling in the field. Must be tedious work.

"Look Whit, um, I don't have much time."

"What's wrong?"

The stories that came from Korea were horrid. Soldiers cheating on their wives, drunken bar fights, prostitutes roaming the streets. She shoved those thoughts from her mind.

Not her Collier. Not ever.

"Remember that piece you heard on the news?"

"Yeah." She rolled her eyes. How could she forget? The media had about given her a heart attack. "News stations need to get their facts straight."

Collier coughed. "Anyway." He coughed again. His tone echoed hints of anxiety.

Whitleigh fidgeted with a piece of tangled wet hair falling from the towel. Collier never hesitated with his words.

"Well, they aren't rumors anymore."

"What do you mean?"

Oh.

Wait.

What?

"War?" Whitleigh slid off the bed. "That's ridiculous. They can't send you to Iraq." She paced the room. The carpet, tan and tattered, had felt more than its share of trampling feet. "No. You've done your year in Korea." She threw up her free hand and stomped her foot. Like that would help. "They can't send you anywhere else but home."

"Whit, calm — "

"Calm down. Calm down? Really, Collier?" She clamped her jaw tight. "They have no right — "

"Whitleigh." The sharpness in his voice silenced her. Her stomach contorted, sending a wave of nausea over her body. She collapsed on the bed, fighting off tears and the urge to continue her rant.

"Listen to me, please."

How could she listen? All of the effort it took to move to Fort Carson, Colorado and transfer her college credits, ready to start her life with Collier, but then a hardship tour to South Korea interrupted. Now this?

Collier released a drawn out breath. "I wanted you to hear it from me before the crazy news people start saying stuff."

Closing her eyes, she softened her grip on the phone. He didn't deserve to be her punching bag. "I'm sorry." Whitleigh shook, drawing the pillows into her lap. "I just want you home. For good. I want us to be together."

A tear fell, and then another.

"I know, Sweets. I'll be home in two days tops."

That was good news to cling to. Whitleigh propped herself against the headboard.

"We've got two weeks of leave. We'll celebrate."

"Celebrate what? Deployment? Spending another year apart?" Whitleigh unraveled the towel from her hair and dabbed her eyes. "This isn't how I thought we'd spend our first anniversary — oceans apart."

"I know, Whit." He probably pinched the bridge of his nose. She listened as he drew in a deep breath. "Two weeks is enough time to take you on a real honeymoon."

Whitleigh held in quiet sobs. Her chin dimpled.

"I know this isn't what we planned." No it wasn't. "But it's gonna be okay." Nothing about this was okay.

His optimism made her scowl.

Collier exhaled. "Please say something."

Her bottom lip protested beneath the grip of her teeth. The tears couldn't be stopped. "I'm not sure I know what to say." Nothing from her mouth would be beneficial. Holding her tongue was the most viable option.

"Listen, Sweets, I have to go. There are others in line behind me." His voice softened. "I'll … I'll see you soon."

LONGEST night ever. Going to sleep wasn't an option right after receiving such devastating news. Whitleigh rolled from bed, grumpy beyond reason. The morning news station didn't help. Twelve soldiers killed in Iraq. She turned the TV off and threw the remote on the floor. Not even a quickly brewed cup of coffee lifted her spirits. She pried the screen door open — dumb thing — and stepped down onto the broken slab of concrete.

The coffee sloshed from side to side with each grumbled movement. Her favorite hooded sweatshirt, torn and faded gray, looked as droopy as she felt. The cracked Kentucky Wildcat emblem provided no reason to discard this cozy cotton article of clothing no matter what Collier said. There were plenty of things he wore and did that she couldn't stand. Whitleigh blew a strand of hair from her face, wishing she had the energy to throw it into a ponytail.

The clinking of nails and hammers echoed through the cul-de-sac. A new subdivision was being built on base adjacent to theirs. Maybe she could convince the construction workers to do some sympathy renovations on her home.

Whitleigh sat on the cool concrete and cradled the steaming mug between her hands. Her tired, puffy, red eyes squinted in the sunlight. She sniffled and refused to let another tear fall. It was time to pull herself together. Suck it up.

Think positive. Maybe a run would help, or maybe a chocolate bar. Either of those always did a pretty good job of clearing her mind. Cookies. She was getting pretty good at baking. Maybe a good book and bubble bath would stop the aching in her chest. A tear threatened to fall but Whitleigh blinked it away.

She took a sip, enjoying the bold flavor as it scalded her throat.

Thinking positive was harder than it seemed.

Whitleigh looked from side to side. It may not have been the wraparound porch like she'd dreamed, but there was room for a chair, sort of. Pink blooming rose bushes, flanking the sides of the porch, greeted her with a fresh floral scent. Whitleigh leaned over, prolonging an inhale. Wonderful. The new housing units didn't have these kinds of flowers.

The chilly wind pimpled her flesh with goose bumps. She crossed her arms. Spring was here, but summer needed to hurry. Like normal, the cannon blast and trumpet call sounded the beginning of a new work day on base.

She yawned and stretched. Collier hadn't spent much time in their brick matchbox, but this was their home now, broken slab of a porch and all. Maybe she could see about having the cracked siding redone and repainted. The once cheery yellow paint had faded with time, along with the grass. She might get it growing again if she could rid it of the overgrown weeds. She'd have to talk to housing about that when they opened later. Their home needed to be cozy and inviting when Collier came home in a day or so.

So much work to do. Whitleigh rubbed her brow. Too much work to do in one day.

Turning her head to the west, the corners of her mouth curved into a slight grin.

The mountains were beautiful.

Those Rockies still took her breath away and made the rolling hills of her Kentucky home look puny. Colorado Springs' pride and joy, Pike's Peak, kept a snowcap almost year around, but today it seemed spectacular, bleached even. It was stunning in the wee hours of the morning.

Whitleigh stood, drinking in the morning mountain air. So far, Fort Carson seemed nice enough. It wasn't her old Kentucky home, that's for sure, but it was military life. Real. Hard. Each day she'd discovered it wasn't exactly what she'd romanticized.

She sighed. A tiny ant crawled along the porch step. She moved her foot to let it pass. Maybe she should skip class today. Professors were understanding people. Sometimes. Besides, there was so much other work. Whitleigh eyed the chipped paint on her fingernails.

The sound of another defiant, creaking screen door caught her attention.

Whitleigh turned to wave at Mrs. Ryan, a sweet woman from across the street if you could overlook her meddling.

She sported a puffy pink robe and at least thirty hair rollers. Most of Whitleigh's neighbors were nice enough. Sort of. Though she wasn't old, this mother of five had a mother hen complex.

Mrs. Ryan hustled out into her lawn to snatch up the newspaper. She flipped a wave and scurried in Whitleigh's direction. The powdery pink fuzz balls atop her house slippers shook with each step. It wasn't the best time for a visit from Mrs. Ryan and her snooping questions.

Whitleigh forced a smile. "Good morning."

"Morning." Her lips bent into a worried glower. "I heard the news." She tucked the newspaper under her chubby arm. The pink material of the robe hid all but a portion of the paper.

Whitleigh nodded. The word that the Second Brigade Combat Team was headed to Iraq from Korea proved headline worthy. News travels fast. Surely Mom would be calling soon, along with the rest of her friends and family from back home. Maybe she should turn off her cell. No. Not at the risk of missing a call from Collier.

Mrs. Ryan's steps were careful as she neared, like the smallest movement would send Whitleigh spiraling out of control. Maybe it would.

Whitleigh sipped at her coffee and gave a half smile as Mrs. Ryan sat beside her.

"This life … these kinds of thing," Mrs. Ryan shook her head and sighed, "they can be unbearable." She picked a piece of fuzz from her robe. It fell from her fingers and floated quite a distance before landing on the sidewalk.

Whitleigh's chest throbbed. She inhaled, wishing three clicks of her heels would take her home — anywhere but here, talking about anything but this. Mrs. Ryan needed to stop prying. Maybe Whitleigh should interfere in her life. Strange how the Ryan family, being higher enlisted, still lived among privates. Strange how she never saw Mr. Ryan. Bet she wouldn't want Whitleigh asking those kinds of questions.

"You know," Mrs. Ryan scratched at her nose, "that last batch of cookies you brought over topped any of the others. All the neighbors agree." She smiled.

Whitleigh's cheeks grew hot. Talk about an insert foot in mouth moment. "Thank you." She bowed her head.

"The kids gobbled them up in minutes. I had to fight for one."

A wave of warmth washed through Whitleigh's body and dulled the ache in her chest. It was nice to be noticed. Her lips twitched upward.

"You lift our spirits with those cookies." She smacked at Whitleigh's shoulders with a hand. "And expand our waistlines." Mrs. Ryan's finely manicured nails clicked against the concrete as she giggled. "I'm glad I could squeeze a smile out of you, Whitleigh." She gave a playful nudge.

Whitleigh rubbed her hand across her forehead, grinning. "It feels good to smile."

"Bit of advice from someone who's been living this life for a while now." She put a steady hand on Whitleigh's knee. "Find reasons to smile and laugh. Keep busy. Make friends."

Easier said than done. She was trying. Trying hard to do all those things.

The coffee in her mug had grown cold. No bother. She took a sip anyway and leaned into Mrs. Ryan's hug, willing herself not to cry.

Sirens sounded in the distance, growing closer by the second.

She and Mrs. Ryan parted, standing to watch as the first police car sped by and took a squealing sharp turn onto the street behind them. An ambulance followed soon after, and then two more police cars. Blue lights ricocheted in the morning hours. Piercing sirens echoed through the housing area. If anyone were still sleeping in the neighborhood, they would be awake now.

THE Military Police arrested a sobbing soldier. Whitleigh reminded herself to blink, clinging to an empty coffee mug. The story on the mid-morning news was horrific. Why had she even turned the television back on? It worsened the day, but her eyes were fixed on the screen, unable to look away. An Army wife dead, neck snapped by her husband who was on leave from Iraq. A tragic accident. Two children left without a mother, their father facing life in prison.

Whitleigh choked back tears. Her throat burned. Through the dining room blinds she could see the crime scene tape stretched across the perimeters of the house behind hers. What was this new life of hers?

She willed her fingers to click the TV off. Except for the low hum of the ceiling fan, the living room was silent. Uncomfortable. Whitleigh sat on the couch, fingers rubbing the corduroy backing of a floral pillow. It was best to keep busy, so why couldn't she move? Collier couldn't get home soon enough.

For the most part the inside of the house was tidy. Dusting could be done in a cinch. Her textbooks and leisure reads were stacked neatly in various places around the house. Laundry could be put away in no time. Dishes were done. It wouldn't take much to run the vacuum. She was sure Collier would want to go out to eat. No need to prep a meal, though she would need to pick up his favorite sugary cereals.

A few cars started in the parking lot. Whitleigh tried not to look out toward the crime scene. Maybe she should go to class. Professors weren't always forgiving. A quick dab of mascara, and Whitleigh rushed out the door.

THE swishing of bristles against the bathroom tile floor equated to therapy. Hard work was a great way to process the news of an impending deployment. Sweat dripped from Collier's forehead and onto the tile. He scrubbed over it and sat against the cool brick wall. It had been a long day. A long year. Sadness from Whit's voice reverberated against the walls of his mind.

"Go to sleep, Cromwell," Pulu grumbled as he launched a pillow in Collier's direction, missing. "Do you know what time it is?" His bunk creaked as he jostled around. "We have to be up in like three hours."

"Sorry." Collier hushed his voice as he stood, sudsy brush in hand. The ancient floor still appeared grimy. So much for his hard work. He clicked the light off and tiptoed to his bed, nearly tripping over a mound of Dock's body weights and Pulu's video game controllers. There went his attempt at being quiet. Collier all but skipped and hopped over laundry and empty soda cans. These guys needed a few housekeeping lessons.

"Shhh. Geez." Pulu's growl brought a semi smirk to Collier's face. If they didn't want someone falling over their stuff in the middle of the night, creating a ruckus, they should've put it all away.

He tossed the pillow back onto Pulu's bed and cleared his throat as he sat onto his squeaking bunk.

"Could you be any louder?" Pulu kicked at his blankets. His voice muffled. "How is Dock sleeping through this?"

Collier laughed underneath his breath and reached for the headlamp on his nightstand. It's amazing what can be built with cinder blocks and plywood. His fingers scrolled across the unsanded surface. Ah. Just where he left it, his *Army Officer's Guide* book, which would be easier to finish if it were on audio.

With a push of a button he had his own personal light source. The headlamp may have been one of the greatest inventions ever. Collier flipped open the book and removed a photo of Whit.

Her smile. Those blue eyes. Collier sighed and turned toward his wall. Each picture taped there deserved its own moment of appreciation. Whit looked like a dream in that floral dress she wore at Basic Training Graduation. A few snapshots from their wedding day … he paused at one of the pictures. It didn't matter how many times he looked at it, he couldn't help but laugh at their funny expressions. No way was he about to eat shrimp stuffed mushrooms. Blech.

He smirked at the self-photo they snapped on their makeshift honeymoon to Niagara Falls. Cheesy grins and wind-burned cheeks, pictures documented more than images. Not a lot in their bank then, still not too much, but Whit didn't care as long as they were together. Collier gazed into the photograph. She was more than enough. More than a man with a childhood like his deserved. Could he be enough for her? He eyed his pressed uniform hanging in the jam-packed closet. Joining the military ensured their future, proved he was nothing like his failure of a father.

And then, beside the photos, sat the list.

Hopes and dreams on paper. Collier lifted a finger and touched each line.

Crumpled and worn, he studied their "Forever List" on many occasions. Tonight, the words tore at his heart. Fitting a lifetime of to-do's into two weeks teetered on the edge of impossible. He and Whit may not be able to mark off many, but they could try.

"I see the light." Pulu sat up in his top bunk, his voice anything but thrilled.

"Finally." Collier snickered, his thoughts diverted. "I've been praying you'd see the light since the day I met you."

"I so want to punch you." Pulu's grumble morphed into a laugh.

Collier clicked his headlamp off and wiggled under the itchy woolen covers. The cozy spot took a while to find.

Dock's snore echoed through the room. Pulu sighed.

"Hey." Collier pushed back a yawn. "Since we're both awake, why don't we get Dock?"

All the men owed Dock a few payback pranks.

An uneven snort worked its way from Dock's throat. Collier held his breath. Dock stirred for a moment, but soon fell back into snore mode.

"So?" Pulu's low voice seeped mischief. "You in?"

Pulu inched down the side ladder of his bunk. "Haden's going to be so bummed he missed out on this." True. Most soldiers jumped at an opportunity to pick on Dock. Maybe it was wrong, but after Dock switched out his toothpaste for hemorrhoid cream, Collier's supply of sympathy shortened.

"I'll get the shaving cream." Collier rolled out of bed. "And hair gel."

Dock was going to have a hairstyle to remember.

"Turn your headlamp on." A grin bigger than Dock's beloved state of Texas streaked across Pulu's face. "I want to see this."

"I'll grab the camera." Collier's somber mood lifted. Pranking Dock seemed more therapeutic than scrubbing bathroom floors.

COLLIER stood at attention alongside the other soldiers in formation, fresh from a morning PT session. His heart rate returned to normal. Sweat running down his back began to dry. The sun hadn't opened its eyes. 'Army early' meant up before any rooster thought about waking up. Chilly air, too cool for late spring, caused him to shiver in place. He pinched back a yawn, resorting to a deep but silent inhale. Staying up late came with a price, but waking up early had its perks, like seeing Dock wake up and freak out over the matted mess of a hairdo they had handcrafted. Classic.

Collier worked to get a glimpse of Dock in formation, hair still unmanageable. A definite outlaw to Army protocol. The First Sergeant would eat him for breakfast. Collier masked his snicker with a sneeze.

A silent breeze passed overhead, carrying with it the smells of gasoline and oil from the military vehicles nearby. The smell of Army, minus the scent of ammo and dirt. That was coming. Their training schedule would pick up after leave no doubt.

Training schedule.

Collier's eyes glossed over, focusing on the distant fog hanging over the mossy green landscape of South Korea. The news began to take root. He gulped. They were going to war.

First Sergeant Gunthrie held his hands behind his back and stood in front of the formation. His demeanor seemed off. Not his usual angry self. He pursed his lips and paced in front of the motor pool. "At ease." His voice sounded as weary as the weathered military vehicles, slumbering in the surrounding buildings, looked. They would roar to life in the weeks that followed.

The men relaxed their stance, hands tucked against the small of their backs, legs shoulder width apart. Collier's chin rose. His eyes focused on the First Sergeant, careful not to stare directly. Delicate business. First Sergeant Gunthrie detested eyeballing.

"You, there." The First Sergeant split through the rank. Oh man, someone was going to get it. "Dock." Collier could imagine First Sergeant Gunthrie standing nose to nose with his roomie. "You better have a good excuse for standing in formation looking like the back end of a shaved cockatoo. What's wrong with your hair, soldier?"

Dock's voice cracked like a twelve year old boy. "I ... I couldn't get it to lay down, First Sergeant."

What? Collier held his breath. Dock didn't rat them out? More than a little surprising.

Collier's collar tightened around his neck. Maybe he and Pulu had gone a tad too far with this prank. He and Pulu exchanged a quick smile. Nah. They hadn't.

The soldiers in formation fought back strained laughs. First Sergeant pegged it. Dock totally looked like a cockatoo. Definitely worthy of any slack his 'ole buddy may dish out.

"Well, you look ridiculous." First Sergeant's voice reeked with disgust. "Do something about that."

"Yes, First Sergeant." Collier could almost hear Dock seething through his teeth. Priceless. He took in quick breaths to keep his laughter in check.

The First Sergeant made his way back into the front of formation and glanced at the ground before lifting a high head to meet the gaze of his men. "We're a nation at war, and duty calls."

The laughter subsided. Collier's collar tightened even more around his neck. His heart thudded inside the cavity walls of his chest. The news sounded more unbelievable the more he heard it.

"You, fine men, have the privilege of fighting for our great nation." His First Sergeant's face grew solemn, or maybe proud. He placed his hands, stiff and straight, at his sides.

Collier blinked. Hearing it the first time wasn't enough. Reality set in. Telling Whit had been worse than a nightmare.

A shout echoed from the back. "We'll show those Arabs how Americans roll."

Collier's brows furrowed. That comment didn't settle well.

"Attention." The First Sergeant's face grew red. His angry voice bellowed among the ranks and echoed throughout the motor pool.

The men snapped into position. Collier swallowed the lump in this throat. First Sergeant Gunthrie's voice and rank demanded respect.

"We're not going to war to show the Arabs anything." The First Sergeant's voice elevated at an alarming speed. Collier stared ahead, stone still, thankful to dodge this man's wrath. Spit spewed from the First Sergeant's mouth as he cursed and muttered words in a Midwestern accent Collier couldn't quite make out.

"Who said that?" No one dared to answer. God help the man that ticks off the First Sergeant. "You listen up. All of you." Collier tuned in as the First Sergeant pointed a stern index finger. "It's the insurgents we're after. You'd all best remember that. "

Yes, they sought insurgents. Bring them to justice. Set captives free. Collier stood taller. This was what he had enlisted for. God's plan for his life caused his stomach to knot.

War.

Collier swallowed.

His chest puffed out a bit more. He wasn't afraid to fight. Dying didn't bother him either, but saying good-bye to Whit, perhaps for the last time?

Don't think like that. Collier refocused on the First Sergeant. The man stood with a hand on his hip and dug a wad of chew from his pocket. He poked and prodded it into place. A large protrusion hung from the side of his face. Collier grimaced and prayed the First Sergeant didn't notice his own disapproving expression.

First Sergeant Gunthrie shot a stream of tobacco into the ground like a live round. "The lives and freedoms of innocent men, women, and children around the world are being threatened by the hands of Al Qaeda." Collier's jaw tightened. They needed to be stopped. "We will deploy to Iraq with intent to win the hearts and the minds of the Iraqi citizens and rid their nation of the grip of Al Qaeda." The First Sergeant scanned the formation.

Collier licked his lips.

"When duty calls, we answer." First Sergeant scratched his head and spit another round into the ground. "You, brave men, have the honor and duty of restoring the lives and liberties to these innocent people. You've been called to make this world a safer place for America's future generations … no matter the cost." His eyes dropped their hold on the men. "Take the rest of the day off. No PT tomorrow. Just get home to your families. Everyone got their round-trip tickets?" He scanned the crowd. "Good. Sign out before you go on leave. Now get out of my sight."

Collier relaxed and shifted his stance. He watched as the First Sergeant marched away. A hard man by any standard, but a good leader.

Two weeks leave. Not much time, but he'd take whatever the Army gave so he could see Whit. He smiled and turned toward the barracks. Maybe he could clear out before Dock, and his retaliation, made it back from morning chow. It wouldn't take long to pack. Not much he wanted to bring home. He'd rather carry Whit from the airport in his arms than some oversized Army duffle bag.

COLLIER rubbed the sleep from his eyes. He neared the end of *The Army Officer's Guide*. A yawn escaped his mouth. Now to just get enough college credit hours to go to Officer Cadet School. It would mean a few more years in the military, but Whit wouldn't mind. They could iron out the details later.

The flight home from Korea took almost an entire day of travel. Traveling in khaki shorts was a welcome change from his uniform. One by one he popped his knuckles, maneuvering his body in an attempt to stretch within the confines of his seat.

At least he'd been lucky enough to score a window seat, and Haden kept him company. For the last few hours Collier entertained his friend by reenacting every detail of the pranking assault on Dock. Haden laughed so hard tears poured from his eyes. Epic joke. Collier missed his old roommate, but Dock and Pulu were cool too.

To ward off the tingling in his legs, Collier wiggled his feet. The tiny tray attached to the seat in front of him fell into his lap. Again. For like the tenth time. It refused to stay shut. Collier huffed. Crazy thing.

He fiddled with the latch, ignoring Haden's chuckle, and managed to rig the handle with a long thin strand pulled from the parachute cord he had tossed in his carry-on. It worked. Not too shabby.

Haden's mouth curved into a sleepy grin. "I've known you since Basic, and it still never ceases to amaze me what you're able to rig together."

Collier tapped at his head. "This brain's always ticking."

"Ha." Haden stretched out his arms. "And it has nothing to do with the fact there's like a million uses for the 550 cord?"

"Who do you think came up with those million uses?"

"I'm guessing, you." Haden reached for his *Hunter's Ultimate Guide* magazine. Yuck. Haden could have all that hunting stuff.

Collier's ears popped. The plane began to descend. Not long now. "You gonna ask Emilee to marry you while you're home?" A lot of soldiers would come back married, engaged, or divorced.

"I want to." Haden puffed. "Had the ring for months now."

Collier peered out the window. He didn't need to ask about Haden's hesitation. The reason was all too clear. "You staying in Oregon the whole time?"

"I think I might." Haden thumbed the magazine against his knee. "Get some good hunting time in, and it'll be nice to see everybody again before … well, before we deploy."

"Yeah." Collier fidgeted with his fingers. It had been awhile since he'd seen his family. Years. He folded his hands in his lap. The ones he cared about were gone.

They were no longer in the clouds. Streets emerged, filled with busy cars, now a bit larger than a soda can. Clusters of buildings surrounded by nothing but endless patches of flatlands appeared.

Colorado never crossed his mind as a duty station. It didn't matter where he lived though, as long was Whit was there.

The airport came into view. Rows of parked cars circled around the building.

He sat up, leaning closer to the window, nose almost touching the glass.

Knots turned in his stomach. Whit would be in his arms soon. Collier closed his eyes, taking in a deep breath. He could almost smell the Sweet Pea perfume she wore, feel her soft skin.

The wheels hit the runway, jolting the passengers.

Collier twiddled his thumbs. His knees knocked.

"I can feel your nerves." Haden chuckled and swiped at his arms. "They're jumping all over me."

"Sorry." Collier laughed and bent to pull the box of chocolates from his bag. Whit's favorite — chocolate caramel clusters.

"I'm jealous. I wish my flight stopped here."

The plane crawled to a stop, and moments later they filed from coach seating into the terminal.

"See ya in two weeks." Collier strapped on his backpack and extended a hand.

Haden eyed the hand, pushed it out of the way, and threw his arms around Collier, putting any bear hug to shame. A head taller than most soldiers, and barrel chested, Haden didn't notice his own strength. "See ya soon, Cromwell."

Collier waved to his friend and ran down the terminal to baggage claim.

Whit would be waiting.

There she was. Arms folded, chewing on her pinky nail, looking at the clock on the wall. She took his breath away in that yellow eyelet dress. Picture perfect. Her hair was longer than he remembered. Still golden. She'd taken the time to curl it for him. Collier picked up his pace, backpack pressed against his shoulder blades.

"Excuse me." Collier pushed by members of the crowd. "Sorry sir. Sorry ma'am. I've got to get to my wife. Excuse me." The people were more than happy to step aside.

He saw her struggling to jump above the flood of passersby. "Collier." Her hands swayed in the air. "Collier."

Collier paved his way through the civilians, closing the gap between him and his wife. Colliding, he swept Whit off her feet, into his arms, and spun her around.

He placed her feet back on the ground and held her close to his body, staring into the eyes of the woman he was more than willing to die for. His hands held her face. She kissed his thumb as he skimmed it over her lips.

She brushed her hands against his cheeks, mimicking his movements. Tears sparkled in her eyes.

Tears of his own started to form.

Whit looked at the crowd gathered around them and then back at Collier. "They're all staring."

Collier pulled Whit's face to his. "You're the only one I see."

IT felt so strange to have Collier in the passenger seat. Whitleigh turned into the cul-de-sac and smiled as she popped another chocolate caramel cluster in her mouth. Yum. He knew her well.

Collier removed his hand from her knee and tugged at the seat belt. He pressed another hand against the door handle. "I'll be glad when I'm more familiar with the place."

"Hey now." She slapped at his arm. His laughter sang. "My driving skills are top notch."

Whitleigh loosened her hold on the steering wheel as the car crawled into its assigned parking spot, cracking bits of broken pavement under the tires.

"Cold?" Collier skimmed his palm over the goose bumps covering her arm.

"Not really." Well, maybe. She smiled and began to roll up her window. A cool breeze hurried through the crack of the window as it sealed shut. She rubbed the chill from her arms.

The sun began to set over the mountains. Brilliant shades of orange decorated the skies, amplifying the majestic outline of the Rocky Mountains. Collier held her hand.

"They're beautiful, aren't they? The mountains." Turning off the ignition, Whitleigh jingled the keys in her hand and picked at the hem of her sunny yellow, eyelet dress. Collier's eyes followed her movement.

He nodded and lifted her hand, pressing it to his lips.

His eyes were tired. Whitleigh looked down at her hand in his. So small. Now stained and callused, his hands were much different from those that held hers on their wedding day, but no less comforting.

Collier grimaced. "I've tried every kind of lotion." He pulled away and picked at a piece of dead skin. "Nothing works. We're out in the field a lot." He shrugged.

Whitleigh skimmed her fingers across the uneven patches of skin. "I love them."

Neighborhood lampposts buzzed and came to life as the sky faded into a deep blue.

"So, um." *What next?* She cocked her head, eyeing their small brick home. Her cheeks flushed.

Collier turned, surveying the area from his passenger seat perspective. "The yard looks nice … from what I can see."

Whitleigh grinned, thankful to feel the redness in her cheeks retreat. "Emma, the little girl from across the street I told you about, helped." Whitleigh's lips slid into a grin. "She planted most of the flowers. Great with upkeep too." Whitleigh pointed at the petite red, white, and blue flowers that outlined the sidewalk. Lovely. Emma worked nonstop that day, all for grape popsicles.

"Very patriotic." Collier nodded.

Flowers couldn't hide cracks and peeling paint. "Housing said they'd be out soon to do some other updates."

"That's good."

Oh, small talk. Whitleigh picked at her polished fingernails, a clear high gloss. Chipped paint went unnoticed when it was invisible.

"So." Collier twirled a strand of her hair around his finger. He smelled nice, better than she remembered. Whitleigh reminded herself to breathe. He reached for her arm, pulling her close, and nuzzled her neck with playful kisses.

Whitleigh giggled and brushed her hair back. Even in an area without humidity, her hair still wouldn't cooperate. "Maybe we should go inside."

"You read my mind."

Collier ran his fingers through the remaining curls and placed a tender kiss on her shoulder.

His hands fell to her hips, and he placed a kiss at the nape of her neck.

Her face grew warm. She played with the collar of his emerald green pullover. Nervous? Maybe. "I've made some changes to the inside. Redecorated." Really? That's what she thought to say?

"I'm sure I'll like them." His voice now low and flirty.

"I've fixed some stuff too." Not many things. Maybe just the caulking around the bathtub and sink. Refurbished old furniture. She swallowed. Any suave word choice she prepared for this romantic moment evaporated. "The screen door still sticks."

Collier laughed and kissed her lips. "Noted." He slid his hand from her hips and opened his door. "Stay there. I want to open your door." No problem. His kisses left a sensational buzzing in her head. Whitleigh couldn't move if she wanted.

He excelled with swift, smooth movements. One minute she sat light headed in the front seat of her Toyota, and the next, Collier had her wrapped in his arms and carried her onto the front porch.

Other than the dim lighting from a table lamp beside the sage colored sofa, the house was dark. Quiet too. Shadows from the front window danced across their faces. Collier helped her from his arms. His eyes held hers.

Perhaps she could manage a whisper. What changes in the house did she want to show him? Her mind raced.

It didn't matter. Their home could wait.

Her fingers intertwined with his as she led him through the living room and down the hall. Her hand shook as she reached for the doorknob of their bedroom. She could feel his steady breath, the warmth of his body behind hers. Collier placed his hand around her waist, turning her to face him. He lifted her chin with his finger and bent to kiss her.

Whitleigh's knees weakened.

Oh, that melting effect.

She missed it.

Missed him.

She cleared her throat. "I'll show you … the redecorating stuff ... later. If that's okay."

He hovered above her for one more long moment, then his lips were on hers. He pulled away for a brief moment. "Definitely okay," he muttered.

She found herself in his arms once more, a place she loved, as he carried her to their bed. She searched his face, so sincere, so handsome, and admired his physical traits. Those ocean blue eyes, dark hair, broad shoulders much wider than her own, and the defined lines of his muscular arms. His kisses were sweet. His touch, warm, attentive.

The moment was so right. Long awaited. Bittersweet.

Whitleigh leaned forward, pressing her lips against his ear. "I've missed you so much." Her voice quavered, and a single tear fell from the corner of her eye.

"Shhh, baby." Collier wiped the tear as it streamed down her cheek and replaced it with a kiss. "I'm here now." He cradled her. His rough hands smoothed over her head as he covered her face with consoling kisses. "It's okay."

She looked up at the man holding her tight. Her husband, a man whose faith permeated from him and steadied her. If she could have an inkling of his assurance. Just something smaller than a mustard seed would do. "I love you."

Collier's soft smile warmed her body. "I love you, too."

WHITLEIGH rolled over to answer her buzzing cell.

Where was it?

Her fingers skimmed over books, a charger, anything but the phone. A few loose papers fell to the floor.

There it was.

Whitleigh propped up on her elbow, careful not to wake Collier. "Mom?"

"Hi, Sweet Pea." Mom's voice rang from the phone, loud and cheery.

Whitleigh grabbed the clock. She rubbed her eyes and scrunched her nose. "Mom, it's five in the morning here."

"Oops." She giggled. "Just checking in on you two. Making sure Collier made it in safe."

"We're good Momma." Whitleigh yawned. "Still sleeping."

Mom's laugh echoed through the phone. "I'll let you go. Tell Collier we love him." Whitleigh couldn't help but smile at her mother's kissing noises. "We're praying for you guys. Got you both on the church prayer list. It's gonna be okay, Sweet Pea." Mom didn't joke around with prayer lists. That woman could move mountains.

"Thanks, Mom." Prayer coverage provided a sense of comfort. "Keep them coming." Lord knows she needed them.

"Bye, Sweet Pea." Mom made a few more kissing noises before ending the call. Whitleigh bit at her fingernail. Everyone knew everything would be okay, everyone but her. She turned her phone off, flipped it shut. No more interruptions.

Collier stretched, his voice groggy. "Who was that?"

"Momma." She sighed away her worry, fluffed her pillow, and pushed a strand of hair to the side. "I didn't mean to wake you."

"Let me hold you tighter." Pulling her close, he folded her body against his and kissed the back of her neck. Another kiss, and then another. He was so warm. Her thoughts spiraled back to the more intimate moments they shared last night. Nothing short of wonderful.

"You're beautiful." Collier traced the nape of her neck and jostled her hair between his fingers.

Whitleigh turned to reach for his face, unshaven, just the way she liked.

His eyes seemed a deeper shade of blue than she remembered. Rays of sunlight began to peek through the blinds, highlighting Collier's bare skin. This man was beautiful.

Collier held her cheek in his palm. "I want to show you something." He rolled to his side, leaning over the bed. Whitleigh's brows knit together. "What is it?"

"Our list."

Whitleigh gasped and clapped. "You brought it."

Collier rolled to his stomach, propping on a pillow. The wrought iron rails clanked against his dog tags. "Thought we could mark some stuff off, add a few things to it." He shrugged. "You know." She knew. "While we've got the time together."

Her excitement couldn't be contained. She bounced under the covers.

He rubbed the back of his neck. "I know we won't be able to spend our first anniversary together." Whitleigh stopped bouncing. "And I know we didn't really have the best honeymoon." Her lips curved to the side. Their weekend in Niagara Falls was … fun. "I'm prepared to take you anywhere you want to go. Name it and we're there."

Whitleigh's chin lifted. *The Bahamas.*

Collier held her hand. "But, before I deploy, it would mean a lot to me if you and I mark off as many things on this list as we can." She watched his Adam's apple bob. "I thought we could spend the two weeks working on our Forever List, you know, in case …."

"Don't say it." Whitleigh glanced away. She swallowed the lump in her throat.

Collier kissed her forehead. "Well, that's what I thought we could do."

Whitleigh moved her fingers with gentle precision and traced the arch of each of his brows, the curve of his hairline, down to the sharpness of his jaw. His lips were smooth to the touch. "I can't think of a better way to spend two weeks with you."

He kissed her fingers as they skimmed over his lips.

Whitleigh blushed and buried her head in his chest.

WHITLEIGH waved to Mrs. Ryan and the kids before flitting back to her yard. The kids would enjoy the chocolate covered caramel truffles as much as she had. Little Emma grinned and leaned from her top floor window from across the street. Whitleigh blew a kiss that Emma caught and hugged tight. Sweet girl.

Collier stood, holding the passenger-side car door open. Whitleigh kissed his cheek and plopped into the seat. "I'm ready."

Collier slid into the driver's side. "Nice to see you getting to know the neighbors."

Whitleigh clicked her seat belt and tucked a loose strand of hair behind her ear. "They're nice folks."

The car sputtered to life. Collier rolled his eyes. "This car."

"Um, this is a Yota-loving zone." Whitleigh smirked.

"Yota?"

"Yep. All cars need a pet name." She rolled down the window and checked her makeup in the passenger mirror. All good. "Can you think of a better name for a compact baby blue Toyota?"

"Rust bucket?" Collier popped open a soda and laughed before taking a drink. Whitleigh nudged him with her free elbow and propped the other on the window seal.

The brakes squealed and screamed as Collier pulled from the drive. "We have to eat before we hit the interstate. The fridge was filled with girl food."

"Girl food?"

"Yeah. A bunch of salad stuff." Collier scowled. "And coffee. When did you start drinking that?"

Hmm. Whitleigh pursed her glossed lips. "I guess when you left for Korea." She shrugged. "I needed something to help pull off late night writing assignments, and a friend for my blueberry scones, which you'll love. I've found the cutest little coffee and pastry shop." Whitleigh unfolded their Forever List from her purse and gave it a shake. "Look. We can already mark off random road trip, stay up all night, and laugh until one of us snorts."

"I didn't put that one on the list."

"Well, it's on there now." She jetted her hands upward in victory. "And you snorted first."

He rolled a shoulder and placed a broad hand on her thigh, covering the worn spots of her favorite jeans. "Where to first?"

Where to go? Whitleigh nibbled on the inside of her lip. So many choices. Just pick. "Grand Canyon." Anywhere with Collier was the place to be. "Ooh. Ooh. We can mark off travel on Route 66 while we're out that way."

"I'm hoping to mark off skinny dip." He gave her leg a playful squeeze.

"Don't see that on the list." Her fingers skimmed across each line.

"Oh, it's there." He laughed as he pulled from the drive. "You're not looking close enough."

FORT CARSON was hours away. The road had taken them further west, through the Rockies, on into the foothills, and now to the plateau. The scenery was surreal. Mountain goats climbed about the rocky ledges. Giant pines surrounded the area. They stood tall defying gravity. Many were white from being struck by lightning.

Whitleigh spent miles with her head hanging out the window, snapping series of photos. How could Collier keep his eyes on the road? Higher and higher the roads continued to wind. Her ears popped more than once from the change in altitude.

Collier bit off a piece of jerky and washed it down with a soda. "You haven't said much about school." She hadn't thought much about school, not since getting word of the deployment.

Whitleigh shrugged and bit off a piece of an almond bar. "Finals are in a couple weeks. Think I got all A's."

"As always." The car rounded a turn, revealing another path of endless pines. "Two more semesters and you'll be a graduate." Collier sat taller. "My wife. College graduate. Teacher."

Whitleigh nodded and smiled. A classroom full of doting children awaited her soon.

"I'm looking forward to graduating one day." Collier rested his hand on the gearshift.

"You mean, you're still going to take classes when you redeploy?"

"On my down time." He looked from her and back to the road. The Yota bumbled along. "I don't think I'll be fighting all of the time." True. At least she hoped it was true. "And they have internet there."

A definite perk. Whitleigh shook her head. "Sounds like a good plan."

"I've been thinking about going the Army officer route."

The officer route proved more unfamiliar than the Army itself.

Wait. Whitleigh scratched her chin. "You're still wanting to get out of the Army, right?" That was the plan. As long as the Army officer program could be wrapped up in two years, there wouldn't be a problem. Army life was not for them.

"Well." Collier's eyes squinted.

"Well, what?" No way was he going to serve more than the three contracted years. Whitleigh could feel her eyes widen.

Collier took another drink. "I've been reading this book, and I think the officer side of this life could be a better fit for us." Was she hearing him correctly? No side of this life was right for them. "I want to go into the medical field. Why not let the Army pay for it and get the best medical training they have to offer?"

Why not?

Whitleigh could think of plenty of reasons why not.

"It's great experience."

For who? Him? Whitleigh bit her tongue. This was not the place or time to start a fight.

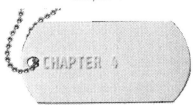

THE wheel shook beneath his palms. Collier grimaced at the sputtering sounds emitting from the hunk of blue rust Whit affectionately called Yota. The vehicle needed to be euthanized. He was surprised it made it to the Grand Canyon, and now he could only pray it would make it back to Fort Carson.

The week spent out west had flown. Collier sighed. Seven days remaining.

He watched Whit, bare feet on the dashboard. Short people can do that. She flipped through one of those how to refurbish old stuff magazines, paying no mind to the Yota's ill snorts.

Whit tapped her toes to the low tune of the radio. Really? She didn't hear the sounds of a dying car?

Collier smiled and shook his head. "I'm getting you a new car when I get back from Iraq." He turned the song up and dug for a pretzel in the bag at his side.

She shrugged, offering a half smile. "You're joking?"

"Guess you'll have to wait and see." Yeah. She'd have a new car soon. Collier pointed toward a small billboard off to the side of the road. "Monument Valley." He slowed down, gaining a better view. "It's about an hour and a half away."

"It's not on our list." Whit licked her finger and flipped a page.

Geez. "You know, we can talk about whatever's been bugging you for the past, oh I don't know, 122 miles." Collier glanced at the odometer. "Don't say nothing's wrong." He may not have been around for their first year of marriage, but he'd learned nothing meant something, and Whit had been gnawing on something for a while.

Collier turned the radio down. Whit huffed and shut her magazine. Huffing was never a good thing. "Just trying to sort out a lot of stuff." That much was obvious. "Sometimes it's crazy being a girl." She gave a quick laugh and stared out the window.

He scratched his head. She had a point, but still left him hanging. "Babes, your brain is like an interstate system, and my brain is like a country back road." He remembered that one from their week of premarriage counseling. "Elaborate for this simpleminded man."

Whit managed a snickering frown combo. "My brain is on overload." She stretched her hands out and gathered in a deep breath. Even upset, she was beautiful. "I don't know what to feel or think about any of this." She cupped her forehead. Collier reached for her hand. Whit intertwined her fingers with his. "I can't stand all this time apart." Yes. He'd thought of that. He'd thought of a lot of things lately. "And now, as if sending you off to war wasn't terrible enough, you're wanting to stay in the Army longer?"

War took home the grand prize as far as terrible goes, at least in his opinion. Maybe he shouldn't say that out loud.

Whit's lips twisted to the side. "This is the first time you've mentioned wanting to stay in longer, and I'm mad at you for wanting to stay..." her voice shook. Oh no. He could hear the tears. "But I don't want to be mad at you because I don't want to be upset at you before you leave." The words sped from her lips, and her chin dimpled. "Ugh, I'm such a mess." She swiped at a tear. Yes, it had to be crazy to be a girl.

Collier blinked. His country back road mind struggled with an answer. "I'm only wanting to stay in for a year, maybe two years more."

Her eyes widened. That was even worse than huffing. He should rephrase a bit. "I thought it would be a good way to get a leg up, earn more so we can save more. Get job experience." Collier licked his lips. He watched her eyes flicker. "I mean, I was going in the medical field anyway, right? It's a great plan. You finish school, get a little teaching experience, and by the time I get my commission and finish with the medical program we can, um ..." She didn't seem too keen on his plan. Collier focused on the road. Her stare pierced the side of his head.

Whit sat up. Toe prints smudged on the window. Not cute. "Why can't you just get out when your time is up so we can move on with our lives?"

He had to admit, the past year hadn't been ideal, but the Army put food on the table and helped pay for her college and his. "You're being kind of negative, Whit."

"How can you say that?" She crossed her arms. Collier frowned. Whit had more trouble fitting into Army life than he. He shrugged. His friends were kind of assigned. Hers were not.

"Collier, I get that you felt God wanted you to join the Army. It was your duty. I get it, but God didn't tell you to stay longer than you have to."

He shook his head. "God also didn't tell us he created dinosaurs, but we know he did." Wow. That didn't come out right.

Whit rolled her eyes. She gave a heavy sigh and ran a hand through her hair.

"What I mean is that some things you just know without God having to tell you, like the sky is blue, and you're beautiful." He flashed a smile in Whit's direction.

"So, you're saying you know you're supposed to stay in the Army?" She cocked her head to the side, eyes too interrogating for his liking.

Careful. She seemed on edge.

This moment demanded calm, wisdom-filled words. "What I'm saying is, as the head of the household, it's my duty to provide for my family in the best way that I can, and it's your job to respect the decision I make in how I provide for us." Well said. Collier smiled to himself. The premarriage counselor would be proud.

Whit's jaw dropped. "You're serious?" The tone in her voice caused a sweat to break out across his head. Were his words not calm and wisdom filled enough? "Do you even hear yourself?" Her voice morphed into a low, terrifying hiss. "You never thought to consider me in this decision?"

He squinted. Think. Think. "No decision was made, really. No contracts signed or anything."

Whit raised a brow. What else could he say? What would the counselor say? Collier's heart rate quickened. "I'm not trying to upset you." Collier bit his tongue, hoping to make a u-turn on a road headed toward a fight. "Tell me what to say." That should stop an argument. "I'll say anything to make whatever this is okay." Relieved, Collier released a breath. Women were trickier than the marriage counselor let on.

Whitleigh threw her hands in the hair. "I can't believe you." Guess that wouldn't stop a spat. "Why don't you start by saying you're sorry you joined. You should've stayed in college." Collier slowed down. Maybe he should pull over. He'd never seen Whit so frustrated. Her voice trembled. "We'd still be in Kentucky with our friends and family, going to school together. We'd be with each other instead of going through all of this craziness."

Did she mean that?

Her point was easy to see, but she could at least show some appreciation.

Collier grimaced. "We'd be scraping by. Is that how you want to live?" There was no way he was going to dig for change in his couch. He'd seen his parents do that too many times.

"I don't care about the money." Whitleigh smacked a tear from her cheek. "I just want you home, safe, with me, instead of fighting someone else's war."

"That's enough." He didn't have much of a temper, but Collier's body grew warm. Whit's mouth snapped shut.

Collier pulled off to the side of the road. Whit was the most compassionate person he knew. How could she not see that this war was helping to free others from militants?

His jaw tightened. The car grumbled to a halt, and Collier tugged the keys from the ignition. "I'm trying to do what God wants me to do, be the man I'm supposed to be for you, for myself." *Anyone but my father.* "All you're doing is complaining."

A tumbleweed rolled across the two lane road. Except for a few passing cars, the mesa area was silent. Whit sat cross-legged, infatuated with the view outside her window. She cried real tears — the big ones.

This was not the ending to their road trip he'd imagined. "Huge Fight" wasn't on their Forever List.

His stomach turned. Maybe he'd been too harsh. Ugh. So this was what a first fight felt like. Collier scratched his head and worked to make eye contact with Whit. She picked at a patch of frayed denim on her jeans.

"Whit. I'm sorry." He placed a hand on her arm. Her skin was cool despite the Arizona heat. "I know there's a lot going on." A huge understatement. "I should've talked with you about wanting to stay in longer." Why didn't he? Whit told him about the things she wanted to do. "And I wish I wasn't leaving you." Her mascara stained eyes drifted in his direction. It would kill him to leave, now even more, seeing her pain, knowing her struggle. He wouldn't be there to help see her through. Collier raised her hand to his lips. "This isn't what either of us planned, but it is what it is, and we have to make the best of it."

She sniffled, peeling away from the window. "You're right. I'm sorry." Whit curled close.

He sighed and drew her into his chest. She seemed so fragile. What was going to keep her from falling apart when he left, and what if he never ... no, God was in control, no matter what.

COLLIER slid the manila folder into the filing cabinet, tucking his will and funeral arrangements away. Whit went through an entire box of tissues when he picked out the songs for his funeral. It wasn't the most upbeat conversation he ever had with her, but it needed to be done just in case the unthinkable happened.

The cabinet door closed with a metallic thud.

Collier glanced around the room. Whit had a knack for refurbishing old stuff. Did she know how talented she was? Photos and letters from their past hung in frames made from planks of aged barn wood from her parents' farm. Their dating years. Those thoughts alone were worthy of a grin.

On the far wall, she had freehanded a pencil sketched large oak tree and painted it with warm bronzed hues and patches of olive green. Their family tree appeared alive. It graced the wall in the small spare bedroom, telling their story. Each leaf boasted a photo or written name of a relative. His mother and his brother shared the date of their death. Collier touched their names with his fingertips, careful to give little attention to the name of the man who had the title Father.

Collier skimmed a finger across an empty painted branch. Whit created room for their family to grow. He smiled and allowed the possibility of children to fill his mind. One day.

He smirked and picked up the strangest sort of picture frame from where it perched on a planter turned end table. It looked as if Whit had attached a frame to a candlestick, then painted the entire thing the same color. He studied the picture of he and his college buddies, being boys. Collier sighed. A lot had changed in just over a year, from single to married, college to combat.

Was Whit right? Should he have stayed in college? No. Collier shook his head, dismissing any doubt. God called him to join the military. Right?

Right. This is where he was supposed to be.

He turned to leave, fidgeting with the locks on the windows for the third time today. Whit needed to stay safe while he deployed, and the old locks proved incompetent. Collier grumbled.

A sweet tune greeted him as he made his way down the hall. Whit's faint voice danced from the kitchen. She didn't sing in front of others, just him. He stood a bit taller and walked toward her voice.

He stopped and stared. A brilliant display of fresh cut roses brightened the center of the dinner table. Candles floated in small glass vases around the dining room. Subtle notes of piano music drifted from the stereo. Whit knew how to set a mood.

Homemade blueberry bread baked in the oven. The delicious smell danced underneath his nose and made his mouth water. His ears perked at the cracking and clattering of hot grease in the kitchen. Whit's fried chicken put any other to shame.

She peeked from the kitchen, the hem of her floral dress skirted around her calves. "Don't just stand there." He stopped, staring. She giggled. "Come help me."

He tugged at his polo, hoping a few wrinkles would fall out as he made his way to the kitchen.

A frilly eyelet apron, too vintage to be new, covered most of her dress. She must've bought it at a thrift shop. Collier folded his arms and admired the way the strings hugged her tiny waist. Whit pulled the last of the chicken from the frying pan with care. She leaned over and drew the loaf of bread from the oven.

It smelled too good not to offer a hand. "I'll take that."

"I figured you'd help with that." Whit laughed and played with the pearls around her neck. He had bought them for her when he first got to Korea.

He placed the bread on the counter. No matter how amazing it smelled, it would have to wait. "It's our last night." He kissed her once and held out his hand in waltz pose. "Shall we?"

"Dance in the kitchen. Barefoot." She nodded and slipped off her heels. "We can mark that off our list."

That's what he had in mind. They'd made a decent sized dent in their Forever List. Not too bad.

Whit laid her head against his chest. He'd miss having her in his arms. Collier fought back the tightness in his throat.

Through the kitchen and into the living area, Collier twirled her amongst the candles, swaying to the music. Though smiling, her eyes carried a deep sadness. Did his carry the same? There wasn't a need to ask for her thoughts. He knew. Sometimes the unsaid words spoke louder than the audible.

His hand cradled the small of her back as he kept her in step.

"I … I'm trying to be strong right now." He loved how her jaw clenched when she tried to be resolute.

"And you're doing great." She was. Much better than he expected. Collier kissed her hand before leading her into a graceful turn. He led with a left step, slowing almost to a standstill. "I know this moment is bittersweet." He swallowed. "But I'm trying to focus on God's plan for our life and remember that it's good." No matter what.

"Do you really believe that?" She toyed with the back of his collar. "That God has our best interest in mind?"

He stopped in mid sway. "You don't?" The uncertainty in her voice allotted for alarm.

"I wonder sometimes." Her lashes batted. He needed her faith to stay strong, but he couldn't fault her. Minutes ago he had doubted his decision to enlist.

She glanced away. "It's easier to believe God has our best in mind when everything's going well."

"True." Very true. He rubbed his thumb across her cheek. Her skin was smooth to the touch. Flawless. Collier lifted her hand back into a proper dance pose. "Dinner's waiting." They began to sway.

She drew in a deep breath. "It can wait a little longer."

Collier smiled. He didn't want to stop dancing either. Her body relaxed in his arms as he led their unhurried steps to and fro, side to side. Maybe they would stay like this all night, letting the music and silence soothe their souls, expressing what words could not.

Their last dinner, none more perfect.

Somehow, saying 'I love you' seemed insufficient, but it was all he could muster as he searched for her lips in the dim lights. Warm against his, soft and welcoming, forgetting a moment like this would be an impossibility.

Her gentle hands lifted to hold his face. "I love you too, Collier."

Chapter 5

SEVEN weeks, one day. Whitleigh kicked off her damp running shoes as she crossed through another numbered square on the kitchen calendar. Each day down meant another day closer to Collier's return. Living without him compared to an infant struggling to put one foot in front of the other.

A week passed since their last correspondence.

Four soldiers from the battalion had been killed in action. No one she knew, but Collier may have. As an adopted duty, Whitleigh attended each memorial ceremony on base. She blinked several times and refused to cry again. Pushing away the faces and sounds of families in mourning only grew more difficult.

Collier would call soon. No news was good news.

Rings of sweat darkened her blue workout shirt. She leaned against the sink and sipped on a glass of water, hoping to settle her stomach. Nothing like a late afternoon run to clear thoughts and work up a thirst. Whitleigh reached for a few crackers and reheated a bowl of homemade alphabet soup. Childish maybe, but a piece of home every now and then felt nice. Not to mention it seemed to be the only thing she could keep down lately. Recovering from food poisoning was no joke. Shortly after Collier deployed, Mrs. Ryan had brought over several casseroles that made Whitleigh too ill to think. Mrs. Ryan meant well, bless her heart.

Regurgitated chicken rice casserole. Yuck. Whitleigh shuddered at the memory.

The spoon clanked against the glass bowl as Whitleigh stirred. She drummed her fingers on a book perched on the counter. *The Army Wife's Survival Guide*. With a sigh, she skimmed through the pages. COLA, CONUS, MIA, ATC, ACU, DCU, LES, DEERS. Learning to speak Army-nese proved to be a challenge, but she was improving. Collier would be proud.

Whitleigh took another bite. The letters in her alphabet soup started to look like Army acronyms. She huffed a laugh and pushed the bowl aside, glancing at the clock. Mrs. Ryan would be over in less than half an hour. She all but dragged Whitleigh to the women's book study at church just days after Collier left. Going beat wallowing in sorrow, and meeting other Army wives didn't hurt.

She scooted to the bathroom, hopping into the shower, and then scrambled for a trusty cardigan to complete her look. A dab of lipstick and a smidge of mascara completed her makeup routine. Whitleigh shoved aside what few items she had in her cosmetic bag, grabbing a bobby pin from the bottom. She leaned closer to the mirror, placing the pin into a tidy but wet French braid just in time to hear a rapping at the door. That would be Mrs. Ryan.

Whitleigh opened the door and was instantly greeted by Mrs. Ryan, whose smile appeared as wide as the dish that held the warm casserole displayed in her hands.

Whitleigh's stomach turned. Oh no. "Wow. Um." She smiled. "Thank you so much, Mrs. Ryan."

"Oh, it's nothing." Mrs. Ryan's cheeks flushed as she shrugged a shoulder. "Just thought I'd fatten you up a bit. Skin and bones."

Maybe Whitleigh wouldn't be 'skin and bones' if she could keep down anything this woman cooked.

"You should eat more of those cookies you make for everyone else." Mrs. Ryan leaned in for a side hug. "Which reminds me. Emma's birthday is coming up and we should make a few of her favorite sweets."

That would be nice. Whitleigh nodded. Emma was a sweetie. She deserved a gift for all the upkeep in Whitleigh's flower bed.

Mrs. Ryan stood in the doorway, fanning herself.

"Um." The casserole taunted Whitleigh. "Come in for a second." She took the dish from Mrs. Ryan's hands. The smell of cheesy vegetables attacked her face. This meal had a rendezvous with the trash can when she got back. "Let me grab my Bible, and we can get going."

"I've got a sitter until 8." Mrs. Ryan's voice danced from the living room. Whitleigh said a prayer for the person watching those children. Sweet but wild. "After the study I was hoping we could sit at a coffee shop where there's nothing but silence."

Whitleigh laughed and dropped her Bible into an olive colored satchel. "That sounds like mother's idea of heaven."

Mrs. Ryan winked. "You got it."

"I know just the place." Whitleigh smiled. The woman had her hands full raising five rambunctious children all on her own, never complaining. If her life was askew, she never let on. Where was Mr. Ryan? Whitleigh reached for her keys. It wouldn't be polite to ask. Most women didn't want to talk about their husband's deployment. "Ready?"

"Honey, I've been ready since I woke up." Mrs. Ryan fiddled in her purse and pulled out a tube of lipstick.

Whitleigh would be ready too if she had that many kids. She reached for the doorknob, but another bout of nausea left her frozen.

"Whit? You're looking pale."

"I'm okay." That may have been a lie. If just the smell of Mrs. Ryan's casserole made her feel this way, she could only imagine what the taste would do. Yeah, that dish needed to be tossed. Whitleigh swallowed the ill feeling and pushed on.

WHITLEIGH licked her finger and flipped through the pages of her Bible. Despite the fact that there were more women than before, the growth in attendance had no effect on their inability to interact. Most sat quiet with clasped hands. The Chaplain's wife, a kind, soft spoken woman, led the study. Her study questions did little to pry the ladies from their shells.

Pretty objective stuff, this study. Learning to be content in all situations. Got it.

Whitleigh scanned the faces. Pleasant expressions worked best to keep up a facade. Were all these women as happy as they appeared? She stopped at one transparent face. Whitleigh focused on the young woman whose arms were crossed. She had never seen her before.

Country as cornbread. Big hair, wide brown eyes. Must've been close to her own age. She sat across the bare chapel room, sporting a pair of cowboy boots, looking rather unenthused by the study of Philippians. Her few abbreviated responses and nonverbal cues proved as much. Still, Whitleigh couldn't help but stare at the woman whose accent was so similar to her own.

Home. This lady sounded like home. She looked like home, though a bit flashier. She passed as someone with whom Whitleigh could become good friends. This could be an answered prayer. Whitleigh sat taller.

"That's Jen." Mrs. Ryan leaned in, her voice a whisper. "She's from Tennessee." Nice. They were probably cousins. Whitleigh chuckled inside at her clever little joke — good old Kentucky humor.

Mrs. Ryan spat out facts like reading from a mental check list. "She's new to the area and engaged to a soldier who's deployed. I think she's a student at the same college you're at."

Nosy, but informative, that's Mrs. Ryan. "Want to invite her for coffee?"

Whitleigh nodded her head. Of course she did.

The Grounds, a quaint café, wasn't far off post. Whitleigh all but chuckled as she stepped through the door. She was doing it. Making friends. Making it on her own. It felt nice. She soaked in the aroma of coffee and slid into the corner booth next to Mrs. Ryan.

"Thanks for making time to hang out with us." Whitleigh fought to restrain the excitement in her voice. Mrs. Ryan chuckled.

Jen smiled. She even looked like a friend or two from back home. "I'm glad someone invited me." That accent was so comforting. "I promised Mark I'd make friends and try to fit in."

"Tell me about it." Whitleigh rolled her eyes. She knew all about that.

Mrs. Ryan placed an elbow on the table. "Well, sometimes fitting in means you have to make room."

"Well, here's to making room." Jen lifted her coffee mug.

Whitleigh held her mug high. "And to new friendships."

One sip. She winced. Ugh. The coffee tasted off.

She tried another. Worse.

Her stomach turned, and a wave of sickness washed over her body.

Oh. Not again. Where was the bathroom?

Whitleigh sprinted down the hall and plunged toward the toilet just as a violent spout of vomit spewed from her mouth. She clung to the commode, stomach muscles heaving. Mrs. Ryan's casserole couldn't be blamed for this.

The room spun. Could it be? Her panted breaths quickened. She hung her head and opened the bathroom door. Mrs. Ryan and Jen still sat, their worried faces staring at her from the booth.

Why hadn't she thought of this earlier?

She counted the weeks in her head since Collier had left. No. It wasn't possible.

But it was.

Jen arched an eyebrow.

There goes a new friendship out the window before it even started.

Mrs. Ryan placed a hand on Whitleigh's. "Whit?"

Beads of sweat dotted along the lines of her forehead. She swiped them away. "I think I'm pregnant."

THERE was nothing much left to talk about with Jen and Layla after two more unattractive bouts of nausea. It was a great girls' night gone wrong. Whitleigh called it a night and then called to make a doctor's appointment first thing in the morning.

The doctor's words played through her mind all day. "Pregnant. Six to eight weeks." His enthusiastic words confirmed her fear.

Whitleigh's fingers trembled as she sat on her bed, staring blankly at the wall ahead. She touched her stomach.

Pregnant. Unbelievable.

Their five year goal to have children, shot. Five years, then start a family. After saving more money. After college. After a few years of teaching. After the Army — if there was an after Army. After Collier came home. Her eyes stung. If he came home.

The bed seemed emptier at that moment. Whitleigh reached for Collier's pillow and gathered it close to her body. His scent lingered. She closed her eyes. The arrival of their first child should've been a joyous occasion, but right now she struggled to find the joy. Tears flowed.

Whitleigh rolled to face the Bible on her nightstand. Her vision blurred through watery eyes. Even if she wanted to pray, would the words come? Would God even listen?

She pursed her lips. Collier needed to know. Not through an email. No. It would be best to wait for his call. Whitleigh nuzzled the pillow against her cheek. If the circumstances were different she would've told him by placing baby booties in his Army boots before he left for work. Little white ones. She smiled. Sending a care package with baby items or a Father's Day card sufficed, but snail mail would take too long.

A baby is a blessing, no matter the timing. True. She knew it, so why couldn't she stop crying?

Whitleigh wiped her tears, gathering her knees to her chest. Home. She wanted to go home, where she wouldn't be alone, where the war didn't reach. Friends and family awaited back home. This life, this Army life, grew more horrible by the moment. She didn't get married to be single.

Done. She felt her eyes narrow as she lurched from the bed toward her closet.

"Don't do it." Mrs. Ryan stood in her doorway.

Whitleigh jumped back. "I didn't even hear you come in."

How silly she must look to Mrs. Ryan.

Mrs. Ryan shrugged an apology. "I knocked and got worried when you didn't answer. You've been hiding out in here too long."

She wasn't hiding. Whitleigh crossed her arms, sat back down, and dabbed at her eyes with a sleeve.

"I know what you're thinking." Mrs. Ryan leaned against the door frame. Lord knows I've packed a few suitcases in my lifetime, ready to walk away from it all." Her eyes sparkled like she enjoyed being an Army wife. Whitleigh fought the urge to huff out loud. "Come on. Let's get outside for a while." That was the last thing Whitleigh wanted to do. Mrs. Ryan gestured toward the hall with her head. "Fresh air will do you some good."

THE neighborhood children ran through the sprinkler in Mrs. Ryan's yard. Their laughter warranted smiles from any passerby. Even Whitleigh smiled. Emma danced underneath the drops of water alongside the Ryan children. Carefree and knobby-kneed Emma was the sweetest child on the block, despite her mother's obvious lack of involvement. Whitleigh's heart warmed at the child's cheery grin.

"See," Mrs. Ryan scooted a chair next to hers and patted the seat, "fresh air helps."

Whitleigh settled into the chair. A few children rolled past on skateboards, chased by a mother's call of caution. Several moms sat, chatting, their lawn chairs in a half circle, tapping their toes to the radio tunes. Mrs. Ryan jumped in on the conversation like a pro. Whitleigh watched and listened as they changed diapers, snapped photos, and kissed boo boos, never missing a beat. Emma waved, and Whitleigh smiled in return.

Motherhood. Whitleigh sighed. That thought demanded a nervous swallow. She placed a careful hand on her abdomen.

Her phone buzzed. Not a moment too soon. She hurried from her seat. "Hello?"

Static sounded from the other end. "Hello, beautiful."

Collier. Thank God. "How are you?"

"The phone lines aren't the best here." His voice faded and then cut out before clearing up. He sighed. "I'm okay. Best I can be." His voice sounded off.

"Yeah?" She didn't dare mention any of the causalities. He would talk about it if he wanted.

"It's been rough the past few days. Lots of, well, war stuff." Whitleigh imagined him running a hand through his buzzed hair.

"Oh." What do you say to that? At least he was safe.

"Tell me about your world." She could almost hear a faint smile in his voice.

"Well, there's been lots going on." She had to tell him about their baby. "Like me getting ready for school, and house stuff." Just tell him. "And like how you're going to be a daddy." Why couldn't she be smoother?

"What?" His voice raised three or four octaves. She held a breath. Was he upset? The phone line crackled and popped like a breakfast cereal. Her heart resumed beating when he released a hearty laugh.

"Hey guys. Guess what?" His voice boomed.

Tears stung her eyes. He was happy. Maybe she could have joy now. Yes, it began to bubble up inside. Everything would be all right.

A thick, low hum vibrated through the phone line. Rustling. Loud, urgent voices reverberated through the phone. What were they saying?

"Get down. Get down." Did she hear that right?

"Collier?" Whitleigh pressed the phone against her ear as tight as possible. Don't panic.

She clasped her hand over her other ear to drown out the neighborhood noise. "Collier. Can you hear me? Collier?"

Clatter or some sort of popping noise sounded over the wire. Gunfire? She wasn't sure.

The line died.

Whitleigh's limbs stiffened. Her joy evaporated. The phone in her hand might as well have been a fifty pound cannon ball as it thudded to the ground.

The Army was right. No news was good news.

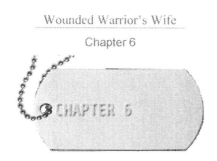

THE phone lay at his side. Collier blinked his eyes, but the thick clouds of rubble and smoke made sight a near impossibility. An RPG attack. Collier growled as he lifted sheets of plywood and plaster from his body. The insurgents of Ar Ramadi, Iraq rarely hit a target, but when they did, it proved deadly.

His head rung. The dense atmosphere swirled with floating debris. Each breath singed the lining of his throat. Where was the doorway? Where were his buddies — Haden, Dock, and Pulu?

Muffled groans sounded in the distance. Maybe closer but he couldn't tell. Exchanged gunfire popped and echoed in the streets. Collier reached for his gun and rolled onto his knees. Sweat dripped from his face. He closed his eyes to steady the spinning room. Covered in dust and wreckage, Collier ran his hands over his body checking for injuries … blood. His blood? A pool of red puddled beneath his knees, covered his hands, and trickled from his chin.

He stumbled back, breaths heavy, moving his hands up and down his body at a frantic pace. All clear. But whose blood? With this type of attack, it could've been anyone's.

Collier low crawled toward the stream of crimson fluid, aware of the pressing weight his bulletproof vest created. He inched around the perimeters of the room, tightening the chin strap of his helmet into place. Still bodies to his right and left. Death. Collier swallowed the lump climbing up his throat. He could hear the pained cries of the injured, but where were they?

His fingers stumbled across the rigid floor as he searched low to the ground for survivors. A soldier stirred beneath his fingertips and groaned as Collier tugged on the man's uniform.

Rays of light peeked beneath a baseboard a mere thirty feet to his right.

A way out.

Collier scrambled to his feet, hacking and spitting out the thick layers of dust. He knelt, lifted the soldier over his shoulders, and with a surge of adrenaline, bolted out the doorway and onto the street. His ears rang, his head pounded, but it didn't matter.

An overturned Humvee provided enough shelter to administer first aid. Valuable even in the daylight, he reached into his side belt pouch for a flare to shoot. The others would be able to locate them that way. Collier laid the man down and scanned for injuries.

A bullet to the hip.

No tourniquet would stop the bleeding, but he had to try. Collier ripped the paracord bracelet from his wrist, unraveling it as he sought a way to tie it around the soldier. He used his hand to push against the wound and tightened the cord with his free hand.

Jesus. Help.

Collier clamped his eyes closed. Could he look into the face of the man he wouldn't be able to save?

A chilled, damp hand touched his.

"Cromwell. Stop."

No. Collier released the breath he subconsciously held. He knew that voice. "First Sergeant."

Collier clenched his teeth together, a failed attempt to prevent the stinging in his tearing eyes.

The First Sergeant's bloody fingerprints stained the top of Collier's hand. Collier smudged the prints as he rummaged through his pouches. Bandages, anything he could use to apply more pressure to the wound. There was always hope.

"Cromwell." The First Sergeant's voice grew low. He struggled to lift his hand. "Stop."

"No." Collier ripped material from his own pant leg and wadded it up before applying pressure to the First Sergeant's hip. "You're fine. You're okay." Collier pushed down on the oozing wound. Thick, dark blood bubbled between his knuckles. Too much blood.

"It's okay." First Sergeant Gunthrie winced. His eyes dimmed. "You can let me go." He wheezed and coughed. "Get the others."

Collier pushed harder on the First Sergeant's hip. He could stop the bleeding. He could. He had to.

Why hadn't help come?

"I'm sending up another signal." Collier plunged his free hand into his rucksack, searching for another flare. "You're going to be fine." He lied. "Help is on the way." He prayed, then shot it up to the sky. Maybe they would respond to that one.

The First Sergeant's breathing slowed. "I'm giving you an order. Go."

Collier turned away at the sight of his superior struggling to speak. With the paracord tied tight around the First Sergeant's upper hip, Collier pressed on the wound with both hands until the muscles in his arms shook. His superior groaned beneath the pressure. Little else could be done. He wouldn't make it much longer without immediate medical attention.

"Go." First Sergeant Gunthrie's voice deepened.

Collier couldn't let go. He wouldn't.

"Go." The First Sergeant pushed Collier away. It must've taken all his remaining strength.

With the crook of his elbow, Collier shoved a tear aside. It was time to let him go.

Clutched in bloodied fists, Collier gripped his M-4 Rifle. He stood to his feet and maneuvered across the street with vigilance, ready to strike down anyone that came between him and those who were trapped and wounded.

He fired his weapon only twice before reentering the building, hitting both enemy targets. Clean kills.

Collier hurried through the room. One. Two. Three. Four soldiers dead. Movement in the far corner caught his attention. Two soldiers, both wounded, one unconscious.

The weight of the second soldier hoisted over his shoulders caused Collier's knees to buckle. He heaved, trying to catch his breath. His muscles screamed in protest as he carried each man to safety and hustled back in hopes of finding others.

One. Two. Three. Four. Five. Six, and no more found alive. Collier collapsed alongside the Humvee, exhausted. Thirsty, but too tired to drink, Collier let his head hang. Reinforcements scoured the area. Finally. Medics tended to those needing attention and moved past those that no longer required their services.

Collier covered his face as two soldiers placed a blanket over his First Sergeant's motionless body. Lifeless fingers dangled over the side of a gurney. This man, once deemed invincible, fell prey to war.

Collier's throat constricted.

BY now, the families of the fallen would've been contacted. Two days was the typical protocol. The phone lines and internet would be running again. He should call Whit. She'd be worried.

Whit. His heart raced at the thought of her carrying their child. He rubbed his brow.

The men gathered outside a makeshift bunker, preparing for another patrol. Their eyes drooped. Constant combat followed his unit. Collier sighed and wiped dirt from his body with a wet wipe. What he wouldn't give for a hot shower and a good night's rest.

"You deserve an award." Haden sat on a cinder block and washed off with a bottle of water. "You saved six men."

Collier shook his head. He didn't need any kind of award. "I couldn't save the others." Their paled faces, vacant and glossed over eyes, scrolled through his mind. Men he knew. Smith. Garret. Jenkins. Swarnson. First Sergeant Gunthrie. Collier dragged the wipe over his face, careful to dodge the scrapes and cuts.

"No." Haden shook his head. "They were already gone."

"You're looking at it all wrong, Cromwell." Pulu crouched at Collier's side. Collier looked at him in disbelief. What other way was there to look at it?

Dock scooted a cinder block over and sat beside Haden. "For once, the child delinquent has a point." Pulu punched Dock's arm. Their antics weren't lifting his mood today.

"Gear up." Their Squad Leader, Sergeant Prowski, walked by. Time to roll out again. Collier lifted his head to the sky, then pulled on his helmet.

He trudged through the city, rucksack on his back. The heavy bag pulled on his shoulders. He paid it no attention. One foot in front of the other kept him going. Their squad's patrol ended soon.

Riddled by war, the rocky ground of Ar Ramadi crumbled beneath his boots. A few scrawny chickens ran loose, clucking and pecking at the ground. Collier's stomach grumbled. Breakfast was long gone.

"No sarcastic comments from you today, Pulu? Dock?" Haden's voice teased. The men were too tired to make any kind of conversation.

Dock threw a grin in Haden's direction. Pulu replied with a sharp dart of his eyes. His bushy eyebrows moved close together, almost seamless.

Collier smirked. Pulu's eyebrows looked like fuzzy caterpillars.

Sergeant Prowski led their squad through trashed back alley ways.

"Alright men." Sergeant Prowski stopped and tossed his ruck to the ground. "We'll rest here for a bit and get some grub." He unzipped his ruck, pulled out an MRE (Meal Ready to Eat), and tore it open with his teeth. "Dock. Pulu. Pull guard. Ten minute shifts." Sergeant Prowski pointed at each alley entry point.

Collier shook his MRE. The burrito was not home cooking, but nothing to sneer at.

"Hey." Haden jostled his MRE in his hands. "This one has Skittles in it. Wanna trade?"

"Sure." Collier hadn't had those in a while. Nice for a change.

Collier licked his lips. His mouth watered as he prepared to take the first bite, but a mound of moving trash brought him to his feet in seconds, weapon aimed. With an unidentifiable enemy everywhere, Collier refused to go down without a fight.

Sergeant Prowski motioned the men with an index finger, assigning them each to a point of attack. Weapons in hand, the soldiers hustled into position with catlike precision. Two on look out, three surrounding the threat.

A light breeze swept through the back street and lifted bits of crumbled paper, tossing them about like a tumbleweed. Collier steadied his breath, ready to shoot, ready to kill the enemy if need be.

From beneath the heap of garbage, a small, filthy hand stretched out. It was just a child.

"Hold your position." The order hesitated from Sergeant Prowski's lips. Even a child posed a threat. Collier's nose flared. The enemy was disgusting and cruel beyond anything he could've imagined. Twisted enough to send a child to do their dirty work.

Haden pushed away the crate with his boot, exposing a terrified and dirty child, no more than five or six years old. She hid her face in her knees and began to cry. There was no way she was a threat.

"Lower your weapons." Sergeant Prowski wiped at the sweat pouring down from his helmet.

"Just a kid? Really?" Dock stomped. "I'm pretty sure my guard duty is over. Could you relieve me? This cowboy needs to eat."

Pulu peered over his shoulder. "What do we do with a kid?"

Sergeant Prowski shrugged. One thing was for sure, they couldn't keep her.

Taking off his helmet, Haden laid his weapon down and eased his way toward the child.

"Careful." The words slipped from Sergeant Prowski's mouth.

"She's just scared." Collier scanned her tiny body. "And probably hungry."

"Yeah." Dock scoffed. "I know the feeling."

Collier ignored Dock's grumbling.

Haden knelt down, grabbed a handful of Collier's skittles, and held out an open palm. "Hi sweetheart." The child eyed the candy. She searched the soldiers' faces and buried hers in crossed arms. Collier looked away. They must look like monsters with all their equipment and weapons. Her sobs tugged at his heart. Didn't she know that her people terrified them?

"Here." Haden placed the candy at her side.

Dock waved an arm. "Seriously. I'm starving over here." He had a bachelor's degree in irritation.

"No. She's starving." Sergeant Prowski rolled his eyes. "You're just annoying."

Collier walked to his ruck. Wind swirled through the alley, carrying with it the putrid smells of incense and must.

"Cromwell." Sergeant Prowski placed his hands on his hips. "What are you doing?"

"The right thing, Sergeant." Collier gathered the food from his MRE and placed it in front of the child.

Haden smiled, nodding. Pulu watched, silent.

The girl peeked from behind her arms. Her petite hand inched toward the food.

Haden pushed his open MRE in her direction. "Do you think she's an orphan?"

The men shrugged. Numerous civilian causalities in this war at the enemy's hand, and unfortunately their own, made this a real possibility.

The girl lifted her eyes to Collier's. Large, brown. A deep well filled with more pain than a child should know. Experiences he'd give his life to make sure his child would never have.

In one swift motion, she shoved the contents of his MRE into her mouth. The pangs of hunger bypassed any trust issues the child carried toward the soldiers. Melted cheese oozed from the end of the burrito, landing on her scrawny leg. She scooped it up, licking her fingers clean.

Sergeant Prowski placed a canteen at her side. She drank, water pouring down her chin and neck, creating rivers of clean skin. The men silently watched. War was cruel even to the innocent. Dock appeared to forget his need to eat. Collier couldn't have eaten if he wanted to. His chest tightened.

Sergeant Prowski picked up his ruck. "There's a school close by. We can take her there."

More gusts of wind blew through the narrow street. Sand smacked against their faces. Bad weather neared. Dust storms lasted from minutes to days.

Sergeant Prowski led the way. "Let's move before the storm hits."

Collier reached out to the child. Her boney arms hesitated, then wrapped tight around his neck. She buried her face into his chest. He held her close, following his squad from the alley, and hummed a lullaby recalled from a few scarce pleasant childhood memories.

THE air was crisp. Too rainy for November in his opinion, but this was Iraq, not America. Not home.

Home.

Collier loosened his hold on the trigger.

Time was flying, but not fast enough. Seven months left in this stinking deployment. He wasn't sure what fueled his desire to leave, his hate for Iraq and its people, or his love for Whit.

Whit.

How was she?

Recent photographs of her growing belly played through his mind and lifted the corner edges of his lips.

Their baby.

He let the word bounce on the tip of his tongue and swirl through his mind like a dream. At times, dreams were his sole companion. God knows he wanted to make it out of this sandbox alive, but who knew if God even listened?

Each fallen comrade made it more difficult to pray. Too many died, and more would fall.

Collier narrowed his eyes as he sat perched in the gunner seat atop the Humvee. He scanned his surroundings. Littered streets and rusty broken down cars. A stray dog scampered from one local market vendor to the other, shooed away by each. An anonymous tip on the whereabouts of an insurgent spurred their patrol. So far, nothing.

Children, much like the frail girl from the alley, kicked tattered and faded soccer balls along the street sides and in between honking cars. Women, concealed by long, dark garments, shuffled past, careful not to make eye contact with any male along their path. The smell of grilled goat lingered in the air. Collier scrunched his nose. He'd rather go hungry than eat goat, or anything those people made.

This place was a mess. The whole country was a mess. Collier huffed louder than intended.

"You okay Cromwell?" Pulu puffed on a cigarette and shouted from the passenger seat below.

"Yeah." Collier leaned against the metal frame of the turret. He was fine. Everything was fine.

He eyed the townspeople. Which one of them plotted the next roadside bomb? The next ambush? Without an enemy brave enough to wear a uniform, everyone became suspect. His hand tightened on the trigger. There was a woman thumping on a melon at the fruit stand. Was she a threat? Or maybe the older man leaning against the rock wall. He looked suspicious. Even children, though the child in the alley proved an exception.

Maybe he'd grown callous, even inhumane, but pulling his trigger became easier, too easy.

With gritted teeth, he peered at the passersby through the crosshairs of his weapon. How many more of his friends were these people going to murder? Winning the hearts and minds of the Iraqi citizens was nice in theory, but that ideology went out the window when bullets started to fly.

Haden may not agree, but Collier knew one thing — the more enemies he could kill, the more of his buddies lived. He swallowed and jerked his hand from the gun. The lines between right and wrong blurred with each passing day, each dead body, and each bullet fired from his weapon.

WHITLEIGH stood up from the pew of the silent and somber chapel. Jen followed behind as they made their way past the photos of the young men killed in combat mere days ago — the fallen. Thank the Lord Collier wasn't among them. She winced at the selfish thought.

The family members, their faces long and tired, stood in a line, greeting those in attendance. How were they standing? Whitleigh's knees buckled as she grew closer to the families. A middle-aged woman dabbed at her eyes. A mother? Whitleigh's lips quivered. What could she say to a mother who lost her child? She placed a palm on her growing abdomen. Losing the life inside was unimaginable. A painful, paralyzing thought.

Whitleigh's heart thudded against her chest cavity as she worked to keep her composure. The woman's worn eyes watered. Whitleigh's arms opened to reach for her as if they operated on their own.

"Thank you for coming." The woman's voice sounded just above a whisper.

Whitleigh managed a nod, but nothing more. She crossed her arms and hurried out the exit. Deep waves of chilled November air filled her lungs.

"You okay?" Jen placed a hand on Whitleigh's shoulder.

"Yeah." Maybe. Whitleigh reached into her black handbag for a mint. Her stomach twisted in a multitude of knots. How many more men and women would die before this war ended?

Jen tucked her arm through the nook of Whitleigh's elbow, and they walked to the little blue Yota without a word. It was nice to have Jen at her side. Knowing her fiancé, Mark, was in Collier's unit experiencing the same travesties, added a level of difficulty to attending the memorial ceremonies.

Whitleigh pried open the creaking car door.

She closed her eyes, taking a seat on the frigid cushion behind the wheel.

"We don't have to keep coming to these you know." Jen slid into the passenger seat. Maybe she was right. Since their first meeting in the coffee shop months ago, she and Jen frequented all ceremonies. Attending drained Whitleigh's emotions.

"That could've been Collier." Whitleigh turned the key until the car rumbled to life.

Jen's eyes flickered away. "Or Mark."

A dull mood, darker than the clouds overhead, floated in their midst and followed them as she pulled from the chapel parking lot.

"I sent Collier a care package a few weeks ago." Her eyes watered. "It's been awhile since he's called, and I can't stop wondering if he'll ever get it, or will I wake up one day and it's been returned?"

"No news — "

"Is good news. I know." Knowing didn't make it easier. Whitleigh ran a hand across the back of her neck. She checked the time on the dashboard. "You got anywhere you have to be before book study tonight?"

Jen shrugged. "I thought maybe you'd want someone to go to the doctor appointment with you."

"I'd like that." Whitleigh smiled, and the atmosphere lightened. Going with someone beat going alone. Collier should be the one hearing their baby's heartbeat, experiencing it all.

Dwelling on what couldn't be changed served no purpose. Whitleigh kept to the road. "Have you thought about going to the women's holiday brunch? They'll be putting together Christmas packages for our guys. It could be fun."

"I don't know." Jen wrinkled her nose. "FRG stuff, that's a little too cliquey for me. Ranks don't mix that well, if you know what I mean."

"Not really." Whitleigh's brow folded. Most of her time was spent at school, giving little thought to the mind boggling rank structure of the Army. "Collier's tried to explain all the levels and their jobs, but honestly it just seems kind of silly to me, and besides, why would the women even care about mixing ranks?"

"Oh honey." Jen all but cackled. "How long have you been an Army wife? Going on two years, and you still don't know?"

"You're not even an Army wife," Whitleigh grumbled. "How do you know how things mix in this world?"

"Um, Hello. I was an Army brat. Remember?"

"Oh. Yeah." Whitleigh shook her head. Jen's life story — Army brat, strict Christian upbringing, rebellious teen; now an on track excelling college student.

"Our husbands, well, my soon-to-be husband and your husband, are enlisted." She stared at Whitleigh. "They're not even NCO's yet."

NCO. NCO. Whitleigh lifted a finger. "Non Commissioned Officer." Well done. "So what? I'm proud of my Private First Class, soon to be Specialist."

Jen shifted in her seat. "That's not the point."

"Besides, it's his rank, not mine." The Army need not force anything else on her.

"You'll find many wives don't see it that way." Jen crossed her legs and smoothed out her pin-striped skirt. "I can feel them staring at us with disdain already."

"That's silly." Whitleigh turned on the windshield wipers as a slow drizzle fell. She stilled the car at the stop sign, looking both ways. "Well, I'm going to the brunch anyway."

"Guess that means I'm going too." Jen rolled her eyes. "Do me a favor and bring those little cakes you make."

"The petit fours?" Delicate baking business, those things.

"Yep." Jen twirled a strand of dark hair around her index finger. She and Mrs. Ryan loved those cakes. So did Whit. "The officers' wives will die of disbelief when they find out a lower enlisted spouse made them."

"Hey." Whitleigh's jaw dropped open. "That's terrible on like sixteen different kinds of levels." Rank didn't matter, at least not to her.

"Just telling how it is." Jen's shoulders boosted. A twisted grin crept up the side of her face. "And tell them you're about to graduate college. They'll never believe you." She tugged on the sleeve of Whitleigh's white woolen sweater. "Ha. They'll never believe you're lower enlisted dressed like that anyway."

"Like what?" Whitleigh scanned her outfit. Pearls. Sweater. Dress pants.

"Like you're a model for *Southern Living* magazine or something." Jen's high cheek bones elevated. "I mean, come on. You have an extensive cardigan collection."

"I'll take that as a compliment." Cardigans were comfy and classy. "And, for your information, cardigans can be dressed up or down. Thank you very much."

Jen raised a brow.

"What?" Whitleigh grimaced. "I dress down." She signaled left, mouth still moving. "You've seen me in my sweats. That old sweatshirt Collier hates is my favorite thing to wear."

Jen held up a hand and cocked her head. "Just saying, I'm going to have a blast watching these women intermingle with you."

"Glad I could make you laugh." A Christmas Brunch with fellow Army wives. How bad could it be? Whitleigh's palms dampened. She tightened her hold on the steering wheel. Jen wasn't the end all, tell all guide to Army wife behavior. Whitleigh dismissed the thought with a quiet humph.

The car piddled along past the corner Shoppette and onward toward the women's medical facility.

"So," Jen plucked Whitleigh's latest design and renovation magazine from the dashboard and scanned through the pages, "I'm wondering when I'm gonna get to taste those little goodies again."

"You mean, the petit fours?" She flicked the turn signal on.

Jen nodded.

"Tonight actually."

"Oh yeah." Jen's voice sank. "I've got class tonight."

"Boo. Well, maybe after?" Whitleigh sat taller in the seat, relieving pressure in her lower back. "This batch came out pretty well. Got to keep perfecting my technique."

"Can't stay too late, got an early bird class in the morning," Jen grumbled, crossing her legs. I'm taking all midmorning classes next semester."

"You just want to sleep longer." Whitleigh's small, rounded belly bounced with her short chuckle. "Can't say I blame you though." As the pregnancy progressed, so did her need for naps.

"What about you?" Jen jabbed a playful elbow in Whitleigh's direction. "You still gonna take next semester off?"

"Humph." Whitleigh's sigh was heavy. "I don't know. Guess I need to decide soon." Baby Cromwell's late February due date put May's graduation in question. "How am I supposed to finish student teaching and take a leave of absence to have this little one?" Her heart throbbed. "I just want to graduate and teach." She'd worked too hard to stop now, but the option to finish out the school year seemed unavailable.

"The professors will work with you."

"Yeah." She clicked her nails on the steering wheel. "You're probably right." Was day care a viable option? Whitleigh's forehead wrinkled. Plans for the future couldn't be ironed out in a ten minute car ride.

"Well, if you decide to take off, I was hoping that would give you more time to perfect your petit fours." Jen waved her hand as the last two words fell out of her mouth with a failed French accent.

"You'd think I'd be the one craving sweets, not you." Whitleigh patted her stomach and stopped at the red light. "Your sweet tooth is almost as bad as Mrs. Ryan's."

"It's important for you to get those bad boys to expert level." Jen's grin was too crooked for her own good. "Since Mark and I are getting married when he comes home on leave in March."

"Oh my goodness." Whitleigh's accent thickened. She stomped the gas pedal and the car lurched forward. "You're kidding! That's so amazing."

"Eyes on the road, my friend." Jen wriggled in her seat. A car honked as it passed.

"Sorry." Whitleigh giggled an apology. "So, you're kidding, right?"

"Nope. Not joking." Jen twirled the diamond on her left finger. "We didn't want to wait to get married until after the deployment."

Whitleigh nodded. That made sense. Memorial ceremonies served as a morbid reminder to embrace life — carpe diem.

"And," Jen talked through squinted eyes, "I was kind of wondering if you would … help?"

"Help?" What could she do?

"With catering, planning, and decorating."

"Me?" Whitleigh paused and looked ahead in time to see the next turn. "Why me?"

"Seriously?" Jen's forehead creased. "I've seen and tasted all those delicious things you bring to our group, and have you seen your house?"

Whitleigh winced. What was wrong with her home?

"It's like a classy, comfy, chic, vintage craft fair exploded in there."

"Um." Whitleigh reached for the heat nozzle, turning it up a tad. "Thanks. I think."

"Please." Puppy dog face wasn't a good look for Jen. "You have to help."

"I don't know, Jen." Whitleigh searched for the expectant mother parking spot at the facility. "I've never done anything like that before." She shook her head. "I don't think I'm the person you want."

"Please. Please." Jen clasped her hands. "I know you can do it." She crossed her arms and laughed. "The only reason I kept coming to the book study was to see what you were gonna bring."

"I noticed you stalking the dessert table." Whitleigh gave a half grin. How Jen managed to stay fit baffled them all.

"It seems like a lot to take on. School. A baby." She tapped her belly. The baby kicked back. He was a strong one. The expectant mother's parking spot was open. Score. Whitleigh's eyes brightened.

"It's a small wedding. Not even sure what day it would be on right now." That's Army life. Jen smirked. "Twenty people tops."

Whitleigh parked and pulled the key from the ignition. Planning a wedding did sound fun. She huffed as her stomach grumbled again. A big juicy burger sounded better.

"I totally get it." Jen's face melted into a frown and then became animated again. "What if you and I start planning now?" Her hands moved faster than her words. "We can design the table settings, flowers, pick out recipes. Do all of it now, and then when it's time for the wedding, I'm sure I can find people to carry out our plan — the women in our group even."

That was an idea. A good one.

Several table setting options swirled through Whitleigh's mind. Pearls. Shades of white. Classy. Even a big haired, gum chomping, loud make-up kind of girl like Jen would appreciate a classic three or four tiered cake.

The baby jostled inside, a sweet reminder of who would be occupying most her time all too soon. Whitleigh's lips twisted to the side. "This could work, but right now we've got to go check out this baby, and then I need to eat before I turn evil."

"I'M going to starve before this lady comes back." Whitleigh's feet dangled from the edge of the examining table, while watching the hands tick on the clock. Her stomach groaned. She swallowed back the nausea. A television, high in the corner, broadcasted low murmurs across the confined area. At least waiting for the ultrasound tech to return proved entertaining with Jen at her side. She listened as Jen chatted on about wedding plans.

"I can't wait to tell Mark you're helping us." The metal chair clanked underneath her. "How much do we owe you?"

"Owe me? To plan? Nothing." No way could she charge Jen. Collier outranked Mark, meaning Mark made less pay.

"We have to give you something." Jen chuckled and placed a hand on her hip. "Wedding planners get paid."

"A wedding planner?" Whitleigh snickered. Maybe a future teacher. She was definitely not wedding planner. "You can't pay me. Just give me a budget and consider the planning a wedding gift from your best friend."

"I can't thank you enough." Jen wrapped her arms around Whitleigh, rustling the paper gown around her body.

"Easy." Whitleigh held the thin parchment clothing closed.

"You better believe I'll be all over babysitting for you. Diaper duty here I come."

"That's payment enough." Whitleigh patted Jen's back with her free hand.

"Hey, look." Jen tore away, her head snapped toward the television. "Isn't that your neighborhood?"

It was. Whitleigh scooted to the edge of the seat, forgetting her hunger. Even with the volume low, another report of domestic violence scrolled across the screen loud enough to hear.

"Your neck of the woods is getting pretty scary." Jen folded her arms across her chest. "Three rape cases on base, and all sorts of spouse abuse reports."

Whitleigh pried her focus from the screen. The news was disheartening. It was more proof she lived in the midst of a very different war.

"Have they found the rapist yet?"

"No." Whitleigh eyed her purse. That's why she carried pepper spray. "And nothing more was ever said about the man who accidentally killed his wife. Such a sad story."

Jen bit at her lip. "You living all alone scares me." She tucked her clasped hands between her knees. "At least I'm in a dorm."

"I try not to dwell on it." Whitleigh licked her lips, her heart quickened. Collier did his best to secure the locks before he left, and Mrs. Ryan lived across the street. Her gun toting habits were quite obvious to everyone on the block.

The door creaked open. Finally.

Whitleigh stilled her jittering legs. Her smile faded as the doctor entered behind the lab tech. "Is everything okay?" His straight faced expression gave little insight to their downcast demeanor.

He pursed his lips and extended a cool hand. Surely hers felt clammy. "It's nice to see you again Mrs. Cromwell." His smile offered some reassurance. "Are you still wanting to keep the sex of the baby a surprise?"

Whitleigh presented a tight grin. "We have our guesses, but Collier and I want to be surprised together."

Jen gave an impish eye roll.

"Very well then." The doctor nodded and jotted a few notes on his clipboard.

"Sir, is everything all right?" Whitleigh toyed with her wedding band.

"I'm not going to lie, Mrs. Cromwell." He rubbed a hand over his graying beard and peered over his glasses as he sat on the rolling stool. "We've seen some things on the ultrasound that concern us."

"Things?" Whitleigh swallowed. "What do you mean?"

"Right now, they are just concerns, nothing confirmed." His voice was kind. "We want you to come back in a few days and do a special test to check your baby's heart." He gave Whitleigh's knee a pat. "We'll know more then."

Whitleigh managed a nod. Jen scooted close and placed her hand over Whitleigh's.

"Ms. Paula at the front desk can schedule the appointment for you." The lab tech slipped from the room.

The doctor stood, his lab coat stretched across a stomach much larger than hers. "Go home and relax. Most of these things turn out to be nothing. We make mistakes all of the time." His words were sincere, but doubt clouded her mind.

Collier needed to know. He should know, but how could she add to his worries? Telling him something like this could distract him. Distraction caused injuries, sometime even fatalities.

"You want me to leave?" Jen's voice shook. "Give you a minute by yourself?"

"No." Whitleigh placed a trembling hand against her mouth. Being alone right now was the worst thing imaginable.

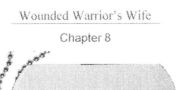

COLLIER reread Whit's latest letter and held the cardboard care package laden with whimsical swirling hearts in his lap. He kicked back on his cot. Dock, Pulu, and Haden lounged on the dust covered floor, devouring snacks from their packages. Collier plunged a handful of tortilla chips into a container of cheese dip and then into his mouth.

Whit's gifts came just in time. Limited food supply created the greatest weight loss plan known to mankind. Twenty pounds lighter and hopefully no more. He chugged the remaining water in his canteen and washed down the last of Whit's homemade sugar cookies. Three dozen cookies were no match for a squad of soldiers. Dock and Pulu wrestled for the crumbs left in the container.

Collier rubbed his full stomach and kissed the latest ultrasound picture, noticing a small watermark on the edge of the photo. Rain, or maybe a tear? Not a tear. Whitleigh had no reason to cry.

He ambled to his sore feet and hung it alongside the others on the tiny bulletin board above his bed. Collier folded each page of the letter with care, returning it to the kiss covered envelope. Emails were great, but nothing beat a handwritten letter. His dirt covered fingers skimmed across the faded lip prints on the envelope. It was the closest he could get to Whit right now.

Haden limped to his feet and toyed with the photos on Collier's bulletin board. "When are you gonna hang up your award?"

Dock and Pulu stopped in mid conversation.

Collier glared at the green document holder on the floor. The Act of Valor. Cruel evidence of his fallen brothers. Proof he couldn't save them. "It's just a piece of paper."

"It's more." Haden shook his head, flopping onto a bean bag.

No need to argue. Opinions weren't in short supply.

Collier crossed off another square from the calendar he had duct taped to the wall and doodled a Christmas tree on the 25th, just days away.

"You know what I want for Christmas?" Dock opened a letter.

Haden and Pulu looked at one another, offering a shrug.

"A warm shower." Dock sniffed his underarms and groaned.

"What? Cleaning off with bottles of water isn't cutting it?" Pulu's second language was sarcasm, but no one liked water bottle showers.

"I guess you don't like feeling baby fresh either?" Haden chuckled, and Collier laughed along. Bathing with baby wipes had a way of making a man feel less manly.

"I told Whit she could stop sending me wipes and just keep them. I'm sure we'll go through about a million when the baby comes."

"The way you're smelling, Cromwell, I'd say you need to keep as many wipes as you can get." Dock covered his head to dodge a slew of playful punches.

The room boomed with their hearty laughter, the kind that was good for the soul. The kind he shared with Whit.

Collier's laugh wheezed to a halt. He plopped on his cot and rolled to his side, Whit's letter still in hand. If he was home, he'd be drinking hot cocoa and watching some corny holiday movie with her, dancing by a fire, or engaging in a snowball fight. They would be marking off all those things still left undone on their Forever List.

After another read, he tucked the letter in the pocket closest to his heart. It was safe there.

She seemed to be doing well. School. Friends. The baby. Even helping to plan Crawford's wedding. Good man, and Jen sounded like a cool girl from all that Whit said.

Whit's life was good. Peaceful even. Collier nodded. She was safe, and that's all that mattered. Better to fight a foreign war than to battle one on home soil. He leaned into his pillow, letting his eyes close.

"You still reading this?" Haden's voice pushed through a yawn.

Collier's eyes lifted into a tired squint. *The Army Officer's Guide.* Hmph. "Kind of." Staying in the Army wasn't as appealing as it used to be, but what choice did he have with a baby on the way?

"Mind if I borrow it?" Haden flipped through the pages and gave the book a thump.

"Be my guest." Collier nestled into the plywood, eyes closing once more. Planning a future during a war seemed like a waste of time anyway. Collier threw the pessimistic thought aside.

Never mind the scratchy blanket, thunder from steady mortar-round attacks on their FOB, and dust ridden conditions. Rest wouldn't come. Collier listened to Dock and Pulu rustling through their packages from home. Mail day equated to Christmas, and every soldier turned into a kid no matter the season.

"Wasabi peas." Pulu didn't smile about much, but he sure sounded happy. "And sea weed."

Ick. Collier grimaced.

"Yo, Cromwell." Dock always shouted. "You've got cheese dip covering up that new Specialist rank. Can't salute you if I can't see it." His laugh was bigger than his personality.

Collier swiped at the cheese and licked it from his finger. Still good. "Now you can salute."

Dock guffawed. Hard to believe he was a grown man.

"I heard it won't take no time 'till making Sergeant, after making Specialist." Haden smacked the book on Collier's hip. Yeah, these guys wouldn't let him sleep anyway.

"That's what I hear." Collier stretched and sat up. "Hope it's true." Specialist pay was appreciated, but Sergeant pay would be a dream come true, especially with a baby.

Collier's heart skipped a beat or two. In eight short weeks he'd be on a plane to see Whit, welcoming their child into this world. This crazy world. Collier rubbed his worn hands over his face.

Haden twirled the black, metal, in-remembrance band on his left hand. "I talked to Emilee about me becoming an officer." He skimmed the pages, marking a spot with a letter of his own. "She thinks it's a good idea. Thinks I'd make a good officer."

"She also thought marrying you was a good idea." Pulu chomped on a mouth full of wasabi peas.

"Whatever." Haden kicked at Pulu with an outstretched leg. "As I was saying, after talking with you about it, Cromwell, I think it's the best route for Emilee and me. Maybe you and I could even go to the school together."

"Maybe." The future — all of it — seemed so unsure. Collier chewed on a hangnail. "We've got to make it outta here alive first." He chuckled at the truth.

"What's wrong with you Dock?" Pulu threw a pea in his direction. Dock's skin paled. His loud mouth shut.

A letter hung limp in his hand. "She wrote."

"Who?" Collier gave sidelong glance. There were lots of 'shes' he could be referring to.

Dock sat on his cot and released a heavy breath. "My wife."

His wife?

The men exchanged confused glances.

"My ... my wife." Dock shook his head. "She says ... she says I have a daughter." His head fell into his hands.

This was insane.

Collier scratched his brow, looked to Haden, and then to Pulu. The men shrugged and stared at the broken man before them. The letter slipped from Dock's hands and onto the gritty floor. An image of an infant girl, no more than a year old, peeked from the corner of the folded paper.

"Wait. This makes no sense." Pulu stood. His voiced climbed an octave or two. "You're married? We've known you for how long, and we're just now finding this out?"

"Calm down." Haden stood and placed a hand on Pulu's shoulder. "It's okay."

"It's totally not okay." Pulu swiped Haden's hand away. "Dock. Dude. The entire time we were in Korea you were sleeping with a new girl almost every night." Collier blushed at the blunt reality. Pulu's face folded, his fists clenched. "I thought I was the one with issues. What's your deal, man? You're a cheat."

Collier's body froze as the color of Dock's neck and face began to redden.

A fight neared. Collier stood alongside Haden, ready to referee just in time to catch Dock as he lunged for Pulu.

"Get off me, Cromwell." Dock was solid. Collier struggled to keep him at bay. "That little punk is going to get it. You're dead Pulu."

"Punk? Me? You're the cheater." Pulu twitched as Haden writhed and wrangled to restrain Pulu's short but stout body. "Let go of me Haden. He's smut. He's disgusting."

"I'm smut? I'm disgusting?" Dock tugged and strained in Collier's clenched arms. "Whose mother was a Korean prostitute that got knocked up by some GI that abandoned him? Huh? Tell me who."

"Shut up. Shut up." Pulu roared and kicked, but Haden held him in place.

"Who spent his teen years in juvie 'cause no foster family would keep him?" Dock stooped lower.

Pulu spit out profanities. Dock deserved them all.

Words continued to fly from Dock's mouth like daggers. "You're the loser no one wants."

"Stop it Dock." Collier gritted his teeth and tightened his grasp. Dock yelped.

Haden's knees began to buckle. Wrestling Pulu seemed to be no easy task either. Pulu shrieked. "Your daughter doesn't deserve to even know you exist." And with that, Dock broke free, colliding into Pulu with a sound clap.

Collier grappled Dock to the floor and pinned him in a hold as Haden ushered a bloodied and bruised Pulu from the room. Other soldiers gathered in the doorway. There was no way to keep this scuffle from the Sergeant.

"I'm gonna kill that kid." Dock struggled beneath Collier's clutch. The veins protruding from his neck resembled a road map.

"Be quiet, Dock." Collier lowered his voice. "You're not mad at Pulu, you're mad at yourself." He flexed his biceps around Dock's neck, beckoning him to relax.

"I give. I give." Dock smacked the floor with his palm. "I'm calm, now get off."

Collier shot a sharp glare at the onlookers. "Nothing to see here guys." They scattered with disapproving moans. The less people around when the higher ups got ahold of this the better.

Out of breath, Dock laid back on the cracked floor, covering his face with his hands.

"You better hope Sergeant Prowski's in a good mood." Collier sat back against the walls of splintered wood and broken plaster. He might as well have wrestled an ox. Collier tugged on his shirt and enjoyed the puffs of air that hit his face. "Pulu didn't deserve that, man."

Dock swiped sweat from his face. Maybe tears too. "He should've minded his own business."

Collier huffed. Dock was so pigheaded. "He had enough guts to say what we were all thinking."

A flicker of rage returned to Dock's face and then faded.

"It's the truth." Collier shrugged. "What are we supposed to think? Seeing you with all these other women?"

"Amy and I are separated." That still didn't excuse his promiscuous ways. Dock looked at the floor and flicked a speck of mud across the room. "I wasn't husband material, if you know what I mean." No joke. That was an understatement. "She came over one night before I left for Korea to try to work things out. That's the last time I've heard from her." He touched the gash above his eye. Pulu got a good hit in. "Guess that's when she got pregnant."

The partially crumbled letter lay inches from the door. Collier crawled over and picked it up, pulling out the photo of the child. She had Dock's eyes.

Dock reached for the photo. His expression softened as he rubbed his thumb across the image of the pudgy infant with sprouting ponytails atop her rounded head. "She's pretty, huh?" Dock's voice carried a strange combination of shock and awe. "Annabelle."

Collier grinned. She was cute. Just the way he'd want his daughter to look.

"I've made such a mess of my life." A big mess. Dock sniveled. "I have to make this right. For her." Funny how someone as small as a child could inspire change in some, but not in others — like his father. Dock turned the picture toward Collier. "For Annabelle."

They sat in silence.

Collier fidgeted with the shoestring of his combat boot. "So where do you go from here?"

"Amy wants to go through with the divorce," he paused, tapping on the photo, "but I don't." Dock knew how throw someone for a loop. "It's time for me to grow up and be the man, husband … and father I'm supposed to be." Sincerity filled his eyes. "How do I do that?"

Collier lugged his arm over a knee. He was still learning those lessons too. "Not sure there's too much you can do while you're here." He scratched his head. "Maybe write to her whenever you can." He did his best to do that for Whit.

"Yeah." Dock smeared blood from his busted knuckle on his pant leg. His leg popped as he stood. "Guess I should go talk to Pulu."

Collier pursed his lips. "Guess you should."

"**GOT** another mission." Sergeant Prowski huddled the squad together.

What's new? Collier rolled his eyes. Merry Christmas.

Dock and Pulu folded their arms, eyes black and still a bit swollen. Luckily, the higher-ups overlooked their scuffle. The new First Sergeant must've been trying to make a good impression.

"Don't know, don't care who keeps giving us these tips." Sergeant Prowski smacked on a piece of gum. "But, it seems we've got us another high profile insurgent hanging around town." Against threat of death, the Iraqi citizens seemed to be letting more and more information seep into the soldiers' hands. Brave.

"Not going to lie." Sergeant Prowski placed a hand on his hip. "This task is more dangerous than the others." Right. They were all dangerous. Collier sighed. Seldom had any of their missions ended without some sort of injury or death.

Sergeant Prowski stood taller. "We leave tonight. B Company will have our backs." Crawford's group. Whit would be happy to know he'd be working with Jen's fiancé.

"Four man teams." The Sergeant eyed his squadron of twelve. "Haden, I want you sharpshooting for me. Cromwell, lead your team: Pulu, James, & Brooks." Haden wasn't going with him? They shared a glance. Haden always went with him. Sergeant Prowski pointed a finger. "Pick your shooter, Cromwell."

Why couldn't he sharp shoot for his own team? Pulu wasn't the best shot. James was decent, but given the selection, Brooks was the best. Not as good as Haden. "Brooks it is."

"Goodman." Sergeant Prowski slapped the soldier of the man next to Collier. "Lead the third team."

"Yes, Sergeant." Goodman gave a nod. He was a decent shot. Good soldier.

"All right." The Sergeant cracked his knuckles. "I'll give you a rundown before we head out. Remember, no man left behind."

Unless they ask you to leave — like First Sergeant Gunthrie. The muscles in Collier's jaw twitched. Leaving the First Sergeant behind wasn't an easy decision. It had to be done.

SO this was the building. Stucco, run down, like the others. Not a surprise.

"You're right, Brooks." Collier moved his team down the alley way alongside a few soldiers from B Company. The stars above provided enough light to maneuver about the sleeping city. "We need men on the roof." The roofs were low, easy to access.

"It's not Christmas without someone on a roof. Ho. Ho. Ho." Pulu earned a few hushed snickers from the men.

"We'll go up top." Crawford knelt and hoisted the first of his men up.

"Let's get in and get out." Collier checked his ammo pouch. Good to go. "Grab our guys. Detain them all for questioning like the Sergeant said." The men nodded just as the first shot rang through the street.

A body fell from the roof and thudded to the ground. Crawford's soldier was down. Collier and his men sprang into action, returning fire. Crawford bellowed and grabbed his side while clamoring to push his men out of the way.

"Go. Go. Go." Collier ushered the men around the corner. They had to take that building. The soldiers busted down the door as Collier and Crawford provided cover until the last man entered.

"C'mon." Crawford's panted breaths were reason for concern. He tugged at Collier's arm.

Collier eyed the alley. No man left behind. "Right behind you."

Bullets buzzed past his head as he crawled to the soldier on the ground. Collier hoisted the man over his shoulders. No movement. "Hang in there man."

Explosions sounded in the distance. Each team must've been hit. What a nightmare.

Gunfire slowed long enough for him to enter the bloody scene inside the house. The medic ran to retrieve the soldier from Collier's shoulders. Women wailed, clawing their faces, and children screamed as the suspected men were detained and dragged through their own blood to the middle of the room. They spouted hurriedly to one another in a language too foreign to understand. Their laughs were mad, sick and twisted. Demented.

Collier turned to their interpreter. "Keep them quiet or I will."

The team lifted their weapons, ready to ensure silence if the need arose.

Collier scanned the room. Soldiers held their defensive positions though the fight seem to have stopped. The medic continued to work on the soldier Collier had brought in. Did he dare look to see who it was?

"Collier, you're bleeding." Crawford coughed and wheezed.

His heart drummed in his ears. "So are you."

Crawford grabbed at his side, then his knees buckled.

THE park was quiet for a Saturday morning. Whitleigh tucked her feet to the side of the bench and dusted away the light covering of snow. She glanced around, desperate for anything to distract her from reading the medical brochure in her hand again. Sporadic footprints in the snow created a patchy brown lace coating for the ground. An icy breeze passed between the housing units and brushed across her face. She buried her cheek into the knitted scarf layered around her neck — a Christmas gift from Mom. The holidays passed and a new year began with little word from Collier. Receiving a sole, short and simple email, made keeping a jolly façade difficult. Collier didn't give many details, but then again, neither did she.

Gloomy, cold clouds stalked the mountain tops. No sign of spring anywhere. Whitleigh exhaled and noticed the puffs of air as they escaped from her mouth. She folded the worn brochure and tucked it in her coat pocket. Hiding it changed nothing, nor did continuing to read it.

Whitleigh pulled the ends of her jacket as snug around her pregnant body as possible. Seven weeks to go. Six weeks until Collier came home on leave.

Baby Cromwell stretched inside, like normal. Why couldn't his heart be the same?

The doctor felt hopeful. So did Jen. Mom. Dad. Mrs. Ryan. Everyone filled to the brim with hope.

"You're going to be just fine." She smoothed her hands over her stomach. Hopefully her voice convinced, and if not, then perhaps soothed Baby Cromwell.

Life would never be the same. Ever.

The doctor had been kind, sympathetic even, but his diagnosis could not cure their child or her heartache.

Hypoplastic Left Heart Syndrome. Their baby had HLHS.

Babies born with underdeveloped heart valves were surviving with greater rates nowadays with surgery. It meant several surgeries after birth, and even the possibility of in utero operation. The risks, well, there were many. Possible death. Severe disabilities. Developmental delays. Chronic health problems.

A newspaper tumbled in the wind and flopped against the bench. Whitleigh groaned as she bent, feeling for the paper. The belly was becoming quite an obstacle. No need to complain since that was the normal part of being pregnant.

The paper rustled in her hands. She shook out the wrinkles, opening it wide.

Fort Carson Rapist Remains At Large

Old news.

Maybe this was the year for bad news. Whitleigh crumbled up the paper and tossed it over her shoulder.

"Hi Ms. Whitleigh."

Whitleigh turned to greet the green eyed little girl whose lips chattered. Emma grinned like both her front teeth were still there.

"Where's your coat, sweet girl?"

Emma shrugged.

"Here, sweetie, take mine." Whitleigh pried off her thick woolen jacket. Emma seemed in need of many things. Warm clothes, a few pounds, a good bath, but a healthy heart was something she possessed.

"Come sit." Whitleigh canvassed the park, patting the bench. "Where's your mom?"

"Her friend's over again."

"Friend?" Emma's mother didn't seem like the friendly type.

Emma slid close to Whitleigh and scooted her way into the coat with a smile. "Yeah." She snuggled close. "He only comes over when Daddy's gone. Momma makes me go outside when he's there."

"Oh." Whoa. "Um." What could she say to that? "You know, you can always come over to my place."

"Yeah. I know." Emma licked her chapped lips. "You weren't there, so I came here. I've seen you sit at the park by yourself a lot."

"Do I do that?" Whitleigh placed her hands around Emma's, willing them to warm. "I'll be home more often now that I'm out of school."

Emma laughed. "You're too old to be in school."

"You're never too old for school." The decision not to return for the spring semester pained Whitleigh. By the time she finally graduated, maybe she would be too old. Whitleigh swished at Emma's long, dark pony tail.

"Can I touch your stomach?"

"Um. Sure."

Emma poked Whitleigh's belly with an index finger, and then placed both hands on top. She pressed her ear against the abdomen. "I can't hear anything."

Whitleigh choked on a laugh. "Not yet, but you will."

"My mom says you're huge, but I don't think you're that big."

"Um. Well, thank you Emma." Helen. That woman. Grr.

Emma's mouth twisted to the side. What else was this child going to say or ask? Whitleigh interrupted any further comments. "You wanna go to my place and bake cookies." Surely Emma's mother wouldn't mind.

"The sugar ones." Emma kicked her legs and sent her tattered shoe laces swinging.

"Why does everyone want the sugar ones?" Whitleigh tickled Emma as they walked through the park, kicking clumps of blackened snow. "The others are just as good."

"No way." Emma whistled through her remaining teeth. "They aren't all sparkly."

True. "The sugar ones it is then."

"WELL, Miss Emma, I don't know where you got your information on Kentucky people, but it's false." Whitleigh snickered and turned up the classic rock tunes on her MP3 player. "I wear shoes, and I have all of my teeth." She flashed a smile in Emma's direction. "I've never used an outhouse, I went to school, and I didn't marry my cousin."

Emma huffed, no doubt unconvinced.

Whitleigh slipped small rounded cookies onto the cooling rack and eyed the laptop screen on the counter. Collier's email still rubbed her the wrong way. Staring at it didn't help. What wasn't he saying? She closed the computer and slid it against the rosy red tile backsplash.

"What about Florida people? I bet they all go to the beach every summer, have perfect tans, and love orange juice." Whitleigh nibbled bits of colored sugar from her fingers, pinching at Emma's scrunched nose.

"No way. I like apple juice and I've never been the beach."

"Never?"

"I will one day though." Emma bobbed her head to the music and added a few more sprinkles to the cooling cookies just as the front door opened.

"Hey Whit." Jen's heels clicked in the foyer, her purse thudded as it hit the ground.

"In here." Whitleigh rolled a pinch of dough between her palms until it formed a perfect ball.

"Well, hey there, Emma." Jen tousled the top of Emma's hair. "You eating my cookies?"

Emma giggled and popped a warm cookie into her mouth before darting into the living room.

"Brought you a decaf." Jen placed the steaming paper cup on the counter and sipped at her own.

"Oh, I needed that." Decaf would have to do for a bit longer. "Thanks." The cup felt right at home in her hands.

Jen cradled the cup near her nose. "Mmm. A bit of sugar and hazelnut creamer. Nothing better."

Whitleigh stretched from the kitchen. "You can watch cartoons, Emma."

"Really?" Emma jumped and danced with the remote control in hand.

Jen sank against the kitchen counter and inhaled dramatically. She fanned a wedding magazine. Little planning had been accomplished. "I still can't believe the women's holiday brunch was rescheduled. Who wants to wait until Valentine's Day to get together, and what makes them think I want to spend that day with them?" Good point. Jen bowed her head. "All those petit fours, gone to waste."

"Waste? You ate all of them." Whitleigh chuckled.

"You know what I mean." Jen rolled her eyes. "I was so looking forward to all the catty army wife drama." She sighed.

"You're evil." Not that Whitleigh was friends with many, but most of the Army wives were pleasant enough.

"To think a little ice on the roads kept me from some serious entertainment." Jen frowned and pouted her bottom lip. "Oh, by the way, Mrs. Ryan is on her way over." Nice. Entertaining Emma, Jen, and Mrs. Ryan sounded like the plot of a reality show. Jen snickered. "She's ranting about self-defense. I wouldn't be surprised if she single-handedly takes down that lunatic running around raping women." Jen eyed the cookies and tucked a wedding magazine under her arm like an accessory bag. She waved a hand and blew back a strand of her big hair.

"She says she's gonna teach us how to shoot." Jen sipped at her coffee. "She should know country girls like us already know how to handle a gun."

Whitleigh winced. Gun toting wasn't exactly on her list of know-hows, but she could pack a mean punch.

"You can't shoot?" The disbelief in Jen's voice was insulting.

"I took kickboxing classes." Whitleigh held up a hand in a karate pose. Kickboxing may not have been on the same caliber as gun slinging. "Put your eyes back in your head. It's not like every country girl can shoot."

"Apparently not." Jen scooped up a cookie. It crumbled in her hands.

"Have you heard from Mark lately?" Maybe he wasn't as vague with his messages as Collier.

Jen frowned. "Not since Christmas Eve." More than a week ago. "Way to start a New Year, right?"

Whitleigh shrugged. Holidays and special events started to lose appeal without Collier by her side.

"Said they were keeping busy." Jen reached for another cookie. "He doesn't tell me what they're keeping busy with though. Guess he can't." Mark seemed a lot like Collier. "Guess the news kind of tells us what they're doing."

"Yeah." A cumbersome thought. Whitleigh placed another tray of dough into the oven. Last batch. She wiped her palms down the green gingham apron tied above her belly. Her lower back ached. Whitleigh shifted her weight but found little relief.

"So." Jen paused, pressing her painted lips together. "Talk. Tell me how you're doing. You've got makeup and pearls on. That's a good sign."

Whitleigh lifted her shoulders and released a faint smile. She chewed on her lip. Not much to say. "I guess I'm still trying to process it all." Talking wouldn't heal her baby's heart. It wouldn't bring Collier home safe. Maybe praying would. Whitleigh rubbed a chill from her arms. "It all just feels like a dream. A really bad one."

Jen crossed her ankles, clasping her coffee cup with both hands now. Her brows inched close. "I think you need to tell Collier."

Whitleigh caught a breath. "I can't bother him with something like that."

"You're his wife." Jen sat the cup down on the counter. Her earrings dangled, mocking the motion of her nodding head. "Something like this is a need to know. Mrs. Ryan's obsession with spying on the neighbors is something he doesn't need to hear about. Whining and complaining about how awful life without him is, well, that's something he doesn't need to hear." She raised a perfectly arched brow. "A serious medical issue concerning your baby? He needs to know."

"I know." *Stop with the advice.* Whitleigh untied the apron and tossed it onto the countertop. "I can't talk about this right now."

"If it was Mark and I — "

"It's not." Whitleigh's voice shook. "You're not even married yet. You don't know what this is like."

Jen bowed her head, fingers dug into her crossed arms.

Cartoon melodies played from the living room. Emma laughed, carefree.

"I'm sorry, Jen." Whitleigh closed her eyes. "I didn't mean to snap at you."

"I get it." She pursed her lips. A genuine, soft smile grew across her face. Jen, the most understanding person in the world. "Come here." The most forgiving too. She opened her arms. Hugs helped.

The front door thudded open. "Whit? Jen?" Mrs. Ryan and her brood stomped about.

Whatever happened to knocking before entering? "In here."

Jen gave Whitleigh's back a quick pat. "Guess who's about to learn to shoot a gun?"

Whitleigh's shoulders sank.

"There you all are." Mrs. Ryan shuffled into the kitchen and untied her scarf. No gun in hand. A good sign. "There's a man outside." She lowered her voice, partially covering her mouth. "He's standing in Emma's yard, smoking."

Whitleigh tilted her head. That must be the friend.

"That's not her father. I've seen her father, and that's not him." Mrs. Ryan's mouth clamped into a fine line. "Of all the men that woman's had over her house, he's the creepiest."

There were more men? Well, Mrs. Ryan would know.

Poor Emma.

Whitleigh shook her head and leaned from the kitchen doorway to cast a warm smile in Emma's direction. Her mom didn't even know her whereabouts.

Jen tiptoed to the living room window and pushed down on the blinds. Spying wasn't her forte. She glided back to the kitchen, unnoticed by the children, contented with cartoons. "He does look creepy." Jen shivered. "Looks familiar, too." She squinted her eyes for a moment. "At least Emma's mother had enough sense to keep her away from him."

Yeah. Better for Emma not to see whatever happened when the friend came to visit. Sickening.

Whitleigh threw a dozen or so cookies on a platter.

"What are you doing?" Jen reached for the dish.

"I'm gonna take a few over to Emma's mother." Nothing eased an awkward conversation like a little sweet treat to chew.

"Now?" Mrs. Ryan's hair bounced with each shake of her head.

"I can't think of a better time." Where were those bows? Cookies couldn't be delivered without being properly wrapped. "Here we go." Whitleigh pulled ribbon from a cluttered kitchen drawer. She cut it, tied a ribbon around the plate, and curled the ends. Very pretty.

She pranced from the kitchen. "Emma, stay here honey. I'll be right back." No reason for this little girl to hear any unpleasant words that may be exchanged — not that she planned on any discord.

The door creaked closed behind her. Whitleigh didn't look back. Mrs. Ryan and Jen were sure to be glued to the blinds. In a few strides she made her way from her yard into Emma's.

The man, tall and tattooed, puffed away, blowing rings of smoke in the cool air. Whitleigh nodded a hello, dismissing the head to toe stare. Who gawked at a pregnant woman like that? No one respectable. At the second knock, the woman answered.

"Can I help you?" She buttoned her blouse. No bra. Caught. Whitleigh swallowed back the judgment.

"I'm … I'm Whitleigh Cromwell, from across the street." She pointed at the end house to her back. The living room blinds snapped shut. Terrible spies, Mrs. Ryan and Jen.

The woman stared, arms folded, looking quite unwilling to open the screen door.

"Emma's at my house right now." Whitleigh paused. Did she care? "We made cookies." Good moms do that with their children. That judgment proved harder to toss aside. "Thought you would like some."

"Thanks." She opened the door and slid out a bony arm to receive the cookies. Emma inherited the skinniness. "I'm Helen." She toyed with the ribbon tied around the platter, unable to look Whitleigh in the eye for more than a second or two. "This is a family friend of ours."

With a twist of his boot, the man put out his cigarette. "Pleased to meet you." His dog tags clinked as he extended a hand. "I'm Ray." Ray. Well, that was redneck sounding enough. Why wasn't he deployed like Emma's father? Seemed like a better place to be than hanging around a married woman with a child.

Good heavens, those snide, critical thoughts kept coming.

"Nice to meet both of you." Convincing enough? Whitleigh almost crossed her fingers.

"I'm sorry my daughter is bothering you."

Bothering?

"Not at all." Whitleigh waved a hand. "Emma is wonderful to be around."

Helen's half smile wreaked of disbelief.

Ray moved uncomfortably close as he slid past Whitleigh and back into the house, giving Helen a smack on her rear. Friend?

Helen's cheeks reddened. "Something else I can help you with?"

Many things. Whitleigh bit her tongue. "Emma was outside earlier. Without a jacket." The woman appeared unconcerned. "In this weather." Flurries danced around the front porch.

"She doesn't get cold." Helen's voice was monotone. "We're from Florida."

Okay. "Her teeth were chattering."

"And?"

Helen missed a few parenting brain cells.

"And …" Whitleigh puffed back a strand of hair, "if you were a little more concerned with your daughter than your friend, then maybe Emma wouldn't have to roam the streets, shivering while she waits for Ray to leave."

"I think you should go." Helen shoved the cookies back into Whitleigh's arms. It would be classless to toss them back. Whitleigh clasped the plate and straightened the bow. "Send Emma home when you get tired of her."

Whitleigh lifted her chin. "I'll send her home after she's had a bath and eaten."

Helen shrugged and closed the door.

Some people.

Whitleigh stomped toward her home. Emma would have the feast of her life. She deserved it. Maybe afterward, she and Jen would take her shopping.

HELEN came late in the evening for Emma. She should've let her stay the night, or forever. Whitleigh hugged and kissed the little girl. Jen gave her a squeeze and a peck on the cheek.

"Take everything with you." Jen reached for the department store bags at the end of the couch, handing them to Emma. Whitleigh gathered what bags Emma couldn't manage to hold. Helen stood in the doorway and stared without expression.

"See you tomorrow, Ms. Whitleigh." Emma bounced from the house, holding a sucker as Helen tugged on her daughter's wrist. "Maybe I can go to church with you?"

"Anytime, sweet girl."

"Thanks for the clothes." Helen dangled the shopping bags from her shoulder.

"It was our pleasure." Whitleigh forced a smile.

Helen stood on the porch for a split moment, as if pondering something else to say. She batted her eyes, and her lips parted, but nothing came. With a nod, Helen followed behind Emma, who skipped across the street, dodging slick spots, taking care to keep her shiny new pink shoes clean.

Whitleigh closed the door. What a day. She'd have to write Collier about it later. The lower back pain returned. Whitleigh stretched tall, arching her back. Baby Cromwell had the same idea. Sweet baby.

Maybe Jen was right. Maybe it was time to tell Collier, but in an email?

"I was so waiting for you and Helen to get into it." Jen chomped on a piece of gum, her bracelets clattered about with each hand movement. "I still can't believe you went off on her earlier."

"I can't either." Whitleigh palmed her forehead. Lord only knew what came over her.

"I knew you had a sassy Kentucky wildcat side." Jen popped a bubble and crossed her arms. "It's been hiding under a set of pearls and a cardigan."

Ha. "Cardigans that won't even button around me now."

Jen popped a bubble. "You'll get your figure back soon enough." True. "Did you see how happy Emma was at the mall?" Jen swiped a tear and began to tidy the living room. "Best day ever."

Whitleigh chuckled, swiping back tears of her own. Emma had a whole new winter wardrobe that included shoes, two stylish coats, and several cardigans. She and Jen were sale searching besties.

"That little pink coat looked so sweet on her." Jen picked up the last of the popcorn kernels from the floor. Mrs. Ryan's kiddos knew how to make a mess. "The green one will look cute too."

It would.

"I'm impressed with all your stylish thrift store finds. I guess mixing the old with the new isn't so bad."

Whitleigh rolled her eyes as she sank into the cushioned recliner.

Jen flopped on the sofa. "I think I'm gonna crash at your place."

"Fine with me." Whitleigh yawned. A quick email to Collier and then off to bed. The next time he called seemed like a better way to tell them about their baby.

"Well, look what I found?" Jen yanked her hand from the couch cushion, waving her phone. "I didn't even know it was missing. Those Ryan kids. Sweet but — " her expression changed. Jen's mouth opened without sound.

"You okay?" Whitleigh forced her legs to move.

"Seven missed calls?" Jen's chin trembled. Missed calls were one thing, but seven indicated something entirely different.

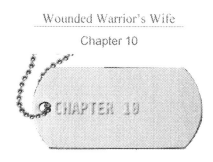

CHAPTER 10

COLLIER stood in the makeshift shower. Shards of plywood stuck out at odd angles, ready to attack anyone who got too close. He ran a hand over his forehead. Just scabs now. Head wounds always looked worse than what they were … most of the time. Nothing to worry Whit with. Collier touched the healing gashes. They didn't hurt much anymore.

What a bust the Christmas mission had been. No deaths, thank God. Private James, shot through the neck, fell from the roof, now paralyzed. Lucky to be alive, if that was lucky. And Crawford. Collier blew out a breath of air. Crawford lay in a hospital bed somewhere fighting for his life. Surely Whit's friend must've heard the news by now.

The target man, Areeb, escaped that night before the others were detained. That wouldn't happen again if he could help it.

All of the planning and fighting, for what?

He shook his wet hair, pouring another water bottle over top his head. He scrubbed in a dab of shampoo — had to make that stuff last. His dog tags clanked and clattered as he washed under his arms and across his chest. A bathtub would be heaven, though anything belonging to heaven would seem out of place in this corner of the world.

He dried his face on a ragged towel and dressed. His uniform, dirty, stiff, and worn, no longer appeared as crisp and promising as it had once upon a time.

"Hey Cromwell." Haden stuck his head in the shower. "Phone lines are up and running again. Lines are somewhat short. I'm gonna give Emilee a call. Wanna come?"

He nodded and stood. Hearing Whit's voice would be a treat, a sign that the whole world wasn't mad.

"ANY word on Crawford?" It wasn't like the troops got updates on the medevaced soldiers. Collier held the phone close to his ear.

"Nothing new really." Whit's voice sounded older, not as bubbly. "Jen says he's still in Germany and out of critical condition. They're going to do another surgery to help repair his intestines."

"Hmm." That bullet messed Crawford up pretty bad. Collier rubbed his chin. "He's lucky to be alive."

"That's what Jen said." Whit's voice faded in and out with the line. "She was going to try to visit him, but they only let family come, so she's praying his folks will go in her place."

"Why wouldn't they?"

"I guess there's just a lot of disconnect there."

Collier shook his head. He knew all about family disconnect and was grateful Whit didn't bring it up. If that was him on a hospital bed, his mother would've caught the first plane over, if she were still alive. Collier swallowed. His father, well, he couldn't say what his father would do.

The silence continued for a moment longer.

"You sound tired." Whit knew when to change the subject. Collier closed his eyes, drinking in the softness of her voice.

"I'm hanging in there, baby." His calloused hands caught on his pant leg. "I'm never too tired to call you."

"Yeah. I know." Whit giggled. "Remember college?"

Seemed like a lifetime ago.

"We used to stay up all night on the phone talking to each other and then have to be in class at seven." There was a smile in her sigh. He could hear it.

"Nothing's changed then, huh?" The corners of his mouth turned up. "I'm still staying up to talk to you."

"It's fun to reminisce."

"It is." Collier rubbed his temple. Glimmers of a memory flickered in his mind. Sweeping her in his arms after exchanging vows, glimpses of a new life they barely had a chance to live together.

"Remember — "

"Let's talk about the new memories we're going to make." A future, whether actual or pretend, existed outside of this place. He knew it.

"Um." Whit's voice caught. "Okay. Well."

"You okay?"

"It's just — "

"Just?" Collier arched a brow. Probably army wife neighborhood drama. Comical really.

"Nothing." Oh, it wasn't nothing, for sure. "I can't stand doing this kind of stuff over the phone."

"What, Whit? Tell me." Collier grumbled and pinched the bridge of his nose. "The phone's all we've got right now."

"Our baby has something wrong with his heart."

"His?" Collier rested an elbow on his knee. "I thought we weren't finding out the sex." Way to leave him out.

"I didn't find out, Collier." Her words bit. "I just say 'his' and 'he.'"

"Oh." 'She' seemed a better fit for their baby, rather than 'he'. The silenced settled. "I'm sorry."

"Did you even hear what I said?"

No. As if Whit could see his head shake.

"Our baby has a heart problem." Her words held tears.

What did this mean? Collier balled his fists. He couldn't help her, hold her.

"I — wha — are you okay?" Was that all he could say?

Whit sniveled. "What do you think, Collier?"

Collier licked his lips. Of course she wasn't okay. There had to be something to say. Why wouldn't the words come?

"This is all my fault." Whit sobbed. "I was upset when I found out I was pregnant. It wasn't in our plans. I didn't want a baby, and now I do and he may not even live."

Not even live?

Collier covered his mouth with his hand. Oh God. So this is his punishment for taking lives. His child to pay the penalty?

"No." Collier cleared his throat. "No. This isn't your fault."

"It is." Her voice cracked. "You … you want to talk about our future, but I can't see it anymore."

Collier's heart sank. What was she saying?

"I'm afraid to think about life with our baby, life with you. What if you don't come home? What if our baby doesn't make it? Why should I keep planning when nothing works out?"

"Because you have to." Didn't she know that? "We have to dream and plan." He had to or at least start again. "Whit you have to keep the faith. We have a Forever List to finish."

"I've been trying to be so strong for you." Whit's voiced wavered with the connection. "You need to know that I'm okay, so you don't have to worry, and here I am just crying my eyes out like a big baby. Like I'm the only Army wife whose husband ever deployed."

"I'm glad you're talking to me." He pressed the phone closer to his mouth. "It's honestly nice to know that I'm not the only one struggling."

"Wha — What do you mean?" Her mascara probably ran beneath her eyes.

"Let's just say I haven't told you how hard it is over here for us." That was an understatement. "But, I'll be home soon to hold you and our baby." That would make the world right.

"I'm counting down." And she probably was, to the day. "I wish you were here."

That made two of them.

"Look." Collier swiped a hand across his forehead. "Our baby is going to be okay. Diagnosis can be wrong." They could be. "Especially with those ultrasound things. How doctors are even able to make out anything but a head is hard to believe."

Whitleigh's laugh hiccupped.

Collier smiled. "I'm glad I could get a laugh out of you." Even if slight, it was better than nothing. Collier turned at the tap of the man behind him. Time's up. "Whit, sweetheart."

"You have to go." The sadness in her voice panged his heart.

Why did he nod? She couldn't see.

"I'll call you again as soon as I can." He pressed the phone to his lips. "I love you, baby."

"I love you too."

There was so much more to say. Collier hung up the phone and worked his way to a computer. A few spots open. Maybe he could catch her on chat, or at least send an email. No need to burden her with the details of war, but sharing the struggles, well maybe that could be a good thing.

THEIR baby was okay. She would be fine. Collier touched the ultrasound pictures clinging to his wall, and pulled one off. Squinting, he brought the photo closer to his eyes. That he could tell, nothing appeared wrong with her heart. She lay perfect with her tiny feet tucked under her tiny body. It was a wonder that anything so small could live.

Collier returned the picture alongside the others. He rubbed his rough hands over his face as he sat back on a cinder block stool. Of course he'd been pulled for a mission a week before going on leave. Dock totally faked the flu. Collier yanked his helmet from the floor and fidgeted with the helmet cam Whit had sent him until he securely fastened it on the front. Gadgets were cool, and it would be nice to shoot some footage for her. Nothing heavy of course. Just scenic stuff. Documentary kinds of things. She'd like that, and in time, so would their baby — their perfectly healthy baby.

He finished knotting a new paracord bracelet around his wrist. It proved handy in combat situations. He grunted and laced up his boots. Time to gear up. The heavy bulletproof vest wasn't the most malleable garment. With a quick swoop, he lifted his rifle and headed out as loudly as possible. No need for Dock to sleep too sound.

"Hey Haden, Pulu coming?" Collier buttoned a few pouches hanging from his uniform.

"He's right behind me." Haden shoved a few snacks in his cargo pants' pockets. Food for the road. "It's good to go on mission with you again."

"For real." That was a plus of being called up. The other guys were cool, but Haden had his back.

"You heard where we're going?" His rugged voice hinted.

"Some sort of school." Did it matter where they were headed?

"It's the school where we dropped off that little girl, remember, from the alley?"

"Oh." Collier blinked. She hadn't entered his mind in, well, he couldn't remember how long. "I must've missed that memo."

"Word has it, our guy is hiding out there." Haden crossed his arms.

Collier sneered. "The one who got away the night Crawford got hurt?"

Haden's lips pressed into a fine line as he nodded. "That's the one."

"Who hides in a school?"

"Cowards." Haden's face reddened.

Whoa. Haden barely spoke an ill word about anyone. Collier cleared his throat.

"I checked in on Dock." Haden fastened his helmet. Guess he didn't have more to say on the subject of cowards. "Didn't look like he was knocking on death's door."

Collier rolled his eyes. "You know Dock."

Haden shook his head. "He and Pulu haven't said much to each other."

"Well, avoiding him isn't going to help." Dock needed to man up and apologize. Pulu was just a kid. "Pulu doesn't need his past thrown in his face." No one did.

The medic walked from the DFAC eating area. Collier scratched his chin. This was gonna be good. "Be right back."

Haden nodded.

"Hey, Doc." Collier grinned as he ran toward the medic. "Dock's real sick. I mean really sick."

"Yeah?" The medic crossed his arms with a sideways grin. "Does he need a thorough exam?"

"The works." Collier tipped his helmet. "Give him the works."

"Roger that."

Ha. It was difficult to contain the laughter lodged in his throat. Priceless. Collier jogged back.

"I'm hoping you didn't do what I think you did." Haden's eyes danced.

"I'm sure Dock will feel better by the time we get back." Collier made a clicking sound with his mouth just as Pulu walked up. "Let's go meet the others."

WHERE was this intel coming from anyway? A lot of information seemed to be leaked to the soldiers regarding the whereabouts of wanted terrorists lately. That's great and all, but still curious.

Collier kept his hand on his trigger and marched alongside Haden and Pulu down the paved roadway. For a cool morning, the sun was bright overhead, its beams reflected off the Euphrates River in the distance. An old beat up truck piddled by, carrying a camel in the bed. Strange. Humorous.

Sergeant Prowski walked ahead, Specialist Tillman and Private First Class Rogers at his flank. Humvees trailed in the rear, and one followed off in the distance for added fire power if the mission called for such.

Children shouted as they darted alongside the crumbling road, kicking soccer balls and chasing the armored vehicles with outstretched hands. The soldiers on board threw a few balls and whatever candy they were willing to part with.

Were all the roads in Iraq dilapidated? Collier stepped over a pit of crushed concrete. The buildings weren't much nicer either. He kicked at a pile of trash on the side of the road.

A few stray, scraggly dogs fought over the contents of an overturned garbage bin. The smoldering smells of the city burned in his nose. The school lay ahead.

Geez. Collier wiped at his nose and scanned the streets through his Army issued sunglasses. The school had to smell better than incense, burnt rubber, and rotting flesh.

"You know what this place needs?" Pulu kicked at a glass jar.

"That list is endless." Paper crunched under Collier's boots. "Grass."

"Agreed." Pulu's hearty laugh was contagious.

Haden adjusted his chin strap. "They do have some nice looking tropical trees."

"In patches, and no suitable beach." Pulu snapped. "I can't wait to get back to Guam. Beaches galore." He stretched out a hand.

"I can't wait to get back to the FOB and watch you all rock out on karaoke night." Collier flipped on his helmet cam. Seemed like a good time to film some stuff. "Say hi to Whit, guys."

Pulu waved his arms. "Hi — "

A furious force threw them tumbling backward. Collier clung to his rifle. A deafening blast thundered in his ears.

He shook and struggled to get to his knees, but the world was spinning. Focus. But he couldn't. His eyes closed, opened, and then shut. Flickers of dust, metal, and flames engulfed the area.

There was no shouting. Collier laid amongst the rubble. No ambush. Just another roadside bomb. Collier groaned and sputtered.

Haden? Pulu?

He had to get up. Had to find them.

The dust cloud consuming the area made maneuvering difficult. The smell of freshly scorched flesh made breathing a challenge. He crawled, slow and steady, low to the ground. Bits of blue sky broke through the dust.

Sergeant Prowski called for help on the radio. Thank God for a voice.

The soil settled, veiling a multitude of broken bodies. So many small bodies. Children. Women. Soldiers. One bomb wouldn't have done this much damage.

Collier worked his way to his knees, lungs aching with each breath. His rifle helped to support the weight of his body as he stood. How had he lived? Why did he live?

Collier shuffled toward two men, lying still, facedown.

"No. No. No." The butt of his rifle hit the ground with each step. Why weren't they moving? "Haden. Pulu." The rifle fell from his hands and thudded to the desert land. His hands ran across their bodies and over their sand covered faces. "Get up."

God please. Collier clenched his teeth, his eyes squinted closed. They were fine. It was okay. His head hung over their still bodies. Warm to the touch, maybe they were unconscious. "Please. Haden. Pulu. Get up."

"Cromwell, they're gone." Sergeant Prowski placed a hand on his shoulder. No, they couldn't be. They were just there. Collier tore his paracord bracelet from his wrist. It could make a lifesaving tourniquet with ease.

Sergeant Prowski knelt down beside him. "Collier."

No. He shook his throbbing head. His chest heaved. This wasn't right.

A ragged groan sounded. Life. Pulu's fingers bent in slight jagged movements on the ground.

Collier's heart pounded from his chest, his ears rang. Pulu. "I'm here. You're okay. You're okay."

Blood pooled around bits of rock and clotted with the dust and dirt.

"Medevac. Medevac." Sergeant Prowski's voice bellowed through the thick air as he yanked medical equipment from his hip pouches. A few soldiers in the distance radioed for help in response.

The choppers would come. They always came. Collier held Pulu's hand and worked to wipe away the dirt from his buddy's cheek. "Hang in there." He had to make it.

Haden's body was too close not to notice. Collier reached out with a free hand and pulled Haden to his side, holding him against his chest. He was still warm. Warm enough to pass as living. Collier held onto his friend. "I'm sorry." He shook, the tears seared his eyes. "I'm so sorry."

WHITLEIGH stretched her back and rolled her shoulders. Sitting too long had its downfalls. The spare back bedroom was nearing its transformation. Swatches of material organized by gender cluttered the floors, stacks of diapers, wipes, and any other item a baby's room could possibly need filled the closet.

She dug around in the tool box. Which screwdriver did she need now? Sometimes labels didn't help.

The Philips fit fine as Whitleigh turned it in her hands. A few more twists and the crib was in working order.

She grinned and placed her hands on her hips. Collier would be proud.

The cellphone buzzed in a circle from across the room. She all but waddled to it. "Hey, Momma."

"Hi Sweetheart, it's getting close." Her voice sounded saturated with anticipation of their first grandchild.

Whitleigh laughed. "Too close. I'm kind of nervous." She swallowed back the doctor's diagnosis.

"Don't you worry about a thing." She could almost see Momma pointing a finger. "Your Daddy and I are so excited we almost can't stand it — can't wait to get our hands on that sweet little bundle. Oh the plans we have for our grandbaby."

"I bet you've got some plans." Whitleigh chuckled and placed another box of wipes in the closet.

"How's the nursery coming?"

"It's coming." Whitleigh glanced around the room. The walls were painted. The crib was up. "I need to get the wall stencil painted."

"I had no clue you could paint the walls while living in military housing."

Whitleigh nodded. "As long as we paint it white before we move, and that's in several years. Don't worry, I wore one of those horrible looking anti-fume masks."

"Very nice. Gotta keep those fumes away from my grandbaby." Momma paused, surely to take a sip of sweet tea. Whitleigh could hear iced cubes clinking against glass. "What color did you decide to go with?"

"Spring Cactus." It was more like a pastel green really. "It's a nice gender neutral color."

"You can always add pops of color once the baby comes."

"Planned on it. Got fabric swatches picked out." She was one step ahead.

"This is all so exciting." Momma's giggle ended with an abrupt pause. Whitleigh squinted. There was no telling what Momma was going to say. "Young lady, you better not have moved all that furniture out of that room by yourself."

Whitleigh shrugged. "There wasn't much, really." A desk, dresser, nightstand, and chair. "Jen helped — even carried in the new stuff. Well, the old stuff we painted new. "

"Bless her heart. When you get a chance, Whit baby, give me her address so I can send her a thank you card. She's been such a dear friend to you." There was no room to get in a word. "Have all the packages come in the mail?"

"You mean the baby shower via delivery?" It looked like Christmas again in her house.

"Well honey, I'd much rather have thrown you a shower instead of send you one."

"I know Momma." Whitleigh shook her head. "I'm surprised you didn't send a cake."

"Oh, that's coming."

"What? You can actually mail a cake?"

"You can mail anything."

"But a cake?" Whitleigh grinned. "You're too good to me Momma." She smoothed her fingers across the newly finished dresser. Only the nightstand and chair left to refurbish. "I wish you were here."

"Me too, baby girl." Momma sniffled. "I'll be there soon."

Yeah. Soon.

"So." Momma sniffled again. "Tell me. Have you picked names? I know how secretive you and Collier have been about all the gender and name stuff."

"We're not secretive, Momma." Whitleigh huffed a smile and arched her back. So stiff. Achy even. "We just want to be together when we find out the gender and then decide on a name, but yes, we've talked about a few we like."

"And?"

"Well, we both like older names, family names."

"Do you want my list?"

"Sure, Momma." Whitleigh stretched again and worked to catch her breath. Baby Cromwell was active today. "Email it to me. No matter what you say, we aren't using Ernest." Whitleigh's nose crinkled.

"Oh, honey, he was such a great man."

"Great grandfather or not, no Ernest."

"Fine. But I'm still sending you my list, and I've mailed one to Collier too." Momma smacked her lips. "Sugar, I'm gonna have to get going, but please take care of yourself. I watch the news, and I know all about the stuff that goes on out there you're not telling me."

Whitleigh rolled her eyes. "Okay Momma. I love you."

"Bye baby."

Whitleigh shut her phone and rubbed her lower back. The aching wouldn't let up. The pressure. This part of the pregnancy was a pain — pun intended.

A ray of sunlight danced across the room. Whitleigh peeked out the side window. A blue sky, even a few chirping birds. Maybe spring wasn't as far off as the winter wanted her to think. Fresh air and a walk around the block would surely ease the cramping joints and muscles of her changing body. She grabbed an old coat of Collier's from college and headed out the door.

Squealing brakes in the distance signaled the mailman. Whitleigh walked to the mailbox, careful to dodge remnants of dirty snow that harbored slippery spots.

Not much in the mail today.

She closed the box and thumbed through the papers. Her heart quickened. The disenrollment confirmation from the University of Colorado had come. It should've been a longer letter, and more hospitable. The words ran together as her eyes glossed over the page. With an official announcement in hand, Whitleigh didn't need further confirmation that the plans for her life had gone awry.

Graduation was within her grasp — the gateway to a successful teaching career. They could've at least said, "We hope to see you soon," or "Sorry about your circumstances, but you're welcome back anytime." No personal touch.

Oh well. It didn't matter. Whitleigh's eyes stung. She wadded the letter and tucked it in her pocket. No sense in hanging onto things she couldn't change, and there was always next semester. No one said rolling with the punches would be easy. She swallowed back the burn in her throat. Crying wouldn't help. Maybe she'd take that walk later.

Other things in life existed outside college graduation and teaching. Many things. Whitleigh lifted her chin. She rolled the junk mail and tapped it against her thigh as she stepped onto her sidewalk. Yes, lots of thing to look forward to. Jen's wedding. Collier would be home on leave soon, baby Cromwell would be in their arms, and if she could stop taking afternoon naps, the nursery would be finished before they both arrived. All good things.

Whitleigh counted the half-gallon paint cans on the porch. Three cans, an assortment of brushes, the paisley wall stencil, painter's tape, but where was that tarp? Maybe the shed? Forgetfulness seemed to be a recurring theme with pregnancy.

She trudged through the yard, making her way around the back. There was no dodging the large chunks of muddy ground that were a by-product of snow and dirt. Warding off a chill, Whitleigh crossed her arms and grimaced with each squishy sound from the earth beneath her shoes.

Strange. The back gate was open. She fumbled with the lock. The silly thing couldn't even keep out the neighborhood kids. They could've just jumped the fence instead of busted the lock.

Whitleigh closed the gate and surveyed the yard. Nothing seemed amiss. Nothing missing. Of course, there wasn't much to steal. Two chairs, a small metal table, and a hand-me-down grill with a mind of its own don't have much criminal appeal.

But there were tracks. One set.

Whitleigh held her arms snug to her body as she moved closer to the prints. Was it the cold or the eeriness of the situation that made her insides shake?

Boot prints? Not a child's.

Her breathing stilled. With one set of footprints, someone was still in her back yard.

The deep, calculated imprints circled the perimeter of the yard and then cut diagonally from the bathroom window and stopped in front of the shed. Whitleigh gasped, her hands flung over her mouth.

The window. Had someone seen her? Watched her? Whitleigh swallowed.

The soppy ground squished with each careful step toward the window, eyes never leaving the shed. She stole glances, noticing the cracks of the window seal.

Profound metallic scratches were not a product of wear and tear, but of a possible intruder.

A thud echoed from the shed.

"Who's there?"

No answer.

Whitleigh rubbed the sweat from her palms and forced a labored breath. "I said, who's there? I will call the police."

A dog barked in the distance, and Whitleigh jumped. She whipped her head around, casting quick glances. The day may have been bright and clear, but the situation grew bleak.

Whitleigh took a step back, and then another, until she could feel the gate beneath her fingertips. She held the sides of her bundled belly. Pains shot across her abdomen as the shed door flung open. Whitleigh screamed as a man lunged toward her, his hands wrapping around her neck. Her vision blurred, her legs kicked. "Collier, help." He wasn't there. Whitleigh wailed, finding strength. She punched and clawed at her attacker's face. She pulled his hair and kneed him in his groin. A fierce yelp yielded from his mouth. He reeked of cigarette smoke. His hold didn't loosen.

A gun shot rang throughout the courtyard. The man released Whitleigh and darted over the fence, speeding past the other housing units. Whitleigh fell to the ground, gasping for air.

"Whit. Oh, Lord, Whit. Someone call the police," Mrs. Ryan screamed. She held her gun tightly as she raced to Whitleigh's side. "Help's coming, Whit. Hang in there."

"I'm okay." Far from true. Whitleigh's stomach contracted in short, sharp spasms. She sucked in a deep breath and worked to regain a normal breathing pattern.

Collier couldn't get home quick enough.

Another pain darted through her body. She winced, contorting. Her lips trembled. Breathing through the cramps neared impossible.

"Did you see who it was?"

Whitleigh shook her head. What had she seen? A man — face covered. Tall. Angry. Terrifying. Her fingers trembled, and deep sobs quaked from her throat.

"Shh." Mrs. Ryan wrapped both arms around Whitleigh, holding her steady. "Help's coming."

Whitleigh closed her eyes and wept aloud, too numb to do much else.

WHITLEIGH rested on Mrs. Ryan's sofa. Pillows of all shapes piled around her head and beneath her knees. Her neck and back ached even three days after the attack. She rolled to her side and swallowed, hoping to wet the dryness in her throat.

"Stay still." Mrs. Ryan sat on the floor amongst a pile of laundry, shaking out wrinkles as she stacked and folded. "I can't believe the hospital released you. Twenty-four hours of observation wasn't enough."

No, it wasn't.

Her attacker still loomed, escaping the police once more.

The hospital meant safety.

Whitleigh hadn't returned home since, well, it happened. Her teeth buried into her bottom lip. Collier had yet to be reached, but Momma should be in soon. Maybe then Whitleigh could enter the house.

"Where's Jen?" Whitleigh scanned the living room through weak eyes. The layout of Mrs. Ryan's living room and home paralleled Whitleigh's with great similarity.

"Right now I'd say Jen's tearing into the housing manager. When she's finished with them, I'm pretty sure all windows on base will have new locks."

"He didn't break in."

"What do you think he was doing, Whit, admiring the shape of your window before he hid in your shed? No." She snapped a shirt in the air and folded it on her lap. "You and your baby are lucky to be alive."

True.

Whitleigh's head throbbed. She smoothed her palm over her stomach, and Baby Cromwell nudged from within. Whitleigh's lips curved upward. "I need to move around." She stretched her legs, propping herself up with an elbow. "I'm getting stiff laying here."

"Stubborn." Mrs. Ryan mumbled, tossing a towel to the side. "Here. Let me help." Her strong embrace provided enough support for Whitleigh to ease to her feet. "Let's get you to the dining room table. The sun is shining through. That'll be good for you."

Whitleigh didn't argue. No need.

"Andrea, from your FRG, stopped by." Mrs. Ryan nodded toward the flower arrangement on a side table. "She brought a few frozen meals too."

So nice of them. Whitleigh winced with each short step.

"Jen was shocked."

"That the FRG helped out?"

"More so that Andrea came by. She's an officer's wife."

"Oh. That's right." Jen and her rank bias. Whitleigh paused to catch her breath, dismissing the all-over-ache. "I'll have to send a card to Andrea and the FRG ladies."

"Later. Right now you can sit here." Mrs. Ryan scooted a heavy wooden chair from beneath the dining room table. Whitleigh sat, back straight.

"Hungry? I've got leftovers from breakfast."

Whitleigh shook her head. Food held no interest to her unsteady stomach.

"You need to eat something. Biscuits. Bacon."

"An apple." Whitleigh reached for the bowl of fruit in the center. "I think I can keep that down."

Mrs. Ryan stacked a few papers and pushed crayons from the woven place mat before taking a seat close to Whitleigh. Whitleigh immersed herself in the scrawled crayon art covering the kitchen table.

"They're something, aren't they?" Mrs. Ryan gazed out the window. Her children, the ones too young for school, ran amuck in the fenced in backyard, bouncing on the trampoline, laughing with each jolt.

Childhood. Whitleigh managed a grin. "They're precious."

"It's the middle of January. Can you believe they even stand it out there?"

"They're tough." Whitleigh shook off a chill. Her eyes roamed the perimeter of the room. Childhood covered the walls of the Ryan home. Photos, drawings of hearts, hands, and houses all strategically placed on the fridge, dining room walls, down the hall, and anywhere the eye could see. Would her home be the same once Baby Cromwell arrived? Whitleigh soothed her squirming child with a touch to her side. Would Baby Cromwell have the chance to decorate their home with drawings and such?

Whitleigh turned her head, casting attention to the living room. It was as tidy as a house with five children could be. Each corner accommodated its own specialty learning center, equipped to educate. Crafts, sensory, science, math, and a closet nook stacked with books — Mrs. Ryan had it all — a miniature classroom.

"You'd make a great Elementary School teacher." Whitleigh crossed her ankles and nibbled on the apple.

"I homeschooled for awhile, and now all this stuff just helps me occupy them in a productive way."

"You've done a great job." Whitleigh turned the apple in her hand. "My classroom would've been set up similar."

"You'll graduate and get a teaching job." Mrs. Ryan gave Whitleigh's arm a gentle squeeze. "Things have a way of working out, sometimes in ways we can't begin to imagine."

So far nothing had worked out. Whitleigh raked a hand through her hair.

Mrs. Ryan glanced out the window once more and stood. "Coffee?"

"Decaf please."

Mrs. Ryan scooted into the kitchen. Whitleigh watched out the window as the children played. Cabinet doors clicked opened and then closed. Coffee mugs clanked together. A robust aroma wafted through the air. Mrs. Ryan appeared, clasping oversized mugs in her hand. She slid the cup in front of Whitleigh and smiled. "No sugar, right?"

"You know me well."

Mrs. Ryan returned to her seat. "I hope Emma comes out to play with the kids after school."

"I'm glad she's got kids her age to play with."

"Well, I've got plenty."

"I'd say so." Whitleigh's lips twisted to the side. "It's hard to keep their names all straight." Chloe, Sophie, Wyatt …"

"Ha." Mrs. Ryan waved her hand. "Tell me about it. The twins think it's hilarious."

Whitleigh wrapped her hands around the mug, absorbing the heat. Almost therapy. Amazing the forms comfort can take.

Mrs. Ryan clicked her fingernails on the table. "I think it's time, Whit."

Another one of Mrs. Ryan's talks? Whitleigh huffed. "Time?"

"I didn't want to do it either, but after Jayson left, and with all these crazies running around, I got a gun."

Jayson? Mrs. Ryan never talked about her husband.

"Then I bought a few more guns." She stretched out her arms and cracked her knuckles. "You have to think about protecting yourself, and a baby soon."

"You sound like my mom." She did, but that wasn't a bad thing. Whitleigh raised a brow. Should she ask? She sipped on the coffee. Strong, but good. "I don't need a gun. I've got pepper spray."

A snort sounded from Mrs. Ryan's throat. "You're getting a gun whether you want one or not."

"Mrs. Ryan, you mentioned your husband, Jayson?"

"You're not as good at changing the subject as you think." Mrs. Ryan leaned over her coffee mug. "And seriously, you have to stop with the Mrs. Ryan thing. Calling me Layla isn't going to kill you, but that crazy man tried. Get a gun, or take one of mine."

"Fine." Guns were scary, but the attack had been scarier. "I guess I can borrow one from you, Layla." Her first name sounded so wrong. "Now can we move on?"

Layla nodded.

"I am kind of curious though, about your husband."

"I've been wondering when you were going to ask." Mrs. Ryan, no, Layla, laid a forearm on the table.

"I … I wasn't sure if I should." Most husbands were deployed, while others were worse — deceased. Whitleigh swallowed. Asking seemed somehow unsafe, unwarranted.

"Jayson has had his share of deployments, and he finally wizened up and got the help he needed."

"You mean, he has PTSD?"

"Post-traumatic stress disorder, yes." Mrs. Ryan fidgeted with a tassel on the place mat. "He's getting treatment at Walter Reed Army Medical Facility. Doing much better now. Didn't know how much more of him I could take." She chuckled, eyes focused on the coffee sloshing around in her mug. "At first it was maddening trying to help him, figure him out. He didn't even know what was wrong, so it's been a relief to both of us to put a name to it."

"I bet." Seemed like PTSD was the new 'it' disease sweeping the military. "The news is always talking about PTSD. I mean, look at all the abuse and murder cases that we've had on base. Collier seems to think a lot of soldiers are just crying wolf. Trying to play the system or something."

"Maybe they are, but Jayson wasn't crying wolf, he was the wolf." Layla scratched her neck. No smile existed on her face.

"This life." Whitleigh released a slow breath. "It's like there's always something to deal with, you know?"

"That's the truth. Army wives even experience symptoms of PTSD. Did you know that?"

"After the experiences I've had, I believe it."

Quick, pounding raps at the front door ricocheted through the house. Whitleigh caught Layla's wide eyes for a split second.

Layla bolted from her seat and hustled to the door. "Jen?"

"I need Whit."

Whitleigh scooted

Layla held the door open, ushering Jen inside. "What's wrong?"

"I need Whit. Get her. Please."

"Jen? I'm here." Whitleigh held her breath. Jen appeared disheveled, her face swollen, red, and streaked with mascara. "Who did this to you? Are you hurt?"

She stood. Shaking sobs escaped her mouth.

Not another victim. Whitleigh drew Jen into her arms.

"Oh, Dear Lord." Layla held a quivering hand over her mouth. "Were you raped?"

Jen shook her head, pushing back tangled hair. "No." Her face folded, shoulders hunched forward. "He didn't make it."

"Who?" Whitleigh held her close. Jen's shuddered movements became her own.

"Mark." Her cries ripped through Whitleigh. "He didn't make it through surgery." Jen's warm tears soaked into Whitleigh's shirt. A serrated pain stretched from her back and tore across the width of her stomach. Whitleigh gasped and crumbled to the ground, pulling Jen with her. The lights faded with the pain. An inviting warmth surged through her body. Whitleigh blinked, closing her eyes. Rest would help.

"Layla, call 911." Jen's voice sounded muffled and washed out. "Stay with us Whit."

THE mess had almost been erased, as if the roadside bombs had never detonated, as if Haden wasn't gone.

The wreckage had been removed, but the craters from the blast remained. Collier held his rifle to his chest as he and the other soldiers canvassed the area, cleaning up any remaining debris.

Haden and Pulu had stood mere feet from him when the first of the bombs discharged. They took on most of the hit.

Collier choked on the burn climbing in his throat. He eyed the schoolhouse in the distance. They had been so close to their target, who had now most undoubtedly fled. Another empty handed mission, and for what? Haden was dead, Pulu barely hanging on, and all Collier had was a sore back. He kicked at the ground. If he had any say in it, those responsible for this would pay with their lives.

"I should've been there."

Collier flinched. When had Dock walked up?

Collier could only stare. Yes. He should've been there.

Dock lowered his voice. "It should've been me, not Haden."

Collier swallowed. It should've been anyone but Haden.

Dock wiped at his eye. "I have to make things right with Pulu."

He should've already done that. "Yeah. Let's pray you get that chance."

"Sergeant Prowski and the Platoon Leader were talking. Said Pulu lost both legs. Pretty messed up inside."

"Yeah." Collier's jaw tightened. The whole ordeal was disgusting and tragic no matter how he looked at it. Life seemed infinitely unfair on all levels.

"Over here." Sergeant Prowski waved a hand. "Found some more."

Fantastic.

Collier gnawed on the inside of his lip. Nothing could brighten a day like picking up body parts mangled by a blast.

Why couldn't the Iraqi citizens pick up the parts? It was their people being blown to smithereens. Collier and the other soldiers had already picked up the parts belonging to the soldiers. An arm, a few fingers. Not much this time.

Collier tucked his nose into the sleeve of his ACU jacket. Sergeant Prowski was right. More body parts remained. He slid his rifle to the side and bent down to pick up a small finger — probably a child's. He pitched it in his trash bag. Thank God for gloves.

A scalp with hair intact. That was a first. Collier shrugged and walked through the swarm of flies.

Dock picked up a foot and gave it a wiggle before tossing it into his trash bag. "That person needs some toenail clippers."

"Not anymore." Sergeant Prowski snorted and spit out a round of tobacco.

Collier grinned. Morbid humor. Laughing helped to cope.

Dock kicked at some unrecognizable fleshy mound. "We seriously don't get paid enough for this kind of junk."

"So true." Collier swatted away the flies. The place reeked.

"You think we could call a maid service or something?" Dock smiled and covered his nose.

Sergeant Prowski shook his head. "You ain't right, Dock."

No one over here was right anymore.

A Private leaned against the brick wall and vomited.

"Toughen up." Dock rolled his eyes. "Crazy Privates."

Sergeant Prowski took the trash bag from the Private and dismissed him. The kid was too young to see that kind of stuff anyway. Collier scooped partially clothed globs of some kind of human remnant into the bag. Almost done. For now.

More blasts were almost a guarantee. Where explosions existed, so did cleanup.

A mangy, skeletal dog cowered close, and then darted in toward the bits of flesh lying about. Collier raised his rifle as the dog scurried away with a hand in mouth.

"Let him go." Sergeant Prowski sniffed. "At least he'll put it to good use."

Collier's stomach turned.

COLLIER ran his shaking fingers over his buzzed head. No emails from Whit. It wasn't like she was in school now. She could've at least sent a quick message, something, anything. He lifted from the chair, knees popping as he stood. His body creaked and cracked like an old man. Twenty one seemed too young for a cane, but maybe it would help. Collier stretched and headed to his room.

He pushed back the hanging camo blanket — their makeshift door.

"You got a letter." Dock leaned against his cot, eyes fixed on the locked black tough-box. Haden's box.

Collier pursed his lips. They would have to go through it soon, and get it home to Emilee. Collier bowed his head and turned, snatching up the letter.

His heart stopped.

Return address: Luther Luckett Correctional Facility. Lagrange, KY.

Did Whit give his father his address? What was she thinking? He tossed the letter to the corner. A roach scurried away. "Don't have time to read that." It wouldn't say anything he hadn't heard before. Pitiful excuses.

Dock lifted his gaze. "Can I read it for you?"

"Be my guest." Collier took his jacket off and threw it on the cinder block table. "I just don't care to hear what it says."

"You're never this touchy."

"Yeah. Well. I guess we all have those things in our lives we don't want to talk about."

"Can't argue that." Dock placed his arms behind his head. "Speaking of such things, it looks like Amy may be willing to give me a second chance."

Maybe Dock deserved a second chance. Some people didn't.

"I hope you get that chance." Collier leaned back on his cot.

Haden's box sat between them.

"You think Whit's heard about Crawford?"

"We just found out, so I'm sure she knows." Collier closed his eyes. She's probably comforting Jen. Maybe that's why she hasn't written.

"Sometimes I feel like death stalks this place. Like it's waiting for us."

Collier shook the chill. Death crept all around like an ever present shadow, blocking out the light.

"If Haden could go, then …"

Dock didn't need to finish. If Haden could go, someone so full of faith and hope, then no one was exempt from death's reach.

"Ready to open it?" Dock fiddled with the lock on Haden's tough-box.

"No." The cot creaked as Collier sat forward. "But I guess we need to."

Dock popped the lock.

Collier blew out a deep breath before standing. This needed to be done.

"I can't." Collier's cheeks warmed. "It's too soon."

"We have to take inventory."

Collier punched a wooden beam along the wall. "I know what we have to do."

Dock's hands dangled on his knees. He sniffed. "He was my friend too you know."

No.

Maybe.

"I know." Collier's knuckles throbbed. Haden was everyone's friend. Collier rubbed both hands across his face … "I don't know how to do this." His shortened chuckle held no humor. "How do I do this?"

"You don't." Dock stood and placed a strong hand on Collier's shoulder. "We do."

They sat, box opened.

Collier wiped a few budding tears from the corners of his eyes and overlooked Dock's snivels. A soldier's tears held no humor.

"Just pull it all out, and I'll write." Dock reached for the clipboard next to the box.

Collier's hand trembled. He could do this. He had to. For Haden. For Emilee.

WHIT hadn't answered his call again. What was so important that she couldn't pick up the phone to talk to her husband at war? Collier huffed. He needed her, her voice, an encouraging word, something soft and familiar to pry the callous from his heart.

Collier squinted as he walked toward his barrack.

As Collier passed, a veiled woman talked hurriedly to the Company Commander, Captain Black, and an interpreter. The woman looked from side to side as if searching for someone, or perhaps hoping to avoid being seen. She was a brave woman to be out in the open speaking to a man, an American soldier no less, especially without being accompanied by male relatives.

She clenched the fabric of her veil with one hand, and with the other, held the hand of a child. A young girl.

Collier's steps slowed. He knew her — the child. The small, hungry girl from the alley.

The child turned and greeted Collier with the wide eyed stare. She remembered.

The girl tugged on the woman's arm, pointing.

"Him?" Captain Black glanced over his shoulder.

The child nodded.

Collier froze. What could this possibly be about?

Captain Black waved Collier over.

"Sir?"

"This woman has been trying to tell me something about soldiers who found this girl. Dropped her off at the school?"

The interpreter shook his head, obviously frustrated with Captain Black's assessment.

"Yes, Sir." Was it the wrong thing to do? "My team found her in an alley, months back, starving, all alone, covered in trash." Collier stood taller. "We couldn't just leave her."

Captain Black nodded.

"This is what I've been trying to tell you." The interpreter held out his hands to the Captain. "This is why this woman dares to tell you what she knows."

What she knows?

Was this the person leaking information to the soldiers on the whereabouts of terrorists?

"Maybe I need a better interpreter." The Captain's brow wrinkled.

"You Americans." The interpreter grumbled under his breath.

Collier stood, arms at parade rest to his side. Should he go?

The child would not take her eyes from him. She smiled. At one time her wide grin would've tugged on his heart, called him to action, but now, nothing. No feelings. Of course he wished her no harm.

"Let me get this straight." Captain Black pointed all five fingers at the Iraqi interpreter. "This woman, from the school, has been giving us intel because we helped a kid?" He frowned. "This makes no sense."

"It's because you — he — showed grace and mercy to the least of these, as no one from the Taliban have done. Therefore you are worthy of help."

The woman spoke again, tears in her eyes.

"She says, 'worthy of all risk.'" The man sliced the air with his hand. "'Free us,' she says. 'Free us.'"

The man's voice was urgent, fervent. Collier's forehead beaded with sweat.

"Sir?" Collier kept his hands tight at his side. "Would you like me to leave?"

This conversation didn't seem appropriate for a Specialist to be hearing.

Captain Black shook his head. "Just speak to no one until I can get this figured out."

"Yes, Sir." No problem.

The child reached for Collier's hand. Her tiny fingers wrapped around his index finger. Collier sucked in a deep breath.

Captain Black rubbed his chin. "How can we trust this woman?"

"She risks her family. Her father has been killed. Sister raped and mutilated." The interpreter tugged on his hair. "She has never led us astray."

"Her information has, however, caused several casualties for our men and your people."

The interpreter stomped his foot. "All worth it for freedom."

Collier's insides lunged. The faces of Haden, First Sergeant, Crawford, and the others flashed through his mind. His knees weakened, but he held his stance. Was freedom worth it? Worth the death? The destruction?

The interpreter continued. His turban moved a bit out of place. "Your country speaks of freedom for all, show us you believe it. See us through."

Captain Black ran a hand across chin. "Specialist Cromwell."

"Yes, Sir."

"Thank you for saving this child. Your team helped us in ways you don't know."

Collier blinked. He was starting to get that picture.

"Speak to no one. The higher ups will need to deal with this situation. You're dismissed."

"Yes, Sir." Collier turned. The higher ups had a lot on their plate. The prospect of Iraqi freedom meant more injuries, deaths for civilians and soldiers.

"Wait." The interpreter held up a hand. "The girl, her name is Nu'ma." The interpreter moved to his side. "She says 'thank you for finding me. For feeding me. For giving me life.'"

Collier froze at the child's tiny voice. A heavy weight pressed on his chest and slowed his breathing. His brows folded together. "Tell her 'you're welcome'." The corners of his mouth worked into a smile.

The child waved as Collier walked away.

Sergeant Prowski jogged toward him. Not another mission. Collier fought the urge to cross his fingers.

"Cromwell?" Sergeant Prowski held a slip of paper in his hand, unable to look him in the eye. The Sergeant never avoided contact.

"Yeah?" Collier's heart thudded. Who else had been killed in action?

He handed Collier the paper. "Whit's in the hospital."

"She's not due for a few more weeks." This was sort of good news. Much better than a death. Of course he'd rather be there when she gave birth, especially given the diagnosis.

"I think there's more to it." Sergeant Prowski nodded. "You're needed home right away."

Collier scanned the words on the page. Attack. Intensive care. Caesarean. Unresponsive. The letters blurred. The lining of his throat thickened. This couldn't be happening. "Wh ...when do I leave?" He managed to swallow.

"Can you be packed and ready in half an hour?"

"Sooner." Collier shoved the letter in his pants' pocket and jetted toward his room.

DULL, brief, steady beeps sounded near Whitleigh's head. She breathed in the stale and sterile scents. The blankets beneath her palms were cool and coarse. Nothing comfortable.

"Has she been under a lot of stress?" The man's voice seemed distant, foggy even.

"Well, of course." When did Momma get here? Where was here? "My goodness. What do you expect? Pregnant, alone, attacked, husband at war." Momma whimpered. "Is my Whit going to be okay?"

"We can never guarantee anything Mrs. Haynes, but her vitals are strong. She's doing a lot better than before."

Before? Whitleigh's eyes shuffled underneath her closed lids.

The man's voice rose an octave. "A placental abruption is serious. She's very fortunate to have been with friends."

Abruption? Yes. Something had torn. Her insides shuddered. The pain had been unbearable. She had fallen. Jen tumbled down with her. Yes, that's how it happened.

"Had she complained about any back, pelvic or abdominal pain? Bleeding or spotting?"

"She never let on if anything hurt." Momma sniffled. "How could this all go so wrong?"

Wrong? Oh no. Whitleigh's eyelids flickered but wouldn't lift. She willed them open. "Where's my baby?" Were her words audible?

"Whit. Oh, Whit. Thank God."

"Mrs. Cromwell, please lay back."

Lay back? This man better move. She swatted at the webs of wires in and around her. "Where's my baby?" Whitleigh grimaced as searing pain ran across her lower abdomen. "What happened to me? Give me my baby. Momma, get Collier."

"Lay back Mrs. Cromwell." The doctor held her arm with a firm grip. A young nurse worked alongside of him. "Your husband's been contacted. He's on his way."

When would he arrive? Whitleigh struggled with the doctor. How long had she been in here? "Get off of me. I don't even know who you are. Where's my doctor?" Her weakened state proved no match for the strength of the doctor and his nurse. She gave up, lying back. Her legs tingled with an unfamiliar intensity as the nurse helped tuck them back under the thin knit covers.

"I'm Dr. Roberts. Your doctor wasn't on call."

Whitleigh's pulse continued to race. Momma smoothed a hand over Whitleigh's hair.

"Momma?"

"It's okay, baby, I'm here. It's okay."

"Mrs. Cromwell, we had to do an emergency caesarean."

That explained the intense discomfort.

"You had some complications. Do you remember what happened?"

"I do." Whitleigh nodded. She looked around the room. The memories weren't as foggy as before. The top of her hand ached as the nurse replaced the IV.

Dr. Roberts jotted something on his clipboard as the nurse plugged in wires and tubes that Whitleigh had torn from their source.

"It's okay Sweetheart." Momma kissed Whitleigh's cheek and held her hand. "Calm down, baby."

It wasn't okay. Whitleigh's chest heaved. Each movement hurt to the core. Nothing was okay. Jen. Collier. The baby.

Whitleigh placed her hand over her tender, swollen abdomen. Her dry mouth made it hard to swallow. "Where's my baby?" Her fingers shook as she lifted them to her cheek. He had to be okay. Alive. His little heart needed to be strong and healthy.

The doctor pushed up his metal frames. "He's in the NICU." Would you like to see him?"

Intensive Care Unit? So this was really happening.

Whitleigh could only nod. At least he was alive. He. It was a boy. She released a long breath. Could she smile?

"If you would like to see him, I'll have the nurses help you."

Whitleigh nodded.

Momma dabbed her eyes with a napkin.

Whitleigh swallowed as her heart quickened. "Is he … is he okay?" The doctor must've known what she meant.

"He's okay for now." Dr. Roberts bobbed his head. At least his smile was pleasant. "We will have to discuss treatment. His heart, well, I'm told you know about his condition."

Whitleigh pursed her lips and bowed her head. "My doctor said ultrasounds weren't always right."

"I know it's hard to accept, but we'll need to take action very soon." Dr. Roberts tucked his clipboard beneath his arm. You do have ... options." His lips formed a thin line. "Hypoplastic Left Heart Syndrome is fatal if not treated."

"I know." Whitleigh closed her eyes. It could be fatal even if treated.

He folded his arms and then took a seat on the rolling stool next to the bed. "Mrs. Cromwell, have you considered Compassionate Care?"

Whitleigh tilted her head to the side. "I've heard so much over the past several weeks." Life blurred together. "What is Compassionate Care?"

"This condition is very serious, very rare." Dr. Roberts leaned forward.

"Yes." No one said it wasn't.

Momma sat on the bed, holding Whitleigh's hand in her lap.

Dr. Roberts coughed. "Undergoing surgery is difficult enough for any newborn to endure, but a premature baby to undergo a total of three major heart surgeries … possibly more … possibly needing a heart transplant down the road … well…" He rubbed a hand over the graying stubble on his cheeks. "And waiting for a heart transplant — there aren't many suitable hearts available."

She should think not. Whitleigh wrapped her hands around Momma's.

Dr. Roberts blinked. "You have to understand the risks involved."

Whitleigh flinched. "Are you saying my baby may not make it?"

Hadn't she known this already?

"I'm saying that death is a real possibility, and even if he makes it, your baby will never be … normal."

What was normal anyway?

Dr. Roberts looked away for a moment. "Compassion Care forgoes surgery."

Whitleigh's chest rose, and her eyes lifted. "Forgo?"

Momma rubbed Whitleigh's hand, silent.

Dr. Roberts cleared his throat and quickly glanced at Momma. "Mrs. Cromwell, he wouldn't need any care. You could go home with him in a few days when you are healthy enough to leave. He could pass peacefully at home."

"Die?" Whitleigh's lips cracked. The nurse placed a cool hand on Whitleigh's shoulder. "You want me to let my baby die? What kind of doctor are you? How is that even legal?"

"It allows him to live his life, no matter how brief, without his little body enduring multiple surgeries that he may not even live through." Dr. Roberts held out an open palm. "Many couples in this situation choose this option."

"We don't."

"In many ways it's more respectful."

"For who?" This man was an idiot. "I want a new doctor right now."

"Understand that your Military insurance may not cover all costs relating to the procedures if you choose the surgical route. Hotel stays, the cost of gas, long-term care, etc."

"Money?" Whitleigh's cheeks grew hot. "Really?" The nurse tugged on her shoulders. "I don't want to lay back."

"Calm down, Whit, sweetie." Momma squeezed her hand.

"Momma, are you even hearing this quack?"

"Compassionate Care is a viable option." Dr. Roberts' brows narrowed.

"Maybe for some, but not us." Whitleigh shrugged the nurse away. She crossed her arms and looked toward the window. "Please take me to see my baby."

The doctor stood. If he wanted to continue their conversation, he could keep standing. "Either way, we need a decision soon."

"I think you know my decision."

"Your husband has a say in this too, Mrs. Cromwell."

Whitleigh held her breath. This man had some nerve. What made him think Collier would choose any other route but life?

The nurse stood at her head, Momma at her side. Each was silent as if they were preparing to handle any outward act of the storm brewing inside Whitleigh.

"Again, Dr. Roberts." Whitleigh released her breath. "You know our decision."

"Mr. Cromwell will be here soon. I'd like to talk to with him too."

Bet he would. Whitleigh clenched her jaw.

"Know that your baby will need to be taken to the Children's Hospital in Denver if surgery is what you both decide. I can make those arrangements when I hear from Mr. Cromwell."

"Then I guess we're headed to Denver." Whitleigh focused her glare on Dr. Roberts. He wasn't the enemy, but it sure seemed like it.

With a sigh, the doctor turned, and the door clicked closed behind him. The nurse tidied up the room and hurried out.

Another battle. Always another fight. No need to stop the tears. Like troubles, they came at their own discretion.

"Come here, baby." Momma drew Whitleigh into her arms. If only she were a child again. Back then, all problems could be solved with hugs, kisses, and a sweet treat.

"How is this fair, Momma?" No baby should have to fight to live.

"It's not."

HE looked perfect, even with wires and tubes attached. He had blue eyes. Of course those could change with time, and his hair was much darker than she imagined. Beautiful. Tiny. The preemie clothes Momma brought hung loose on his small body. Even his sounds and movements were short.

Baby Boy Cromwell slept in his clear, plastic crib. What would they name him? Whitleigh touched the strip of blue paper taped to the outside, her finger scanning across each line. DOB January 15th. Four pounds, eight ounces. Sixteen inches long.

She counted his fingers and toes. All there. She kissed his sweet wrinkled feet and placed her hand on his tiny chest. His heart thudded beneath her palm. How could anything be wrong with him?

"Mommy's gonna make it all better."

His hand held onto her index finger, barely able to wrap around, but his grip was strong.

"Am I able to feed him? Even if he has a feeding tube?"

A nurse scurried around the room. "We can bring you a pump if you'd like?"

Pumping wasn't in the plan, but whatever worked. "Could you show me how to use it?"

"Well, of course." The nurse, round and jolly, helped ease the trying situation. "Give me a moment and I'll make sure to get you squared away."

Whitleigh eyed her name tag. "Thank you, Nurse Trish."

The woman smiled and scooted out the door with a nod.

Whitleigh sank back into the pillow, ignoring the bland, clinical room features, though a few balloons painted on the wall added a splash of hope. The rocking chairs added a nice touch too. Whitleigh leaned forward, eyes gaping at this child — her son. "I wish I could hold you."

His little leg twitched.

"I hope you're having the best dreams in the world."

"Knock, knock." Momma stepped through the doorway. "Mrs. Ryan is here."

"Oh." Whitleigh kissed her baby's hand. "Mommy will be right back." She rubbed his head and kissed him again before unwinding his finger from hers.

"I'm ready, Momma."

Momma wheeled Whitleigh from the NICU, through buzzing security doors, and past many rooms in the silent halls. How many couples shared their journey? How many hearts ached?

Her room was small, but at least she didn't have to share with anyone.

"Whit, you look lovely." Mrs. Ryan held a bouquet of flowers. She didn't lie well. "When is Collier coming in? Do we have time to fix you up?"

Momma glanced at the clock. "In the next couple of hours I'd say."

"Oh that's plenty of time." Mrs. Ryan reached for a large duffle bag. There was no telling what that woman had crammed in there.

"He called a few hours ago."

"He called? Why didn't you tell me, Momma?" Whitleigh tried to stand from the wheelchair. No luck. "Where was he? Was he okay? What did you tell him?"

"He's fine, dear." Momma smiled and helped Mrs. Ryan pull out a cosmetic case. "He was in New York. Had a layover. There wasn't much to tell him, only that you were okay, and the baby was okay."

Whitleigh rolled her eyes. Okay seemed to be her new favorite word. It was quite annoying since nothing was okay.

"Your Daddy will be here soon." She unzipped a side pouch, digging around. "He had to tie up some things at work."

Whitleigh puffed her cheeks. "Dad never misses work."

"Running his own business is tough stuff, but that man would miss anything for you, sweetheart."

"I know." It was true. Though, there was a time, not so long ago, she would've doubted that.

Whitleigh closed her eyes as Mrs. Ryan, or rather, Layla as she always reminded her, and Mom dabbed on layers of concealer. She must look terrible.

"I've already emailed him pictures of our sweet little grandson." Momma sighed as if she were past cloud nine.

"Hold still, Whit." Layla bit her lip as she smoothed foundation underneath Whitleigh's eyes.

"Ladies, I think I'm fine." Whitleigh shooed them away. "I just had a baby. I think Collier will cut me some slack." At least he better.

"Let me get a bit of mascara on you, oh and," Layla pulled a few garments from the bag, "I brought some cardigans for you to choose from in case you wanted to change your clothes." Layla eyed Whitleigh's hospital gown. It wasn't the most fashionable thing she'd ever worn, but it served its purpose.

"You went to my house?"

"I even finished the nursery for you."

"Surprise." Momma clapped. "Layla worked all night on it for you." Momma squeezed Layla into a choke of a hug.

"Please stop." Whitleigh shook her head. "Stop pretending everything's fine. We can talk about the bad stuff. I'm not going to fall apart." Not now at least.

Momma ran a comb through Whitleigh's hair and tucked a few strands behind her ear. "Hard times are everywhere honey, but we choose to focus on the good things."

Layla stepped forward, envelope in hand. "Emma made this for you."

Whitleigh tugged out a pink construction paper card, bedazzled with stickers, hearts, and balloons. A pink princess bandage fell from the page and into her lap. Stick figures adorned the inside. "The Peeple I Love." Emma, Whitleigh, Jen, and Mrs. Ryan along with a slew of stick figure children sure to be the Ryan kids, all surrounding a broken heart. She wrote, "This band aid can fix n e thing."

Maybe it could. Whitleigh picked up the bandage and held it close. "How's Jen?"

No pleasant answer existed.

Momma sighed and wiped her eyes.

Layla sat in the straight back chair. "She's a mess, Whit."

Whitleigh could've guess as much. Whitleigh held her hands loose in her lap. "Is she … I mean, has she gone back — "

"She left for Tennessee."

"Oh." She couldn't blame her for leaving. "For his funeral?"

Layla nodded. "And after."

They sat in silence. The light in the room dimmed as gloomy clouds formed outside. Rain began to splatter against the window.

What a dreary day.

Layla's smile was soft. "She's called a couple times to check on you."

"She would." Whitleigh arched a brow. "Jen shouldn't be worried about me." She had so much to deal with already.

The door clicked open. "Excuse me, Mrs. Cromwell." Nurse Trish peeped into the room. "Your husband is here."

"Oh." Whitleigh's eyes widened. Her stomach knotted. "Let him in."

CHAPTER 14

MINUS a few articles of clothing strung over a high backed chair, the hospital room appeared squeaky clean, making the medical stations in Iraq look like a rundown traveling circus. Collier stood in the doorway, mere feet from Whit.

Mrs. Haynes and Mrs. Ryan gave kind smiles as they walked past him and into the hall. Collier nodded. He willed his heavy feet to carry him forward, stopping at the foot of Whit's bed. Hat in sweaty hand, Collier clasped a bouquet of the hospital gift shop's most expensive arrangement. He pressed his lips together. Why couldn't he speak?

She looked tired and pale. Her lips were dry and a washed out shade of pink. Always beautiful, but more worn than he'd ever seen. Nevertheless, she was okay, alive, and staring right at him. Her eyes filled with tears. A woven white blanket lay over her still swollen stomach.

This wasn't how their life should've played out.

He'd missed it all. The whole pregnancy. Everything.

Collier tucked his bottom lip under.

Time passed without him, so cruel in many ways.

Her blue eyes searched his. Surely he looked quite a mess with his dirty worn out ACU's. Remnants of Iraqi sand clung to the creases of his boots and underneath this nails. The quick wash-up in the airplane restroom didn't prove much help.

The clock on the wall ticked.

He lifted his shoulders in a half shrug. "I'm home." After almost eight months away, that's what he came up with?

Whitleigh's lips quivered as she lifted her arms toward him.

Was it safe to touch her? Collier moved to the side of the bed and placed the flowers on the vacant nightstand.

She winced at his embrace and he loosened his hold around her warm body. He breathed her in.

"Whit, I'm sorry." Collier brushed his hands over her hair. "Are you okay? Hurt?" He scanned her arms and neck for bruises from the attack. "I should've been there to protect you. You're safe now."

"Kiss me." Whit's voice muffled into his shoulder.

He pulled away. "You never have to ask."

"I wasn't asking."

Assertive. Wow. Collier raised his brows and rubbed the tears from her cheeks with his thumb. He drew her lips to his.

Time in Iraq never permitted him to remember how much he missed kissing her. There wasn't much time for anything but trying to stay alive. Were those his tears or hers on his cheeks? It didn't matter. He held her lips to his. Let the clock tick, he had all day, all week, and then another.

Collier moved a hand to the small of her back. With the other he held her face and cradled her neck. Her hair tangled between his fingers. Too close wasn't close enough.

Whit's body tensed.

He pried his lips from hers. "I'm sorry."

"You're not hurting me." She didn't lie well.

"I can't keep kissing you like that. At least not right now." He brushed a hand over his face, mindful of the stubble.

Whitleigh sighed and tugged on his collar. "I understand."

Collier held her hands and kissed her cheek. She held her forehead to his chin. He'd waited months without intimacy, a few more wouldn't hurt.

"Tell me about our baby." Did he want to know? Of course, but seeing their child only to say good-bye so soon seemed unfair.

"It's a boy."

"I could've sworn it was a girl." Collier grinned. "A boy. Wow."

Whit squeezed his hand with a gentle touch. "You're going to be the best dad in the world."

Was he? His heart skipped a beat, maybe two. What did he know about being a dad? His father had been a terrible example. How could Collier be a good father when his son only had no more than a few days to live? Collier's breathing slowed. Why did his son have to die?

The joy drained from his face. He knew why. His son was dying as punishment for the lives he'd taken in war.

"Hey." Whit placed a tender kiss on his lips. "You okay?"

"Yeah." He cleared his throat. "Let's go see our boy."

"Don't be shocked when you see him. Lots of cords and wires."

"Oh." The doctor in the hall had stopped him on the way in and said the same thing. "We can't hold him then?"

"I'm thinking soon." Given the doctor's dreary report, Whit seemed way too positive. Maybe she needed to be in denial a bit longer. She'd been through so much already.

They could talk about funeral arrangements later. For now, they could enjoy what little time they had with their son.

He helped Whit from the bed, steadying her with his hands. Her legs shook for a moment as she stood, holding her stomach. "It feels like my insides might fall out at any second." She laughed through the pain in her eyes. He couldn't prevent her pain. Seemed like he should be used to that by now, not being able to help others when they needed it most.

"Here, let me get the wheel chair."

"I want to try to walk. The nurses say I need to as soon as possible." She took an unsteady step forward. Collier extended his arm — the least he could do.

"I'll bring the wheelchair just in case."

Whit nodded a smile.

"Let's go see our boy." Collier kissed her hand and pushed back a yawn. Sleep, among many other things, would wait.

MONITORS beeped at a low steady pace. A few muted conversations in the NICU drifted past the curtain barrier. They weren't the only couple dealing with seemingly insurmountable obstacles.

Their baby slept in a case of plastic, complete with armholes, and covered with tape and tubes. Collier held his breath. How could he not be shocked and awed?

"He's mine." Collier sat at the edge of his seat. He placed his hand into the hole of the transparent crib and worked his pinky into the palm of his son's teeny, wrinkled hand. "I can't believe he's mine. Like a tiny little miracle."

Was the doctor sure he wouldn't make it? His little chest rose and fell with each breath. Maybe hope existed. "I know he's small, but he looks okay to me."

Whit frowned. "That's what I keep thinking. I've read some parents take their baby home, not knowing they have HLHS, and a few days later, the baby dies."

Unimaginable. Collier's stomach knotted.

For months death was his reality. That's war.

"Do you think he's in pain?" That mattered. If a way existed to allow his son to go in peace with no pain, they would take that route. His son wouldn't suffer in death like his mother, brother, and brothers in arms had.

"He seems very much at rest." Whit smoothed her hand over the dark hair that stood up all over their baby's head.

"Poor kid. He's got cowlicks like me."

"That's one of the first things I noticed."

"Fixing my hair used to drive my Mom crazy in the mornings." The distant memory lingered. Collier's grin faded. Whit rubbed his shoulder and intertwined her fingers with his.

"She'd be so proud of you."

Would she? He nodded, his mouth too dry to speak.

"I know you may not want to talk about it, but would you like to let your dad know about the baby?"

No way. Collier gnawed on the inside of his lip. "He's not my dad anymore."

"I just…," Whit sighed.

"Did you give him my address?"

The muffled conversations around the room hushed. Collier's cheeks grew hot. Maybe his voice had been too loud and harsh.

She stared. Her words stuttered. "I … I … no, I didn't."

Collier slid his finger from his son's palm. "He wrote me a letter."

"Oh."

"He's still in jail — can stay there for all I care." Collier twirled the wedding band around his finger. "I didn't read it if you were wondering." Maybe he should've.

"Everyone deserves a second chance."

Collier blew out a ragged breath. He wasn't home to hear a sermon. "He's had plenty of chances."

"Your Mom wouldn't want — "

"She wouldn't want to be dead, Whit. That's what she wouldn't want."

Whit sat back, pulling her hand from his, looking about the room.

There it was, pain on her face, embarrassment. Why did he snap? She only tried to help. "Can we not talk about this right now?" He reached for her hand. "Maybe later, but not now."

She gave a slight nod, her focus on the baby.

"I brought you something." Collier stood, digging deep into his pocket. He pulled the paper out, careful to unfold it.

"Our list." Whit covered her mouth. "You kept it."

"Always." His heart warmed at her bright smile. "I thought we could add a few things to it while I'm home." He held it in the air. The lights overhead highlighted worn spots. "Maybe we need to rewrite it on some new paper."

"It has character." Whit would say that. Always turning something old into something new.

"Naming our first child would be a great addition." Collier gave the list a slight shake.

"That's definitely something worthy of our Forever List."

"He said he wants his name to be Sam."

"You must be hearing things."

"Sam's a good, strong name." Collier eased back into his seat. "You got anything better?" She probably had a mile long list. Sam, along with a handful of family names, were the extent of his. "I know your Mom has several suggestions."

"Way too many, and I've pretty much dismissed her ideas." She rolled her eyes. "I don't know if you'll go for it, but I like Anderson."

Hmm. His grandfather's name. A great man. Collier bobbed his head. "Anderson what?"

"Well, I was actually thinking Anderson as the middle name." Her voice squeaked. "And I thought Haden for the first name, after …."

"My Haden." The Haden he loved like a brother, the Haden he couldn't save. He swallowed and ignored the ringing in his ears. A dull pounding in his head brought him to his feet. "I'll be right back. Just need some water."

"Over there." Whit lifted a pale hand. "The nurses said we could grab any of the water bottles in there." A small refrigerator sat perched on a half-sized counter in the NICU.

"Thanks." Fresh air would've been better than bottled water. It would do. Collier crossed the room in two strides and snatched a bottled water. The cap rolled off with a twist and Collier guzzled until the room temperature cooled down.

"There are a lot of other names we could go with." Whit lowered her gaze. "It seemed like a nice way to ..." her voice trailed off.

Collier took another sip. Her intentions were good.

"Let's just forget it. I was silly to — "

"You weren't silly." Collier lifted the bottle to his lips, finishing off the water in one large gulp. He wiped his mouth. Sand and grit from the sleeve of his uniform grated across his lips. "I'm not sure how naming our son after Haden would honor him."

Whit's eyes squinted. "What do you mean?"

Collier tapped the empty bottle and took a seat at her side. "Haden didn't live, Whit." He touched her cool hand. Her pulse quickened under his fingertips.

She stared, as if not understanding. Her eyes glistened.

How was he going to help her see the truth? Speaking the truth in love seemed impossible. His mouth went dry. He shook the bottle, but no water remained. "Whit, you have to accept that our son isn't going to live either."

She gasped, and the hushed conversations about the room halted once more.

"He's not strong enough, and even if he were to survive all of those surgeries, he's never going to be normal or have a normal life." Collier leaned forward. "How is that fair to him?" It wasn't fair. She had to see that.

"You talked to the doctor."

It sounded more like an accusation coming from her pouting lips.

"He said the same thing to me as he did to you."

"He's not even an expert."

"He's a doctor, Whit."

"He's a doctor with no experience in this condition, and you sided with him. A death sentence for our baby." She positioned her wheelchair in front of the plastic crib. Collier frowned.

He crossed his arms. "You're not thinking logically right now, and I understand that. You've been through a lot." They both had. "Putting our son through surgeries is cruel, and there's no reason for him to suffer when we can make him comfortable and happy right now."

"Who are you?"

Collier stepped back. Her words, hardly a whisper, were deafening. *Who was he?* How could she ask such a thing? He ran his hands across his face, and then let them fall to his knees. "I'm the man that wants a quality life for his son, no matter how long or short that may be."

Her lips were a stiff line. "Then give him the chance to live."

The woman infuriated like no other. Collier shook his head. "Do you not get it?"

"You're the one missing it here." She gripped the sides of her wheelchair. "You're denying our son the chance to live for a possibility he may die in surgery. He's dead without surgery, Collier, but with it there's hope he can live."

"Live to do what? Be a special needs child? Depending on everyone his whole life, never getting married, never having a family of his own? I've seen men fight to live, and it's ugly. I couldn't stop their suffering, but I can stop our son from hurting."

"What scares you most Collier?" Her voice hissed, and her body shook. "That our son may have obstacles in his life to overcome, or that he won't be able to depend on you to help him overcome them like you couldn't depend on your father?"

Collier froze. Her words exploded and proved more devastating than any roadside bomb. The ringing in his ears returned. She could've said anything but that.

He rose from his chair, legs heavy as he walked from the NICU. There was no need to fight. She'd won.

WHAT an ugly sight. Whitleigh closed her eyes as the nurse changed the dressings covering her abdomen. Though she seemed to be as careful as could be, Nurse Trish couldn't prevent the staples from sticking and pulling.

"I'm glad to see you back in your room. There is such a thing as overdoing it, you know." Nurse Trish focused on applying the new bandages.

"I guess." Whitleigh flinched and bit her lip.

"Almost done. I know this isn't pleasant, but you're doing well."

Her smile convinced. She must've said that to all her patients.

"I'm glad you're getting me fixed up. I gotta get back to my baby. He needs me."

"He also needs a relaxed momma."

Whitleigh blew a messy tuft of hair from her face. "I'm as stress free as they come."

"Mm hm."

"My stomach looks like Frankenstein." Maybe she should've kept her eyes closed.

"Oh honey, this is nothing compared to the things I've seen." Nurse Trish laughed with a lift of her hand. "Shew! I bet your husband's seen worse."

Whitleigh swallowed and grimaced through the last staple as it caught. Collier probably had seen worse, and her wound would be nothing compared to the stitches their son would have when he underwent surgery.

Collier would come to his senses. He had to. Their baby needed this surgery.

"All done."

"You're a peach."

"You know, Mrs. Cromwell, we take good care of that little boy of yours.

You just worry about getting yourself back into working order."

Whitleigh nodded.

Nurse Trish winked and waddled out the door as Momma entered.

She kissed the top of Whitleigh's head. "Mrs. Ryan will be here soon."

"She doesn't need to drive out here again. She's got all those kids to take care of."

"The FRG ladies are taking turns watching them." *Lord help those women.* Momma dug through her purse. "I guess there's some neighborhood drama she's helping clear up."

"Drama?" What now?

"Gum?" Momma held out a stick. Whitleigh declined with a nod. "The police showed up and arrested some guy from across the street."

"Was there a little girl involved? Emma?"

"Not directly, but Mrs. Ryan did want me to tell you that Emma is okay."

"What happened?"

"Some man was arrested for domestic violence. Mrs. Ryan said the soldier drug that little girl's mom out of the house and beat her right there in the front yard. Can you believe something like that?"

Whitleigh covered her mouth. Poor Helen.

It wasn't easy to believe, but the news confirmed atrocities like it all too often.

"I'm telling you Whit, these soldiers are just snapping."

Yes. Snapping too often, and too close to home for comfort.

"God help them." Momma shook her head. "I'm afraid this war is doing something awful to our soldiers and their families in ways we may never understand."

Whitleigh's chest tightened.

"Mrs. Ryan is taking care of Emma right now until her next of kin can be contacted."

"What?"

"Well she can't stay with her momma right now can she? Or her Dad?"

"Was it her Dad who was arrested?"

"Honey, I don't know. I told you what I heard from Mrs. Ryan."

Of course Whitleigh resided in a hospital the one time Mrs. Ryan decided to hold back details. She huffed.

"Anyway. She'll be here as soon as she can. I'm sure she'll tell you more." Momma pulled a hairbrush from her purse. "Wanna talk about what's bothering you while I fix your hair? Lord only knows how you messed it up again."

"Nothing's wrong."

"Sure there's not." Momma shook the brush. "I've known you long enough to know when something's the matter.'

Moms were so prying. Whitleigh glanced about the room. "Maybe later, Momma."

Momma hummed a tune and ran a brush through Whitleigh's hair. No matter how lulling the melody, it couldn't still her thoughts.

Collier was angry, or hurt, maybe both. A fight was no way to say welcome home, but he gave her no choice. A homecoming should've been a time of celebration, but no joy existed. It went out the window before he came home, mired by anything that could possibly go wrong — and that doctor had some nerve. She gritted her teeth. How sneaky of him to speak to Collier before she had, and how disgusting for Collier to listen. Whitleigh sighed.

"Where's Collier?"

No telling. She shrugged. "He's probably getting some rest."

Maybe sleep would rid him of the Dr. Jekyll behavior.

Momma continued to brush. Its soothing effect helped a bit. "He's been through a lot Whit, and then he traveled a long way home only to go through more." Momma patted her arm.

He had been through a lot. She'd seen it — proof in his eyes that he was different, aged, burdened. No matter, condemning their son to a death sentence was inexcusable.

"We all go through tough times. Give it time, honey."

There wasn't time. Each tick on the wall clock made her shudder. Whitleigh pressed her lips together.

"Did you decide on a name?"

"Not yet, Momma." She and Collier couldn't agree on surgery for their child, let alone a name.

"I'm fond of Lincoln." Momma let out a short chuckle. "Our little Linc."

Whitleigh's brows lifted. "I actually like that name. One of the higher ranking on your list?"

"The fact that you ask proves you didn't look at it."

Whitleigh smirked, folding her hands in her lap.

"But yes, Lincoln was on the top."

"I'll have to ask Collier about it." If they ever talked again. The way he walked away from her earlier resembled an end of some sorts.

"No need." Momma stood and tucked the brush into her purse. "He likes it too. Loved the names I suggested."

"Of course you sent him a list too. Why wouldn't you?" Whitleigh shook her head. "You meddle more than Mrs. Ryan."

"I knew I'd love Mrs. Ryan the moment you first told me about her." Momma crossed her arms, her smile wide and pleasant. "We don't meddle, dear. We just care a whole lot about you, and Collier for that matter."

Whitleigh rolled her eyes. Meddling is meddling no matter if it is, at times, appreciated. Momma and Mrs. Ryan knew no limits to intrusion.

Hmm. Whit strummed her fingers. Could it be?

"Momma? Did you give Collier's address to his father?"

Her silence provided enough proof.

"What were you thinking?" Whitleigh palmed her forehead. Their marriage was stressed enough without Momma stirring things up.

"I'm thinking I've known Charles all my life. He and your Daddy grew up together."

"I know all of this."

"That man's been through the ringer, Whit."

"So has Daddy. He grew up in an abusive, alcoholic home just like Mr. Cromwell, but Daddy didn't do us the way Mr. Cromwell did his family."

"If you only knew — "

"It doesn't change anything. You can't force Collier to make amends. What you did was wrong."

Tears glistened in Momma's eyes. "Whit, honey, he's dying." Her shoulders sank.

"What?"

"He has pancreatic cancer." Momma's chest rose and fell in a defeated manner. "The doctors are giving him two to four months to live."

This was terrible. Whitleigh closed her mouth for a split moment.

"Is there treatment? Can he even get treatment in jail?"

"He's refusing anything." Momma shook her head. "He only wanted to talk to Collier one last time, maybe get a glimpse of his grandson. That's all. What was I supposed to do? How could I not try to help?"

Whitleigh lowered her eyes. This day kept going downhill.

"I'm sorry if I caused trouble for you, sweetheart. You know that wasn't my intention."

Whitleigh nodded. Momma's sweet spirit never meant harm.

She dabbed her eyes. "Your Daddy called a bit ago. He was able to get off work sooner than we thought." Momma grabbed her purse from the floor in a slow movement. "I'm gonna go on up to the airport." She kissed the top of Whitleigh's head and turned. "Whitleigh, honey, I know it's not any of my business, but don't you and Collier shut each other out. You need each other. Keep talking. When you stop, well, that's when the real trouble starts."

Whitleigh nodded. Momma would know.

FADED sunlight slid through the sides of the pulled shades. The room filled with a warm orange glow. For the time being, the rain stepped aside.

What a day. Whitleigh pressed her cheek into the bed pillow.

Collier's shadow entered the hospital room first. His steps were light and courteous.

"I'm awake." Whitleigh worked to sit up.

He raised a hand. "Please lay down." His eyes appeared red. Allergies this time of year? Whitleigh swallowed. Her words cut him deeper than she thought. How could she bring up his father right now, or ever?

She eased up with an elbow. "You look relaxed." In all honesty, he looked handsome, even when wearing sweatpants.

"I came in earlier." His Adam's apple bobbed as he toyed with some sort of rope bracelet around his tanned wrist. "You were sleeping."

"I wish you would've woke me."

Sigh. Their tone sounded too formal.

"You need the sleep." Nurse Trish probably shooed him away. "Hope you don't mind, I uh, dug around and found some of my clothes in your bag and thought why not? Sure beats my uniform."

"I bet." Whitleigh scrunched her nose. "These days I guess I can't help but want to wear your old sweats." A slight laugh escaped her lips. "They fit better than most of my other clothes."

Collier smirked. "I bet you look nice in my clothes."

"Better than this hospital gown." He was too kind. Forty pounds heavier, and he handed her compliments. "I'm sure Mrs. Ryan packed plenty of clothes, so help yourself."

"She's taking my uniform home to wash." He rubbed the back of his buzzed hair. "She's not one to say no to."

"No, she's not."

Silence fell between them, ending their cordial conversation. Which one should apologize first? Whitleigh lowered her gaze and opened her mouth.

Collier's voice took her place. "I'm sorry for earlier."

Whitleigh held out a hand. Her heartbeat matched each of her quick breaths. "Come here."

"I don't want to lose him, Whit. I can't say good-bye."

Something about his voice seemed childlike. Whitleigh smoothed her thumb over the back of his hand. "You don't have to." She lifted her hands to his face. The stubble on his cheeks scratched her palms. "He can make it. He's the son of a warrior."

"And an Army wife."

"Two of the strongest types of people on this planet." Whitleigh wiped a tear from his cheek. "I'd say our boy's got more than a fighting chance."

His blue eyes held her captive. Did he know the effect he had?

"Baby Cromwell needs a name." Whitleigh tapped on her chin. "I hear you're pretty found of Lincoln."

His smile rang with sincerity. "I also like Anderson, and Haden."

"Are you sure?" Whitleigh grimaced. "I don't want — "

"Haden would be honored." Collier bowed his head and kissed her hands. "I wish you could've known him. Best guy ever." It was hard to imagine anyone better than Collier.

He chuckled. "The things we would do to Dock and Pulu, Dock mainly."

Whitleigh laughed along with him. She'd heard the stories. They'd make a great novel.

"So, if you're sure," Whit squinted, "then I think we've decided on a name?"

Collier's chest puffed. He stretched out his neck. "Lincoln Anderson Haden Cromwell."

"That's a mouthful."

"It's a strong name."

Indeed.

"So." Collier fidgeted with his hands. "How does this all play out? What's the next step?"

"The doctor needs to know we plan to move ahead so he can make arrangements for us in Denver."

Collier licked his lips. His hands shook for a moment. "When can we bring Linc home?"

Linc. Whitleigh smiled. "A week? Two months? It depends on how he does."

"I don't know if I can stay longer than two weeks."

Whitleigh's hand swung to her chest. Did her heart stop? "What do you mean?"

This wasn't an overnight fix. Several surgeries spanning months and years lay ahead.

"I only have two weeks of leave."

"But this is an emergency."

"I have to go back. It's my duty."

"Duty?" His family was his duty. "I'm sure they will let you stay longer. Our son is in a life or death situation, Collier."

"So are all of the soldiers in Iraq."

She winced. "Are you saying you can't stay or you don't want to stay?"

"Don't do this."

"Do what?" Whitleigh's jaw tightened.

He sighed and ran his fingers over his crew cut. "I'm saying I will do what the Army tells me to do."

"This isn't some minor situation."

"I understand that, Whit, but we're not the only family that has an emergency." He pinched the bridge of his nose. "The war doesn't stop for us."

Apparently. She folded her arms.

"I've sworn to defend this country against all enemies — "

"Foreign and domestic, yes, I know." Knowing didn't make it easier.

"My battalion knows what's going on. I can ask to stay, but …."

"You don't want to."

"That's not fair, Whit."

"It's true."

"You're twisting this all around."

"Please explain." Her chin dimpled. "Tell me how I'm supposed to feel when my husband would rather be fighting a war than at home with his wife, who has a newborn baby struggling to live."

"There's no way to explain. There's no winning this argument with you. This is my job. It's what I signed up to do. You're an Army wife, and this is what it is."

She bit her lip, eyes stinging with tears. "What if that man comes back for me? How will I defend myself and our child?"

"Don't go there. They'll find him. There's a bigger world out there than just us." So she realized. Collier interlocked his fingers. "A very ugly world full of terrible things that I can't even begin to describe to you. There are problems greater than the ones we are facing and it's my job to help." He groaned, pacing the floor. "I don't like this, Whit, but I can't help it. I have to do my duty."

She faced the window. So this was what it was like to be on the back burner, putting the world's needs before their own. "What about us?"

"I need you to be strong."

She clenched her jaw, offended he thought otherwise.

"Whit, I can't stay focused over there if I don't know you're all right; that you've got it all under control."

This was true, very true, but irritating at the same time.

"I'm fine." Or at least she would be. "I can take care of it all." And more. Whitleigh's lashes touched the top of her cheek. She blinked a few times and then rubbed her arms to ward off a climbing chill.

"That's my girl." Collier kissed her forehead.

She might as well have been stone. Maybe the key to surviving this lifestyle resided in becoming a rock — unfeeling, cold, and solid. Whitleigh gathered the blankets up under her chin. "Promise me you'll try to find a way to stay, if for no other reason, then for our baby."

Collier closed his eyes. "I'll try, but I can't promise."

She nodded. At least he would try.

Collier kissed her cheek. The warmth from his lips helped to melt her skin. She closed her eyes. When would this war be over? When could they have a normal life?

WHIT slept, but Collier's attempts failed. Morning would arrive soon anyway. Thanks to the Army, he could function on little sleep. Collier tried to recline, but hospital chairs weren't designed for comfort. Too many things going on, and too much at stake for his mind to stop racing.

The news made it worse, like an irritating itch that couldn't be scratched. As he sat, crazy terrorists were setting off roadside bombs and killing his comrades and innocent bystanders. Maddening. Nothing could be done from a hospital room, except watch reports. Collier clenched his fists. Why was he even watching? How many times had he told Whit to stop watching the news?

He was home, even if for a short while. It's what he wanted, so why the tense sensation growing in his chest? Collier stood and paced the perimeter of the quaint room. The room in Denver would surely be bigger, but compared to his glorified broom closet in Iraq, this resembled a resort.

Collier scanned the room. Bouquets, bigger than the one he bought Whit, sat on every corner and crevice. Friends and family from back home, and members from her book club and FRG, sent their love and support. He scaled the walls with his eyes. Mrs. Ryan tacked up at least a dozen or more handmade cards and drawings from her children and that little girl from across the street that Whit talked about all of the time. Whit had plenty of vital support, lots of hope.

Everyone hoped for the best, and so did he, but what if the best didn't happen? What then? It seemed better, safer even, to expect the worst and be surprised with the best.

The door cracked open.

"Is Whit awake?" Mr. Haynes peeped his head in more than once over the past couple of hours, checking on his daughter.

"Not yet."

Whit stirred in bed, mumbling something about Linc in her sleep.

"Do you mind if I come in and wait?"

Mr. Haynes always proved good company.

"Be my guest. This recliner isn't the most inviting though."

Collier extended a hand. Mr. Haynes pulled him into a hug and gave Collier a nice slap on the back.

"You look good, Collier." His voice was a kind whisper. "Last time I saw you, you had a boy's body. Look at those muscles." Mr. Haynes gave Collier another firm pat on the back. He was pretty stout himself.

"Guess carrying around a lot of stuff has that effect."

Mr. Haynes smiled and walked to Whit's bedside. He knelt down and gathered her hand in his, kissing it. There was no doubt, Whit was still a daddy's girl. His words were soft. "Daddy's here, Whit baby."

Collier looked down at the pile of washed, dried, and neatly folded clothes Mrs. Ryan had delivered earlier. Should he go? He was intruding on their moment.

Whit slept on, but a faint smile appeared on her peaceful face.

So this was the effect a father was supposed to have on his child. The role of a father always seemed sort of ambiguous, but cleared as he watched Mr. Haynes dote over his little girl.

Mr. Haynes stood and turned his head. He must've wiped a tear.

"You hungry?" Mr. Haynes cleared his throat. "Cathy's with Linc right now. She's there every minute Whit can't be. I figured she wouldn't be up to grabbing a bite, but you look like you need to get out of this room."

"Yeah. Food sounds good. If anything's open."

"Twenty-four hour cafeteria, best invention ever." Mr. Haynes gave his stomach a quick pat. "Big day coming up."

They both ran their hands over the back of their heads. No need to elaborate. Linc's surgery could only go two ways.

Collier bit his lip. "We leave for Denver sometime in the morning. We'll know more about the surgery time when we get there."

MR. HAYNES put his hands in his pocket as he walked to the door. He gave a thoughtful nod. "Pizza sound good?"

Collier grabbed his wallet from the nightstand. "Anything's fine with me."

"After eating all that Army stuff, I'd say you'd eat almost anything now."

"Almost."

"Collier." Mr. Haynes scratched at his ear. His face seemed to redden. "I don't know if you and Whit have talked, or how much she's told you."

Collier crossed his arms. "About?"

"About your father."

Who cared about him? Collier chewed on the inside of his jaw. "I don't mean any disrespect, but I don't think this is the time or place to bring him up."

"I'm guessing she hasn't talked to you then?"

Collier tilted his head. "She knows how I feel about Charles."

Mr. Haynes sighed. He eyed the floor and then lifted his head. "Collier. Your dad is dying."

Collier's chest sank. He stepped back, trying to control the burning in his chest. Didn't his father deserve to die?

"He'd like to see you, Collier; see his grandson."

Collier's cheeks were quick to warm. "I'm not traveling back to Kentucky on my leave just to visit that man in jail, and Linc sure won't be able to make that kind of a trip for a long while."

"You don't have to go anywhere." Mr. Haynes placed his hand on Collier's shoulder. "He's here now, in the hall, waiting."

Collier's head spun. He swallowed, grasping for composure. It had been years since he'd been in the same building as his father. The courtroom was his last recollection.

"Serving five years doesn't sound like a life sentence. How did he get out?"

"There's a lot of compassionate people out there, Collier."

Collier huffed. He wasn't one of them. "Did Whit know about — "

"No, she didn't." Mr. Hayne's bushy eyebrows lifted. "Your Dad's prepared to leave if you say no, but think about it."

This was too much to deal with. Collier pinched his lips together until they throbbed.

Whit would want the peace and the closure for his sake. Did he want it? No. Collier rubbed a hand over his mouth. He wouldn't have to say much to him, maybe a hello and a nod for Whit's sake. For Linc's sake. He could do this.

COLLIER wiped his palms on his sweatpants. The thudding of his heart made it difficult to hear. His father waited outside the door. There would be no bars between them, no guards. He'd played this moment out a thousand times, and they all ended with him bashing in his father's face. He had to remain calm, keep the upper hand. Collier wasn't a boy anymore, and he wasn't afraid of this man.

He stepped from the room and into the well-lit hall. A few words, that's all he needed to speak. No elaborate conversations. Nurses strolled by, assisting a few insomniac patients. An older gentleman, clean cut, shaven, middle aged perhaps, sat in a chair against the wall. This couldn't be his father. The man eased to his feet, facing Collier.

It was him, though different.

His skin now boasted a hue of yellow, perhaps a side effect of his disease. Dark circles hung around his eyes. He was thinner, no beer belly. Spearmint replaced the smell of smoke and alcohol. Rage no longer surfaced in the crevasses of his face. His once distant and cold eyes now appeared caring and warm.

Yes, it was him, but the memory of the man who killed his mother and brother did not mesh with the man standing before him.

"Son."

Collier's mouth dried. "Dad?"

"My son." The man's hands trembled.

He knew this man. Collier stepped forward. The urge to hug his father created a force stronger than gravity, but he couldn't. No. This man would sober up long enough to make everyone think he'd changed, but he proved the same, always letting others down.

Collier crossed his arms. "I know why you're here, Charles."

"You're safe." The man's eyes watered as he nodded. "Thank God you're safe."

When did Charles thank God? This man threw Bibles and ripped out the pages. Collier kept his arms folded.

"When Mike and Cathy told me you were being sent over there, all I could do was pray."

So Whit's parents were keeping this murderer informed.

"Pray? Since when do you pray?"

Charles wiped his eyes. "I had to see you. I had to see Lincoln."

"I'm not sure what you think it's going to change?" Collier shrugged his shoulders and kicked out a leg. "You come here, dying, all cleaned up and talking about God. It doesn't change anything. I know who you are and what you've done. Mom and Erik should be here, not you."

Charles winced. Good. The words were intended to inflict pain. "I play that night in my head over and over." Charles covered his face for a moment. "I shouldn't have drove."

"You shouldn't have done a lot of things. I would never lay a hand on my wife and son like you."

"I deserve all your anger and judgment."

Collier ground his teeth. He wasn't above punching a dying man. No fight remained in the man standing in front of him.

"I wasn't the father or husband I should've been."

"Ha. That's an understatement. I'm no priest, and I think it's a little too late for your confession. You won't find forgiveness here."

"I could never expect you to forgive me. Your mother was the most wonderful — "

"How dare you talk about Mom? You took her from me. And Erik. He was just a kid. You took everything from me." Collier shook his fists. If only he could've gotten Erik from the car in time. The buckles were bent, glass everywhere, and the flames were so close. "You didn't mind saving yourself." Collier lowered his voice as a few nurses looked his way. "I can't believe some sympathetic judge let you out of jail. You deserve to die in prison."

"I know. I'm ready to die. I need to die for what I've done."

"I hope it's painful. More painful than any car crash."

"I'm sorry, so sorry." Tears flowed freely down the river of wrinkles on Charles' face.

He seemed immune to Collier's venomous one liners. Infuriating.

"I'm so sorry they're gone, and I'm sorry I'm the reason they aren't here. I'm sorry, and maybe it doesn't change anything, but I want you to know that from the bottom of my heart I wish I'd been the dad and husband I was supposed to be." His voice broke. "I'm proud of the man you've become and thankful you're nothing like the man I was."

Collier closed his eyes. His father took two lives on accident. In Iraq, Collier pointed, aimed, and shot many people on purpose. Maybe he possessed more similarities to his father than he once thought. Collier shoved the notion away.

"Please don't ever be like me." His father reached out and Collier pulled away. "I could never see past my own mess and notice all of the blessings right in front of me."

"I know a blessing when I see one." Collier pushed past Charles. "Linc is this way. He has surgery soon."

COLLIER watched Whit, a true picture of beauty. Her pin-striped maternity top hung a bit looser today, which must've brightened her day even if just a tad. Whit stood in front of the hospital room window, looking over the town. Denver was large, much larger than any town she'd probably ever seen. She held her arm, rubbing one hand mindlessly over her shoulder. Quiet seemed to be the theme of the day.

"We'll come back here one day. Me, you, and Linc." Collier wrapped his arms behind Whit and gently pulled her back against his chest. "I hear Denver has a lot of things to see. The guys at work talk about how great the museums are."

Whit nodded and placed a hand on his.

"He's going to be okay, Sweet Pea."

She turned, face solemn. "It's been awhile since you called me that." Whit held her arms close to her chest.

"Yeah?"

"It feels nice."

He tried to smile, offer some sort of comfort.

"It's been hours, and we've heard nothing."

"No news is good news." He ignored her eye roll at the clichéd Army expression and reached for her hand. "These are some of the best, most skilled surgeons in the world." He almost convinced himself. Collier kissed her cheek. "Maybe you should rest."

She huffed and turned back to the window. "I've been doing that for days."

"Just three."

Whit grinned. At least he got some sort of smile out of her.

She brushed her hands along the colorful drapes. Busy cars scurried along the roads below, oblivious to the lives hanging in the balance above.

"How did things go with your dad?" Whit blushed and lowered her eyes. "I mean, Charles?"

Collier drew in a lengthy breath. "It was a start in the right direction."

Right direction? Even his subconscious knew he needed to forgive. "He's staying in your parents' hotel room."

"How long?"

"We didn't talk much about length of stay."

"He seems different from what you've told me."

"Yeah. I guess." Collier clicked his tongue against the roof of his mouth.

"Feeling hopeful?"

He rolled his neck. "I don't have the energy to sort through it all — the years of neglect and abuse and how it all ended." Like his fallen comrades, no way existed to forget the screams of his mother and brother. He swallowed hard. "I've wanted to hear 'I'm sorry' from that man my whole life, and now it's too late."

"Nothing is ever too late."

"I dunno, Whit. It seems like it is, and it doesn't even matter now."

"You don't mean that." Whit turned in his arms, gazing up at him.

"All I know is that I've wasted too much of my life hating him. I don't have time to do that anymore, it's not worth it, but I don't have the time to make things right."

"There's still time."

"You don't understand." Collier shook his head. "I don't want to take the time. Maybe if we had years ahead of us I could've, but now, with just weeks or months, no way. Not now when so much of my attention needs to go to you and Linc and bringing my men home safe."

"Your men aren't family."

"They're mine." He stood tall, releasing his arms from around her. How could she be so blind? "They gave their lives for me and I would gladly give my life for any one of them."

She didn't get it. How could she not get it? These were his buddies, his friends — his family.

Whit's cheeks flushed. "You're not hearing me."

"And you're not hearing me."

"I need you to be here with me right now, just me. I can't compete with soldiers for your affection."

Collier sneered. "You're jealous?"

"I don't know. Maybe I am."

Insane. Completely ridiculous.

"Whit, you're my wife. No one comes before you."

She lowered her gaze and then lifted her watery blue eyes to his. "Sometimes it doesn't feel that way, Collier."

His heart sank.

Whit's arms hung to her side. "Be completely here when you're home, not there with them in your mind."

His breathing slowed. "I don't know how."

It sounded like a confession.

The sadness in her eyes caused his heart to ache. He would never get used to letting her down.

THE day carried on longer than any other. Whitleigh clasped her hands together, holding them close to her chest. She drew in a deep breath, inhaling the scents of the room — hand sanitizer and flowers. A strange but fitting combination for a hospital. Whitleigh took careful steps around the room, admiring the floral arrangements. She stopped in front of a cluster of yellow Gerber Daisies by the window and rolled the silky petal between her fingers. Maybe its bright cheeriness was contagious. She let her head rest against the cold windowpane.

Momma and Daddy sat close, chatting amongst themselves on the sofa. The doctor should've been in an hour ago. What was the hold up? Whitleigh snapped around, ignoring the pulling sensations from her abdomen, as the door opened

"Hey." Collier waved.

Her lips lifted and then fell.

"Glad to see you, too." His sarcastic smile grew heavy. He'd been out for a while. "You look nice."

Whitleigh tugged on the sleeves of her cardigan. "Momma always said looking pretty makes you feel pretty."

Momma winked.

"I'm not sure it's working." Whitleigh shot a crooked grin toward the sofa and turned back to Collier. "You okay?" She opened her arms as he walked forward. "That was a long coffee break."

"Since I don't drink that stuff, it was more of a water break for me." He walked into her embrace, kissed her forehead, and tousled her hair. "I pretty much sat there and listened to Charles talk." He pressed his lips together. Perhaps he would say more when they were alone. "Any word from the doctors?"

She looked down at her reflection in the tile floor. "Not since the last time." Whit eyed the clock. Hours ago.

"Well, they said everything was going better than expected. That's good news enough."

"For now."

Collier touched her cheek. "Stop worrying."

Easier said than done. How that man remained calm was a mystery. Whitleigh eyed the clock again. Whoever said time flies never waited in a children's hospital.

"Doctors are always late." Dad stood from the corner sofa, knees cracking and popping. He groaned. "I hope Linc takes better care of his body than what I did growing up."

"Growing up?" Mom took a sip of her iced tea. Her nails clinked against the glass. "You've never fully grown up, dear." Mom and Dad laughed. Whitleigh couldn't help but snicker a bit.

"Whit and I used to run through the back fields." Dad looked at Collier. "I climbed trees with that girl. Remember that, Whit?"

Whitleigh nodded. In her mind's eye she could still see Dad running at her side. Good times.

Dad puffed out his chest. "I bet I could still climb that old oak out back."

Momma's smile sparkled. "You were, and still are, a rowdy man." She held her tea glass, pointing it at Dad. "Remember that picnic you planned for me when we were dating?"

"Ha." Dad slapped his knee. Whitleigh rolled her eyes, but no matter how often she'd heard that story, it never got old. Collier propped himself against the window and pulled Whit into his chest. He may not have heard this one, though she wasn't sure how he could've missed it.

Momma crossed her legs. "Honey, you were so bound on catching and cooking that catfish for me yourself.

"I even made my own fishing pole. That old tobacco stick worked just fine. Thought my skills would impress you." Dad double flexed his bushy eyebrows.

"It did." Momma leaned forward, hand on her knee, looking at Whitleigh and Collier. "He's always been good with repurposing old things and the like."

"Guess we know where Whit got that from." Collier's compliment warmed her mind.

Whitleigh nestled her head under his chin and watched her parents relive their past. One day she and Collier would do the same with their children and grandchildren.

Momma threw her head back, laughing. "I still remember you down on that riverbank, spitting and spewing."

"Those boogers were slippery and the pole just wasn't doing what it was supposed to do." Dad folded his arms, grinning.

"Well, there he was, trying to be all suave when he gets those long legs of his stuck in the mud." Momma covered her mouth but failed to hide the laugher.

Collier's chest quaked against Whitleigh's back as he chuckled along with the family. "How did you get out?"

Dad shook his head, face turning red. "It took a while."

"Awhile?" Momma swatted at Dad's arm. "It took more than awhile. I go to help, get tangled up in that mess, and before I know it, there we both are, covered in mud while a catfish flaps around near our heads."

"I'm guessing you didn't get that romantic catfish dinner?" Whitleigh raised a brow. The story never changed, but it always entertained.

"Well, let me just tell you." Momma held up a hand. "We'd been trying to get out of that mud for Lord knows how long, and then over the hill comes Charles, holding up a whole mess of catfish, and we …."

Collier's body tensed as he sucked in a sharp breath. Momma stopped the story. It must've been one thing to know Dad grew up with Collier's father, but another to hear the memories retold.

"Those were good times, dear." Daddy kissed Momma's forehead and the room grew quiet.

Whitleigh gave Collier's arm a squeeze. He offered a faint smile in return, but then looked away. It wasn't fair Collier had been robbed of so many special moments and memories. Regardless, Linc's life would overflow with wonderful times, cherished for a lifetime.

A knock at the door broke the silence. Whitleigh reached for Collier's hand as the doctor entered. "You may see your son now."

Whitleigh stood, fingertips to mouth, frozen. She should've run out the door, but her feet wouldn't move. Collier seemed just as immobile.

Momma stepped forward, but the doctor's outstretched hand signaled her to stop. "Only the parents right now, please."

Momma nodded and turned into Dad's embrace.

The doctor held his clipboard at his side. His eyes were kind, hopeful even. "It's okay. There's no need to be worried." He tugged on his white coat. "The surgery went very well. We can all relax for the time being."

For the time being? Would they ever be in the clear?

Whitleigh inched forward, Collier in step.

They followed behind, clammy hands clasped tightly together. This was it. Whitleigh twisted her lips. Linc would surely be asleep, but he would know they were there. Her heart raced. What if he never woke up? A seventy five percent survival rate after the first surgery were incredible odds, but a twenty five percent chance of sudden death remained. She chewed on her thumbnail.

Collier gave her hand a gentle squeeze. "We got this." He looked straight ahead and didn't let go. He was right. They had this, and it would be okay. Whitleigh focused on her breathing, calm and steady like her steps.

A Wall of Courage to her left grabbed her attention. She and Collier paused for a moment. Photos of smiling families, holding their children, hung in gallery style from ceiling to floor. Short, handwritten testimonies were posted alongside each framed photo. More room existed for stories like theirs.

"You've got a fighter on your hands," the doctor chortled as the thick, metal NICU doors opened with a buzz.

"We already knew that, Sir." Collier gave her arm a playful tug.

Whitleigh nodded. Maybe it was okay to smile, laugh even. Weren't they both laughing just minutes ago?

Whitleigh intertwined her fingers with Collier's and fidgeted with the hem of her yellow cardigan with the other hand.

They passed a tidy nurses' desk. An oversized empty coffee mug, stained with pink lip prints, nestled close to the computer. Someone worked hard, all hours of the night, for her son. A lump formed in Whitleigh's throat. No expression of gratitude would ever be sufficient.

Monitors beeped, but other than the soles of their shoes squeaking on the waxed floor, the NICU was rather quiet. Not just quiet, but serene. Calming shades of green and blue flowed like water along the walls and down the hall, filling the rooms. Yes, if Linc couldn't be home, this was an ideal place for him to rest and heal, in this cozy, nursery-like place.

"The next forty-eight hours are the most critical, but so far he seems to be doing great." The doctor pulled back the curtain. "Not too bad for a premature baby, who survived a violent birth and major heart surgery at five days old."

Whitleigh released Collier's hand and touched her abdomen, still tender and sore from the caesarean. With the other hand she covered her mouth. Tears pricked her eyes like needles.

"I know he looks a little beat up, but trust me," the doctor placed a firm hand on Whitleigh's shoulder, "he will look much better as he heals."

Together she and Collier moved closer to the clear, plastic crib. More tubes than she cared to count sprang from his sweet, tiny body. Layers of vertical surgical tape made a stripe down his torso.

Ten fingers, ten toes. His belly rose and fell with each breath. So precious. So strong.

Whitleigh held out her hand. She had to touch him. "May I?"

The doctor nodded.

If only she could hold him. Whitleigh closed her eyes.

"You can hold him soon."

Her heart leapt. "Really?"

"Give him a few days, and I think it will be fine."

Whitleigh didn't bother to wipe her eyes. Who cared about tear stains with news this wonderful? "We get to hold our son soon, Collier." She turned to the doctor. "When can we take him home?"

"Don't get ahead of yourself." Dr. Simpson rocked on his heels. "Every child is different, but he will still need around the clock attention for quite some time. Maybe four weeks at a minimum. It's hard to say."

"Oh." Whitleigh glanced back at Linc. "Well, at least we'll be here with him."

Collier stood at her side, stone-like. "Dr. Simpson? Why is Linc blue?" He gazed at their son, his expression aloof.

"Oh, that's typical."

"It's just, um," Collier coughed. "Um, it's just when I've seen people turn blue it's never a good thing." He rubbed the back of his head. "I know I'm not a doctor, but um," Collier's voice cracked, "I … I've had some experience with medical situations."

Whitleigh's eyes drifted from Linc's face and scanned Collier's. His forehead wrinkled and dotted with perspiration.

"Understandable, Mr. Cromwell, but this is quite usual." Dr. Simpson adjusted his glasses. "As you both know, for whatever reason, the left side of his heart was underdeveloped and unable to allow for adequate blood flow through his body. As a result, his oxygen supply was limited, hence the blue-ish tint. This surgery, the Norwood, rerouted the blood flow through his strong, right heart chamber, and now allows enough oxygen through the bloodstream for him to survive."

Collier's eyes widened.

"I know it's a lot to process." Dr. Simpson smoothed his hand over Linc's head. "But his color will return."

Whitleigh peered down at Linc. He didn't appear too blue.

"I know you both must have a million questions and concerns." Dr. Simpson pulled a stack of pamphlets from his lab coat pocket. "But in this day and age, I see no reason to be pessimistic about the long term implications for Linc's life."

"Long term?" Collier clasped his chin in his hand. "You mean, he could live a long time? A normal life?"

Was it possible? A long, normal life for their son. Whitleigh stood taller, focusing on the monitors.

"I don't want to mislead you. Linc has a lot to overcome. You know the statistics."

Whitleigh's grin broke. Forty percent of babies with HLHS would not make it to their first birthday. She skimmed a finger across Linc's cheek. His skin was so soft and warm.

Dr. Simpson held up an index finger. "But, medical technology is improving every moment. Twenty years ago this condition was a death sentence." He shook his head. "Are we in the clear? No. Will Linc ever be in the clear? No. He will always have doctor visits and medicine to take, but there are now more adults living very normal lives with a congenital heart defect than ever before."

They stood in silence for a few seconds. The monitors beeped a rhythmic tune that sounded a lot like hope. Whitleigh reached for Collier's hand. "We got this."

A stack of congenital heart disease and defect instructional pamphlets sat on the night stand of the hospital room. Whitleigh folded the last brochure and passed it on to Collier.

"You know, most parents don't get an instruction manual for their new baby." She pushed back her hair. "I guess that's a plus."

"True." Collier chuckled and leaned back on the pillow next to her. "I'm pretty sure I could write a decent research paper after reading all of this."

"You and me both." She eyed the mound of papers and packets. "This is so overwhelming."

"It is a lot of information, but — "

Whitleigh jostled her hair with her hands. "No, I mean yes it is, but that's not what I meant."

"I know what you meant." Collier kissed her cheek and wrapped an arm around her shoulder. The hospital bed, though small, allowed just enough room to cuddle. "All new parents have to feel bombarded, terrified even."

Was that true? Whitleigh sighed. "It's scary enough bringing home a newborn, but I don't know how to take care of Linc."

"We're looking at a million and two brochures that can clue us in, and the doctors here have already said we can call them anytime."

"What if I hurt him on accident? How do I take care of a baby with a serious heart condition?"

"You love him, Whit, that's how. You're already a pro at that."

"How in the world will I ever be able to discipline this child?" She slapped a palm to her forehead. "He's gonna be a little stinker."

"Our little stinker. Nothing wrong with that."

"And what about babysitters? Who can watch him if we want to go on a date?"

Collier shrugged. "Nothing wrong with dinner and a movie on our couch." He winked. That deserved a playful elbow to his side.

"I'm being serious." Whitleigh held her head in her palm. "What if I don't schedule his next surgery in time? What if I don't notice the signs that something's gone wrong?"

"You're forgetting that I'm here too."

"You won't always be." She pulled his arm around her neck. He tried to yank it away. "I'm not being mean, Collier. I need to know I can do all of this on my own too."

He sat up.

"I'm really not trying to hurt you, baby, but if you're wanting to stay in the military longer, then I can't be dependent on you all of the time."

He had to know that. No military wife can be totally dependent on her husband. Common knowledge.

"I don't know if I can stay in the Army anymore, Whit."

What?

Whitleigh let go of his arm. He hadn't mentioned this before. Her bottom lip tightened. All of these months preparing herself to embrace military life, working to deal with it gracefully, for what? She swallowed and sorted through her thoughts. No need for an unnecessary argument.

"I know you've been through a lot, but is this what you want? I've stood beside you and will continue to do so." The sheer prospect of a normal civilian life compared to a dream come true, but it was important to support him and the way he chose to provide for their family. "You seem attached to your soldiers."

"To my friends, yes. To the Army … I just don't know." Collier hung his head. "I can't explain it. It's like I'm torn between serving and leaving. I hate it and hate that I love it. It's like I need them and they need me."

"You mean, the Army needs you?"

"Yes. No." He groaned. "My men need me. The Army needs me. It's hard to explain."

Apparently. Whitleigh crossed her thumbs, rubbing one over the other.

"But, no matter how bad I want to leave, I don't see any other way than to stay."

Whitleigh held her breath, waiting for him to continue.

He clutched at his dog tags tucked beneath his shirt. "There is no other way for me to provide for you and Linc."

"You're going to finish school. Get your degree. There are lots of jobs out there for veterans." He had to see that. A life existed outside of the Army.

"Whit, it's gonna take longer than I thought to finish school." He huffed. "There's hardly any downtime over there, not enough to study, and half the time the internet is down because of all the casualties."

Whitleigh paused. "Well, I'll be done with school soon. I can get a teaching job. That will help."

"And put Linc in day care with all of his medical needs?"

"I'm just saying that there are other ways to make a living besides the Army."

"Ways that will provide the kind of health care Linc will need?"

Whitleigh froze. He'd made up his mind. Nothing she said could change it. For better or for worse, that was Collier's character.

"I have to stay in, Whit." His voice fell from his mouth in a whisper. Months ago he was excited about the prospect of extending his time in the military. Things changed. He turned toward her with eyes too sad for her to look away. His rough hands held her face. "And, I don't know how to say this any other way, but my request has been denied. I can't stay home with you past my two week leave."

Whitleigh's breath caught. They were sending him back to Iraq, even with their son's life hanging in the balance. How could they?

COLLIER tapped his fork against his plate. The hospital cafeteria food wasn't half bad. Smelled good, tasted even better. It only took a few minutes before the Salisbury steak was devoured. Whit picked through a leafy green salad, staring at her food like it talked. She always did take longer to eat.

"It's nice being out here with you. Kind of like a date." Collier nudged her foot against his under the table.

She gave a slight smile and then continued to fluff the rabbit food.

The silence was uneasy. She had every right to be upset.

"Dock emailed me. He's doing good." Collier smirked. "As good as anyone can be over there. Said they're closer to getting the dude responsible for so many of the roadside bombs." He cracked his knuckles. "I wanna be there when they get that guy so bad I can taste it."

Whit stared at him and continued to eat.

Collier drummed his fingers on the tabletop. Maybe war wasn't the best date conversation. "Do you know what your Mom wants to talk to me about?"

"No." Whit shook her head as she swirled the greens in some sort of glazed dressing.

"She pulled me aside before we left."

"Hmm."

Just a 'hmm' and a shrug was all she had to say?

"It's probably something about my father." That would get her to talk for sure. Collier leaned back in his chair for a good stretch. "I don't know what else they want me to do. I'm talking to him. That's a solid start."

"Yes, it is."

The silence continued.

He'd whistle a tune if not for her piercing glare. Collier settled on tapping his foot instead. He looked right and left. It wasn't where he would've chosen, but hospitals were in short supply of the kind of places girls liked to go for dinner. At least they had their own table off to the side, next to the fruit vendor. Whit liked fruit, and apparently her salad tasted real good too.

It wasn't too busy either. A few people, most getting their food to go.

Enough silence. "Look, Whit." Collier sighed. "I wasn't sure when to tell you. I waited until we were alone."

She munched on. So maddening.

"C'mon Whit. They called me back right after I finished talking with Charles." He placed his elbows on the table. "How do you think that made me feel? Chatting it up with the man responsible for my mom and brother's deaths, and then finding out I have to go back to Iraq?"

She lifted her eyes, parted her lips, but said nothing. Instead, she stabbed a tomato hiding under a leaf and shoved it in her mouth.

"Please, Whit. Can't we enjoy the week we have left together?" Even silly questions deserved to be asked.

Whit stopped chewing and laid her fork on the napkin. Her expression hardened. "What you mean is, we pretend that life is peachy for the next week and never deal with the issues 'cause you're always gone.'" She folded her arms. "Sure. I can do that." Had she always been this outspoken or was this something new? Collier scratched his head.

"I can't help this, Whit. I did my best, jumped through the hoops, called everyone I was supposed to call." Collier licked his lips. "The Army needs all the manpower they can get and there aren't many exceptions for getting out of war."

"I understand it's your … duty." That last word fell out of her mouth with a heavy thud. Her jaw clenched. "Don't they realize the seriousness of this situation?"

He wiped his hand over his face. "Your health has improved and Linc's surgery was, by all standards, a success. The next surgery is several months away, and we will all be back home by then." God willing. Collier wet his lips.

She looked too angry to cry. "None of this seems to end. One issue after another. It's overwhelming."

Overwhelming, yes. She'd go home without him again, to care for their son, who might not live. "I know there's nothing fair about this. How do you think it makes me feel?"

"You know, it's hard not to need you." She covered her mouth and shrugged. Her face aged in front of his eyes. His choices affected both their lives in destructive ways.

Collier spread both hands over his face and rubbed his temples. Many more deployments and more deaths at his hand or the enemies' lay ahead. All of this for the sake of providing for his family. Staying in the Army seemed like some kind of a warped trade-off — a trade-off he'd make all over if it took care of Whit and Linc.

"Collier, I can't do this. I can't do eighteen more years of this life."

He lifted her hand, holding it between his. "We're gonna make it. We have to. You've told me over and over that we can do all things through Christ who gives us strength."

Her chin dimpled and her cheeks flushed.

"We can do this, Whit. This is the best option we have right now. Maybe down the road things can be different."

She pushed her plate aside.

Collier shuddered. The look on her face said too much. "You're not thinking of … of leaving, are you?"

Her eyes stared past him.

His cheeks warmed. "Whit?" Soldiers got dumped and divorced all of the time, but not him. Not Whit.

She covered his hands with hers, locking her eyes with his. "Letting go isn't something I do, no matter how hard it gets."

"Good." He could breathe again. "We have to keep the faith." Collier led her hands to his lips. "I need you. I can't do this without you."

She nodded, but didn't smile. His stomach twisted. It wasn't fair how much he needed her when she had to learn not to need him.

ANOTHER day closed. Five days remained of his leave. Collier tossed the thought aside and sat in the NICU room rocking chair, all washed up, ready for his turn to hold Linc at last. The leather from the chair stuck to his pant legs as Collier scooted forward. Whit took pictures as a nurse helped place Linc in his arms, a bundle of plastic tubes and wires.

Collier's palms dampened. "I've never held a baby before."

"You'll be fine." The nurse adjusted a few wires and gave Linc's bottom a tender pat.

"Well, I held my brother when he was born." Collier swallowed. "But I was just a kid."

"Smile, Babes." Whit snapped a few pictures, and light from the camera lit the dim room.

Collier kissed Linc's forehead. "He's so small. Can you believe he'll be a full grown man one day?" Unreal.

Whit knelt at his side, silent.

Collier stared. "Some baby books said his hair could fall out." Not Linc's. It remained thick, dark, and unruly. No need to try to keep it from sticking up.

The nurse raced about the room, pulling curtains and arranging monitors before leaving.

"I think it's sweet you were reading baby books." Whit placed a hand on his knee. "I could stare at him all day."

"Me too." It was true. "I never thought I could love until I met you, Whit." He fought the lump rising in his throat. No time to cry. "I knew I wanted kids one day, but … well."

"I know." Her hand brushed his face, soft against his cheek.

"I wasn't sure if I could be a good dad. Truly love my kids."

"You don't have to say any of this. I already know."

No. He needed to say it and so much more.

"You were right, Whit. I was scared to be a dad and I can't believe I ever...," his voice cracked. "What I mean is," Collier cleared his throat, "I'm sorry for not wanting this surgery for Linc."

"Collier, it's okay."

"I was going to let my son die, Whit. It's not okay."

"But you didn't. You chose life just like you're choosing to be a good dad."

Were good choices all it took to be the man he wanted to be? He could make those. Collier nodded. "How can I leave you guys? Is that a good decision?"

"It is what it is." She sighed. The hint of aggravation did not go unnoticed. "Let's not talk about it right now. Let's make the best of the time we have left together."

"That's a big mission."

"I think we've faced worse."

True. Collier traced Linc's face with an index finger. So perfect. "When Daddy gets home, I'm gonna take you to the zoo and the park."

Whit giggled and took another picture.

"Your momma can teach you to climb trees." Collier leaned into the blue leather chair and rocked. "And when you're old enough, I'll teach you how to low crawl."

"Seriously?" Whit chuckled and smacked his arm. "How about teaching him to catch a ball or fish?"

"All in good time." Collier rocked on. Maybe he would start a Daddy-To-Do-List. "Hmm. You know, Whit? We need to add this moment to our list. Holding our firstborn child."

She tilted her head. "I love it."

"And when I get back, we'll add surviving a deployment."

"I think we're going to need a notebook for our list instead of a sheet of paper."

"I'm sorry to interrupt." The nurse stepped in, wrapping her long nails on the door frame. "Mr. Cromwell, your father would like permission to come in."

Collier stopped in mid-rock. It couldn't hurt to let Charles see his grandson, but not because he deserved to. He pursed his lips.

The nurse arched a brow, waiting for a response.

"I'm sorry, Ma'am." Whit smiled. "Could you give us a min — "

"It's okay." Collier lifted a hand. "He can come in."

Whit's eyes widened.

"Well, ok then." The nurse smiled. "Two at a time."

"I love my boys." Whit kissed their cheeks before leaving. "I'll be back. I'm sure Momma will fill me in on Fort Carson's news. Layla calls her daily."

"Of course." Collier forced a smile, his underarms already sweating. Being in a room with his father trumped any encounter with an insurgent.

Whit hugged Charles in the doorway and thanked the nurse for all her hard work.

"She's quite a catch, Collier." Charles stepped into the room, holding a baby gift in his hands. Unexpected, but sweet.

"Yes, she's too good for me, that's for sure."

"I understand that." Charles blushed and Collier looked away. At least he knew Mom had been too good for him.

"Would you like to meet Linc?" Collier raised his brows. Charles stood there, shirt pressed, buttoned to the top. The dark circles under his eyes resembled half-moons. His expression, solemn and sunken, tugged at some long lost cavern in Collier's soul. "It's okay … Dad."

Charles' steps were slow. His eyes focused on Linc. He stopped mere inches away, setting the gift bag on the floor.

"I'd let you hold him, but — "

Charles waved his hand, aged with spots. "No, son. I'm too sick. I wouldn't want to hurt him. He's been through so much already."

"Cancer's not contagious." Collier chewed on his jaw. "I can ring the nurse. She can help with all of these wires and stuff."

"Just seeing him is enough." Charles held a shaking fist to his mouth. "He looks like you when you were born."

Collier nodded. No much to say to that.

"I was good then." Charles folded his arms. His eyes sparkled with tears. This man was too tender to be his father. "Your Mother and I were happy. I was a good man." His head bobbed. "Held down a steady nice paying job. Had it all."

Collier looked from Linc to his father. He drew in a deep breath. The drinking. The fighting. The bruises. The cruel words. He and his mother endured much. "Why?"

Oh, he'd heard all the back stories — the reason for Charles' behavior. Charles shook his head.

"That's it then?" Collier huffed. "The abused become abusers — that's what I'm going to have to believe."

"Nothing excuses the things I did."

"I always thought it was my fault. If I could stay quiet enough, out of your way, you wouldn't be mad. You'd stop. Be better." Wishful thinking. "You know how many times I prayed you'd die?"

"I prayed the same thing, but God had other plans."

Other plans. Nice. "That's what you're going with?"

"I was full of hate, Collier. Hated my father for what he did to me when I was a boy, hated myself, hated anyone who wasn't full of hate, and then hated thinking that way."

Collier's heart thudded against his temple walls. "Why me? Why Mom? Why not Erik? You never hurt him." Like puss from a festering boil, questions from deep within spilled to the surface. Collier never wanted Erik to be harmed. "I always tried to protect him. Hid him in closets. The dryer once during one of your tirades." Collier clung to the corner of Linc's baby blanket.

"Erik was my new start." Charles held his arms close to his chest. "He was the one person I hadn't hurt and I tried to keep it that way. I know it's sick sounding son."

Sorta. Collier winced.

"But that night." He stopped. "The night they died, I hit him."

"What?" Collier's brows folded. "Where was I?"

"You hadn't come home from school yet. Your mom was working a little later and I got Erik off the bus."

Collier pressed his head into his hand. His stomach turned.

Charles let out a sigh. "When we got inside, he didn't have much to say to me. Acted scared and that set me off."

Collier clamped his jaw together until his teeth ached. If only he hadn't stayed after school that day. He could've changed it all.

"Your Mom walked in as I was shaking him." Charles lowered his gaze. "It was the last straw, and I knew it. She should've left me long ago. Tried several times, but I always straightened up long enough to get her to stay."

Collier's breathing slowed. His chest burned. "Why did she get in the car with you?"

The night sky crept into the room. Charles cast his eyes toward the window. He didn't respond. Maybe he couldn't.

"You hit her didn't you? Knocked her out, then put Erik in the car, didn't you?"

Charles stood, looking out into the night. No response.

"Didn't you?"

"Yes." Charles' voice trailed off. His shoulders shook. "I wasn't in my right mind."

"And I got to drive up on the wreckage." Collier shut his eyes, but couldn't black out the sound of the roaring fire, cracking glass, and smell of burnt flesh. Erik's face, small and cut, morphed into Sergeant First Class Gunthrie's, into Crawford's, Haden's, and Whit's as she fought to evade her attacker. Erik and his mother happened to be the first of many Collier couldn't save. Would Linc be next?

Collier rang for the nurse. "I need to get out of here."

WHITLEIGH took her time moving about the hospital room, tidying up after Mom and Dad retired to their hotel for the evening. With Collier visiting Linc and his father, the TV provided her with company. She bent to pick up water bottle and grimaced. An eight week recovery period from a C-section made total sense. Whitleigh tossed the water bottles into the trash and folded a shirt before tucking it in the small, narrow closet.

The door clicked open. Whitleigh swung her head around. "You're back." Seemed like Collier was getting good at long absences. "I'm guessing you and your Dad had words?"

"Something like that." Collier screwed the cap on his empty soda bottled and tossed it into the trash can with a thud.

"Is that from Charles?" Whitleigh pointed at the bag hanging from Collier's wrist. Tissue paper stuck up like peaks of blue icing.

He nodded, dropping it to the floor. "You know how you said it just seems like it's one thing after another? Well, you're right." He let out a half growl and sank into the recliner.

"Care to elaborate?" Whitleigh fluffed a pillow on the bed.

"Not really."

"Did you open the gift?"

He stared at it, twisting his mouth to the side.

"Well, what is it?" Whitleigh kicked a leg out.

"My baby blanket and a photo album for all our new happy memories with Charles back in the picture."

"Oh." Whitleigh glanced at the blue dotted bag, ignoring Collier's sarcasm.

Though he sat close by, Collier seemed far away, perhaps visiting places in his past she may not want to travel.

People walked the halls outside their room at a quick pace. The soles of their shoes squeaked against the floor. Doctors, nurses, hospital staff, and visitors kept this place running all day long. Whitleigh clicked her tongue on the inside of her cheek. She needed to finish picking up, but not much remained.

"Whit?" Collier's voice broke the strange silence. "Why didn't you tell me about the rapist running around base before you were attacked?"

She stopped mid-step, balled fist firm against her hip. "Is that what Mom wanted to talk to you about?"

"You should've told me."

"So you could've worried? Yeah, I'll pass on that." Whitleigh arched a brow and smoothed out the linen wrinkles. He had a lot to worry about already. "Wanna give me a hand?"

"Why are you cleaning?"

"Layla called Momma earlier. Jen's flying in tomorrow." She dusted off the night stand with a tissue. It worked well enough. "I don't know how long she's staying. Ugh. I bet she's still a mess." Whitleigh blew back a strand of hair. "I don't even know what to say to her."

"It's hard losing someone you love." Collier put his hands through his hoodie pocket. "But you don't have the time or energy to carry her baggage, Whit."

"She's my friend." Whitleigh crumpled the tissue in her hand. "And what do you mean by baggage?" Picking battles could be difficult.

"I mean, does she need a ride from the airport?"

That was more like it. "Would you mind?"

"No."

"Good." Men. Whitleigh shook her head and took a seat on the edge of the bed. "I've been thinking." She pressed her cold knuckles to her cheek. "Poor Jen. I don't know what's she been through, but you can relate."

Collier tilted his head. "And?"

"Maybe you could talk with her. You'd be better than me."

"I don't know, Whit." He scratched his head. "That stuff's hard to talk about."

"I'm just trying to help her."

"And that's great of you, but maybe she's not ready."

"It's just a thought." Whitleigh sank forward.

"Keep being her friend, Whit. If she brings it up, I promise I will try to help the best I can."

That was fair. Whitleigh smiled. Maybe Collier would find his own healing by helping Jen find hers.

"Um, anyway." Collier moseyed from the recliner and sat down at her side. The mattress sank lower. "You can't change the subject. I think you need to move home until I get back."

Whitleigh huffed. "Like you said, they've probably caught him by now."

"I still think you need to go home. It would make me feel better."

"I appreciate your concern. Really, it's sweet." She patted his knee. "I took kick-boxing and self-defense classes."

"It was an elective with a bunch of your goofy college friends."

"So?"

"So, now you're a mom, by yourself with a defenseless child."

"Even more reason to fight harder." Whitleigh flexed her arm muscles. Granted they needed some toning.

"This isn't a joke."

"No one's laughing." She smacked her lips shut. Life seemed too serious and drained of all fun. She laid her head on his shoulder, wrapping an arm around his biceps. So strong. Much stronger than her mosquito bite of an arm muscle. "I know you're concerned, but I'm not leaving Linc's doctors."

"Louisville has a children's hospital. It won't even take an hour to get there."

"Denver isn't much farther away from Fort Carson than Louisville is from Mom and Dad's."

"You should go home, Whit."

She shook her head. "I've already talked to Mom." It was amazing how attractive and annoying he could be at the same time. "She's making plans to live with me for the next few months."

"She didn't mention that."

"Just decided right before she left. She's flying back with Dad in a couple of days to get her things ready. Between Layla and Mom, I think I'll be fine. Jen will need me around too."

"I don't know."

"You know how your soldiers are your family over there?"

Collier nodded. Maybe she could get him to understand.

"Well, Layla, Jen ... the others from my book study — if I ever get to go again, and the FRG have become like a family to me." She lifted her shoulders. Strange to admit. "Even though I can't choose who's in the group and some of those wives are just plain crazy, well, I guess that makes them even more like family."

"I can't argue that. Can't choose who's in your family and most of them are nuts anyway."

"See?" Whitleigh laughed. "I'll be fine." She rolled her eyes. "I'm sure Layla has plenty of her own weapons of mass destruction to share with the neighborhood. Her stockpile would scare any kind of offender away."

"Really?" Collier held out an open palm, an invitation. "She doesn't look like the gun toting type."

"Oh, you have no idea." Whitleigh placed her hand in his. "I guess nail polish and ammunition is her kind of thing." Collier tugged on her arm, pulling Whitleigh closer. She couldn't help but grin. "I know, I know. I'm your kind of thing."

"That's right." Collier kissed her cheek. She leaned into the stubble on his face and welcomed the subtle prickles. "I've been wondering. How did it end?"

She scrunched her nose. "Huh?"

"The story. The one with your parents on the river bank, stuck in the mud with the catfish. I'm just curious."

"Oh." Whitleigh flapped her hand. "I can't believe you didn't ask your dad."

"We weren't having the most lighthearted conversation."

"I guess not." She squeezed his knee and nuzzled closer. "My dad sent your dad away. Told him he couldn't be a third wheel on his date." Whitleigh smiled. "It's funny imagining our parents as young, dating and doing silly things."

"Yeah."

"Anyway, Charles knew Dad wasn't much of a fisherman, so I guess he decided he was gonna go over the hill and fish, thinking he could help Dad impress Mom."

"How did he get them out of the mud?"

"With a cow."

"What?" Collier's jaw dropped. He chuckled and Whitleigh giggled alongside.

"True story." She held up a hand. "Your Dad tied a rope to one of the cows

grazing in the field. My parents held on, and your dad pulled them out, only ...."
Whit slapped at her leg with a loud laugh. She groaned and held her stomach.
Nothing hurt stitched up abdominal muscles like a hearty laugh. "Only, the cow
pooped just as they were being drug out and Mom and Dad landed right in it,
face first."

Collier guffawed. Whitleigh held tight to her stomach and chortled along.

"It took Momma awhile to agree to another date with Dad."

Collier's face reddened, displaying a bright grin. It had been too long since
she'd seen him laugh like that. He shook his head. "And I thought our first date
was bad."

"We were just teenagers. Who knew spaghetti dinners were first date
no-no's?"

"That marinara sauce looked great on your white dress."

Her stomach ached, but she laughed anyway. "I'm glad you've stopped
getting so nervous around me that you drop whole dinner plates in my lap."
Those were good times, much better than the multitude of present concerns.
Whitleigh sighed. "Do you think we'll ever be carefree again? A happy family,
living our happily ever after?"

He pursed his lips. "I'm not sure happily-ever-afters exist."

Whitleigh lowered her gaze. Maybe he was right.

"It's funny how life changes us." His hands pressed into the mattress. "It
changed my dad ... from good to bad, and back to some form of good. Even
your dad went through a transformation." This was true. Emotionless
Workaholic to loving Father. Whitleigh palmed her knees. "This war, our
experiences, Linc's birth — we've changed too." She couldn't deny that.

He placed a warm hand over hers. "Maybe happily-ever-after isn't what
we're aiming for. Maybe it's something more."

Maybe. Whitleigh played with her side ponytail, letting the strands slip
between her fingers. Her eyes focused on nothing in particular.

THE morning light broke through the blinds, creating a kaleidoscope of
shadows that danced about the hospital room. If only the windows would open.
The room needed a breeze, or maybe she did. Whitleigh batted her lashes. Sleep
stuck to her eyes. Time ticked away. In some ways not fast enough, and in

others, too fast. Two days. That was all that remained of their time together. Collier had to leave so he could return. What an oxymoron. Maybe she could sleep through all of life's hard parts and awake to enjoy the good.

"Good morning, sleepy head." Collier greeted her with a sweet smile — a wonderful way to start a new day. "What are you thinking about?"

"Nothing specific." Whitleigh pushed back a yawn, careful to cover her mouth. Morning breath was a deadly weapon.

"Charles is leaving today. He's flying back with your parents."

"Will he ...," Whitleigh paused. What was the polite way to ask?

"Go back to jail?" Collier shook his bowed head and sat on the rolling stool next to the bed. "No. He's living out the remainder of his life back on the farm."

"You okay?"

"I think so. Some sort of closure is good." He puffed his cheeks. "I'm ready to get this deployment over, get back to you and Linc, and start our lives."

"It does feel like we've been pushing pause a bit too much. Wish I could find life's remote control. It needs new batteries."

Collier grinned. "You're funnier than you used to be."

"Thanks." Whitleigh sat a bit taller against the headboard. She reached for his hand. "I'm here if you need to talk."

"Right now, I'm not the one who needs to talk."

She squinted her eyes, noting his suspicious behavior.

"Mrs. Ryan did the honors of picking up Jen from the airport."

Whitleigh gasped and covered her mouth. "Really? She's here?"

"Come on in, ladies."

"I just woke up." Whitleigh whipped her head to the side. "Hand me my makeup and toothbrush." Too late.

Layla flew in first, heels clicking, red lips wide open. Jen followed with slower, unsteady steps. No high heels. No makeup. No jewelry. Much too thin. Her dark hair hung in strands from a loose side bun. Whitleigh tried, but couldn't force a smile. Jen's grief wouldn't allow it. She stared past Whitleigh and focused on Collier, as if he were familiar. Jen's watery eyes tore from his face and Whitleigh's skin prickled.

Layla clicked her way to the bedside. Her clamp-like hug caused Whitleigh to cough. She fought to offer an embrace in return.

"It's so good to see you." Layla did a little jig. "You look fabulous." She dropped a few bags on the floor. Collier tucked them under the bed, nodded at each of the women, and rushed toward the door. She couldn't blame him. Layla clasped her hands together. "I brought your mail, some books to read, pictures the kids drew for you, lots of little goodies from the gals, which reminds me to tell you we're starting our spring book study in March." March. Whitleigh swallowed. Jen was supposed to get married in March. Layla didn't miss a beat. "Now I know you may not be home yet, but if you are, Jayson is back from Walter Reed, and with all his medical experience, he is more than equipped to look after little Linc."

"I'm so glad he's home." Whitleigh pressed her back against the headboard. No escape. Jen stood at the foot of bed and for a split moment they shared a smile. Whitleigh placed her hands in her lap, pinching the diamond from her wedding bands between her fingers.

"It's good to have him back." Layla smiled and wiped a tear. "He's becoming the man I remember and even better. God is good."

Jen held her arms close to her chest. A black V-necked shirt that once fit the curves of her body nicely, hung limp without form.

Whitleigh wet her lips and eased from the bed, reaching out her arms. "Jen."

Jen lifted her eyes, walked to Whitleigh, and fell into her embrace. She was more than fragile. Jen shook beneath her sobs and Whitleigh held tight to her friend.

"I'm so sorry, Whit." Jen buried her head, muffling the cries. "Look at me falling apart after everything you're going through."

"Shh." Whitleigh swayed side to side. "I'm here for you. We're all here for you."

"It's been so hard. I can't stop thinking about him." Jen wiped her eyes and took a step back. Layla rubbed her long nails in a circular motion across Jen's bony shoulder blade. "And now Mark's parents are taking me to court over his life insurance."

Whitleigh covered her mouth as Layla handed Jen a tissue.

"How was I supposed to know Mark was going to leave everything to me?" She blew her nose. "I can't believe all of this is happening. He was a good man, and they're just greedy people. Did you know he bought a house for us?" Her bottom lip trembled. "It was a wedding present, but I'm not his wife, and now I'll never be."

"Come sit." Whitleigh led Jen and Layla to the bed. The women sat, cross legged, no smiles. Real life unfolded in their midst. "This isn't easy, and I don't know how to help you, but I can sit with you. I can sit with both of you and listen." Whitleigh held out each of her hands. Layla latched on to the first and then Jen to the second. "We can do this, make it through anything, together."

CHAPTER 20

Date: March 4
Re: Leaving the Hospital

Hey Baby!

We're finally going home! Linc is doing really well, what a trooper! He is eating like a pro and up to 6 lbs now. Don't have much time, mom's helping me pack up, just wanted to share the good news. I'm attaching a few pictures of us. He looks so much like you! Stay safe and know that I pray for you and your soldiers every day. Let me know how you're doing.

Love me always,
Whit

PS. I hope you don't mind, but I gave Jen your email address.

Date: March 10
Re: I Miss You

Hey Whit,
I'm so happy you and Linc are home. Thank you for the pictures. I'm attaching a few of my own. I hope you like the one of the camel in the

back of the truck – it's my favorite. Things are kind of slow here right now, which is a good thing so I won't complain. Even so, we are always on guard, never really sleeping. And it's hot. Real hot.

Dock says hey and wants me to tell you that his wife, Amy, will be moving up to Carson in a couple of months. Maybe you could hang out with her. Dock's a good buddy of mine. All of us here talk about everything we are going to do when we get home. These guys are crazy talking about wanting to go sky diving and stuff like that. I just want to get home to you and Linc. I love you.

Love me always,

Collier

PS. I don't mind you giving Jen my email address. She's written a couple of times asking things about Crawford. I feel bad for her.

Date: March 11

Re: Four Months Left

Hey Baby,

I've been marking the days off the calendar. Four months, and then you're home! Time can't go fast enough. Can you believe Linc is almost 2 months old? He's been keeping me very busy, and I don't know how I could do it without Momma. I worry about him a lot and don't get much sleep 'cause I keep waking up to make sure he's still breathing. He's such a happy baby. His scar doesn't even bother him, neither do the breathing tubes. That kid is a warrior.

Haven't been able to get back to my book study group, but I did get good news from UCCS. My counselor says I have enough credit hours to graduate with a degree in History, and when I'm able, I can finish my teaching degree. I'm pretty excited about that option. Jen and Layla keep telling me to stay at home and do event planning and catering for the people — make my own hours and stuff. I've got to admit, it sounds like a way for me to stay at home with Linc and still have something of my own. Anyway, we're sending out a care package to you. Need anything?

Love me always,

Whit

Ps. Sorry I attached so many pictures. Recognize the baby blanket? Yup, it was yours!

Date: March 25
Re: Missing You

Dear Whit,

I'm sorry it's been awhile since I've called or written back. Things got a little crazy, a few casualties, but we're okay now. I guess the insurgents went back to plant their crops or something. I'm cool with that, as long as they leave us alone. I can't give details, but I'm pretty sure we caught the insurgent responsible for Haden's death. He got what was coming to him.

Dock got bit by one of those huge spiders right on his big toe. He screamed like a girl. It's all swelled up and red. Funniest thing ever. We all needed a good laugh. I attached a picture of it for you, and of one of the desert sunset — I think you'll like it.

I'm happy to hear about your degree. I know how hard you've worked to finish school. I'll get there one day.

I'm sure you've already mailed the package out, but when you get a chance, could you send me some more baby wipes and a big bag of beef jerky? Keep sending pics. I love them.

Love me always,

Collier

MARCH ended. April, May, June — all marked through with a purple sharpie. The emails continued, back and forth, for weeks and months. A few calls here and there. Pictures exchanged, packages sent. Monotonous at times.

Whitleigh hung over her laptop, rereading the last line in Collier's latest email, *"I'll see you soon."* There was no 'I love you.' She scanned once more. Not there. Maybe he was tired. Long, perilous days surely had the ability to shorten emails, or could it be something else? She sighed. Her imagination went crazy at times. Whitleigh touched the screen before closing it with a click. She toyed with her hair and moseyed into the kitchen.

Care packages, emails, letters — had she sent enough to Collier? It didn't matter now with less than four weeks remaining until he returned. Whitleigh stared at the calendar. In her peripheral, Momma sat on the couch, folding laundry and humming a tune. Linc babbled on the floor, chewing on his little balled fists, oblivious to what the next few days would hold.

July 7th, circled and underlined. Whitleigh tapped the date with an index finger. Linc's next surgery. Collier said he'd be home. She leaned against the kitchen counter, folding her arms.

"He'd be home if he could." Momma bent over the couch arm, straining her neck.

"You were always good at reading my mind."

"Hang in there, Whit." She shook out a shirt. "You going to help with the homecoming ceremony?"

"Haven't given it much thought." That may have been a lie. Whitleigh bit her tongue as she slouched into the living room. "I'd like to help, but it may be too much on my plate with Linc's surgery and all."

"True, but it may give you an outlet — sort of a stress reliever while you're in the waiting room."

"Maybe."

"Jen is helping."

Jen — a whole different topic. "She feels like she has to. That's her way of honoring Mark."

"You should invite her over for dinner."

"Momma, I've called her, emailed, sent letters — she's in a world of her own right now."

"People grieve in their own ways."

"She could at least reach out." Whitleigh adjusted her pearl necklace and smoothed out a wrinkle on her peach colored cotton and lace t-shirt. "I miss hanging out with her. And when we do talk, it's short and awkward."

"Give it time." Momma blew kisses at Linc and continued folding. "Is she seeing a therapist?"

Whitleigh shrugged. "I know she's talked with Collier a few times."

"Hmm."

"What?"

Momma held a towel in her lap and paused mid-fold. "Oh, it's nothing. Just worried about her is all. Anyway," she crossed her ankles, "I think the FRG Leader is only wanting advice, direction, some sort of layout and decor ideas for the ceremony. That's right up your alley."

"I wish all I had to think about were parties, ceremonies, and centerpieces." Whitleigh puffed. "Instead, I'm worried sick if my son is going to live and if my husband is going to make it home alive." She palmed her forehead. "I don't even know if I'm going to be able to make it to the welcome home ceremony."

Momma gasped.

"Don't look at me like that Momma." She held out open palms. "Odds are Linc will still be in the hospital when Collier gets home."

"And you'll take time out to go see your husband return." Her curly hair bobbed.

"How can I leave Linc? What if something happens?"

"These doctors are more than equipped to take care of little Linc. I'll stay in Denver with him, but your place, at that moment, is to be with your husband, Whitleigh Cromwell."

She was right. Whitleigh pressed her hands deep in the back pockets of her jeans. Boo. They were still too tight.

"Your husband is priority, even in this situation."

"I know Momma." Whitleigh sighed. "You sound like Layla."

"Stop worrying. Your little Linc is gonna be fine. Look at him."

He kicked his feet and rolled side to side, looking nothing short of sweet in his blue onesie. Whitleigh grinned. He was something special for sure. She fidgeted with her shirt, maybe she could stretch it out a bit. Nothing seemed to fit right anymore.

"And I'm gonna tell you one more time." Momma pointed a finger with her free hand. "It took nine months to put that weight on, so don't expect it to come right off. You're beautiful."

"I'm nervous. So nervous." She dug her hands deep into her jean pockets.

"Psh." Momma waved her hand. She leaned forward. "You think that man is gonna care if you have a few extra pounds hanging on you? Not a chance. That's just a little love chub sweet girl."

"Momma." Whitleigh felt her cheeks warm. She batted her eyes. "That's not the only thing that worries me."

"I know that honey." Momma bunched a towel in her lap. "You've both been through a lot. You've both changed and your circumstances are challenging. The two of you have never had the chance to live together as a married couple and really get to know each other. Now you're new parents with a child who has some serious health issues."

"Thanks for the recap." Whitleigh hunched over.

"Just breathe, baby. It's a lot, yes, but love is more than all those walls you feel like you have to climb."

Love. Collier forgot to mention anything about loving her in his email. Maybe it was silly to let such a small thing damper her mood, but then again, maybe it wasn't. Whitleigh wiped the corner of her eyes. "We want different things."

"What married couple doesn't? But you want the same things too." She lifted Whitleigh's chin. "I'd say, if you took the time to think about it, you want more of the same things, than different."

Whitleigh squinted, twisting her lips to the side. Momma had a point. She and Collier wanted a lot of land one day. A home with a big wrap around porch. What else? Travel. A love of history and learning. Hole in the wall restaurants.

Momma pushed the pile of clothes away and patted the couch cushion. "Marriage is work, but worth every minute of it. Compromise, dear."

Whitleigh sat in place of the clean pile of laundry. Momma made everything all right. Over thirty years of marriage must've given her that ability.

Sirens sounded. A clap of thunder shook the frames on the wall. Whitleigh whipped her head toward the window. Another lightning storm.

Momma jumped. "This is the only place in the world I've ever heard of sounding off sirens to warn people of lightning."

"It gets pretty severe up here." Whitleigh shuffled to the blinds. A car door slammed across the street. She leaned closer to the window, her breath creating a circle of fog. Two shadowy figures walked up the sidewalk and onto the front porch of Emma's house. Whitleigh tilted her head. Emma's house had been empty for months. A swirl of smoke wafted from the soft glow of a cigarette. Who could it be? One figure waved from across the street. Whitleigh jerked back. Her heart thudded. She closed the blinds tight, checked the window locks, and turned toward Momma. "You'd be surprised how many people get hit by lightning out here."

"This place is downright rugged, in the most beautiful way of course."

"It's the Wild West." Whitleigh snickered and took a seat on the floor at Linc's side. Her face felt flushed, but Momma didn't seem to notice.

Momma eyed the window. "I feel like I'm a part of the food chain out here."

"No bear or wildcat would come near you. Too much hair spray."

Momma scrunched her nose.

Whitleigh chuckled, pushing the jitters aside. She'd have to check on Emma tomorrow.

"**IT** escaped my mind." Whitleigh rushed through the door of the community center on base. Running in heels, no matter how short, didn't go well. "I'm so sorry I'm late. I was checking in on a neighbor." Waste of time. No Emma. No Helen.

"Whitleigh Cromwell, it's so good to see you. Love those pearls." Becca, the FRG Hospitality Coordinator, stood behind the sign in desk, striped button up tucked into a professional looking pencil skirt. How did she stay so skinny after three kids? "We miss you at our book study."

Whitleigh scribbled her name on the sign-in sheet. "I've been meaning to come back, but it just hasn't happened." She scanned the list of names. No Jen.

"You have your hands full." Becca's red lipped smile faded. She handed Whitleigh the FRG meeting itinerary. "Layla keeps us updated."

"That's Layla." Whitleigh shook her head, grinning. "She seems to know everyone on base."

"I'm so glad your mom has been able to stay with you."

"Me too." Whitleigh bobbed her head.

"And how's little Linc?"

Whitleigh swallowed. No matter how sincere the person, it was difficult to answer that question. "He's hanging in there."

"And his next surgery?"

"Um." Whitleigh pressed her lips together. "Friday."

"Oh, that's soon."

"Two days." Whitleigh clasped her purse, holding it close to her side. Next subject.

"Well, we will all be praying." She took in a deep breath. "The meeting won't be too long today. They're just finishing up refreshments — oh," Becca pawed at the air, "we really miss your baking skills around here. God bless these women for trying, but nothing beats your goodies."

"Thanks, Becca." Whitleigh adjusted her purse strap. She hadn't turned on an oven in months. "I'm sure I'll be up and baking treats in no time." Maybe.

"That's good news for us." She held up a finger. "Almost forgot. Will you be helping with the homecoming ceremony decor?" She hovered, eyes glistening as if no wasn't an answer.

Whitleigh forced a smile. "I'm sure I can help with something."

"Goody." She clapped. "Andrea would like for you to design table settings. Three styles. Just tell us what they should look like and we will do all that work."

Whitleigh raised a brow. "I'm sure I can do that. I'll have that done and emailed soon."

"Soon, as in?"

"Well." Whitleigh pursed her lips. "I guess I can whip something up tomorrow. I'm preparing for the hospital stay, so no promises."

"Excellent." Becca reached out, locking Whitleigh in a hug. "We can never repay you."

Knowing their FRG budget, that was a true statement.

"Oh, and one more thing." Becca yanked back. "A lady asked about you, her name …." she tapped her bottom lip, holding the sign in sheet close to her face. "Amy. Amy Dock. Know her?"

Whitleigh folded her arms. "I don't think so." Dock. Why did that sound familiar? "Oh, yes, it's the wife of one of Collier's buddies."

"She's in there." Becca bent back, peering into the meeting room. "Last table on the right. First seat."

"Thanks." Whitleigh hurried past the sign in counter and eased into the meeting room. There sat Amy, with the most beautiful auburn hair she was sure she'd ever seen. Amy seemed nervous and out of place with her arms folded in her lap, eyes scanning the room. Her Texas Longhorns t-shirt was about as faded as her blue jeans.

"Hi, Amy." Whitleigh extended hand. "I'm Whitleigh Cromwell."

"It's very nice to meet you." She stood and returned the shake. Freckles dotted across her nose and cheeks, creating a childlike appearance.

"May I sit with you?"

"Please." Her green eyes widened.

"It's nice to sort of know someone at these kinds of things." Whitleigh offered a smile.

"Let's get started." Andrea Baker, the FRG leader, took the stand. "Just a few things to cover tonight. Take a second to look over the agenda, take a deep breath, and then we'll talk about it."

Whitleigh skimmed. Homecoming ceremony — food, decor, volunteers. 2 BCT expected arrival date — July 21st. Next scheduled deployment. Whitleigh blinked, pinching the paper between her fingers. What did 'next scheduled deployment' mean?

Mumbles from the deployed spouses grew in volume across the room. Andrea cleared her throat. "Let's look at the good news first. They will be home a week earlier than expected, give or take twenty-four to thirty-six hours, and we'll celebrate. Fantastic news for us."

A few frustrated shouts from the crowd rang out. Andrea sighed into the microphone. The speakers cracked and popped. "I understand the last point on our agenda is frustrating." Yes, by all standards. "While we do not know many details, we do know that our unit will deploy for another tour to Iraq one year after returning home."

Whitleigh took steady breaths. Amy covered her mouth.

Andrea bowed her head and inhaled as if refocusing. "We also know, and please understand that this is the Army and things change all of the time — hurry up and wait, right?" She chuckled, but no one in the room laughed along. "We also know," Andrea licked her lips, "that this next deployment will more than likely be fifteen months instead of twelve months."

The women gasped. No air remained for Whitleigh to breathe.

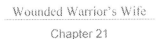

THE clothes were folded and the laundry basket empty — a rare occasion. Whitleigh yawned as she carried the pile into her room. What a day. She sank into the bedside, placing a few articles of clothing and toiletries into the suitcase. The length of the hospital stay depended on the outcome of Linc's surgery. Whitleigh patted her knees and stood, making her way to the hall.

It wasn't often Linc slept in his nursery. The hall light seeped into the room. Whitleigh scooted the wooden glider over to his crib, slipping her hand between the slats. She kissed her fingers and placed them on his forehead. Linc slept on. Even with small round oxygen nasal prongs and a scar the length of his chest, he slept as if he hadn't a care in the world. His belly rose and fell and his damp pouty lips pressed together, causing his chin to dimple. So sweet. So innocent.

Whitleigh held her face to the crib. She couldn't get close enough. Both of the men in her life, one just an infant, were fighting for their lives, and she could save neither. Whitleigh bowed her head. Prayer worked. It did. So why weren't the words coming? She covered her face, eyes locked, breath held. God would have to interpret the silence.

"Whit, honey?" Momma's shadow drifted from the hall and into the nursery. "You need to get some sleep."

Sleep didn't matter. "He's perfect, isn't he?"

Momma wrapped her robe tight and tiptoed in, nestling on the footstool beside Whitleigh. "He will be okay, and Collier will come home."

"And he'll leave again, and Linc will have more surgeries."

"Army orders change more than the direction of the wind." Momma nodded. "I can only tell you that you're surrounded by family and friends who love you and support you."

She couldn't deny that truth.

Whitleigh bit at her thumbnail. "I've been asking, 'why me?' but I think that's the wrong thing to ask." She held the armrest of the glider. "I think I need to know the right way to respond to everything life throws my way. How do I do that, Momma?" Whitleigh crossed her legs, clasping the cotton material of her nightgown in hand. "What's the right way to respond to this, Momma? To Linc's condition? The surgeries? To more war? More time apart? I know the distance is driving a wedge between me and Collier — I can feel it growing with each on-the-surface conversation we have." Whitleigh rested her chin on a balled fist. There were no tears.

Momma shook her lowered head. Weren't moms supposed to have all the answers?

"You're so strong." Momma brushed her hand over Whitleigh's cheek. Whitleigh closed her eyes. Even as a grown woman, her Mother's touch soothed.

"Strong feels a lot like enduring."

"Yes. That's what it is. It's perseverance. So keep hanging on. God will bless that."

Whitleigh sat back, gliding at a slow steady pace.

"You know," Momma reached for her hand with a solid grip, "I would say Collier feels that wedge too. He feels this struggle you're describing. Maybe talking about it with him doesn't help, but perhaps acknowledging it would."

"Maybe." Whitleigh arched a brow. "We've talked about it. I think we both know life is hard right now."

"This distance you feel will get better when he gets home. I'm sure of it. This surface level stuff you're talking about is part of hanging on. It's a temporary thing. The good stuff is coming."

"I hope you're right." Whitleigh squeezed her mother's aging hand.

THE sun was up whether or not she was ready for the day. Whitleigh shoved the Ladies' Day Out at the Gun Range flyer into the over engorged trash bag and then plunged the entire load into the trash can. She couldn't pull off a lady's day today. Not the day before Linc's surgery. What was Layla thinking, inviting her to something like that? That woman.

Whitleigh rolled her eyes and smiled. She tugged the garbage can with one hand outstretched behind her back and waved to the neighbors out and about in their yards with the other. The wheels bumped along on the uneven sidewalk, smashing a dandelion that dared to peek through a crack in the concrete.

Whitleigh paused for a moment, wiping her brow. Though it was hot, the heat could be tolerated more than the humid Kentucky summers. She winced as she looked over at the sun, hovering above the mountain peaks.

She dragged the trash bin a bit further, planting it on the side of the curb with a handful of others. A few children from across the road waved in her direction, dancing and hooting through a makeshift sprinkler. Smells from the neighboring charcoal grills swirled about the air. Whitleigh waved back, her smile fading. Summer was well underway. It snuck up somewhere during the deployment and Linc's birth and surgery. She sighed and knelt to tie her tennis shoe.

A walk would do her some good. But maybe she should get back to the house.

Whitleigh stood on the curbside, crossing her arms. It was just a walk. Momma said she had everything under control. Whitleigh huffed and shook her ponytail. Walking relieved stress and promoted relaxation. It was okay to do something relaxing. Right?

Right, but there were so many things that could go wrong. Linc needed her. She'd already left him once yesterday to attend the FRG meeting, which hadn't been the most chipper meeting. Whitleigh grimaced. The news of another deployment — even longer than the present, caused her stomach to turn. She gnawed on her lip. There really wasn't time for a walk. The list of things to do didn't end. Laundry, dishes, trying to fix that silly leaky bathroom faucet, packing, and attempting to make contact with her elusive best friend, Jen, again demanded attention. Then there was table decor to design for the welcome home ceremony, and no time to sleep before pumping and storing more breast milk. Whitleigh groaned.

On second thought, a walk — fast paced — seemed like a good thing. Whitleigh dug the toe of her shoe into the sidewalk, twisting it around a few times. Yes, she could take a few minutes for herself. After all, Linc was eating well, breathing well, and his skin color, though still a bit on the blue side, looked more normal every day.

She lurched forward, sprinting more than walking, and then slowed to a jog. Her feet refused to stray from the path, and she pushed on behind the housing complex and onto an adjacent street. Onward, breathing in, breathing out, Whitleigh passed barking dogs, other spouses with distressed expressions, and carefree, barefoot children. Rounding the corner she could see the officers' quarters in the distance. The higher ups. Did their spouses feel the burden of the war and wear it on their faces as the spouses of enlisted soldiers? Whitleigh held the stitch in her side, breathing through the pain.

Her muscles ached and her breaths quickened. How fast was she going? How long had she been jogging? It didn't matter. She ran further until the buzzing of her cellphone brought her to a sudden halt.

Collier? Whitleigh's hand, sticky with sweat, shuffled about the pocket of her shorts. She hadn't heard his voice in over a week, but no news was good news.

"Hello." She sucked in a deep breath, careful not to sound too winded.

"Whit? That you?" The line wavered in and out.

"Collier?" Whitleigh exhaled and the line crackled and popped. She smiled, licked her drying lips, and wiped away a few tears. "Thank God. I've missed you … missed your voice. Tell me you're okay."

Her words echoed with the time delay of the phone line.

"I'm good. Just stinking hot over here."

"Everybody alright?" Whitleigh raised on the balls of her feet and lowered back on her heels. Her breathing steadied.

"Yeah. Yeah, we're all fine." His voice strained.

Whitleigh tilted her head, hand on hip. "Something wrong?"

"Just ready to get back home. Get back to normal, you know?"

"I know a little something about that feeling." Did she ever? Whitleigh grinned, nodding as if he were standing by her side.

"Humph." The sound came out as a semi scoff. Whitleigh wrinkled her nose. What was that about? Maybe his exhaustion spoke for him, or could it be something more?

"We're ok, right?" The words slipped from her mouth almost without realization. Whitleigh gritted her teeth. No reply came. "Collier?" Her voice echoed across the distance.

"I don't think I'm okay." He sighed.

Whitleigh stumbled back, her heart sank. "What do you mean? Is it me?"

"No, no. All I mean is that I think I will be fine once I get home."

"Oh." Her lungs expanded. "I'm sure you'll be fine." She tried to giggle. "I know I'll be fine once you get home."

"Yeah." His tone couldn't reassure. Whitleigh's brows inched closer together. "I don't have much time, Whit. Got a line of guys waiting. Can you fill me in real quick? How's Linc? Any word on Charles? Talked to Jen?"

Why did he want to know about Jen? "Oh uh, sure." Whitleigh's eyes rolled from right to left. "Haven't heard anything from Charles, but Dad called the other day and said he's doing really well. Linc's so strong." Whitleigh's throat tightened at the mere thought of their son. "He's such a happy guy. Loves his toes." She chuckled.

"His surgery?"

"Friday … tomorrow." Whitleigh cradled the phone with her shoulder. "The doctors say he's healthy and the odds are in his favor." Whitleigh shifted her weight. "We've got everyone and their mother praying for him."

"Let's hope God answers their prayers more than He's answered mine."

Whitleigh gasped. "Collier. You don't mean that?"

"Yeah, well. Babes, my time's almost up."

Whitleigh's chin lifted. He called her Babes — a good sign. "Oh. Uh. Okay. Tell Dock that I met his wife Amy. Real sweet. Looking forward to getting to know her better. And, um, you asked about Jen." She twisted her lips to the side. "Not sure what's going on with her. Don't know if I've upset her, but she's not responding to any of my calls. I think she's in a real bad place."

"Keep reaching out to her. I've tried to encourage her, but I'm worried she might, well, you know?"

"Kill herself?" No way. Jen would never do something like that.

"Just try to keep an eye out."

"Will do."

"Whit?"

"Yeah?"

"I love you."

She patted the corners of her eyes. They were okay. He still cared. "I love you too."

The line clicked. He was gone, but prayerfully, not for too much longer.

WHITLEIGH steadied her arms as she aimed the handgun at the paper target. Layla won. Saying no to the silly ladies' event at the gun range became more difficult when she found out Jen would be there. How Layla managed to convince Jen to go, Whitleigh would never know.

Whitleigh's eyes shifted. Jen stood to her side, staring off in the distance. Maybe she was a little depressed, but not suicidal.

"I still can't believe they dropped the news of another deployment like this.

Your guys haven't even gotten home yet." Layla popped the top of a soda can. Jen flinched.

"Don't really want to dive in to that right now." Whitleigh eyed the target. Whoever drew the outline of this person needed a few art lessons.

"Crazy things happen during wartime." Layla couldn't catch a hint. She shook her head, chomping her gum. "I know what war can do to a man." And she did. Layla popped a bubble. "They can come back bent on self-destructing."

"At least some come back." Jen's words were a whisper. Did she intend for them to hear? Whitleigh pursed her lips, trying to keep her eye on the target.

Layla gave Whitleigh a quick pat on the shoulder. "Now focus and shoot."

Easier said than done. "I should've invited Amy, Dock's wife." Whitleigh inhaled, pushing out the breath. Her hands wouldn't steady.

"Never mind that. You can invite her next time." Next time? Layla's words drug out in that New England sort of way. "Now concentrate. You can do this." Her words were encouraging, but the uninjured target had different things to say. "Just take a deep breath in and shoot on the exhale."

"I thought you shoot on the inhale." Those were the first words Jen had spoken most of the morning. She flipped her hair back and continued to gaze toward the mountain peaks.

"Which is it?" Whitleigh rocked on her heels, side to side. The gun grew slippery in her palms. She swallowed, lowering the weapon. "I don't think I need to be here. Linc's surgery is tomorrow."

"Which is why you need a nice day out." Layla palmed her hips, big hair blowing in the breeze. "It's definitely on the exhale."

"This day is too beautiful to be on a gun range." Whitleigh closed her eyes. She could be taking Linc for a stroll.

"And don't close your eyes when you shoot. The purpose is to hit the perpetrator."

"It's a piece of paper." Whitleigh's words fell from a sigh.

Layla waved a finger. "You won't be thinking that if it's some crazy person coming at you again. You of all people should know that."

"Fine." The whole thing was crazy. Whitleigh groaned and widened her stance. She lifted the small, coal black handgun. "Why are we wearing these business suits?" She rolled her neck. "This isn't gun range friendly."

"But we look pretty incredible." Layla winked. "No other way to go to a gun range."

Jen managed a snicker.

Whitleigh grinned, gripping the gun tighter. "I do kind of feel like a Charlie's Angel, or maybe a Special Agent."

"Exactly." Layla lifted her hands to the side. "It's all a part of my plan to build your confidence and get you sharp shooting. I promised Collier I'd teach you well."

"Guess I missed that conversation, but you can tell him you succeeded."

"Not until you finally hit the target."

Whitleigh adjusted the not so attractive shooting goggles that clung to her face. "Ugh. I'm sweating." She wiped her hands on her pants.

"Don't you get sick of complaining?" Jen's words all but smacked Whitleigh in the face. Jen held her arms as if they were life preservers. "You play the victim well."

Whitleigh hunched her shoulders, tugging at her blazer. "Um. It's a business suit, lighten up. I'm just having fun. You could've at least played along and dressed the part too." Whitleigh laughed, but Jen's sneer didn't budge.

Jen shook her head, rolling her dark eyes. "This isn't about how ridiculous the two of you look."

"Hey now." Layla pushed out a hip. "We're hot mommas."

Whitleigh squinted and turned from the target. Her tongue was thick, too heavy to respond. Jen sounded homicidal instead of suicidal. Jen's face hardened. Her glaring eyes formed menacing lines around her eyes. The wind blew between the three women and the range seemed too empty.

Whitleigh held her breath, searching for the best way to respond. "Jen, what's wrong? Talk to me."

"Like you care. All you do is complain about everything."

Whitleigh blinked. "Ok. Fair enough. Maybe I do complain too much."

"Jen." Layla's face contorted. "You're being incredibly rude. Everyone has hardships. Talking about them with your close friends isn't complaining, it's called doing life together."

"Whatever." Jen pierced Layla with a half glance and then focused back on Whitleigh. "You're too caught up in your own world and your own troubles to recognize how blessed you are." Her eyes glimmered as she slapped a tear from her face. "You have a man who loves you and would do anything for you, but all you talk about is how hard Army life is, and your son, and all the plans in your life that went wrong, and all the things you want to accomplish. What about his goals and dreams?" Whitleigh shrank as Jen's voice rose. "What about being there for him after all the horrible things he's been through?"

Whitleigh's chest tightened. "I'm doing the best I can." Suicidal or not, Jen had no right to talk to her like that. Whitleigh pulled her shoulders back. "Where's this coming from?"

Layla's mouth all but touched the ground. "We know you miss Mark and you're hurting — "

"This isn't about Mark." Jen stomped the ground. "It's about Miss Thing not being appreciative. You don't know what it's like to lose someone you love. You just know how to complain about things." Whitleigh clenched her jaw. Jen stepped forward, inches from Whitleigh's face. "You don't deserve Collier, Whitleigh."

"Excuse me?" Whitleigh leaned into Jen. There would be no backing down.

Layla's laugh broke into a nervous pant as she tugged on Jen's elbow. "Jen, you're really trying to tick off a lady with a handgun?"

Whitleigh let the gun fall to the ground. "I'm going to let whatever's wrong with you go, 'cause I know you're going through a lot right now, but you're way out of line here, Jen."

Jen didn't blink. "Collier doesn't seem to think so."

Whitleigh froze. "What?" Her stomach coiled within at a nauseating rate.

"Hold up." Layla pushed between the women. "Have you been talking to Collier behind Whit's back?"

"She knew he and I have been in touch." Jen kept her arms intertwined across her body. "We've been able to help each other out, dealing with the stuff she doesn't want to deal with."

Whitleigh's heart fell through the floor of her chest. She stepped back. Her ears rang for a moment. It was hard to hold it together when the pieces kept falling. Whitleigh balled her fist, stood tall, and planted her heels into the ground. "You have no business talking with my husband about any personal matters." Her knuckles whitened and her cheeks grew hot. "Stay away from my man."

"Um, Jen." Layla's voice cracked. Her eyes grew large and round. "I think you should go."

Jen's lips were a fine line. Her eyes narrowed. She turned, hair whipping behind.

Whitleigh sucked in sharp deep breaths. War, time, and distance plotted to keep her away from Collier. She couldn't prevent those obstacles, but if Jen thought she could step in, that girl needed to think again.

CHAPTER 22

TABLE decorations for the welcome home ceremony could wait. The FRG would understand. Whitleigh typed furiously from her bedroom. Collier was going to get a piece of her mind. The keys of the laptop clicked under her fingers. She eyed the door. Yeah, it was locked. Momma wouldn't interfere anyway.

Dear Collier,

How much have you been talking to Jen, 'cause it's not like I hear from you all that often. And what have you been saying to her, 'cause she's under the impression that you're not too happy with me right now. If you think it's okay to go airing out any marital issues we may have with someone else, especially a female, and my supposed best friend at that, then we do have problems. If you think war is bad, you just wait 'til you get home."

Grr. She couldn't say mean things like that — especially while he was deployed. What if he got hurt? She'd never forgive herself. Whitleigh deleted the paragraph and let her head fall on the keyboard.

"Breathe Whitleigh." Great. Now she talked to herself. "How do I confront this issue?" Maybe it would go away. Maybe it wasn't a problem — a misunderstanding. "C'mon. Who are you kidding?" Awesome. Now she answered herself. Next stop, the looney bin.

Some advice would be nice. Momma didn't need to hear a ranting rundown on the whole situation, which could create more issues in the long run. Whitleigh tugged at a pillow propped against the headboard and shoved it under her chin. "A little help here God. What do I say? Or do I say anything at all?" Letting it go wasn't going to fly. "Okay. I'm just going to type. Help me with the words."

Dear Collier,

I saw Jen today. She is definitely not herself. She said some things that alarmed me and made me want to check in with you. I know the both of you understand loss, and I'm grateful you're able to help her, but I'm concerned with what you may have confided in her, even if unintentional.

Did that sound all right? Offensive? No. Whitleigh leaned into the pillow and continued to type.

She seems to be under the impression that I'm putting you on the back burner — even said that I wasn't good enough for you. Ouch, right?

Whitleigh smirked. The last line seemed to keep the message upbeat.

I love you. I'm here for you, and I'm doing the best I can while we're apart. Please know you can always talk to me. Just wanted to lay that all out there. Stay safe baby, and know that I pray for you all of the time.

Going to get some sleep — long day of surgery ahead. I'll keep you posted.

Love me always,

Whit

Sigh. Click and send. Whitleigh buried her face in the pillow.

Tap, tap, tap. Whitleigh lifted her face to the door. "Hold on a sec." She rolled from the bed.

"Hey Momma." Whitleigh forced a smile. Momma's face paled. "You okay?" Whitleigh leaned against the door frame. "Is it Charles? Is he — "

"No, baby." Momma tapped Whitleigh's chin. "He's actually doing rather well. Baffling the doctors."

Whitleigh released a long breath. Relief. How horrible it would've been to tell Collier something of that magnitude after the email she'd sent. "So, what's wrong?"

"Layla's here." Momma lowered her voice. "And she has Emma."

"Emma?" Whitleigh pushed passed Momma and made it up the hall in a few strides. There she sat, the same brown eyed, scraggly little girl. She jumped from the couch and into Whitleigh's arms. Layla sat on the couch, holding a pink butterfly suitcase. She tossed a bewildered look in Whitleigh's direction.

Whitleigh squeezed the child and lifted her from the ground in a half spin. Emma was thinner. Whitleigh kissed her cheeks and fixed her feet on the floor, wiping dirt from the child's face.

"Oh Emma, I'm so glad you're back." Even happier that she appeared safe. "Are you hungry?"

Emma giggled, bobbing her head.

"Momma, can you fix her some popcorn?"

"Come with me, Ms. Emma." Momma smiled and nodded. "I think we have a soda in the fridge you can have too."

Emma skipped into the kitchen, rubbing her belly.

Whitleigh sat on the floor, jaw dropping as she turned to Layla. "What's going on? A suitcase? Emma's?"

Layla shrugged, adhering her elbows to her knees. "I am not sure what happened. One minute I'm cleaning up supper, Jayson's getting the kids into bed, and somebody starts pounding at my door."

"Yeah?"

"It was Helen."

"Was she ... drunk or strung out?"

"No, but she was terrified." Layla's mouth hung open. "Kept looking over her shoulder. Freaked me out, I can tell you that much. I almost got my gun, but not with little Emma just standing there."

"What in the world?"

"I know. Bizarre." Layla sank back into the couch, crossing her legs. "She begged me not to call the cops, said her life and Emma's life depended on it, and that the cops weren't safe."

"What? That's crazy talk."

"I know, but funny thing is, I couldn't help but believe her."

"And then what?"

"She handed me this bag, pleaded with me to take care of Emma for a few days. Said it wouldn't be long, she just needed to figure things out in a safe place."

"What about school?"

"Guess she's trying to homeschool her now. Said there's some resources in the bag. Kindergarten isn't too hard to teach. That won't be a problem."

"Do you think it has anything to do with that boyfriend of hers, what's his name, Ray? Maybe her husband?"

"Good chance for both. Her husband found out about the affair, got drunk, and beat her up real bad."

"Yeah, I remember you telling me that. Then Emma went away for a while."

"She spent time with her grandparents in Florida." Layla clicked her fingernails against her teeth.

"Well, they just got back not long ago." Whitleigh bit her lip, tilting her head. "Does Helen's husband smoke?"

"Not that I ever remember seeing. Why?"

"Just wondering." Whitleigh tugged on her ponytail, wrapping a strand around her finger. The whole ordeal grew more suspicious. "I saw someone, definitely a male figure, at Emma's house talking with Helen, I suppose. He was smoking, and when he saw me staring through the blinds, he waved." Whitleigh shivered. "Gave me the creeps."

"All of it is giving me the creeps." Layla scooted from the couch and took a seat on the floor next to Whitleigh. "As it turns out, Ray is Military Police."

"No!" Whitleigh covered her mouth. "That must be why Helen doesn't feel safe? What happened to make her take off like this?"

Layla's shoulders rose and fell.

The microwave beeped. Emma's claps echoed through the kitchen and into the living room. The scent of popcorn floated through the air.

Whitleigh rested her chin on folded arms. "So what are we going to do?"

"We aren't doing anything."

"What do you mean by that?"

Layla shook her head, pulling her pink fluffy robe close to her body. "I'm going keep her for a few days. See what happens. At least I know she's safe."

"Poor girl." Whitleigh gathered her knees.

"I know that look on your face." Layla slapped at Whitleigh's arm. "There's no way you can help right now, nor do you need to. Linc needs your attention, and Collier will be home."

"You're right." Whitleigh blew out a puff of air. Her hands were tied in this matter. "I love that little girl. It kills me to think of what she could've went through."

"She's safe. She's happy. Listen to her."

Emma giggled, begging for a bag of popcorn all her own. Momma obliged.

"You're right, again." Whitleigh smashed her cheek atop her knee.

"I'll keep you posted. Don't you even worry about any of this."

Whitleigh nodded. "Oh." Her head shot up. "I still need to get those table arrangement designs to Andrea." Whitleigh rocked back on her tail bone, palming her forehead. "I'm just running out of time."

"For the coming home ceremony? Andrea, your FRG leader?"

"Uh-huh." Whitleigh bobbed her head up and down.

"Let me help."

"Seriously? You have like a million plus one kids."

"Which makes me an amazing multitasker. Let me help. Just tell me what to do."

"I owe you big time." Whitleigh pressed her fingers against her temples. *Think. Got it.* "All the tables will need is a burlap runner. Centerpieces — way too easy — just a mason jar, yellow ribbon tied around the mouth, and a couple of small flags. Boom, done, simple. Tell Andrea one table setting design will be sufficient instead of three."

"You threw that together fast."

Whitleigh grinned. "It's not like people are really going to be sitting at those tables outside anyway."

"I know, right?" Layla tossed her hand to the side. "Well anyway, consider it sent to Ms. Andrea."

"Thank you, thank you, thank you."

Layla arched a brow and scooted closer. "Heard from Jen?" Her voice hushed.

Whitleigh chewed on her lips which refused to smile. She shook her head. "Not a word. Probably a good thing."

"Thought maybe she'd have it in her to apologize."

"I don't know, Layla." Whitleigh tapped on the carpet, picking up one of Linc's stray Cheerios. "Maybe Jen's right. Maybe I haven't been there for Collier."

"Don't think on it for a minute. You and Collier are doing the best you can while you're apart. It's difficult to know what to share and when to share things that are happening in your lives. You only have each other's best interest at heart. She's the one that's out of line."

"Yeah." Whitleigh drummed her fingers on the side of her knee.

Emma bounced into the living room. "Wanna share with me, Ms. Whitleigh?"

"You bet, sweet girl." Whitleigh yanked the chuckling child into her arms and shoved a handful of buttery popcorn into her mouth. Giggles and buttery popcorn were a nice way to break from life.

THE Denver Children's Hospital hadn't changed and neither had the room where they would be residing for an indefinite amount of time. Each room must've been fashioned from the same design — low to the ground leather sofa, chair, kitchenette, and squeaky clean floors. Whitleigh blinked. Her room could be a hotel room, if only this were a vacation and not a hospital stay. She sat her suitcase on the bed. She clung to Linc's carrier holding him close to her side.

"It's nice to see you both again." Dr. Simpson entered the room with a kind smile. He held a model heart in his hand "I take it you've read the pamphlets on this procedure."

Whitleigh nodded.

She'd read all of the brochures on the second surgery known as the Glenn procedure, but it still baffled her.

"Good. Good. Let's recap." Dr. Simpson stood in front of the wide window. His fingers skimmed the surface of the heart. "We're taking away that extra volume the heart has to pump by getting rid of the shunt and connecting the veins from the upper body to the arteries to the lungs which essentially provides Linc with another source of pulmonary blood flow."

Whitleigh swallowed. Her grip tightened on the carrier. Did any of what he just said make sense?

"I understand this is a lot to take in, a lot of technical doctor talk." Dr. Simpson smiled, but Whitleigh couldn't find it in her to return the gesture. "Take a deep breath and know that your son's heart will be in good hands."

Whitleigh blinked the dryness from her eyes. She believed, but the doubt remained tucked in a corner, ready to pounce. Chill bumps raced up her arms. Whitleigh shook them away. Everything would be okay. Linc would be fine. Her marriage was solid. Jen was having a breakdown. Emma's home would be happy.

"Your Mom is in the hall, Mrs. Cromwell. When you're ready we can begin prepping Linc."

"May I have a few minutes alone with him?"

"Of course." Dr. Simpson patted her shoulder and drifted from the room.

Whitleigh set the carrier on the corner chair. She knelt in front, removing the green froggy and firefly blanket that sheltered her sleeping son. His pudgy legs stuck out from his onesie, looking like rolls of dough. Whitleigh ran a hand over each soft leg, tiny foot, and hand. Linc's lashes fluttered and his sea blue eyes opened.

"You have your Daddy's eyes." And he did. Whitleigh gazed into them, more than willing to get lost. She kissed his cheek. "You're going to be okay, Linc." Tears rose in the corner of her eyes.

He squealed, rounded cheeks stretching into a one toothed grin. Whitleigh cradled the carrier between her forearms, cooing back. "Mommy loves you so much. So, so, much."

Linc babbled out spit bubbles, smiling. Whitleigh wiped her tears. Sobs worked their way from her throat. Her chest knotted, lips fought to smile. She raised her eyes, closing them tight. "Keep him safe, Lord."

She held Linc's sweet hands, kissing each dimple. She studied his face, memorizing every detail. Minutes passed, but it didn't matter. Each tick of the second hand accumulated, documenting Linc's life.

"Mrs. Cromwell?" Dr. Simpson peeked through the doorway. "It's time."

Whitleigh nodded, but her jittering insides were anything but ready.

"You can hold Linc while we put him to sleep."

Whitleigh's voice caught. "I ... I ...." Was she strong enough to do that? "Yes, I would like that."

THE wee hours of the morning slipped into early afternoon. Whitleigh balanced Linc's baby book on her knee. She tucked her legs at her side and she shifted her weight in the armchair. Hours in the same sitting position resulted in numb toes and tingling calf muscles. She eyed the clock and then shifted her glance to the door. No news was good news. Linc must've been hanging in there.

Momma slept on the sofa, knitting needles still in her hands. The blanket pattern book had fallen to her side. Whitleigh snuggled against the armrest. Maybe she should try to rest.

Whitleigh rolled her neck along the back of the chair, the cool leather stuck to her skin. Her thoughts drifted.

Surgeons were simply amazing. Whitleigh smiled, closing her eyes. Cutting, rearranging, and healing. That took serious skill. It must've been difficult for doctors to operate under such stressful conditions, like that of Linc's, but they did it. So brave, like Collier and his soldiers, fighting, never stopping, even under the most desperate circumstances. And Linc — he was brave too without even knowing it.

The room stilled with her thoughts. Maybe sleep was possible. Whitleigh reached for her phone, turning it on silent just as it buzzed in her palm.

"Hello?"

"Whit?"

"Collier?" She sat up, leaning forward.

"How are you? How's Linc?" His voice strained over the distance and cracked and popped with the connection. "I've done nothing but think about you guys."

Whitleigh leapt to her feet. "We're okay. You just focus on being safe and getting home." Whitleigh pressed the phone closer to her ear. "Linc's still in surgery. Hopefully we'll know something soon."

Collier's sigh sounded a lot like relief. "I wish I would've never left you guys. I don't know if I can keep calling to check in, but you can send a Red Cross message to me when you get word."

Whitleigh nodded. "Got their number on speed dial."

"So." Silence hung between them. "How are you really doing?" His voice probed.

"I take it you've read the email I sent?" Whitleigh all but growled. Maybe she shouldn't have sent it.

"A few times actually, and you're right." He huffed. "I didn't mean to talk to her about us. I thought sharing some of my struggles would help."

Whitleigh put one foot in front of the other, slowly pacing the perimeter of the hospital room. She searched for the right response.

"Whit, baby, I see how that was harmful to you and to our relationship. I'm so sorry. Jen is going to have to find someone else to help her out."

"Why didn't you talk to me about your struggles? Your life goals?" Whitleigh's cheeks flushed. She worked to keep her voice down. "I want to hear those things."

"You're right and I don't have a good answer for you other than I was just being a dumb guy."

Whitleigh rolled her eyes, tucking a strand of hair behind her ear.

"Whit, I promise to talk your ear off when I get home. You'll hear all about my goals, issues, and everything else."

She couldn't help but smile. Whitleigh cradled the phone close. "Is that right?"

"You better believe it." The excitement in his voice gave her stomach a case of the flutters. "You'll get to hear my voice, oh, in, I don't know, seven days tops."

"What?" Whitleigh stopped mid-pace. "You're kidding."

"Just found out. Flights got bumped up and we're heading out of here within thirty-six hours. Thought you'd want to hear that straight from my mouth."

"Oh Collier, it doesn't get better than this." Whitleigh bounced on her tippy toes.

The door clicked opened, stirring Momma. She locked eyes with Whitleigh as Dr. Simpson entered the room. Whitleigh gasped. Time stopped. She held her breath. This was it.

Dr. Robinson's slight grin widened. "Success." He bobbed his balding head. "Linc's doing fine."

"I heard that." Collier's voice shouted over the phone.

"Collier, it just got better." Whitleigh embraced her Momma and the doctor with her one free arm. She hopped and hollered or risked bursting. Her fingertips shook while holding the phone. "He's okay, and you're coming home."

CHAPTER 23

JUST as sure as a rooster crows at the crack of dawn, a bugle recording sang Reveille across Fort Carson each morning. Whitleigh stood on the sidewalk in front of her house, keys clasped in her hands as she stood in reverence. *Wait for it.* The cannon blasted and then she stepped up onto the porch, yanking a handwritten note taped on the screen door.

Today's the day. Don't worry about a thing. Take a deep breath and have fun! Love, Layla

Crayon doodles and smiley faces dotted and outlined the paper. Each of Layla's children and Emma had signed their name. Emma still lived with the Ryan family. Whitleigh brushed her fingertips over the drawings, giving a backward glance to Layla's home. Tricycles, bouncy balls, and water guns littered the front yard. Emma must've been having a blast.

Whitleigh tucked the note in her back pocket, closed her eyes, and smiled. Layla was right — today *was* the day. Collier would be home. All was well. She glanced up to heaven and gave a nod. Two years of waiting, over in a few short hours. Talk about perseverance. Whitleigh stood tall, her lungs filling with mountain air. They made it.

She flipped her phone open, keying in the numbers. Momma would be calling soon if she didn't beat her to it.

It rang only once. "Hello?"

Whitleigh balanced the phone between her fingers, vying for the house key. "Made it to the house."

"Good, good. Now get yourself all prettied up."

Whitleigh chuckled. Her stomach knotted. She blew a puff of air, rattling the phone reception.

"Don't you worry about a thing."

So she kept hearing.

"You and Collier have a good time and Linc and I will see the two of you sometime tomorrow."

Whitleigh raised to her toes and rocked back on the heel of her sneakers. "How is L — "

"Perfect. Wonderful in every way."

"Momma, be serious."

"You've been gone an hour. He's fine Whit. You know I'd call if something important was up."

"Yeah." She'd call all right, but her definition of important varied. Whitleigh gave her keys a jingle. "Anyway."

"You know, I wish you and Collier would stay away a bit longer ... maybe two nights to yourself and then come up here."

"Momma." Whitleigh frowned.

"I'm just saying it won't hurt anyone's feelings if you do."

"Gotta go."

"Be safe, Whit. Check the window locks and the doors."

"Momma, I'm fine. Collier's coming home now. I'm safe."

"I know, sweetie. I worry, what can I say?"

"Gotta go."

"Oh, remember to take pictures of the ceremony if you can. Film it too."

"Okay, Momma. Love ya, bye." Whitleigh flipped the phone shut and dropped it into her purse. She surveyed her surroundings. No attacker. No boot prints. Safe.

The neighborhood continued to sleep in the early morning hours as Whitleigh walked in the front door. She placed her keys and purse on the closest table and stood in the entryway. Minus the steady humming of the refrigerator, silence reverberated through the room. She held her arms as her eyes scanned the familiar surroundings. Thanks to Momma's help, the little house remained tidy. Maybe she'd light a few candles, but other than that, nothing needed to be done before Collier's arrival.

Whitleigh eyed the walls. Pictures, most documenting she and Collier's life apart, grew in number. Many boasted refurbished and repurposed frames that hung in patterns and collected on top of the entertainment system. Several others perched on side tables.

Whitleigh wiped a tear. Soon, new photos of them together would join the ranks. Happier times immortalized.

Whitleigh pried the shoes from her feet and reached for the Bible on the coffee table. She couldn't ask for anything more. What else was there to pray for? Linc thrived, and their family would be united. God was good. She gave the Good Book a kiss, sat it back down, and skipped down the hall.

She let her fingers skim along the hall wall in a childish manner until reaching the bedroom doorway.

What to wear? Whitleigh stood in front of her closet, chewing on her twisted lips as if she hadn't eaten breakfast. Her stomach growled. Maybe she hadn't eaten. Oh well. There would be time for that later.

Duty called and duty said to find a dress to impress.

The red one? No. Floral? No way. Whitleigh slid the hangers across the metal rod.

Blue?

She lifted it from its spot, holding it against her body as she turned to the full length mirror.

Grr. Maybe.

Whitleigh shuffled through the colors, clanking hangers against one another. All of these prepregnancy clothes were unrelenting with their taunting.

Sigh.

She shoved the green striped dress to the back of the closet, knocking loose a box on the top shelf. It tumbled to the floor, spilling out a mess of satin and lace. Whitleigh's cheeks grew red. She knelt down, picking up each revealing piece.

The black one — short and translucent, dangled between pressed fingers. When had she worn that? Whitleigh arched a brow. Oh yes. The night before he deployed. She giggled, covering her mouth. Her laugh ended just as she caught her reflection in the mirror.

Whitleigh walked closer, her face folded into a frown. Mirrors didn't lie.

How could she ever wear something so revealing for Collier again?

She leaned in, turning from side to side, lifted her shirt to the naval and stopped. So pudgy. And the stretch marks. Her stomach no longer laid flat. Her thighs were closer together than she would've preferred. Even her arms — Whitleigh lifted them. They jiggled more than they used to. Breastfeeding alone changed her chest in a manner that need not be described.

Whitleigh slouched forward, heart sinking. She let the lingerie fall from her grip. Collier couldn't see her like this, but there was no more time. Surely he would want to be intimate as much as she, but — Whitleigh slumped on the floor, still looking in the mirror. How could she let him see her?

She shook her head.

Collier wouldn't care. He loved her and spoke of her beauty. She had a woman's body now. Maybe some baby weight needed to go, but it took more than nine months to put it on, and it could take more to take it off. Whitleigh nodded and stood to her feet. She bore down on her bottom lip with her teeth.

"Geez." She ran her finger through her hair and pointed to the mirror. "Stop being silly."

No mandate existed for wearing the most revealing piece of lingerie she owned. She knelt back down, digging through the pile of flirty apparel. Something suitable existed somewhere in the midst of the fluff.

"Yep." Whitleigh clawed at an elegant white laced gown. "This one will work."

Now for a dress. She swatted at her hair, pushing it over her shoulders. Back to the closet.

Gray. Taupe. Ten shades of green, three shades of orange. Pinks of all hues. Whitleigh pushed each dress aside. Maybe a cardigan would be the best choice — with her pearls of course.

No. She tapped her toes against the worn carpet. It had to be a dress.

Whitleigh snapped her fingers. "Jen." She'd be great at helping pick the perfect outfit. Whitleigh grappled for her phone and jolted to a halt. No use in making that call. Jen wouldn't answer anyway. It wasn't like they were on the best terms.

Whitleigh sighed. "Here goes nothing." Choosing a dress came down to this. She closed her eyes and extended an open hand toward the closet. "Eenie, Meenie, Minie, Moe …."

Yellow it was. "Hmm." The wrap dress. Not bad.

She slid the dress into place, tying the wide strings until they rested on top of her hip. Slipping into a pair of taupe peep-toed high heels, Whitleigh posed in front of the mirror. Not bad at all.

SIGNS, banners, wreaths, ribbons, and flags adorned the gates surrounding Fort Carson. Whitleigh mounted her red, white, and blue fringed bedsheet banner alongside the others. Letters nearly two feet long had been freehanded in shades of camouflage: *Welcome Home Specialist Cromwell! Love, Whit and Linc.* Red hearts formed from Linc's hand and foot prints scattered across the sign. Whitleigh touched his tiny prints. So precious. She stepped back, admiring their sign and hurried back to her car.

The sun shone overhead. Under an hour to go. Whitleigh sat in the recreation center parking lot, glossing her lips in the rearview mirror for the fifth time in five minutes. Nervous new habit.

Local camera crews gathered. Cars filed in from all directions, parking where the Military Police motioned, directing the flow. Whitleigh tapped her steering wheel. Michigan tags. Washington State. Texas. Kentucky. She grinned. People came from all over.

No doubt Collier and all the other soldiers from 1-9 had landed. Somewhere they probably sat, unpacking, all abuzz, hooting and hooah-ing. That sort of excitement was earned and well deserved from a deployment completed. Whitleigh leaned her head against the headrest, careful not to disturb her curls. She should head inside. The FRG gals could use a hand setting up, or she could at least find someone to chat with. Whitleigh rolled the pearls of her necklace between closed fingers and reached for her purse before sliding from the driver's seat.

Deep breath.

Sunglasses on.

She glossed her lips one more time and rubbed them together as her heels clicked forward.

A group of family members, or perhaps friends of a returning soldier, carried a sparkling welcome home banner. Glitter dusted to the ground as they passed. Children sported patriotic outfits and gallivanted in the gravel, waving flags. Round tables scattered close to the entry way and off to the sides for families to gather around after the ceremony. Whitleigh peered over her shades. The centerpieces looked fantastic. Each table displayed a Mason jar with a yellow ribbon and a small American flag. Layla relayed the instructions to Andrea, the FRG leader, to perfection.

A blast of heat greeted Whitleigh as she inched through the doorway. Industrial fans hovered close by but offered little comfort for a growing crowd.

"Whitleigh? Whitleigh Cromwell?"

She removed her shades, squinting. It was difficult to make out the voice amongst the sea of others.

"Up here."

Whitleigh glanced up at the set of bleachers to her right. "Oh, hi." She gave a quick wave. Amy, Dock's wife, sat, appearing quite lost. A young toddler aged girl clung to her arms. That must be Annabelle. Whitleigh worked her way through the crowd, taking her time to carefully step up each bleacher step. No time for injuries.

"Can you believe how many people are here?" Whitleigh dabbed the sweat from her forehead and tucked her dress beneath her as she sat.

"I don't know what I expected, but it wasn't this." Amy wrung her hands atop her jittering knees. "How in the world are we ever going to find our men?"

Whitleigh crossed her legs, brushing her hair to the side. "Collier said for me to stand on the bleachers and wait for him. He'll find me."

"I think I'm going to copy that plan." She crinkled her freckled nose.

"Have at it." Whitleigh laughed and smiled at Annabelle. "She's so cute. You look too young to be a momma."

"I guess that comes with being a teen mom."

"Oh." Whitleigh's voice caught as her throat constricted. Hello foot in mouth. Collier should've said something. "I'm sorry, I didn't mean anything, I mean, I thought — "

"It's okay. Promise." Her small laugh dismissed Whitleigh's embarrassment. A couple of Army wives gawked in Amy's direction, eyebrows arching. They turned, hands hiding their hushed whispers. She knew their faces from a few FRG gatherings, but their names escaped her. Amy's cheeks flushed. She smoothed the green pleats of her dress around her knees. "It's kind of a long story. We got pregnant in high school, got married, miscarried, and then …."

Whitleigh's face continued to warm. "No need to explain a thing." Hopefully she said it loud enough for those women to hear. She tossed a glare over her shoulder and bounced her purse on her knees. "So, um, the place looks nice." Amy nodded, rubbing her arms. Groups of red, white, and blue balloons perched along the back wall and alongside the guarded doors. "I bet our guys are behind those doors." Whitleigh's stomach fluttered.

"I hope." Amy squirmed, tapping her toes on the bleacher beneath her feet.

Unit and Brigade banners hung from the banisters. On the floor, front and center, stood a platform equipped with a microphone — ready for the Commanding General to give his briefing. A large screen gave way to a slideshow filled with snapshots from Iraq, minus the combat of course.

"I think Collier took that picture of the camel in the back of the truck." Whitleigh pointed as Amy gave a shy shake of her head. "Andrea does a fantastic job with these kinds of things."

"Our FRG leader? Yeah. She seems cool. This is my first time being a part of an FRG."

"Me too."

"Really?" Amy's auburn lashes fluttered a few times. "You seem so experienced with all of this Army stuff."

"What?" Whitleigh scooted closer, grinning. "Trust me, I'm still learning. This is year two and I feel like a beginner."

"You could've fooled me." Amy lifted bag of cheese crackers from her purse and gave them to Annabelle, who seemed thrilled at the gesture. "I still have a long way to go."

"Don't we all?" Whitleigh glanced at the women still whispering. She exchanged a kind smile with them, which halted their discussion.

The lights lowered. The crowd hushed. They stood as wounded veterans, perhaps from the current deployment, and limped and wheeled their way onto the floor. Most appeared quite young, baby faced even. Many were missing limbs.

"That's Pulu." Amy leaned in, her voice a murmur.

Wow. Whitleigh brought a hand to her mouth. Pulu, thinner than what she could recall from the pictures Collier sent, saluted the flag alongside his wounded comrades. He stood on two metal rods that now functioned as his legs, and leaned on a cane — a strange but awe inspiring sight to process. She exhaled, almost forgetting she'd even taken a breath.

Whitleigh's fists were damp. The anticipation grew thick enough to touch. Any minute now. Any second. She strained her neck, focusing on the barricaded back set of auditorium doors.

When?

The yellow material of her dress stretched as she wiped her palms.

Now.

The guarding soldiers stepped to the side. Patriotic music blared from the speakers, and the doors swung open with a thunderous force. Hundreds of soldiers spilled forth in a rhythmic procession. Whitleigh threw her hands in the air, her screams aided in the deafening roar. Her heart thudded in erratic beats against the walls of her chest.

The men filed into formation, facing the crowd, standing tall in their desert uniforms. Where was Collier? Whitleigh strained and squinted. Her eyes raced up and down each row. No use. They all looked alike. The Commanding General walked toward the podium.

"Thank you, thank you." At the sight of his raised hand, the cheering began to subside. "These are the finest bunch of men I've ever had the honor of commanding." The crowd applauded. Whitleigh rapped her fingers against her shaking legs. This man needed hurry up with the speech. "They've been away from you for two long years and I refuse to keep them a minute longer." Best speech ever. He turned to his soldiers. Whitleigh pursed her lips. "Men of the 2nd Brigade Combat Team, ATTEN — TION! You've fought well and were victorious. You are America's best and brightest. This day has been a long time coming, and we're excited, but we remember our fallen. Live your lives worthy of their sacrifice." He raised his hand to a salute. Whitleigh stood on the tips of her high heels. "Dismissed."

His command released the wave of loved ones from the bleachers. They poured out onto the gym floor until they each crashed into their soldier's arms.

Whitleigh held her position. Collier would find her. Besides, higher ground seemed safer than the monsoon below.

Where could he be? Her head whipped from side to side and then back again to the familiar frame tucked in the corner of the room.

Jen.

She stood, wiping her eyes, wadded tissues in hand.

Whitleigh looked away. Jen's pain was too difficult to witness. Whitleigh raised her eyes again but swarms of people now blocked Jen from view. Maybe she had left the building all together. Whitleigh shook the chills away and warmed at the gentle brush from a calloused hand.

"I'm home."

Collier's voice broke through the convivial crowd, his touch unmistakable. She turned, knees weakening as she lunged into his embrace. His hands ran through her hair. He lifted her from the bleacher, twisting her from side to side. The tears came. Whitleigh let them flow, not minding the salty kisses.

"You found me." Whitleigh managed to mutter through jagged sobs.

"Always." His strong hands cradled her neck. He stared, intertwining his fingers with hers. She kissed him again. Talking could wait.

Collier shooed away a news reporter.

Whitleigh giggled and stumbled back a bit. "We've got time to talk with them."

"No way." Collier waved the reporter off and placed his hands around her waist. "I've got a few friends I want you to meet, and then I vote we get out of here."

"Deal." Whitleigh wrapped her arms around his neck. He lifted her in his arms and jogged down the bleacher stairs with her.

Three Months Later

WHITLEIGH awoke. She reached out to her side, grabbing a handful of soaked pillow. Collier was gone, but the sweat rings remained. His nightmares worsened since his return and happened more frequently. Whitleigh rubbed her hands down her face and slid from the cool cotton sheets, careful not to disturb Linc in the bedside crib. He slept sound and breathed well.

With a flick of her wrists, Whitleigh draped a knitted afghan blanket around her shoulders to fend off the crisp October air drifting in the open window. She slipped down the hall, following the sound of an inaudible muddled conversation.

"Collier?" Whitleigh pulled the blanket close, bundling it under her chin. Collier stood, facing the living room window, cellphone dangling from his hand as he stared ahead. "Collier?" She raised her voice above a whisper. Still no reply.

He wasn't one to sleep walk, but the distant and vacant bouts became more and more frequent. Whitleigh inched forward.

"Collier?" She tapped his shoulder and gasped as he spun around with a lifted fist. Whitleigh dodged, dropping to the floor. "It's me." The words stumbled from her mouth.

"Whit? I'm so sorry." He fell to her side. "You scared me." His arms wrapped warm and tight around her back. Whitleigh shook. He didn't mean to almost hit her. Accidents happened all of the time.

"Whit." His words and embrace hardened. "You can't sneak up on me like that."

"I said your name — a few times actually." She pulled free.

He helped her up. Whitleigh clung to the blanket as if it held her together.

"Maybe you should be louder next time."

"Maybe it's time to get help Collier. I'm worried about you."

"I'm fine." His icy glare and tone sent a wintry breeze through her body. "Why are you up anyway?"

"I, um — wait, who were you talking to?"

"Talking? No one. Nothing."

"Then why can't you look me in the eyes? Who do you talk to at five in the morning?"

"I said I wasn't talking to anyone." Collier tucked his cellphone into the pocket of his pajama pants, face reddening.

"Whatever, Collier."

"Are you really trying to pick a fight this early?"

"I don't have the energy to argue with you."

"There you go making me mad." A crooked vein protruded down the side of his forehead. "You keep on. You want me to make yell, don't you?"

"I can't do this again, not now. I don't even know why you're so upset. Please tell me. Talk to me. I'm here, please talk." Whitleigh folding her arms and blanket over her chest.

"There's nothing to stay."

Nothing to say? Whitleigh pushed her fingers through the holes of the afghan, clinging to the yarn like a lifeline. "Why are we doing this — fighting all the time? It's been this way since you've been back."

"I'm sorry life's not living up to your expectations. Join the group."

Whitleigh blinked, refusing to cry. She ground her teeth. Sometimes keeping quiet kept the peace. She turned, wadding the ends of the blanket in her fist.

"Where you going?"

She paused, considering her words. "Figured I'd get breakfast started. We've got church in a few hours."

"You guys can go without me."

"Again?" The question flew from her mouth.

Collier tilted his head and Whitleigh lowered her eyes. *Please not another blow up.* The hall walls couldn't handle more holes. Picture frames concealed the evidence of his erupting temper well.

"I've got things to do around here. Get the grill ready and stuff." He raked the back of his head with open palms. "Pulu, Dock, and his wife will be over for dinner, remember?"

Crisis averted. Whitleigh relaxed her shoulders, releasing a short breath.

"Well, we're only having chili and hot dogs. That won't take too long." Why couldn't she keep her mouth shut? "Layla and Jayson are coming too." There it went again.

"And all those kids? Why didn't you tell me?" Collier groaned. "I didn't plan on feeding Fort Carson."

"Seriously?" Whitleigh raised a brow. Relax. She shook her head, running a few fingers through her tangled morning hair. Tiptoeing across his short fuse required the skill of an acrobat. "I invited Jen too, but haven't heard back. Nothing new there."

Collier snapped to attention. "Why would you invite her?"

"Uh," Whitleigh sneered. "She's still my best friend. I have to keep reaching out to her until she snaps out of whatever funk she's in. What's it matter anyway?"

"I didn't say it did." Collier slid his hand into the pocket of his pajama pants. "I'd like to know how many people we have to feed. Food isn't free."

"I'll be in the kitchen. I'm sure Linc will be up soon." She gave a half shrug. "Looks like we both have a busy day."

Collier scratched at his eyebrow. "You know, you don't have to go to church to be a Christian."

Now who was trying to pick a fight? Whitleigh held her chin and tapped on her bottom lip.

"I'm going to pretend you didn't say that." Her nostrils flared. Who in the world did this man think he was? She stuck out a hip. "If Jesus went to church, then we better have our hind ends there too."

Collier rolled his eyes and yanked on his dog tags. "We've been down this road before, Whit. I'm not going to argue about God-stuff."

"No one's arguing. You've made your feelings about God quite clear, but you know where I stand. I'm not the one who's changed."

"That's right. It's always me."

Oh, that man. Whitleigh puffed her cheeks and bobbed toward the kitchen, quick to shake and rattle the pans. What was wrong with him? Staring out windows. Secret phone conversations. Nothing much to say. Nightmares. Night sweats. His temper flared over the littlest things, and rude — just plain rude. He didn't put the toilet seat down or clean his facial hair from the bathroom sink. Whitleigh slammed the silverware drawer and tossed the blanket from her shoulders onto a vintage stool. Her eyes narrowed, both hands now on her hips. Soda cans hung out on the countertop, hugging an empty bag of chips.

She folded her arms. "I'm not a maid." Her voice rose from the kitchen and into the dining area.

"Sorry."

Oh, he heard that? Amazing. She rolled her eyes and dug in the refrigerator for the eggs. Couldn't hear his name, but heard that. "You need a Belltone."

"I don't need a belt on."

Her bad mood lessened. Whitleigh snickered, head in the refrigerator. The poor guy needed a hearing exam. How he managed to pass any of his redeployment evaluations was a complete mystery.

She lifted the egg carton, placing it on the counter. Maybe she and Collier needed a day out, enjoying the fall weather. Sounded like a prescription to remedy the rising tension. Whitleigh rapped her fingers on the counter and called out. "You have a half-day tomorrow, right?"

"And?" His tone varied in degrees of frustration — an all too common theme.

"Why don't we go down to Turkey Creek? I heard they have hayrides, pumpkins — fun family things this time of year." She tossed an apron over her head, tying it at the waist. "We haven't done much since you've been home." She squinted.

"You know crowds bother me."

Whitleigh bit at her lip. She folded her arms, moving from the kitchen into the living room. "I'm sure Mondays are less crowded. We can go early too."

Collier sat on the couch, soda in hand. He flipped on the TV, not bothering to make eye contact with her.

The cloud of angst that seemed to hang over their heads needed to dissolve. Whitleigh walked closer, kneeling on the floor in front of him. Couldn't he see her? See how much she cared?

"You're okay, Collier. It's safe here. Linc and I are with you. I love you. He loves you. There's no war going on around us."

His eyes narrowed as he stood. The slamming of the back door served as his only reply.

Whitleigh buried her face in the fold of her floral apron. Linc cooed over the monitor sitting on the coffee table. She listened, her tears soaking into the apron's fabric. Whitleigh tucked her knees beneath her chin. This couldn't be happening. She'd gotten her wish. Collier came home and they were together, but the man who stormed out the door no longer resembled the man she married.

WHITLEIGH hurried from the mailbox. Saturday's mail still sat in the box. Sunday afternoons were usually low key, but with guests coming, many things remained on her to-do-list, including more desserts to bake. Linc's nap only lasted so long. She scanned through the mail.

Junk. Coupons & Special Deals. Ooh, another letter from the University — good news. More junk and yet another return to sender.

Jen wouldn't even take the time to open a card.

Whitleigh smacked the envelope against her leg. Why did she still reach out to her when Jen obviously cut ties? No replies to emails, phone calls, or snail mail. Oh well. She didn't have time to give it any more effort right now.

Whitleigh tucked the mail under her arm and moseyed onto the front porch. The door handle wiggled about in her hand. Just a loose screw. Whitleigh gave it another shake. Yeah, that little Philips screwdriver would do the trick.

Whitleigh slid her sandals off at the doorway. She shuffled from the living room, through the dining area, and into the kitchen. Coupons went in their reserved folder on the counter amongst bills and the like, but the rest, including the card meant for Jen, got tossed in the trash. If Jen wanted to be left alone, Whitleigh would give her space.

Whitleigh scooted down the hall, tiptoeing as she neared Linc's room, and then bounced into their bedroom. "Hey Babes, have you seen my pink shoes?" She dove under their bed, pushing past a variety of footwear. No reply. "My pink shoes. Have you seen them?"

"You know I don't like rhythm and blues."

"What? Ouch." Whitleigh bumped her head on the iron bed frame. "Found them."

"Oh." Collier pulled on a green striped polo shirt, pointing to his ears as Whitleigh emerged. "Guess roadside bombs have left their mark on me." He smiled.

There it was — a glimpse of the old Collier. Smiling. Joking. The Collier she craved. As much as she enjoyed snippets of the past, they served as cruel reminders. Whitleigh's smile dissolved with his, their eyes locking.

She raised on her toes, planting a kiss on his cheek.

His hand brushed her face. "Maybe tonight?"

Whitleigh nodded. Her lips parted and then sealed. He hadn't touched her in weeks. "I've missed you."

"I know. I'm sorry. The last time was …."

Robotic. Unfeeling. Detached. Whitleigh pressed her forehead to his chest.

"It'll be better."

"Have I done something?" Whitleigh lifted her eyes to his.

Collier sighed, shaking his head.

"I know I look different after having a baby, but I'm back down to my normal size now." After months of kickboxing classes, daily walks, and hearty salads. "I work hard to look good for you."

"It's not you at all. It's me. You're beautiful, Whit."

Collier raised her hands, his gaze gentle as he intertwined his fingers with hers. Whitleigh's body warmed.

He leaned in, lips touching hers. "Maybe we don't have to wait until tonight."

"Maybe." She kissed him back.

The baby monitor rattled. Linc was awake. Sigh.

Collier leaned against the wall, rubbing a hand over his mouth.

"A baby changes things." Whitleigh smiled, surely failing to hide her disappointment.

"Yeah. Guess it does." Collier gave her hand a squeeze. "I should get the grill going anyway." He slouched out the door.

"You and me. Tonight." Her words chased him down the hall. Definitely tonight.

WHITLEIGH pulled the last batch of cookies from the oven and added another dash of salt to the simmering pot of chili on the stove.

Layla cleaned the face of her youngest son with the bottom of her navy sweater. "It's nice to see you baking again, Whit." She patted his bottom as he skipped from the kitchen.

"I guess it's been awhile." Perhaps months. Whitleigh wiped her hands on her paisley patterned apron. "Anyway," she sighed, "fall always puts me in a mood to bake."

"Funny thing, 'cause it puts me in a mood to eat what you bake." Layla propped herself against the counter with her elbows. "What is all of this stuff?" She scooted a narrow wooden toolbox from its place against the tile wall and dangled it from her hand. "Vitamins? Herbs? You have a toolbox for this stuff."

"Found the old toolbox at a thrift shop. It's small, cute, and works great." Whitleigh filled the sink with dish soap and water. "Threw on some yellow paint, roughed it up a bit. Cute, huh?"

"Cute? When did you start taking all of these supplements?"

Whitleigh shrugged, washing out a batter bowl. "Trying to stay healthy. Most are teas and powdered vegetables to add to smoothies."

"Gross." Layla shuddered and held the largest bottle close to her face. "Green Foods Digestive Aide. For your digestive health." She tapped the cap and placed it back in the toolbox. "Really, Whit? You eat enough fruits and vegetables that your digestive tract probably twinkles."

Whitleigh laughed out loud, placing the wet bowl in the drying rack. "I'm keeping healthy, lowering stress, you know. A happy digestive system means a healthy immune system."

"Everything okay? Vitamins are great, but this seems like a lot. Anything going on you want to talk about?"

"I'm good."

Layla squinted, her lips twisted to the side.

"You know … it's just." Whitleigh patted her forehead with the backside of her hand. "Things are different with Collier and me. He's, I don't know, not the same, and we're not the same." How insane did that sound? "It's probably nothing really, me just overreacting, complaining."

"None of this sounds silly to me."

Whitleigh held onto her arms, hugging them to her. The kitchen grew quiet. Sizzling sounds from the grill out back played in the background.

"Has he hurt you?"

"Collier? Never." Whitleigh huffed and bit her lip. The hall walls were the only victims in the house.

"I put up with a lot before Jayson got the help he needed, and it wasn't an overnight fix, that's for sure." Layla's brows lifted, creating creases in her forehead. "You've heard the sirens in our neighborhoods, seen the news reports. War does things to people, Whit."

"It's fine. We're fine. He just needs time."

"He may need more than time."

Whitleigh ran her hand along the back of her neck. Layla spoke the truth, but a manual on fixing redeployment issues didn't exist.

"Sometimes these guys come back and subconsciously self-destruct." Layla rested her head on her raised shoulder. "He's seen things, awful things. Of course he's going to struggle a tad." A half snicker slipped from her mouth. "I'd worry if he didn't. Odds are he hasn't just seen things, he's done things."

"What's that mean?" Whitleigh pressed her palms on the counter. Her mind raced.

"Look." Layla stood close, her hand on Whitleigh's shoulder. "Many of them have to do things that would normally go against their moral grain. The constant battle, lack of sleep, lack of emotion. It wears on them."

"So what are you saying?"

"Be careful. Be patient. Sometimes it's hard to love them."

Yeah. Whitleigh blinked her eyes, clenching her jaw as if that would stop the tears forming in the corner of her eyes.

"But keep loving him. He needs it." Layla gave Whitleigh's elbow a squeeze. "Remember love is an action word, not a feeling." She extended open arms. "I'm always here for you if you need me."

Layla gave a hearty squeeze. "You think our hubbies are hitting it off outside?"

"I can't believe this is the first time they've met." Whitleigh sniffed and dabbed her eyes. Thank goodness the subject changed. She strained her neck, peeping out the window over the kitchen sink. Collier and Jayson stood, staring at the grill. "Better than it could be I guess. Collier's not too talkative anymore." The metal sink clanked beneath her tapping. "I'm sure he'll liven up once Pulu and Dock get here." Whitleigh hung a dish towel over her shoulder. "So, what were you saying earlier about Emma? I got a little sidetracked getting things ready, and it's not like I can hear you when you whisper anyway."

Layla rolled her eyes in a dramatic fashion. "Haven't you been watching the news?"

"You know me better than that."

"That guy, what's his name?" Layla snapped her fingers. "Helen's boyfriend, well, ex-boyfriend. The one she was having an affair with."

"Ray? What about him?"

"He's on the news. He's wanted for questioning."

"What?"

"They have reason to suspect he has information regarding several counts of rape."

"Oh my goodness." Whitleigh slammed a hand over her heart. The shed sat outside the kitchen window in her peripheral view. Her hand inched to her throat. Large, angry hands once attempted to squeeze the life from her. Whitleigh gasped.

"I'm thinking the same thing, Whit. You were lucky to have gotten away from him."

"What about Emma? Did he … hurt her?"

"No, no, no. Emma's okay."

"Thank the Lord." Whitleigh sucked in masses of air until her normal breathing pattern returned.

"I knew there was something off about him." Layla rotated, turning a hip toward the counter. "And to think he's serving as a military policeman. It's disgusting. Probably thought he could get away with anything."

Whitleigh shook her head, still rubbing at her throat.

"I know Helen brought a lot of trouble on herself, but my heart still goes out to the woman. She seems to be straightening up."

"Yeah?"

"When she came back for Emma, she was a different person. Happier. At peace. Her husband is going through with their divorce, so she and Emma will be moving back to Florida."

Whitleigh sunk forward. "As much as I am happy for both of them, it kills me to see Emma go." She clasped her hands over her heart. "I wish I had more time to spend with her."

"We're here. The party can start now." A deep, jolly voice echoed through the house. Whitleigh grinned. That must be Dock and the crew. "Come on in."

"Sure smells good in here." Dock rubbed his stomach.

"I bet Cromwell can't even hear us — deaf old man." Pulu cackled, limping forward with his cane.

"You've got the deaf part right." Whitleigh hid a smile.

A shy Annabelle clung to Amy's leg. Amy's cheeks lifted as she held out a grocery sack. "I'm not much of a cook, but I can buy chips."

"That's perfect. Thank you." Whitleigh hugged Amy and took the plastic bag. "Amy, Dock, Pulu, this is our neighbor and friend, Layla, and her husband, Jayson," she pointed toward the back door, "is out back grilling with Collier. They have a whole pack of kids running around." Whitleigh chortled along with Layla.

Pulu and Dock gave Whitleigh a hearty side hug and shook Layla's hand.

Dock wrapped an arm around Amy. "Collier did a good job of picking out a new vehicle for you, Whit. Amy likes that pearly white color. We need a little SUV like that."

"He got a good deal." Whitleigh supported the bag of chips in her arms. "I'm loving the extra room, but I miss driving my little Yota, which is still for sale if you know of anyone interested."

"No way." Pulu thumped his cane on the living room rug. "I barely survived Iraq. I'm not going near that car."

Whitleigh swatted at Pulu as he and Dock shuffled around, guffawing their way to the backyard. Whitleigh peeked after them. Collier's eyes lit up at the sight of his buddies. Her heart warmed and then hardened. She tucked her hair behind her ear and toyed with the pearl earring. His eyes hadn't lit up for her in quite some time. She shook her head and smiled at Layla's touch.

"You okay?"

Whitleigh nodded. "A little hungry, that's all." Linc wormed his way across the living room in a half crawl. She scooped him up in to her arms. "Let's sit down and chat while the guys finish up outside."

Whitleigh avoided eye contact with Layla. That woman could read souls.

"I love your home, Whitleigh." Amy scanned the living room, peeping into the hall for a moment before taking a seat at the dining room table. "You're so creative, and I love how you've arranged the photos down the hall."

Whitleigh gulped. Her stomach flipped. "Oh yeah?" Act cool. Be calm. She sat, shoving a cheese cracker in her mouth.

Layla tapped her knuckles on the table. Whitleigh reached for another cracker, handing one to Linc who ground it in his small fists. Be cool, and Layla won't notice a thing.

Amy's face lit up. "It's like there's no particular pattern to them, but it just clicks."

"Yeah, Whit's real good at stuff like that." Layla's stare held Whitleigh in a death grip.

"You're too nice, Amy." Whitleigh swallowed. "I get a decor idea in my head and kind of throw it up. Sometimes it works." She fanned her face and squirmed in her seat.

"The real food's ready." Dock's voice carried through the screen door.

Whew. "That was quick." Whitleigh let out a silent breath and launched from the table, plopping Linc on her hip. "I'll grab the plates."

"Hey, Collier." Pulu limped inside as Dock held the door. "Where's that pretty brown headed girl? I'm thinking about asking her out."

Whitleigh stopped. Brown headed girl?

Layla and Amy created an assembly line of food and paraded the children through one at a time. They grabbed a juice pouch and bolted outside once more.

Collier mumbled. Whitleigh strained to hear, rustling through silverware and napkins.

"You know, man." Dock crashed down into a chair at the table. "That chick that came to visit you at work the other day. Whit's friend. What's her name?"

"Jen." Whitleigh darted into the doorway of the dining room. "Her name is Jen." She pierced Collier with her eyes.

"Oh, um, I didn't mean anything by it, ma'am." Pulu fidgeted with his cane.

"No worries." Whitleigh let her eyes fall from Collier. "Chili's in the kitchen. It's ready." She untied her apron, urging the knot in her stomach to unravel. The attempt failed. Getting through the meal wouldn't be easy. Whitleigh forced a smile and laid a tray of cookies in front of the hungry guests.

WHITLEIGH took her time chewing her food and refused to make eye contact with Collier for the remainder of the meal. He carried on conversations with Pulu and Dock like her cold shoulder didn't matter.

She bounced Linc on her knee, spooning him bits of chili with a small spoon.

"I don't mean to be offensive," Amy squinted, raising her shoulders. She smiled at Linc. "But, I can't believe how norm …" her voice trailed off as Dock shot a semi-discreet look in her direction.

"It's okay." Whitleigh bobbed her head, offering a slight grin. She welcomed any conversation to take her focus from Collier. "He looks very normal, and he is normal other than his heart. Of course, there are some developmental delays, but he's on track and doing fine."

Collier wiped chili from the side of his mouth. "No one would ever know about his heart just by looking at him."

Whitleigh pursed her lips. Didn't she basically say that?

Collier held out his arms toward Linc. "Come see me, big boy."

Linc whined and nuzzled his face into Whitleigh's pink shirt collar. She rocked him, patting his behind, a little too content with Collier's disappointment. Collier's face sank. He didn't wear embarrassment well.

"Don't feel bad man." Dock whapped Collier on the shoulder. "Annabelle is still getting used to me."

"Deployments do that." Layla nodded, handing one of her younger children a chip from the table. "Each one of our kids were affected in some way, but it gets better. Give it time."

"Yeah." Jayson lifted his chili covered hotdog. "And then it's hard to get them away from you."

Whitleigh chuckled along with the guests.

"I'd like to make a toast." Pulu grinned as he pushed away from the table. Though he winced when standing on his titanium legs, his wide smile never faded. "To family. To old friends," he nodded to Dock and Cromwell. "To new friends," he bowed to the others. "And to the friends we miss." He looked up toward the ceiling. "Here's to Sergeant First Class Prowski, Crawford … Had —" his voice caught. "To Haden, and all of our other buddies. We love you. We miss you."

Linc stretched to grab Whitleigh's water bottle as she lifted it, clanking it with each soda can.

"Man, I can't believe he's gone." Collier cleared his throat, his face just a shade lighter than his crimson shirt. Whitleigh sat straighter. Collier never said much about his buddies that were killed. He didn't say much about the war in general. Collier sniffled, wiping his nose." I still can't believe they're all gone."

Whitleigh drew in a silent breath, pressing the tips of her fingers to her mouth. Interrupting the solemn silence in the room seemed almost sinful and disrespectful at best.

"Crazy times." Dock interlocked his fingers and gazed out the window. "The other day I thought about that little girl, Nu'ma, we rescued from the alley. I wish things would've ended differently."

A little girl? Whitleigh shifted Linc on her knees.

Collier's legs trembled beneath the table. "Let's talk about something else."

"So, Whit, didn't Linc have some sort of a breathing tube?"

"Seriously, Amy?" Dock's face reddened.

"Sorry." Amy lowered her head, stirring at her chili.

"Really, it's okay. I'm glad you're asking. Most people don't talk about it. Guess they don't want to offend us, or maybe they're embarrassed." Whitleigh shrugged. "But yes, he needed oxygen for a while. His last heart surgery helped reroute things so he'd be able to breathe better." Linc yanked away as Whitleigh planted a kiss on top of his head.

Collier leaned forward, folding his fingers. "The surgeons literally rerouted his heart so the working half didn't have to pump so much blood, which allowed for somewhat normal blood flow and oxygen to be passed to all parts of his body."

Was there an echo in the room? Whitleigh tightened her grip on the spoon. Keep calm. She smiled and Collier tossed a grin in her direction.

"Wow." Amy's mouth hung open. "So? He has half a heart."

"Oh my goodness, Amy." Dock's voice strained.

"I promise. It's okay." Whitleigh snickered and worked to ignore the irritatingly pleasant expression on Collier's face. He wouldn't get to her. "Yes, essentially Linc has half a heart."

"But, it's a strong one." Collier chimed in as he dipped the end of his hotdog into his chili. Sometimes smiling proved challenging. Whitleigh settled for a pleasant grin and nodded in agreement.

"I'm really amazed and curious." Amy wiped her hands on the crumbled napkin in her lap. "I want to go to nursing school." She frowned. "Eventually."

"That's a great plan." Whitleigh winced as Linc twisted his dimpled fingers around her hair and sucked on his fists.

"You were in college, right?"

Whitleigh nodded, wiping chili from the corners of her mouth.

"She graduates in December." Layla toasted the air with her soda can.

"Oh yeah? That's so exciting. I can't wait to finish. I mean, I haven't even started yet." Amy's face lit up. She hovered close as Whitleigh untangled Linc's fist from her hair. "So what's your game plan?"

"Game plan?" Whitleigh shrugged. Good question.

Collier left his side conversation with Dock and Pulu. Guess he wanted to know the game plan too.

"Well, teaching is out of the question right now." Whitleigh twisted her lips to the side.

"Guess that means I'm staying in the Army then?" Collier's flippant tone begged a retort.

Whitleigh smoothed a palm along her denim skirt. She rested her hand at the knee. "Staying in was your game plan, right?"

"Guess it is now." Collier clanked his spoon against the chili bowl. Did he have a point to make? Whitleigh wet her lips.

"Staying in is not even in our vocabulary." Dock hee-hawed, shaking his head at Amy who appeared in complete agreement.

"I'm loving the desk job." Pulu used his cane to bang against his prosthetic legs. "I'll ride the Army roller-coaster a bit longer."

"We're lifers." Jayson put his arm around Layla, pulling her closer and placed a kiss on her cheek. Layla blushed.

Whitleigh folded her arms around a drowsy Linc. Layla and Jayson had fought hard to end up so affectionate toward one another. How hard would she and Collier have to fight? Would he even fight? Whitleigh sighed, her shoulders lowered.

"So, Whit," Amy swung a leg, "you were telling me about your career goals."

"Goals." Whitleigh held a breath captive. "I'm thinking teaching will be down the road, you know? When Linc gets a bit older, stronger. Right now, I'd be too scared to leave him with anyone for long periods of time."

"She's not joking." Collier rolled his eyes. "We haven't had a date since I got back."

"That's not true, we — " Whitleigh scratched at her brow. "We had the first night alone."

"Because your mom made you."

"We've been out to eat."

"Linc with us — all three times." He leaned against the back of the creaking chair.

"We can't leave him with a sitter yet." She talked past Collier and arched a brow. Linc didn't seem to mind the movement. "And the slightest cold could be a very bad thing for him."

"You can't keep him in a bubble. He'd probably be walking right now if you'd put him down once in a while."

The room hushed and filled with awkward silences.

Whitleigh chewed on the inside of her jaw. Yeah, he wanted to pick a fight. They glared at one another until reaching a stalemate.

Their friends took advantage of the tension by raking their spoons against their chili bowls. Coughing and looking about the room, they were the definition of uncomfortable.

"Whit, I would love to watch Linc." Layla broke the tension with her sincere offer. "He likes our kiddos and we love him like our own." The woman was a saint, not faultless, but a saint just the same.

"I guess we'll have to set up a date soon." Whitleigh wagged a leg, her tongue pressed against the inside of her cheek. "Maybe Pulu would like to join us. He can invite Jen."

Pulu's head shot up, opportunity written in his wide grin.

Whitleigh glowered at Collier. "Since she hasn't returned any of my calls, maybe you'd like to see if she's available for a double date. You have her number, right, Collier?"

Layla ushered a few of her children back down the hall. Collier sat motionless as Whitleigh steadied her breathing.

Pulu hunkered down in his seat. "I'm good, really. Not much on double dates." Poor guy. Pulu wouldn't like Jen anyway. No one liked a plotting, backstabbing home-wrecker. Whitleigh kept her chin high, refusing to break her eye grip from Collier. She needed to stay strong.

Collier broke away from their stare down first. Victory. Whitleigh hid a grin. She pushed her shame aside and focused on the half eaten hotdog on her plate, the most nonthreatening thing about the entire dinner.

The heavens rumbled.

Pulu turned his head to the back window. "Guess the weatherman was right." His lighthearted tone helped lighten the mood, but dark clouds formed over top Pike's Peak, creating a misty haze of rain. A few strikes of lightening targeted innocent trees.

"Crazy how we can see the bad weather coming down from the mountain at us." Jayson swallowed the food in his mouth with an audible gulp.

Yeah. Crazy. Crazy like her husband. Whitleigh crossed her ankles, resting the side of her head in her palm. Linc cradled his cheek on her shoulder.

Layla dismissed herself from the table and opened up the back door. "Time to come in kiddos."

The herd clambered in, stampeding down the hall to join the rest of the children. Whitleigh willed the corners of her mouth to lift. If only she could get through the meal, then she and Collier could hash out their issues later.

"Stay in the baby's room," Jayson called after his kids. "Share. Play nice."

Amy giggled. "What do you think, James? Should we have more?"

Dock's eyes bulged from their sockets. "No way."

"Parenthood changes things." Collier's words launched in her direction. They exploded like a grenade inside of Whitleigh.

Her chin dimpled, but a quick smile kept the tears from coming. "Marriage changes things."

No one moved.

"You know, it's getting kind of late." Jayson eyed the watch on his wrist.

In a few gathering motions, all of the guests were up and heading for the door.

Amy tugged on Annabelle's shoe strings as she squirmed. "Whitleigh, I had a great time. Thank you."

"You and Dock are always welcome in our home."

"I understand what you're going through." Amy embraced Whitleigh, her words a faint whisper.

"Thank you." Whitleigh returned the squeeze.

Dock gathered a reluctant Annabelle in his arms and held Amy's hand as they walked out the front door. They appeared better off than she and Collier at the moment.

Pulu high-fived Collier and bumped chests before exiting. *Men.* Whitleigh huffed.

Jayson rounded up their crew, leaving Layla to linger behind.

"You call me if you need me. Understand?" Layla held onto Whitleigh's forearm, her tone stern and low.

"I'll be okay." Whitleigh smiled, hardly convincing herself.

"Remember, pray and pick up your Bible. There's more wisdom and peace there than in any of your herbal teas."

"You're right." Whitleigh nodded, letting her arms dangle at her side.

"It's hard to love someone when they're being unloving." Layla tugged on Whitleigh's arm. "And frankly, both of you were being pretty nasty to each other."

"What?" Whitleigh folded her arms. Did Layla even hear Collier's comments? "He's seeing Jen. Behind my back."

"Talk to him. Calmly. Get the story straight before you're ready to kill him."

Whitleigh nodded.

"And seriously, call me if things get out of hand." Layla held up two pistol fingers. "I'm not afraid to come packing."

Whitleigh managed a brief smirk. "Deal."

WHITLEIGH planted her feet in front of the kitchen sink, plunging her hands into the searing soapy water, scrubbing each dish as if it were the object of her fury. The last of the dishes were done. What else could she wipe down?

"We need to talk." Collier's voice sounded too kind, too full of remorse.

Whitleigh turned. She wouldn't fall for those deep blue pleading eyes. "Talk."

"Don't be this way, Whit."

"How else am I supposed to be?" She planted her hands firm on her hips. "You've been talking to Jen. Again. After you said you were done speaking with her. Remember that conversation we had months ago? Now you're meeting her. With … without me knowing."

"We met a few times, for dinner and lunch — it wasn't anything."

"Not anything?" Whitleigh's stomach turned. "You're dating her?" She swallowed back the vomit. "What else are you doing with her behind my back? Sleeping with her? 'cause you're sure not sleeping with me."

"I love you." He ran his hands alongside this head. "She doesn't mean anything. I never slept with her."

"You're disgusting." His words stung more than any shrapnel from an explosion. She knocked a cup from the counter. It shattered on impact, shooting a thousand shards of glass in all directions. "How could you? Get out. Now." Her blood boiled. She clenched the counter, willing her legs to stand.

"Whit, please. I didn't sleep with her. It wasn't like that."

"Don't." She shoved him away. "You think it's okay 'cause you didn't have sex with her? You're still a cheater. Get out."

"I love you. I just — I couldn't talk to you."

"Get your hands off of me."

"Whit."

"What? I don't understand. Is that what you're going to tell me? I don't get it." Her stomach churned. "And she does?"

"She listens."

"I'd listen if you'd talk."

"I don't want you to hear."

"Hear what?"

"You don't need to hear."

"I want to hear whatever you have to tell me. I'm your wife."

"You won't understand."

"She doesn't understand."

He covered his face. "You'll hate me."

"Please, just talk to me. I'm trying so hard to help. To make us work." Whitleigh's tears burned hot against her cheeks. Her eyes stung as mascara melted from her lashes.

Collier groaned, he clenched his fist, a vein popping from his forehead.

"Talk." No way would she step back, no matter how mad he got. No matter how tense the situation. "What can she hear that I can't? Huh?" Whitleigh waved her hands in the air, firing bits of dishwater across the kitchen. Collier stood, head against the doorway. "Talk to me." She stomped her foot, throwing a sopping dishrag at him. It fell to the tile floor without any response. "What is it?" The question tore from her throat. "Tell me."

In one swell swoop, Collier clamped ahold of Whitleigh's shoulders. She lunged back, but couldn't break free. "I've killed people. On purpose. Too many to count. " His face now inches from hers. "It didn't bother me and still doesn't."

Her mouth went dry. This was it. She'd be on the news like other Army wives whose husbands killed them in a fit of rage. Collier loosened his hold, and Whitleigh snuck in a quick breath. Her mind raced and slowed with her heart rate. "It's your job. You did what you had to do."

"Don't you think I know this?"

She kept still and silent.

"It doesn't keep me from being a monster." His jaw clamped shut. "God can't forgive me and I don't want his forgiveness anyway."

She managed to swallow. "What else? Talk to me."

"I can't relax. Ever. I don't sleep, and when I'm awake I'm always planning an escape route wherever I go, looking for suspicious behavior, or worrying something on the side of the road is going to blow up."

She fixed her eyes on his face and thought better of speaking.

He stepped back. "And while I'm constantly scanning perimeters, Whit, I feel nothing but anger and numbness. I'm a machine. Are you understanding that?"

Not entirely. Whitleigh managed a slight shake of the head. "I'm listening."

"I'm telling you that I feel nothing. I can't feel." He palmed his forehead, face distorting. "I can look at you and our son, and … and I don't feel a thing."

Whitleigh stumbled back, both hands covering her mouth. How could he say this? She caught her balance on the dish drying rack. Silverware clattered and crashed to the floor.

"Something's wrong with me." His shoulders shook. "I'm trying to feel again, but I can't. Nothing works."

"Except Jen." The words slipped between the fingers pressed to her lips.

"You do everything on your own. Taking care of Linc. Even fixed the screen door handle by yourself." Collier's arms hung limp to his side. "She needed me. You don't."

Something snapped within. Whitleigh lunged forward. "I needed you. I've always needed you." She slammed her fists into Collier's chest. "Where were you when I was almost killed? And for Linc's birth? I've had to be independent. It's how I've survived. It's how all Army wives survive. Don't put all of this on me."

Collier thudded against the kitchen wall and slid to the floor.

Whitleigh gazed at the hunched over defeated man at her feet. Broken pieces of her soul fell to the ground, leaving sizable wounds.

She dissolved to the ground, holding her head between two trembling hands. "How do we fix this?"

"Can we fix this?"

"I don't even know where to start."

The night sky poured in from the kitchen window. Whitleigh closed her eyes. At least Linc was safe and warm, tucked in his crib, far from ground zero. Divorce had never been in her vocabulary, but it danced on the tip of her tongue. Did any other way exist? Whitleigh released a ragged sigh that matched Collier's.

A series of quick, sharp knocks at the door jolted them both to their feet. Collier reached the door before Whitleigh even thought to try. No good news came at this hour.

"Mrs. Ryan?" Collier held the door open.

"It's Jen." Layla held her pink robe tight around her body.

"What about her?" Whitleigh pushed through, brows woven together.

"She tried to kill herself." Layla burst into jagged sobs.

Whitleigh held onto Collier's shoulder. "Don't walk out that door, Collier."

He shrugged her off.

Layla wiped her eyes. "I'm heading to the hospital. I thought you needed to know, Whit." Layla hurried from the porch and into the glow of the buzzing streetlamp.

Collier fidgeted with his dog tags, pacing the living room floor. He untucked his polo shirt.

"Don't think about it. She can wait until tomorrow." Could she? Whitleigh bit at her thumbnail. Jen had been her best friend. A good one. For a while. "You and I still have to work things out."

"Do we?" For a moment he froze. Whitleigh stood near the front door as if she could physically keep him from leaving. "I have to go. This is all my fault. I have to make sure she's okay." Collier grabbed his wallet and keys from the side door table.

"You can't."

Collier pushed past. "I won't be long."

"If you leave this house to see her, don't think about coming back." Her chest heaved in an uneven rhythm that matched the blood pulsing through her body.

Collier didn't look back. He stepped outside with too much ease. The door slammed a mere inch from Whitleigh's face.

JEN listened. She cared. That's right. She cared a lot. Collier slammed the car door shut, sending a booming echo in the hospital parking garage. Jen couldn't die. She shouldn't want to die. He picked up the pace. She needed him. She'd be happy to see him. There'd be no fussing and no insurmountable expectations that he could never meet.

He could put Whit out of his mind anytime he wanted. Way too simple. Yeah, simple. The past was the past. He and Whit were over, but what about Linc? He knew what it felt like to have an absent father. Collier filled his cheeks with air and puffed a cloud into the night. The situation grew even more complicated. Nearing the emergency room entryway, he swiped a hand over his brow.

Whit. That smile. Collier pushed it from his mind and pressed forward. She infuriated him, but he couldn't deny his love for her. He paused, almost tripping over his own feet. What about the commitment he'd made to her on their wedding day?

None of it mattered now. It was over. He'd messed up anyway.

The automatic hospital doors parted, but Collier couldn't enter. His body refused to allow his feet to move.

He vowed before God, his friends, and family, to love and honor Whit until death made them part. Since when did breaking promises become his thing? Shattering hearts and hopes belonged to his father.

Collier panted as his throat constricted.

"What've I done?" An autumn breeze floated past. The icy nip in the wind manifested regret. "What've I become?"

His feet might as well have been heavy mortar rounds. "I shouldn't be here." He couldn't go home. Not now. No way would Whit take him back, nor would he expect her to. Did he want to return to Whit? Collier's head spun.

And Jen? Collier lowered his head, dropping his chin to his chest. Seeing her tonight would only make the situation worse. He'd done enough damage leading her on. Collier muttered to himself, smacking his thighs with an open fist.

People walked around him with caution. What did it matter if they thought him crazy? He must've been insane to walk away from his wife and child.

"THANKS for letting me crash here tonight." Collier caught the pillow Pulu launched in his direction.

"Like old times again, back in Korea." Pulu clicked off the small light at his nightstand and the box sized barrack room went dark.

"Yeah. Like old times." But different. Very different. Collier propped the pillow behind his neck. The pillowcase, musty and faded, reeked of Army — an unmistakable odor. The stubborn sofa pushed against his back, allowing for no comfortable positions.

"I'm glad Whit kicked you out. You deserved it."

"I walked out." Collier kept his eyes shut, embarrassed to admit.

"What?" Pulu tossed about his twin sized bed and clicked the lamp on once more. "You're an idiot. Over some dumb girl."

"I know. I get it." Pulu never could keep his mouth shut. Collier grumbled and sat, bringing his elbows to his knees, biting his tongue until the metallic taste of blood proved too much to handle. "I've made a mess of things."

"That's the biggest understatement of the year, dude."

Collier dodged a crusty French fry and an empty Styrofoam cup. Whit had better aim than Pulu.

"I can't believe you." Pulu yanked his dog tags from his neck and

hurled those too. Collier swatted them away before they hit his face. "I'd throw my legs if I thought I'd actually hit you." Pulu growled. "So did you do it? Did you really have an affair?"

It was what it was, sexual contact or not. He nodded, unable to lift his eyes. Of all the things he could've done, why this? Why step out on Whit? Collier swallowed back the sour bile from his stomach.

"Idiot. For real, totally dumb." Pulu slapped the bed sheets where his legs should've been. "And to think I wanted to date that chick. I almost went out with a home-wrecker."

Pulu's words stung and added to the guilt. "Jen's not a home wrecker, she's just lost right now."

"Oh, please. And what? You're the person to help her find the way? That's a joke." He rolled his eyes. "Have you forgotten about Dock's affairs? You're about to be a Sergeant. You have to lead by example, not going around doing idiotic, immoral things. What would Haden say about this?"

Haden, his faith-filled friend. Collier's heart cracked. Haden would've been crushed by the news. Collier tugged on the thin, coarse, Army green blanket stretched over his body. His skin itched from the material, but at least he was warm. Warmth provided some source of solace from the chilling reality.

Collier's knuckles whitened. "I totally understand why Dock clocked you in Iraq."

"That was a lucky shot. I could take him any day." He snorted, shaking his head. "So how are you going to fix this?"

Collier laced his fingers behind his head. He stared at the wall as if it would give some sort of marching orders out of this mess, but the walls were stone, silent and bare.

"If I were you, I'd be begging for forgiveness. I mean, beg-ging." Pulu's head moved up and down in slow motion. "Your wife is hot, dude, and an amazing cook. She's put up with you being gone for two years and your craziness. And don't think all of your soldiers haven't noticed your mood swings. It's like you're PMS-ing or something."

"You've got to learn a little tact." A hotel room would be better than staying with Pulu. If only it was payday, Collier could check in somewhere else.

"You want me to sugarcoat the truth? Nah. Not my style."

Of course not. Collier rocked his neck from side to side.

"You really think the two of you are over?" Pulu's voice softened.

"I don't know how it couldn't be. I blew it. Bad."

"Why didn't you come to me or Dock before you did this? Aren't we friends?"

"The best." Collier's brows lifted as his heart deflated. Pulu's eyes and mouth cast downward.

Great. As if disappointing Whit wasn't enough. He'd let down one of his best friends.

Collier scraped a palm over the stubble on his face. Whit loved that rugged look. He sighed. Why didn't he talk to his buddies? "I didn't think to tell anyone. Maybe I knew what the two of you would say. Maybe I didn't want to hear it."

"That's honest." Pulu's lips folded into a thoughtful pout. His stocky arms crossed. "You're not alone, you know that? You're not the only one who's going through things. We all experienced a lot of awful stuff over there, man."

"I know that. I do." Collier pressed the tips of his fingers together until they turned white. "You seem to be handling things fine for losing both your legs."

"Some days, some days not. I do my best not to focus on what I lost or who I lost."

"I used to think you were just a troubled kid. Sounds like you've got it all together."

"Nah, Haden just introduced me to the only one who does."

"God?"

Pulu nodded, hands folded over this stomach.

"I'm not ready to talk about God or even go to Him about anything." Collier's shoulders sank. He stared at his palms, unable to lift his eyes.

"You're still blaming yourself for that little girl's death, aren't you?"

Collier's lips sealed. His breathing stopped. Nu'ma — the orphaned girl they'd rescued in the alley, the one who risked her life to provide intel to the Americans on the whereabouts of insurgents. "She didn't deserve to go that way." Held as a human shield. "It was my bullet that hit her."

"That's impossible to know."

"I know it, without a doubt. I killed her." Nu'ma's body went limp after he'd pulled his trigger. Collier urged the memory to move, but it stayed put like a wall of steel. "I tried to hit him, but — "

"Dock said it could've been anyone."

"We got that man though." Collier nodded. Justice had been served in some sense.

"You blame yourself for the others too? Haden. Prowski."

"How can I not?" Collier's body shook.

"You talked to Whit about any of this?"

Collier's head sank between his shoulders. That should suffice as a no.

The heater kicked on, blowing a steady stream of warm air through the randomly placed vents about the barrack room. Collier bit down on a piece of skin on the inside of his jaw. "Why am I still alive? Do you know how many times I should've died?"

"Too many to count." Pulu's face sank. "And you wonder why you need to look into therapy."

Collier drew in a long, jagged breath. "Pulu, there's something wrong with me. Really wrong." Saying it out loud helped, like releasing a valve. "I'm some sort of freak."

"You're not a freak, but you need to get help, man."

"I can't. That's a career death sentence. I'm an infantry soldier, not some weak link that has to cry to someone about my war experiences."

"This isn't just about your war experiences."

Collier slouched back into the couch cushion. "What else is it about?"

"Really? Come on." Pulu scratched at his head, eyes growing larger each second. "I'm the son of a Korean prostitute and you're the son of a man who killed your mother and brother."

Collier's ears rang, drowning out the beating of his heart.

"Calm down, Cromwell." Pulu held his palms out. "My point is, our life experiences combined with our war experiences is reason enough to get some help. There's no shame in that." His shoulders rose and fell in a swift beat. "I'm starting counseling next week."

"You?"

"Surprised?"

Collier ran a finger over the top of his lip. This was good news, but strange. Weak people sought help, right?

"Dock and his wife are looking into getting into a program too."

"What?" No way would Dock see some shrink. "I don't want to be one of those people, blaming war for all my problems, just trying to make a buck and take the Army for a ride."

"I think you've got a pride issue."

"Maybe I do, but I've got a family to think about."

"Not if you don't get help. You think Whit can stay with you the way you are? You think Linc wants some distant ogre for a father?"

Collier bared his teeth, cracking his knuckles. He didn't want that for Linc. Linc deserved more. Everything he never received and beyond.

Collier tucked in his upper lip, rising to his feet. "Seeing some head doctor won't get me promoted. No pay raises, maybe kicked out of the Army, and then how can I take care of Linc? What about health-care for him?" Collier pointed his finger. "Don't even try to tell me you haven't seen guys getting kicked out for this PTSD stuff."

"Look." Pulu's sigh teetered on the edge of exasperation. "You can't keep going on like this. You need to find a way to get better, and then try to make things right with Whit. Hey," he gasped, his mouth morphed into an oval. "That guy, your neighbor. The dude who was over your house tonight. Jayson."

"What about him?"

"He was at Walter Reed for a while for PTSD, right?"

"No. I'm not asking him for help or advice or anything."

"You want to get better?"

Collier nodded.

"You want Whit back?"

"She won't — "

"I asked if you wanted her back."

"Yes. No." Collier smacked his hands over his face. "I don't know what I want anymore."

"You better figure it out." Pulu's voice grew serious. "There are lots of guys out there that would be willing to take your place in her life and be a father to your son."

Pulu's stare lasted a little too long for Collier's comfort. Collier coughed and interlocked his hands. "You're right."

"I know I am. Now get some sleep." The light clicked off and the night spread through the room. Collier prayed. Unfamiliar and awkward, he lifted his clasped hands until his knuckles touched the tip of his nose.

THREE days passed since their blowout, with little word from Whit. Was she happy? Collier circled the neighborhood for the fifth time in twenty-four hours. Whit's midsized SUV parked in its usual spot. Her Yota sat in the back of the parking lot with the For Sale sign still intact.

He slowed at the entryway of the cul-de-sac. Stopping might not be in his best interest. If she took his calls sparingly, then she probably wouldn't open the door. Communicating in voice mails made their parting seem more like an indefinite deployment.

It could be a good time to check in with Jayson though. Collier flipped on the right turn signal and pulled into the neighborhood. He eyed the dashboard. Forty-five minutes still left in his lunch break. Yeah, forty-five minutes allowed time to chat with Jayson and maybe check in on Linc.

Collier rolled to a complete stop, parking in front of Jayson's housing unit.

Breathe.

His chest tightened.

What was worse: asking Jayson to hook him up with some Army shrink, or seeing Whit? Collier slid his hands up and down the steering wheel. Both scenarios were terrifying.

"Long time, no see. Can I help you?"

Collier jumped in his seat, nearly strangled by the seat belt. Layla came out of nowhere.

"Um, I um, was uh." He unbuckled and cleared his throat, sliding from the driver's seat of his pickup truck. "I was hoping to catch Jayson. Is he around?"

"Hold on a sec." Layla's laugh lines looked hard at work, her face dotted with paint. "Wait for me, kiddos. Put the lid back on the paint. We'll finish the pumpkins in a second." She seemed genuinely happy for a woman with too many kids to count and a husband who went loco on her for a bit.

Maybe hope remained for him and Whit.

"Sorry about that, Collier." She smirked. "Getting ready for the Fall Festival."

"We have one here?"

"Whit's going. Several of the FRG's planned it. You know, a fun family thing."

"Oh. Then maybe I shouldn't go."

"Or maybe you should."

"Um, anyway. Is Jayson here? I'd like to talk with him about … stuff." Collier fiddled with the cuffs of his uniform.

"He'll be in around five. You want to stop by for dinner?"

"Uh." Collier focused, but his eyes continued to stray toward his home. The blinds moved in the front window. Was Whit watching? "Yeah. Dinner would be nice." He shoved his hands in his pockets, managing a grin. "Sure beats the DFAC meals."

Layla chuckled. "Could you help me with something?"

"Sure." Collier was positive his voice cracked.

"I've been aiming to get these pumpkins over to Whit to paint, but I've been too busy with all the kids. Fall break wears me out." She swiped her forehead, smearing the paint. "Could you please take them over?"

"I, um, not sure that's the best idea."

"It's the best one I've had all day. Here." Layla laid a pumpkin in his arms. "There's more."

Before he could agree, his arms were filled with pumpkins of various shapes and sizes. Guess he had a solid reason for seeing Whit and Linc now, but did he want to? Of course. Why else had he been stalking the neighborhood? Collier nodded and marched across the street.

The front door flew open before his boot hit the first step. Whit's face appeared, devoid of any emotion except utter disdain. Her eyes, a shade of red, narrowed as she stood in a closed-off stance that said many things without uttering a word.

Collier's legs trembled beneath him. "I was just in the neighborhood." He lifted the pumpkins. "Brought these over." His throat dried.

"Thanks."

"I was hoping to see Linc." He sat the pumpkins down, arranging them neatly on the small front porch. "Thought maybe you and I could talk."

"Not much more to say."

She was wrong. Much more remained. Words tore through Collier's mind, but couldn't find their way to his mouth.

Collier's arms hung to the side. "Can I see Linc?"

"I'll bring him out." She leaned from the doorway. "Oh. You've got mail. It came certified." Whitleigh pointed an envelope. It slid from her hand into his. "I didn't open it."

Collier gave the manila packet a shake and tucked it under his arm. It felt too heavy to be divorce papers and those wouldn't come so soon.

Her long hair bounced around her shoulders as she turned once more. "Don't expect to stay too long. We're going out soon."

"You and Linc? Where you going?" The words popped out. He didn't reserve the right to ask those kinds of questions anymore.

"I took an event planning job for our FRG leader."

"A job?"

"I've got to find a way to make it on my own now."

Maybe the envelope did contain divorce papers. Collier's knees weakened. Heat tingled in his face. She was moving on. He swallowed. "I'm happy for you." Lie.

"It pays well. A change of command ceremony."

"Oh. Officers." Collier huffed. "Moving on up, huh?"

"It's a job, Collier." She rolled her eyes. Even disgusted, the woman was beautiful. She licked her lips and rubbed her arm. The material from her green cardigan sleeve bunched. "Look. I've seen a lawyer."

Collier held his hands to his hips, bracing himself.

"It's just better this way. We've grown apart." Her words were the harshest kind of soft. "Let's stop kidding ourselves and call it what it is … over."

It couldn't be. He shook his head. "Maybe for you."

Collier bit his lip. How could he have been so stupid?

Whitleigh's long lashes lowered. Her face grew solemn. "I'll go get Linc."

"I'll wait." Collier stood at the doorway. He'd wait forever if he had to.

WHITLEIGH ignored the red flashing light on the answering machine and sulked down the hall and into her bedroom. Collier stayed longer than she should've allowed. She stopped in front of her dresser. With care, she overturned the photos. The ones from their travels out west, others of their wedding and honeymoon, face down. They served as reminders of a shattered happily ever after. Their Forever List, tattered and dust covered, filled with a lifetime of things left undone and unresolved, rested behind a small wood jewelry box.

Whitleigh clasped the sharp edges of the antique vanity piece and peered into the mirror. Her worn mascara highlighted the dark circles beneath her eyes. Daylight poured into the room, but shadows were all she could see. She tugged at her wedding band, slipped it off, and shoved the set into the top drawer. Collier could still wear his if he wanted, but she wouldn't.

They weren't supposed to end this way. She chased another tear away with her fingers. They weren't supposed to end at all.

The mirror projected the reflection of their bed — her bed. One side laid untouched. Collier's Army PT uniform draped over the end as if he were in the shower, preparing to go to work, but he was gone. They were over.

His belongings intermingled with hers. A black tie hung alongside her beaded necklaces on the wall. His boots sat beside her heels. On the nightstand, her glass of water perched next to his empty soda can. Unraveling their lives seemed impossible. Yesterday, the lawyer spoke of divorce as cut and dry, a painless surgery, but it was much more.

Much, much more. Like a ripping or tearing of her very soul. Whitleigh's sigh hitched in her chest. She doubled over. The aching in her chest throbbed unbearably. The memories, kisses, touches, fights, angry words, and betrayal sent her pulse racing. Loving and hating someone at the same time once seemed impossible.

She willed herself to face the mirror. Linc needed a mother, not a moping mess. Whitleigh wiped her chagrined cheeks, her eyes welling with another bout of tears. Linc needed a father too.

The way Collier played with him today — it was bittersweet to watch. Whitleigh reached for the hairbrush resting on an antique laced doily and ran it aimlessly through her hair. Custody battles would be in her future. She slumped forward as another sob escaped from her sore throat. When would the crying stop?

Whitleigh clenched her fists and sent the hairbrush flying. It crashed into their wedding picture mounted on the wall. The glass shattered and the frame fell to the floor with a thud. Broken. Just like her.

Why did Collier do this?

She clutched the Forever List in a white knuckled grip and tore it apart as she crumbled to the floor. Tiny pieces of aged paper floated about and coated the carpet. Her hands trembled. Whitleigh fell prostrate, chest heaving with each deep sob.

Linc toddled, slid, and crawled his way into her room as only innocence could do. He'd be walking soon for sure. She lifted him in her arms and rocked, struggling to hum a tune.

His resemblance to Collier grew on daily basis. She hugged him close. Keeping the good memories alive for Linc was essential. Not all her times with Collier were bad. Maybe hard, but not bad.

Whitleigh ran her cheek alongside Linc's. So soft. So precious and worth going on for. No matter how difficult, she must go on. After all, many others suffered as much, if not more, than her.

Good times would return.

Whitleigh rose to her feet, moved Linc to her hip, and walked to the closet. An Event Planner needed to look the part, if not feel it.

"What do you think, Linc?" She kissed the top of his head, breathing in that sweet baby scent. "What should I wear? You like this one?"

Whitleigh pulled a navy seersucker blazer from the closet ranks. Linc babbled, more amused with the texture of the fabrics at his disposal than anything else.

She needed something professional, but not too over-the-top.

Did it say soon-to-be divorced? How many people knew already? How could she go on with her life, or even focus enough to make a living?

Deployments made her a single mom, but divorce would make it a sentence. Whitleigh pushed the tension rising in her chest aside and clung to Linc. "We'll make it through this." Her eyes cast upward. "Please God, help us make it through."

Her phone rang, buzzing in a half circle on the nightstand. Mom again. Whitleigh blew at a tuft of hair matted to her tear streaked cheeks. She couldn't keep hiding from the calls. Whitleigh grabbed the phone.

"Whitleigh Jane Cromwell." The middle name always served as a bad sign. "You've been giving me heart spasms not answering your phone. Do I need to fly out there?"

"I'm okay." Her tone dropped octave. "Or I will be."

"You can't just drop this kind of news to me on a voice mail and not return any of my calls. What's going on?"

"There's not much else to say mom. I told you everything there was to tell in my message." Whitleigh laid Linc on the bed and sat beside him as he rolled between pillows, giggling to himself.

"Collier must be a mess."

"Really, Momma? You're taking his side?" Unbelievable. Whitleigh folded her legs. "After everything he's put me through? Haven't I been through enough? Sacrificed enough?"

"I'm not taking sides. I'm concerned how he's dealing with his father's death, and — "

"Wait? Charles died? What? When?"

"Whit, honey, I left you messages."

"Does he even know?"

"How should I know? Your Dad said he mailed off a letter a couple of days ago, but we haven't heard from Collier."

"A letter?" The certified envelope she didn't open. "Oh, Momma." Whitleigh bowed her head, her body sliding lower into the mound of pillows at the headboard. "This is terrible." Not only had Collier received word of his father's passing, but his divorce papers would arrive soon.

"You and Collier have to fix things. Work it out, baby. Please."

"Momma you don't know what you're asking." Whitleigh tucked one arm under the other, laying her head back.

"Whit, honey, is there any part of you that wants to fix this?"

"Yes. No." Whitleigh slammed her eyes shut. "I don't know. I just want it all to go away or go back to the way it was, before the Army, before I ever met Jen or moved out to Colorado."

"Those aren't options."

No, they weren't.

"Even if I stayed, even if we tried to work it out, how can I ever look at him the same after what he did?"

"God is in control, baby. It takes time and a lot of prayer."

Prayer. She'd know. Being married to a man whose life once compared to Collier's father, required many hours knelt by a bedside talking to God.

Whitleigh rolled her eyes. Hadn't she prayed enough?

"Momma, I can't right now." Whitleigh glanced at the broken frame against the wall. "Emotionally, I'm off the charts."

"You're wounded, Whit, and so is he."

Wounded. Right. She was the wounded warrior's wife. It was true. Whitleigh wet her lips. She'd seen Collier's wounds with her own eyes. The desperation and fear on his face. They were both two hurt people, inflicting more pain on each other. "I can't stay with him. It's doing more damage than good."

"You made a vow to love him for better or worse."

"He broke his vow, Momma."

"But you didn't."

Whitleigh pressed down on her folded legs. "I've already made up my mind. I'll talk with you later." The phone went silent, but her thoughts couldn't be hushed.

THE late Saturday morning sun punished her tear swollen eyes. Six days after her fallout with Collier and the crying hadn't subsided. She balanced Linc on a hip. An overstuffed diaper bag and purse hung like lead from her shoulder. "I won't be gone too long." Whitleigh placed Linc into Layla's outstretched arms.

Layla drew in a deep breath. For once, words escaped her.

"Thanks for keeping him for me." Whitleigh managed a smile. "Are you sure it's okay? I've never left him before."

"Whit, I got it. I wouldn't have offered to watch him if I wasn't serious."

Whitleigh nodded. Good point, but it was still hard to leave. She bit at her lip, extending a hand for Linc to hold.

"Seriously, Whit. I can do this. You just go on and do whatever it is you need to do."

"Yeah." Whitleigh drug the toe of her heel into the sidewalk. "So, anyway. Um, I was wondering, you know, since Collier's been stopping by your place, if he's okay? I mean, does he seem alright to you?"

"What do you think?"

Whitleigh scratched at her chin. "I want to make sure he's alright."

"Then you're asking the wrong person."

"Layla." That woman. Whitleigh frowned.

"You been baking? There's flour on your collar."

"Oh." Whitleigh swiped at her blazer collar. "Sort of." She dug in the diaper bag and pulled a square plastic container from its depths. "Can you give these to Collier? I'm sure he'll be stopping by your place again, sometime soon."

So what if she did make those cookies with herbal ingredients bound to clean out his colon? Paybacks could take on many facets.

Layla's mouth slid into a sly grin. "Cookies? You baked him a treat?" She scoffed, taking the container in hand. "What's this, a peace treaty?"

"Something like that." Whitleigh smudged her lips together and loosened the sweater around her neck.

"You planning to poison that man?"

Whitleigh huffed. Not poison. Just a day hanging out with the toilet. Revenge. "Thought I'd be nice."

"Right." Layla sniffed around the lid. "They smell harmless."

"Just make sure he gets them."

"Of course."

Wasn't the death of his father and divorce papers enough for Collier to handle? Why sentence him to more grief with laxative laced cookies?

"By the way, I knew you noticed him dropping in. You're a terrible spy."

Whitleigh raised her brows. "I've learned from the best."

"And while I've got you here, don't do anything crazy while you're out."

Whitleigh gulped, her laugh a tad bit too nervous. "What makes you say that?"

"I know that look."

Huh. Whitleigh held her purse to her side, kissed Linc, and stepped from the porch. "Be back in an hour. You know what?" She reached back of the cookies. "I'll take these and give them to him later or something."

"Sure. Right." Layla waved Whitleigh on. "Oh. Wait. You still need me to watch Linc tonight?"

Oh. Tonight. "The event planning meeting." Whitleigh's heels caught in the grass. "Yeah. I'm only checking out the layout of the community center. Getting ideas, you know? Shouldn't take hardly any time. Oh." Whitleigh held up an index finger. "That reminds me. Do you mind if I use the painted pumpkins for the ceremony? The white ones with gold glitter. I can come get them after the Fall Festival."

"Of course. You're still going to the festival, right?"

Whitleigh nodded. "If I can get Linc's costume finished by Friday." Depression consumed most of her time. "I can't believe how fast this year has flown. We'll be celebrating Thanksgiving and Christmas before you know it." Though, no telling where. Would she move back to Kentucky? Whitleigh paused, glancing at her bare left ring finger.

"Just so you know, Collier will probably be here when you get back from the community center. He's coming over for dinner."

"Again? You're doing this on purpose. We're through, Layla."

"So you keep saying, but nothing's ever over until it's done." It was no good talking to her. Layla tilted her head in a nonchalant manor. "Besides, he and Jayson have been hanging out."

"I bet." Whitleigh rolled her eyes. What was Collier up to?

It didn't matter.

Whitleigh clenched her purse as she stomped toward the car.

"Have fun."

"You know it." Fun. Yeah, that's what going to confront a home wrecker was.

WHITLEIGH lifted her chin and marched through the emergency room doors to the front desk.

Visiting hours were in session and Jen was about to receive the visit of her life. Whitleigh secured the family and friend pass — what a joke — to her pocket and pushed through the thick metal doors. Her heels clicked, punching the tiles beneath with each swift step.

What would she say first? Maybe nothing needed to be said. Maybe a good old fashioned drag out would ensue. She could show Jen what a cardigan & pearl wearing Kentucky girl could do. Whitleigh pushed her hair in place. Such things were fun to imagine, but not worth the aftermath.

She entered Jen's room, giving a quick, quaint smile to a nurse who appeared concerned.

"Why?" The words sped from Whitleigh's mouth faster than a bullet from its chamber. "Tell me why?"

Jen nodded and the nurse shuffled from the room, closing the door on her way out.

Jen's dry, cracked lips parted. She whimpered. Monitors beeped at her bedside, and white bandages held her wrists together. Her eyes glimmered as a few tears began to trickle down her cheeks.

Whitleigh stepped back. Jen looked worse than she could've imagined. The fighting spirit that fueled Whitleigh's entry into the hospital dissipated. She dug her fingernails into her hips. Why did she still have to care? Jen was a backstabber. Whitleigh swallowed hard, working to keep a stoic expression — not to feel.

Jen's face sank. Her creamy skin paled to the exact color of the sheets on which she lay. The low, oval neckline of the hospital gown did nothing but accent her skeletal chest. What did Collier find appealing about that? Whitleigh frowned. It was easy to see why he pitied her, but any other attachment stretched beyond her imagination.

"Answer me." Whitleigh lifted her chin higher.

"I ... I never meant to hurt you." Her voice was hoarse. "I never planned any of this."

"You've ruined my marriage."

"I'm so sorry."

"Sorry doesn't cut it." Jen knew that. Why else would she attempt to take her own life? Whitleigh bit her tongue. "Collier was my husband, not yours." She formed her eyes into slits, scanning the room. "He hasn't sent you flowers yet?" She huffed. "That's surprising."

Jen's lip quivered. "He ... He hasn't even been here."

"What?" Whitleigh flinched. Maybe he still cared. "Whatever." She crossed her arms. "I'm here for an answer."

Answers didn't change things.

"Never mind." Whitleigh pressed her fingers into her temples. "Why am I even here? This is a waste of time."

"Please don't go."

"I can't even begin to think of anything kind I could possibly say to you right now." Oh, there were plenty of evil things she could spout off. Whitleigh tapped her toe.

"I know you hate me."

"Ha."

"But I honestly don't know how this happened. You gave me his email address and he and I shared innocent emails back and forth. Just a friendship."

"That led to you sneaking around behind my back, visiting him at work?" Whitleigh's breaths quickened. "How stupid did you think I was?" Her voice caught. "I can't do this with you." She covered half of her face. There were no time for tears. "We were friends. Friends don't steal husbands. How could you?"

"Whit, I'm — "

"Don't." Whitleigh balled her fists. "I was there for you. I reached out to you when Mark died and this is what you do?"

Jen lifted her bandaged wrist to her eyes, soaking up the tears. "There's no excuse for what I did."

Whitleigh bit at her thumbnail and paced the floor. It would be easier to tell Jen off if she argued.

"I don't deserve to live." Jen let her head fall back onto her pillow.

"I can't say what you deserve."

Whitleigh held her hands against her abdomen. She couldn't stay much longer. No way could her stomach tolerate much more without vomiting.

"You cut me out of your life, Jen. You cut the world out."

"You're right." She lifted a frail, shaking hand to her cheek. "All of the legal battles Mark's family put me through over his insurance money. Missing him. Hating him for leaving. Being jealous of you and Collier." Another tear fell. "I messed up in the worse way possible."

Whitleigh gazed at Jen's bandaged wrapped wrists, letting her vision blur. Jen made sense, but it didn't justify her actions.

The monitors kept rhythm with each of their breaths. Jen sniffled. Laying there, she appeared childlike — like a small child who had misbehaved very badly, desiring nothing more than forgiveness.

Whitleigh closed her eyes, releasing a long, worn breath. For a moment she cradled her head in her palms, sending up a silent prayer.

She slid into a chair near the doorway. "I'm not sure why I'm here. Guess I needed to confront you." She slouched forward and chewed on the side of her lip, fixing her sights on Jen. "I was angry enough I could've attack you, but now I only feel sorry for you."

Jen held tight to the edge of her blanket, chin dimpling.

Whitleigh stood, hand on the cool, metal door handle. "I pray you get the help you need, and I ... I for — "

Was that true?

Whitleigh tucked in her bottom lip. No, not yet. Forgiveness could be a process.

"Whit?"

"At this point, Jen, there's nothing else to say." Whitleigh opened the heavy door in her hand, looked back only once, and moved on.

CHAPTER 28

SATURDAY night and Collier sat alone in his pickup truck. He parked behind the barracks, waiting for the concealment of night to release his emotions. He lifted his phone, eyes forward as his fingers dialed the number by memory. It rang — and rang.

"Please answer, Whit. I need you." He talked to the robotic answering system and hung up before the beep. He'd left enough messages she wouldn't listen to.

Collier let the phone slip from his hands and into the passenger seat of his car. He eyed the clock on his dashboard. No way could he do dinner with Jayson and Layla tonight.

Should he call?

No.

Collier closed his eyes. He'd rather sit, waiting on the darkness.

Jayson and Layla would understand. They had too. Taking a risk on seeing Whit wasn't worth it. Not right now. Not when he held a request for divorce in one hand and the news of his father's death in the other. He'd crumble at her feet for sure. Then what would she think?

Collier balled his fist, pushing it to his parted lips. His life derailed, like his father, left with nothing and no one. A small envelope peeked from the packet Whit's parents sent. He smoothed it between his fingers — words from his father, spoken from the grave. Nothing his father could say mattered now.

At this point, maybe closure was all Collier could hope for. Something nice and neat to make the news of a departing family member, the horrors of war, and a broken marriage easier to process.

He slid his finger underneath the sealed parchment and tugged the letter from the envelope. The paper shook in his hand. Collier blinked, drew in a deep breath, and began to read.

Dear Collier,

By the time you've read this, I will have already passed, and been laid to rest with your mother and brother. I don't deserve to lay next to them, but I admit, I'm honored to do so.

A tear fell to the page. Collier's face warmed. He hadn't been to see his mother's and brother's graves in quite some time. A visit was overdue. Collier rubbed his eyes and continued to read.

Please don't be angry with Whit's folks for not getting in touch with you sooner. They were only carrying out my request. I wanted to go this way – with no one around, no one to cry over me. It's the way it should've been – the way it needed to be.

As if a prison sentence and a painful death wasn't enough, Charles wanted to die alone as further punishment. Collier pinched the bridge of his nose. His Dad had changed. More than that, his father was truly sorry for all he had done. Collier gasped, pushing back a bottomless lament.

Regarding my things, well, there isn't much, but you're entitled to all of it. A little money, an acre of land, and that's about all. I only ask you take what money I do have left to give, and put it up for Linc. That little boy brought more hope to my life than I can begin to explain.

Linc. What a fighter. Collier smiled through blurry eyes.

I lost a lifetime with you, the ability to speak truth and instruction into your life because I was too lost to begin to know how to direct myself, let alone my son. If I could do it all over, I would, and if I could've given you words to live by, here's what I would've said:

Collier gulped. Like water to a desert, he held the letter close to his face, drinking, absorbing.

Love God, and love others. It's that simple. Put others before yourself. Be eager to forgive those who have wronged you, and learn to forgive yourself. It took some time for me to learn to forgive myself, but it was well worth learning. **You'll find freedom in forgiveness, in truth, and in love. If you ever find yourself lost in life, the path home is in God's Word.**

Love,

Your Dad

The words didn't make his life realities easier to swallow. They spotlighted the chaos. Collier's eyes stung. All the errors of his ways swarmed through his mind. The sun sank low over the mountains just in time to hide the steady flow of tears.

"I forgive you, Dad." A callous fell from Collier's heart. He winced at the pain and let the tears free fall. "I love you."

It was time. Time to stop pretending he could do it all on his own. Time to get help before time ran out — before he was doomed to write a letter like this to Linc.

Collier snatched his phone, dialing.

"Jayson?" Collier sniffed, wiping a tear with the cuff of his sleeve. "Yeah, it's Cromwell. Hey, um, that program you went to. Yeah, for PTSD. How do I get enrolled?"

WEDNESDAY morning came, marking the middle of the longest work week of Collier's life — field training. Over a week had passed since he and Whit split — almost two weeks. Collier stood, wiping sweat from his brow as dust settled atop his boots. When he and the other soldiers weren't in combat, they trained for it outside, all day and most of the night, no matter the weather.

"That's what I call some good grappling, soldiers." The Platoon Sergeant smacked Collier's back. "Now go again."

"Yes, Sergeant." Collier swung back into position, hands up, body angled. He could go another round, maybe more. The divorce papers filing through his mind provided enough fuel to keep him fighting.

Dock grinned, sweat dripping from his chin. "Gotta admit, Cromwell, I'm impressed." He faked a lunge forward. "You've improved since the last time we fought."

Collier spat on the ground. Nature served as their arena. "I must've damaged your brain cells, 'cause I'm certain I held you back." Though barely.

"Get to it." The Platoon Sergeant circled.

Soldiers clapped and jeered, dog tags rattled. Collier licked his lips, eyes settled on Dock. There they were, arms locked, grunting and teeth grinding. Dock was strong, but so was he. Collier pushed back, twisting Dock until his neck fit into the nook of Collier's elbow. Collier locked the hold, forcing Dock to his knees.

The stress of life emptied from Collier's pores with each strain and stretch of his muscles. Collier closed his eyes, brows touching.

"I'm not going down that easy." Dock broke Collier's hold, flipping him onto his back.

Collier coughed and somersaulted back to his feet. Staying down too long mean defeat.

Their bodies collided. Knotted knees. Bended elbows. Saliva. Sweat. Minute after minute and neither of their strength waned.

"Just tap out, Dock." Collier's words seeped through gritted teeth.

"Not on your life, Cromwell."

"I won't lose to you." Collier grimaced, his hands grappling to hold Dock in place.

"And I won't lose."

"That's what I like to see. A soldier never gives up. " The Platoon Sergeant clapped. "Take notes, Joes. Alright. Dock. Cromwell. Enough. Well done."

They broke apart, out of breath, sitting on the dirt. Collier shook his head. Dock laid back on the ground, laughing.

"You fought like you had something worth fighting for." Dock rose, extending a hand.

"I used to." Collier grabbed hold. With his father gone and his marriage failing, what else remained?

"Naw, man, you still do." He gave Collier a playful punch in the arm. "See you at the Fall Festival this weekend?"

Collier shrugged. "I guess I'm going." It would be odd going to a family event with no family.

"You can hang with us if you want. I'm wearing a cape."

"Of course you are." Collier chuckled, rolling his eyes.

"You know I'm here for you, right?"

Collier nodded, a lump rising in his throat. "Thanks, man."

"You're not having any crazy thoughts, right?"

"What?" Collier's voice rose a full octave. "I'm not suicidal or homicidal for that matter."

"Good. Good." Dock squinted his eyes as the autumn sun poured down on the field. "Making sure you're squared away. Life gets, well, you know."

"Tough." Collier sighed through a half smile. "Yeah, I know all about that." All too well. "But, I have to say that sleeping outside here in the mountains sure beats rooming with Pulu. Things are looking up in that regard."

Dock cackled, slapping his knees.

Glad he found it funny.

Dock's voice strung out in a laughing wheeze. "So, Amy's been wanting to have a girls' night with Whit. Maybe we could watch the kids for them. Let them hang out. Talk and stuff. Whatever girls do."

"And you're wanting me to set that up with Whit?"

"Look man." Dock dropped a heavy hand on Collier's shoulder. "If you're brave enough to enroll in a counseling program, then you can talk to your wife. This isn't time to let pride or fear get in the way. Swallow it. Don't let her walk away 'cause you didn't open your mouth."

"She's filed for divorce."

"So did Amy and we're still together."

"Because she wanted to work it out."

"Because I was willing to change and she was generous enough to give me another chance." Dock pressed down on Collier's shoulder. "Pursue Whit. Don't let her go. You want your family back, right?"

"More than anything."

"Then show her you want her — that you're willing to do what it takes to make things right."

"How?" Collier palmed his forehead. "I can't believe I'm asking advice from you. Since when did you and Pulu become marriage counselors? The world has gone mad."

Dock dug a piece of jerky from his pocket, broke it in half, offering it to Collier.

"Come on Cromwell. Let's get back to the campsite. We've got some brainstorming to do. I'm going to call it …," Dock held a hand in the air. "Operation Win Back Whit."

"It's got a nice ring to it." Collier nodded, tearing off a piece of the jerky as he dusted off his pant legs. Maybe he did have a chance. If Dock could win back Amy, then surely he had a hope with Whit.

Collier matched Dock's wide stride. Yeah. All he needed was a plan. Another day or so out in the field should give him plenty of time to create a list of tactical maneuvers guaranteed to mend their relationship.

CLEAN shaven and freshly showered, Collier welcomed the weekend, the end of their field training, and a chance to see Whit. Be brave. He stood outside their home, heaved a deep sigh, and shook his hands. "You're a soldier. If you can go to war, you can win back your wife."

Collier marched over a small crack on the sidewalk and onto the front porch. "I can't believe I'm actually taking advice from Dock and Pulu."

Pulling an index card from his khaki pants, he adjusted the top button on his collar and scanned under his arms for sweat rings. All clear.

"Step 1: Dress to impress her." Collier arched his brows. Whit loved him in yellow. She loved yellow in general. "Step one complete." He cleared his throat. "Step two: Make the first move. Find a reason to see her. Fall Festival. Okay. Got it. I can do this. Consider step two done."

He lifted a fist, ready to knock. Should he have worn a tie? No. No. He stood as straight as the soldier he was and rapped at the door. It crept open.

"Collier?" Whit appeared thinner — tired. The glow he'd grown to love, the one that always radiated from her face, no longer shone. Her light hair was gathered in a messy bun on top of her head. "What are you doing here?"

"Um." What was he doing here? His eyes scanned the perimeter. Fall decor adorned many of the presiding porches in the area. "I like the mums." He flinched. "I mean, what I meant was, would you and Linc be willing to accompany me to the Fall Festival?"

Her tired, blue eyes searched his face. "We're not going."

"Well, then, may I take Linc?"

"I don't have his costume ready."

"I'm good at improvising. I know you're the creative one, but I'm pretty good with face paint."

"Don't smile at me like that, Collier." She folded her arms. "Like everything's okay. Like ...."

"Like I love you." His heart raced. Collier held the screen door with one hand and reached for Whit with his other. "Because I do, Whit. I do love you, and I'll spend my whole life making up for everything I've done wrong if you give me another chance."

Her face flushed as she pulled away into an almost cower. Whit wasn't one to shy away. Collier inhaled, placing a hand to his chest. Her invisible wounds were as deep as his.

"I'm sorry, Whit, for everything." Collier stepped back, giving her room. "Can we at least talk for a bit? No fussing or yelling, just talk?"

"I don't know if I'll ever stop being angry at you."

His lips folded into a narrow line. That was understandable.

She waved him inside. "I'm sorry the house is a mess."

It was. Quite a mess. "No worries." Collier removed his shoes. "You should see Pulu's barrack room. This is nothing." Toys sprawled about the living room, and a blanket and pillow from their bedroom lay crumpled on the couch next to an open Bible. Their house, once filled with music, lit candles, and the scent of something baking in the oven seemed dull and empty.

"I'm sorry I haven't been answering your calls."

"I get it."

"It's not okay. I should've been there for you when I found out about your dad." Her bottom lip quivered. She sat in the rocking chair, holding her arms around her knees. "I wasn't sure how to respond or what my reaction should be now that we're separated."

Collier nodded as he shuffled past toys, pushing them to the side.

He sat on the ottoman, the leather squeaked beneath. "I walked out when I shouldn't have. I carried on a relationship with another woman when I shouldn't have. Yes, those things happened." Collier relaxed. It was important to keep his voice even keeled. "But I feel like things are moving too fast here. You filed for divorce before we even had a chance to talk."

Her eyes narrowed and her lips twisted to the side.

Linc toddled down the hall.

Collier leapt to his feet. "He's walking. Whit, he's really doing it."

She grinned, cupping her face. "Linc. Baby. Sweetheart."

They sped to their child, clapping and hugging, covering his chunky cheeks with kisses. Collier's throat tightened. He'd experienced a first for his son, but how many more would he miss if the divorce proceeded?

"Whit." Collier grasped her hand. "Is there any way we can fix this? Fix us?"

Her eyes watered. She kissed Linc. "I can't. Not right now." Tears raced past her lashes. "Please give me some time."

It wasn't a no, but it wasn't a yes. Collier bowed, scooping Linc into his arms. "Daddy's so proud of you little man."

He cleared his throat, choking on emotions thought to be killed in action during the deployment. "I'll wait for you, Whit. I'll fight for you too."

Holding Linc tight in his arms, he stood. "Do you mind if I get a few things from our room?" He offered a shrug and half smile. "Running out of things to wear."

A spark lit in Whit's eyes, he was sure of it. "Go ahead. And, Collier? You can see Linc whenever you want. Just call." She huffed, grinning. "I'll do better about answering."

Down the hall he ambled, Linc in tow. At least Whit smiled. There was hope. Hope for friendship and then maybe more soon after. Collier passed through the threshold of their bedroom and stopped mid stride.

Shattered glass. A broken frame. Their wedding picture lay lifeless on the carpet. Collier rubbed Linc's arm, but the child was not the one who needed the comfort. Torn scraps of paper littered the floor. Collier knelt, turning over a piece with an index finger.

Their list. Their Forever List.

He blinked, mouth parting.

It was going to take more than five steps on an index card to mend their marriage.

WITH an elbow, Whitleigh opened the front door. It clicked behind her, muffling the late morning sounds of an early November Thursday. She held the glitter covered card in her hands, opening it yet again, while standing in front of the door. She smiled, cheeks growing warmer than the smoke rings lifting from her coffee mug. Another note from Collier. This one wrapped with a ribbon and taped to the screen door. An invitation to attend the Military Ball the week of Thanksgiving. Tempting.

Boisterous grumblings from a moving truck disrupted her thoughts. The bumbling vehicle beeped as it backed into the neighborhood. Whitleigh's smile fell. Emma would be leaving by the week's end. She shook her head, sighing a prayer for a happy life for Emma.

Whitleigh held the card close, pried her eyes from across the street, and scanned the words once more.

It would be an honor to waltz you around the dance floor.

Their first Military Ball. Sigh.

Flecks of glitter fell from the card as she fanned herself. If Collier was serious about winning her back, the daily love notes appearing seemingly from nowhere, were working in his favor.

"I see you over there grinning."

Whitleigh jumped, slamming the card shut. The coffee in her hand sloshed from side to side but didn't spill. Relief.

Layla appeared from the hall, holding Linc's fingers, aiding him as he walked at her side. Her youngest son, Wil, chased after, making car noises. "I bet I can guess who that's from." Her voice filled with an annoying level of flirt. "Care to share?"

Whitleigh shrugged, lips sealed. "Not much to tell."

"Looks like a lot of things have been going on here." Layla's grins had become increasingly sly. "You've redecorated the hall too."

"Collier, um, gave me a hand." Whitleigh worked to lift the corners of her mouth.

"Mmmhmm. Nice paint job and excellent patchwork."

Whitleigh tucked loose strands of hair behind her ears. Layla could be so prying.

"Looks like Collier's been helping a lot around here."

"And?"

"Nothing. Just never knew he was so handy. I see he's fixed the cracks on the sidewalk."

"And caulked the windows." Whitleigh cleared her throat. "He's been very helpful around the house lately." There went her cheeks warming again. "I keep telling him I can do all this stuff by myself."

"Looks like he's finding good reasons to come see you guys. I hear his unit has a ball coming up soon." She tapped her cheek with a single finger. "I wonder who Collier will invite."

"You know too much."

Layla giggled and knelt in front of Linc as he stacked blocks on the living room floor. She swung him into a hug. Wil pushed cars around her legs. "You're doing such a great job, Linc. Ms. Layla's so proud of you."

Everyone was. The whole neighborhood supported Linc. Whitleigh's smile widened as she strolled over to her son, who clapped as fast as his chubby hands would allow.

"Layla, we really need to get back to work." Whitleigh placed a palm low on her hip. "We've got to get things for this change of command ceremony event ready."

"All work and no play."

"We're having a girls' night tonight. That's play." Whitleigh folded a table cloth and snatched up a mound of color swatches. "The event is tomorrow." She held her breath. "I have to get this ready. It's kind of a big deal."

"I get it. I get it, but you skipped the Fall Festival, and now — "

"I didn't skip. Collier ...." Whitleigh smacked her lips together. She'd said too much.

"Go on. Go on. He came over and you two are working it out."

"He cheated. End of story." Whitleigh let the ivory tablecloth fall to the dining room table.

"I think there's more to it than that."

"I'm not sure I even want to entertain that comment. It could mean way too many things." Whitleigh shuffled around the dining room table, dodging white painted and glittered pumpkins of various shapes and sizes lying about on the floor. She lifted a hurricane glass, placing it in a wooden crate. It clanked against the other vases with a chiming effect. Whitleigh sipped at her coffee.

"Whit, you and Collier have had a rough go of it. Linc's health, two years apart, the stresses of rediscovering each other, another deployment looming over you, and his bad lapse in judgment." Layla rolled a table runner, placing it on top of the vases. "It's easy to see why you'd want to be done with Collier and the Army."

"It's not easy. Nothing about this is easy."

"You're right, but don't let his screw up be your excuse to bail."

"Layla, it isn't about that." Was it? Whitleigh shook her head, strands of hair falling into her face.

"This is real and your choices have real consequences good or bad. A poor choice on his part doesn't require you to make the same kind."

There she went again. Whitleigh shook her head, filling the boxes and totes with decor at a quicker pace. "This really isn't any of your business, Layla."

"Whit, you're my friend. I can handle your evil looks."

"What looks?" Whitleigh crossed her arms, eyes narrowing. "And I can handle your honesty, even if I don't agree with what you're saying."

"You love him. I see it. He loves you. Yes he messed up, but we've all been in a position to need a little grace."

"A lot of grace. Much more than I think I can offer."

"That's the problem. You're trying to do something you haven't asked God to help with."

"You're walking the line." Whitleigh closed one box, plopped it on the ground, and reached for another. "I know it must've been hard to work things out with Jayson when he was dealing with PTSD, but our situation is different."

"Please." Layla's wave was dismissive. "Yeah it was hard. Real hard. But it was easier once he forgave me."

"You?" Whitleigh stopped packing, letting her fingertips slip down the side of the cardboard box. Jayson needed to ask for forgiveness, not Layla.

Layla's face reddened. That Whit could recall, Layla never wore an expression of embarrassment.

"Collier cheated on you, but I was the one who cheated on Jayson." Layla released a jagged sigh. Whitleigh froze.

"In my mind I had every reason to." Layla studied the floor. "Anyone would've understood why I did it, but it didn't make it right." Her eyes moistened. "He forgave me even after," she wet her lips, "Even after I found out I was pregnant."

Whitleigh openly stared, jaw unhinged.

"Wil, our youngest, isn't Jayson's child."

Whitleigh swallowed back the dryness in her throat. Her eyes, now wide, couldn't muster a blink.

Layla grew quiet. She took a seat at the dining table, her manicured nails shook as they covered the top of her quivering lip. Wil danced about in the living room, moving in circles around a giggling Linc. He looked like Jayson, but then again, maybe not. The dark eyes were in deep contrast to his or Layla's.

Whitleigh dragged a chair over the tattered carpet, sitting it closer to Layla. She touched her shoulder because no other response suited.

Layla ran her teeth across her bottom lip. "Emma's mom and I had much more in common than I ever wanted you to know. I've been where Jen's been, unhappy with her life, grasping at someone else's." Her chin tilted downward. "I almost destroyed my family, my husband, myself."

"Layla." No other words came. Many descriptions applied to Layla, but not adulteress.

"I'm here to tell you that if I can be forgiven, then anyone can be."

Whitleigh rubbed absently at her arms, her woolen cardigan unable to ward off chills. She hadn't forgiven Jen or Collier. She bit at her thumbnail, releasing a breath. It didn't matter if they deserved it. How arrogant to deny them grace when she'd been the recipient more times than she cared to count.

Whitleigh's words fell as a whisper. "He stayed with you."

"And here we are, three years later."

"Was it worth it?"

Layla didn't have to answer, her smile said it all.

Whitleigh jolted to her feet, pacing the floor. "We need time away from each other. Think things through, you know?"

"You've had nothing but time apart." Layla snapped her fingers. "That's not what you need."

Maybe she was right. Whitleigh ran her fingers through her hair. "Let's just get this stuff packed up and over to the event center."

WHITLEIGH gazed past the glowing bulb lights outlining the top of the bathroom mirror. She lifted her lashes with the mascara wand and dusted on a sheer coat of powder, added a bit of blush and a hint of tinted lip gloss. She dabbed her neck with perfume. Collier's favorite. An old habit. Maybe she should try a new fragrance.

Not tonight. Maybe later.

Besides, Collier would be at the door any moment. Turning his head wouldn't be a bad thing. Her stomach knotted. She wasn't dressing for him. Whitleigh lifted her chin. Tonight was all about fun. Girls hanging out. Eating. Laughing. That's right. Maybe she'd even order two desserts.

She slipped into her black peep-toed shoes and reached for her pearl earrings on the bathroom counter, then stopped. Pearls were her default. There wasn't any harm in wearing something different. Something that dangled. Sparkled.

Yes, those would do. Whitleigh moved side to side, watching the silver, teardrop shaped earrings skim the length of her neck. Not bad.

She smoothed her hands down the tea length black dress. Oh yes, it was definitely worthy of a girls' night out. Better yet, it was sure to turn Collier into a stuttering mess. Whitleigh giggled, flipped her hair in place around her shoulders, and brushed graham cracker crumbs from the dress hem. Oh motherhood.

She called down the hall toward the knocking at the door. "Coming." It was difficult to run in heels. She hopped over blocks and tiptoed past all manner of play things before reaching the door.

Be calm. She drew in a deep breath and let it go as if it were on a time release and opened the door.

"Wow." Collier stood, holding a bouquet.

More flowers. Whitleigh arched a brow, unable to hide her grin. There was a little more room on the kitchen counter.

"You look, um, uh, you look …." Collier wiped a hand over his face.

A stuttering mess. Whitleigh nodded. Success.

"You look incredible."

She pressed her lips together, hips swaying in a playful manner. "Thanks for watching Linc tonight."

"My pleasure."

"You got everything under control?"

"Sure. The guys may come over. You know, order pizza. Let the kids play."

"The guys?"

"Dock. Pulu. Jayson."

Whitleigh's hand flew to her forehead. "Oh my word."

"Don't worry." Collier lifted a hand. "I promise to have the best time with my little man and keep the house from being torn apart. It will be spotless when you get home."

Oh, that helped. Whitleigh huffed and tapped the toe of her shoe.

He winked, holding up a bundle of thick, green string.

She ignored the fluttering in her stomach. "You plan on tying up our son?" She chuckled. "I know he can be a handful but, geez."

"This here is 550 paracord. You can do about anything with this stuff. Makes good fishing line. I even used it as a tourniquet in Iraq."

"Impressive, but unless you're teaching Linc medic tactics 101, I'm still clueless."

Collier's wide smile exposed those gorgeous teeth. "I'm pretty good at using this stuff to fix things."

"You mean, rig?"

"Fix, rig. It's all the same." He rubbed at his chin, still grinning. "Thought I'd fix the clothes line in the backyard while you ladies are out and about tonight."

"I didn't know it was broken." Whitleigh placed a hand on her waist, the other arm dangled at her side. It wouldn't hurt to have a clothes line. Saving on energy costs was a nice thing to do for the military base. "Guess you can fix it if you want to."

"What I really want is for you to accept my invitation to the Military Ball."

Whitleigh shifted her weight to one leg, averting her eyes from his.

"Hear me out, Whit." His words were smooth, but could his actions be trusted? "I've been going to counseling and I qualify for a three week rehabilitation program out in Washington DC. The guys are encouraging me to go."

Whitleigh lifted her face. Collier's eyes had never been more sincere.

"You should." His wounds needed to be mended. Whitleigh offered a soft smile.

He cleared his throat. "I've been learning how to combat my symptoms with diet and exercise. Cut out the sodas." That was a miracle. "I'm even praying again. Been picking up my Bible too." Even more of a miracle.

The bouquet rustled in his hands. Whitleigh extended an open palm and received the flowers. She nudged her nose across the fragrant yellow and orange petals.

"Whit, for the first time in a long time, I'm filled with hope." He placed a hand over his heart. "Tell me I'm too late and I'll go. I'll do my best to let you leave, if that's what you want, but it's not what I want, and if you're honest, it's not what you want."

"Collier, don't." Her heart leapt, urging her arms to embrace him, but her mind couldn't relay the message. "Not now."

"I'm not asking for us to pretend like none of this happened. I'm asking for a chance." He moved closer, the sweet, subtle scent of aftershave lingered. "Let's go to counseling together. Start over. Date again. Get to know each other." His eyes scanned the length of her body. "Lord knows we've both done some changing."

There would be no future for them if she couldn't let go of the past. Whitleigh tucked her chin, eyes closed. It was time.

"Collier, I forgive you." Yes. It was true. Finally. Her chest filled and fell — she could breathe again.

"Does this mean ...?"

"It means I took a step in the right direction." More steps were to come.

"Can we take another tiny step tonight?" Collier rocked on his heels, mouth turned upward. "Be my date to the Military Ball? Please."

It wouldn't hurt to say yes.

"I can do that." She touched her fingertips to his collar, drinking in his smile. "I should be going." She pushed past him, cradling the flowers, nudging his shoulder with hers. Letting go of the past was off to a good start.

HERE. Of course. Jen's favorite coffee shop would have to be the place Amy would want to wrap up a perfectly good girls' night out. Ruined.

Maybe The Grounds closed early on a Thursday evening. Fat chance.

Whitleigh stood tall. She could do this.

Amy interlocked her fingers, almost drooling. "I've heard this place has the best desserts."

No arguing that truth.

So, perhaps the night wasn't ruined. Chocolate cake fixed a lot of things.

Layla dug through her purse. "The guys haven't called once."

"No news is good news."

Whitleigh cracked a smile. "Amy, you've spoken like a true Army wife."

"Score." Amy fist pumped the air, opening the tall, glass door. "It all smells so delicious. I have no clue what to order."

"Start with coffee." Layla eyed the homemade desserts displayed in a glass case like prized, edible jewels.

Whitleigh tapped her bottom lip. Her gaze couldn't be kept on a mere single treat. "Let's each get something different and split it amongst the three of us."

"Genius." Amy touched the glass.

Jen would've wanted the triple layer chocolate cake. "I'll go with the praline cheesecake." She walked toward the register. "And a black coffee, no sugar."

Jen liked hers with sugar and hazelnut creamer.

Whitleigh swiped at her forehead like it kept unwelcome memories away. She paid the cashier and grabbed a seat near the back of the narrow coffee shop. Layla slid in beside her.

Amy grabbed the seat across the table. Her green eyes danced. "Tonight has been so much fun."

It had.

Layla nodded, cupping her coffee mug. "Funny movie, fabulous dinner, and great company."

"Can I just say that I'm so happy to get to know you ladies?" Amy scooped up a piece of carrot cake. "I've got friends and it feels crazy amazing."

Friends. Yes, friend potential existed in Amy. However, it would be wise to proceed with caution. Whitleigh crunched the pralines between her teeth. Layla laughed along with Amy. Choosing friends could be a risky business.

"Ooh, can I try a piece of that fudge pie?" Amy held out a spoon, ready to dive into Layla's dessert. She grinned, face lit up in delight. "Whit, I have to tell you how much you've inspired me as an Army wife."

"Me?" Had she not received the memo? Things at the Cromwell house were shaky at best.

"Of course."

Layla sipped at her coffee. Whitleigh could almost imagine her ears perking up.

Amy's mouth parted. "You've been through so much, and you're still going. Still hanging in there. It's incredible."

Whitleigh held onto her fork, her stomach knotted. "Thank you."

"And how you reacted when Collier volunteered to go back to war after Linc was born. Wow. You're amazing."

"What?" The fork fell from her hand, clattering against the white plate.

"You dealt with that with such grace." Amy made a puffing noise, tossing a hand in the air.

Layla stiffened at Whitleigh's side.

Whitleigh forced herself to breathe. A lump, larger than her throat, began to rise. "Amy, I don't know what you're talking about."

"You know. After Linc was born and Collier went back when he could've stayed home."

"No." Whitleigh shook her head, chest tightening. "No, he was forced to go back."

Layla reached for Whitleigh's hand, but she yanked away.

Amy blinked.

"He was forced, Amy. That's what he told me."

Amy stared at her dessert.

"The Army made him go back, Amy."

"I'm sorry, Whit. I thought you knew." Tears fell from Amy's eyes. She bolted from her seat, running out the front door.

Whitleigh covered her mouth. How could she have been so blind? The military would never have forced Collier to leave his family in such peril. What a fool to think he cared, and how ignorant of her to let him weasel his way back into her heart.

No more.

SHE gathered a handful of hair on top her head and sighed. Last night was terrible. She hadn't even let him speak, just booted him out. Served him right, though. Her bags were packed. They sat next to the front door, moping.

Whitleigh placed her fists on her hips as she walked through the house. Collier kept his promise. The house was intact. Pizza boxes gone. Toys off the floor and in their designated woven basket. Horizontal lines from the vacuum cleaner stretched across the carpet. Spotless. None of it mattered now. Nothing he could fix or clean would make her stay.

Whitleigh flung the spare house key on the dining room table. Collier could take both once she was gone. She opened her wallet, counting the cash. There'd be enough money for gas back to Kentucky, but little else. Maybe she'd get paid after the ceremony today, then she'd jet. No reason to stay. Her diploma would come in the mail after graduation. She could get a job anywhere, even work toward her teacher certification. Nothing and no one stood in her way now.

Whitleigh eyed the clock. Nine in the morning.

Time to go.

She zipped Linc up in a fluffy, hooded jacket and bundled a blanket around him. The November mornings were growing colder, and though winter hadn't arrived, the chill had been around for quite some time. With a loud click, the front door closed as she walked from the house.

"This can't be happening," Whitleigh grumbled, chewing on her jaw. "Not today." A large moving truck sat, unmoving, behind her vehicle. "This is crazy inconsiderate. Excuse me, sir?" Whitleigh bounced Linc on her hip, adjusting the diaper bag draping from her shoulder. "Excuse me."

The man, bearded, middle-aged, and half asleep in the front seat, came to. "Oh, hi there, ma'am." He wore the mark of the steering wheel across his forehead. Whitleigh would've laughed under better circumstances.

"Sir, I have to be somewhere soon and you're blocking my car."

"I'm sorry, miss, but we're helping that family move." His long, bony finger pointed to Helen's home.

"You were here yesterday. How much stuff does she have?"

"The moving process is a long one."

"I'm aware of that." Whitleigh placed her hand on Linc's head and swayed him on her hip. "Is there any way you can move so I can get out."

Lines appeared around his eyes. His shoulders lifted.

"Guess that's a no. Great."

The man shrugged an apology. Whitleigh stretched, peering around the massive hunk of inconvenience. Helen stood at her door, arms folded, scanning the area. Maybe she could get them to budge.

Whitleigh marched across the street, waving. "Good morning." Sort of. She shivered, holding Linc close.

"Morning." Helen gave a soft smile, lifting her hand. She looked over her shoulder. "Emma, look who's here." The screen door creaked open. "Please, Mrs. Cromwell, come in."

"Oh." Whitleigh licked her drying lips. Helen did appear different. Still shaky, but different. Nicer. Healthier. "Thank you."

Emma darted down the stairs, dark hair trailing behind. "Miss Whitleigh." Her high pitched voice carried glee to another level. What an angel.

"Come here. I need a hug." Whitleigh knelt down, Linc clinging to her neck. "You've grown so much." She had. Her face was fuller. Her legs were longer.

"I'm almost as tall as you."

"That wouldn't take much." Whitleigh giggled, brushing back Emma's bangs.

Helen closed the door, secured a series of chain locks, and then glanced out the window.

"Everything okay?" Whitleigh placed Linc on the floor. Emma bounced at his side, happy to play with him.

"Sure. Yeah." She rubbed at her tiny arms. "Of course."

"You looking for someone? You're safe, right?"

Her dark eyes filled with shock.

"It's okay." Whitleigh's mouth slid to the side. "I know about … everything." What other word could describe an adulterous, violent love triangle that made headlines?

"They haven't found Ray."

Whitleigh refused to cower at his name.

"I'm ready to get out of here. Get back home. Start over."

"I know that feeling." Whitleigh inhaled. "You think he's going to bother you? No one's seen anything around here, since I was, well, anyway. I'm sure Layla and her weapon arsenal would let us know." Whitleigh lifted the corners of her mouth, holding a hand to Helen's shoulder.

"It's not me I'm worried about." Her eyes fell to Emma on the floor.

Whitleigh followed her line of sight. "Emma?"

"He told me if I ever left him, ever told anyone what I knew, what he'd done, then …."

"He threatened Emma?" Whitleigh's voice lowered. Her body tensed. "Where's your husband?"

"He's done with us right now." Helen covered her face, fingers falling to cup her mouth. "When you tell so many lies, the people who used to love you don't know what to believe." She shook her head. "I've put my family in this situation."

"Hey." Whitleigh clenched Helen's shoulder. "Stop kicking yourself. Come on, let's go sit over here." Whitleigh blew kisses to Emma and Linc. She glanced at the clock. There were a few minutes to spare.

Helen sat at a tiny breakfast nook near the kitchen. "The faster I can get out of this place, the better for Emma."

"And what makes you think he won't come after you in Florida? If he puts this much fear in you, I don't think that will stop once you move." Whitleigh scooted closer. "That will only go away if he's behind bars."

Helen bit at her broken nails.

"Can you call the military police? Ask for protection until you're gone?"

"He was with them, remember? I'm sure they'd try to protect him. They band together like brothers. To them I'm a harlot who makes up lies."

"He's raped women. He's hurt you, attacked me, I'm sure of it, and now he's threatened to hurt Emma." Whitleigh smacked at the table. "He was on the news, Helen. They're looking for him."

"Based on my testimony. The evidence I knew to share with the media off base."

"Have you shown this evidence to the military police? Not all of them will root for him." Whitleigh's lips curled. This man needed to be in jail.

"I can't do it. They'd see me coming."

"Then let me." What was she saying? She was leaving, today if that giant truck would ever move. "I can do it on my way to work. I'm sure it won't take long." Whitleigh bit her lip. *Stay out of it.*

Helen hunched forward. "Would you?" Her words flooded with relief — desperation even.

Emma rolled on the floor alongside Linc, making stuffed animals dance. So innocent.

"Yes. Give me what I need and I can drop it off." Whitleigh swallowed.

"I'll be right back." Helen slipped from her seat and tiptoed up the stairs.

Whitleigh crossed her legs. Getting more involved in Colorado was the last thing she needed. She rested her cheek in her palm. Emma needed help and so did Helen. Standing aside was unthinkable.

Whitleigh yanked her phone from her back pocket and dialed. "Hey, Layla. Yeah I'm okay. Yes, I'm still bringing Linc over. I know I'm running behind. Yes. We'll talk later. No, I can't now."

This wasn't the time to talk about Collier and all the reasons she should listen to his side of the story.

"What? She's gone? Already?" Whitleigh leaned into the phone. Jen had checked out of the hospital. "They cleared her? She's headed back to Tennessee? Okay."

Whitleigh pinched the bridge of her nose. Her brain was on an emotional overload and overflowing with to-do lists. "Look, I have a few huge favors to ask. Can Helen and Emma come over and stay until the movers are done? Why? Because. She'll fill you in. And, may I please borrow your van?" Whitleigh groaned under her breath. It really wasn't the time to answer a million questions. "Thank you. Yeah, the movers are a pain. Okay. Need to go. I'll be there in a few. I know. I'm hurrying." Whitleigh checked her watch. She'd still be early. Plenty of time remained to make sure everything was ready for the ceremony. "Thank you, thank you. I owe you a bunch."

Helen returned as Whitleigh clicked the phone shut. Her eyes were deep and wild as she sat at the kitchen table, slipping a CD case into Whitleigh's hand.

Her heart thudded against the walls of her chest. What information did it contain? Photos of victims? Letters filled with evil intentions? Whitleigh shuddered.

"That's everything I have." Helen's eyes closed for a moment. "Found all of it on his computer."

"Thank God you thought to copy it."

Helen sat hunched over, watching Emma laugh on the floor. She inhaled, releasing a jagged breath. "I want a do-over. Be the mom I never was to her. Be a great mom and wife, if Taylor will ever have me back." She turned, locking eyes with Whitleigh. "I want to be like you. Like Layla."

"Oh Helen." If she only knew. "I'm no one you want to be like." Whitleigh's cheeks burned. "Don't be me, or Layla. Be who God wants you to be."

"I'm trying."

"And you're succeeding." Whitleigh reached for Helen's hand. "Let's get you and Emma over to Layla's. No sense in sitting here scared."

Helen dabbed at her eyes, her smile grateful.

"And I'll call Collier." Whitleigh paused. Maybe that wasn't the best idea. "I'm sure he and his buddies can help keep a look out tonight." No matter her current feelings, Collier was the kind of man who would come to the rescue.

WHITLEIGH pressed her lips together and picked up the pace. Her black leather boots brushed at the knees. The event center sat a hundred feet away, but it might as well have been a mile. Had anyone seen her drop the CD off at the Police Department? The Commander had appeared surprised by her visit, but not as shocked as the receptionist when Whitleigh demanded to be seen.

Whitleigh shuddered. A burst of wind whipped past. Naked trees and limbs twisted in unnatural positions hung above her head. Discolored leaves lay dead. They crunched with each step, releasing a musty scent unique to fall. The sun peeked past thick, gray clouds, shedding little light on the day. Rain threatened in the distance.

Whitleigh tugged on her plum wool blazer, fidgeting with the thick ruffle down the center. She kept her face forward, but her eyes wandered to the right and left. Helping Helen and Emma was the right thing to do — but scary.

The event center was quiet. Whitleigh clicked the light switch. Large, long lights suspended from the rafters hummed to life, filling the center with a warm welcome glow.

Hardwood floors. Tan walls. Eleven round tables covered with ivory and white linen. A strip of burlap laid across each table. Atop many of the tables sat a trilogy of pumpkins. Several painted white, glittered with gold in various patterns, while some boasted their natural hue. Breathtaking centerpieces. The three tables in the center of the room held bundles of twigs, dusted with bronzed glitter, tied with twine, and filled with twinkling white lights.

Whitleigh grinned, soaking in the atmosphere. No fear existed in this place, just a sense of accomplishment. It started with a vision. Hard work, persistence, attention to detail, and support from many brought it into a realization.

"You've surpassed anything I could've imagined." A soft voice carried from the corner of the room.

Whitleigh gasped. "Andrea, you about gave me a heart attack." She walked over, hugging her FRG leader. "You're the Commander's wife. You should be enjoying a relaxing morning."

"Relaxing?" Andrea's laugh echoed. "I needed to see this place before the big event." She bobbed her head. "Yep. I knew it would be you."

"Me?"

"I need an event planner. I'm terrible at hosting and decorating. The job's yours."

"But."

"After I saw how quickly you were able to throw together something cute for the homecoming ceremony, I just knew I could count on you for this." She outstretched her arms. "My husband is going to have the most beautiful banquet ever."

"Andrea, I'm — "

"The Military Ball is coming up next." Her mouth opened with an excited huff. "I can only imagine how you would put that together. You bake. You decorate. What don't you do?"

"Stay."

"What?"

"I'm leaving."

"Do you need a raise? Please don't leave because I'm not paying enough."

"It's enough. It's great actually. I'm grateful, it's just, well …." Whitleigh held her tongue. Discussing personal matters with the Commander's wife wasn't wise.

"I see." Her straight posture stooped. "So, what's next?"

Whitleigh pressed her fingertips to her forehead. "I wanted to teach. Well, I thought I did." Her future fogged. "And still kind of do, but with my son's health issues, it would make it hard to hold down a career with set hours. So, event planning seemed like a natural choice. Something I enjoy and can make a living at. We'll see." She licked her lips looking away for a moment.

"You've got the talent." She tapped her a hand against her hip. "So, you and your husband …."

"Are separated." The words felt wrong, like mismatched puzzle pieces.

"Ah." She tilted her head back. "That's what I thought. Rob and I did that years back. Army life made both of us crazy." She chuckled.

Whitleigh frowned. There wasn't anything funny about how crazy Army life can make a person.

"But we made it." Andrea stepped back, leaning against the wall. "This life will be what you make it."

True. Maybe. Whitleigh nodded, cradling her arms.

Andrea continued. "I love that man, and I've come to enjoy making plans just to see how the Army will help them evolve."

Evolve. An interesting word choice.

"I don't mean any disrespect, ma'am, but you're the Commander's wife. Seems like a pretty nice life to me. Parties and such."

"I guess it does seem like that." Her smile shortened. "But there's more to it. Long hours. A lot of accountability. So many people rely on him. It wears on a man and marriage, you know?"

Yes. Whitleigh knew.

"And then he comes home to us." Andrea's teeth glistened. "We keep him busy and I have to remind him we're not at his command."

Whitleigh choked on an unexpected laugh.

"Hang in there. Something tells me you've got a lot of fight in you."

"I'm not sure about that anymore."

"Do something for me." Andrea clasped her hands as if in prayer. "Think about what you want. Where you want to be in a year, five years, ten years down the road. What do you see? More importantly, who do you see?"

Whitleigh closed her eyes. She willed them to open. Collier wasn't welcome in her mind.

Andrea nodded. "The strange thing about faith is it's almost impossible to have if you stick with the possible." An elegant, jeweled bracelet dangled in place as she talked. "To me, Army life has always dealt a hearty dose of the impossible, which means we've got an even bigger dose of faith."

A worthy thought. Whitleigh straightened. She tucked in her bottom lip.

"That's definitely a new way of looking at it."

"I'll get out of here." Andrea reached for her purse on the floor. "The caterers will be here soon. Got to get them squared away." She smiled and turned.

"Andrea?" The words leapt from her mouth before she could command them to return.

"Yeah?"

"Thanks."

She nodded and continued on her way.

Whitleigh leaned into the doorway, gazing out at the stunning room. If only she could envision her life in such a manner. Planned. Organized. Something beautiful. Something less chaotic.

THE van ambled on past intersections, stopping when necessary. Police cars sped past, lights flashing. Whitleigh kicked a sippy-cup from beneath her feet. Leaving this place, the sirens and craziness, couldn't come fast enough.

She was almost home.

Home. Now there was a relative term.

She checked her mirrors, recounting fragmented memories, working to keep them at bay. An ambulance hurled by.

By all standards the Change of Command Ceremony and event was a success, not to mention how nice it was to have the check in her wallet. Andrea's husband assumed a new duty, would eventually move up in rank, and everyone enjoyed a lovely and elegant celebration.

Emma and Helen would start over, brighter days lay ahead. Layla and Jayson would continue to be a disgusting level of happy together and have another five children. Pulu would always be joyful, and Dock and Amy were probably enjoying a lunch break in some corner café.

Happy. Good for them.

Life goes on. So would hers.

She turned into the cul-de-sac, greeted by the Big Rig. "It's still there." And Collier. Great. Even better. "What's he doing?" There he stood, in uniform, on the front porch, arms folded. Was that blood on his face? Whitleigh whipped into a parking lot. How had she not seen the flashing lights? The police. The ambulance.

"Linc. Oh, Lord, please let Linc be okay." Whitleigh pushed her way from the van. "I shouldn't have left him." She ran, full stride. "Collier. Collier." Her voice strained.

Her body collided against his chest. "Linc."

"He's okay, Whit. Calm down. You left your phone at Helen's."

She did? No matter. "Where's Linc?"

"Inside with Layla and the kids."

"You're bleeding. What's going on?"

Collier touched his face. "It's nothing. Just a scratch from work. Grappling."

That was more than a scratch.

Police walked about the area, interviewing neighbors. The ambulance silenced its siren. A medical team appeared from Emma's house across the street. They held the sides of a stretcher and rolled a body bag into the back of the vehicle. Whitleigh held her stomach, but the churning continued.

"Helen?" No. Not now.

"She's inside with Layla and the kids." Collier's face was stone, matter of fact. This was Collier the warrior, the defender.

"Then, who?" Whitleigh stared at this man, someone deserving of admiration.

"Ray. It's the guy the police were after."

"What?" Whitleigh drew her trembling fingers upward, covering her mouth.

"The police said they got a tip or something today. They've been on high alert."

Whitleigh gulped. The CD must've gotten to the right person.

"Looks like he broke into Helen's home. Guess he saw Emma playing over in Layla's yard."

"The kids." Whitleigh couldn't hold back the tears.

"It's okay." He pulled Whitleigh close. "Everyone is safe." She buried her head in his chest, the safest place on earth. "Layla ran him off with a gun. Looks like he decided to barricade himself in Helen's house until the police came, and well, you know."

She nodded, his uniform pressed against her cheek.

"Whit." He pried her away, lifting her chin. "I need you to know something."

She looked up into his face. Stern, but nonetheless loving. He could've said anything.

"When I couldn't get a hold of you today, I about lost it." His eyes watered. "I heard all of the sirens. Heard where they were going, and I couldn't get here fast enough. You and Linc were all I was thinking of and I was ready to fight to get to you, to save you."

Whitleigh swallowed. Her lips parted.

"Let me finish." His hands held her upright. "I should've told you I volunteered to go back, but I couldn't bear to see the look on your face."

"Then why?" Her eyes narrowed. She stiffened in his grasp.

"I did it for you and Linc."

"That makes no sense."

His shook his head. "If I stayed home we'd lose the extra deployment pay."

Whitleigh's eyes glazed over. Now it made perfect sense.

"Whit, I knew Linc would need things, special equipment. I knew we needed more in our savings for emergencies."

Her throat tightened. She'd been wrong to assume the worst of him. "You sacrificed yourself for us."

"I went about it the wrong way. I know I did, and I'm sorry." Collier lowered his face inches from hers. "But I'd do it again if it meant taking care of my family."

His hands held the back of her head, his lips crushed against hers.

"Don't." Mumbles were all she could manage as she hit at his shoulders, but it was no use. She couldn't move, nor did she want to. As her knees crumbled, her arms grew in strength, stretching around his neck.

Whitleigh sighed, now the one refusing to break the kiss. She could see it, their life in one, five, ten years and more in the future. Smiling. Dancing. Rocking chairs. Rocking babies. She held his head between her hands, finding the will to pull away. There was something she needed to say. "I'm sorry."

His thick, dark brows furrowed. "For?"

"Being so stubborn and selfish. Being afraid."

"Afraid?"

"Of getting my heart broken again, future deployments, Army life in general." She rubbed a thumb over his cheek. "I'm sorry for urging you to help Jen."

"Don't make excuses for my behavior."

"I need to own up to the part I played." She cradled his arms in hers. "I thought she'd be able to help you deal with the loss and pain you were experiencing. I was wrong. I should've been the one helping and encouraging you, but many times, I was too wrapped up in everything else. "

Collier nodded his head. His cheeks flushed. "You've made a lot of sacrifices."

"So have you, Collier. That's what we do. Make sacrifices for each other and compromise. I see that more than ever now."

He folded her hands in his, lifting them to his lips. "I want to make your dreams come true. I want you to finish school, teach, and do the things you want to do."

"Dreams change. Mine have and all I want is you and Linc." She drew his face to hers, kissing him once more. This was right. The way things were meant to be.

WHITLEIGH licked the envelopes, sealing them shut. One for Emma and Helen, and the other to right a wrong. She held the warm flaxen faux fur tight around her bare shoulders. The letters slipped from her freshly French manicured fingertips and into the mailbox. Jen would get hers in a week or so. Not that they would ever be friends again, but no longer enemies. Forgiveness was a start. A good one.

"You ready?" Collier straightened his tie. His arm rested on the car window seal.

Whitleigh gathered the golden layers of organza material, lifting the dress enough to keep it from skimming on the ground. Her heels shimmered as she stepped from the sidewalk.

"Allow me." He strode from the car, rounding the front of the vehicle and opening her door. A vast array of metals fortified on his chest sparkled in the setting sun. Whitleigh tilted her head, soft curls falling forward. Handsome couldn't quite describe Collier in his Dress Blues.

He straightened the deep blue jacket, bowing at the waist as she sat in the passenger seat. The light blue infantry cord secured around his right shoulder moved with him. Whitleigh's cheeks warmed as fast as her heart quickened.

"Our first Military Ball." She patted her lap, smoothing out the beautiful gown beneath her fingers.

"Our first Thanksgiving together in a couple of days. A first Christmas too. Then Linc's first birthday and soon after that a first anniversary." He laughed and fished for her hand. Whitleigh obliged and interlocked her fingers with his.

"Married two years and having all of these firsts now. That's a riddle."

"It's our story." That it was. He squeezed her hand. "We're here." Collier made a quick left into the parking lot.

"Wow." Whitleigh all but pressed her face to the window, the seat belt refusing to let her any closer. "The event center looks incredible."

"Thanks to you, Fort Carson's greatest event planner."

Whitleigh's chest ached with joy. She grinned. This night couldn't get much better. Pieces of her life meshed together in ways she could've never imagined.

Collier was quick to open her door, helping her from the car with an extended hand. Whitleigh stared, taking time to drink in the atmosphere. The once naked trees outside the center now served as a grand entrance. Wrapped in hundreds, perhaps thousands of lights, they lit up the walkway just as the sun sank over the mountains. Her chest rose, filling with cool mountain air.

"Magical, isn't it?" Collier kissed her cheek.

"You read my mind."

Car doors closed, echoing across the parking lot. Whispers of accolades followed suit. Couples in their best attire held hands, laughed, and enjoyed one another's company. A fun, romantic evening awaited all in attendance.

Whitleigh waved as Andrea and her husband paraded past. Andrea flashed a smile and a quick thumbs up. Dock high-fived Collier as he and Amy skirted past. Pulu followed behind with a lovely woman on his arm.

Collier nodded as they passed. "Before we go in, I have something I want to give you."

Whitleigh clung to the fur still draped around her shoulders. "Was I supposed to get you something?"

Collier's smile was cool. "Don't worry, this isn't a custom." He knew her well. "I wanted to surprise you. Nothing big."

Whitleigh exhaled, slouching a bit.

He unbuttoned his jacket, pulling a small, brown leather book from the inside pocket.

"A book?"

"A journal." He held his hands over hers, the soft leather between their palms. "We said our Forever List would turn into a notebook one day, but I say, who needs a Forever List?"

Whitleigh pushed a loose curl aside. What did he mean?

Collier held her arms, looking into her eyes. "A list — those are just surface dreams and goals. I want to give you more. I found a way to share my thoughts with you in this journal. Everything I have trouble saying, I write." He sighed. "I hope it comes out right, Whit. I don't want to hold anything back from you, ever. I'm yours, for better or for worse."

She held it, skimming through the pages. Dates. Ink. It was all there, his time and effort to connect with her. Whitleigh blinked the tears aside.

"I have to say something." He brushed her tears away with his thumb. "You have to hear this, not read it."

"Okay." Whitleigh grimaced. His serious tone gave her cause to worry.

"I need to thank you."

"For?" Whitleigh tilted her head.

"For the sacrifices you've made for me, for us — "

Whitleigh opened her mouth.

"Please, let me finish. You've sacrificed for this country too. I'm sorry I never took the time to count the ways you've served."

Whitleigh lowered her head. Collier gathered her into his arms. A giggle worked its way up her throat and out.

"What?"

"You amaze me Collier Cromwell." She held the journal against his chest. "This is a treasure. You're a treasure."

"There are a few days I didn't write in it." He rubbed a hand across the back of his head. "I got real sick after watching the kids on that girls' night out. Thought it was my nerves, well, 'cause you know how the night ended."

"Yeah. What a night." Whitleigh held a hand against the gold beaded sequins across her waist.

"But then all the guys got sick, so who knows."

Whitleigh pursed her lips. "What did you eat?"

"We think maybe you made a batch of cookies that went bad or something."

"Cookies?" Oh no. "Where were they?"

"In the microwave. Figured you made them for us."

"Oh." Her pulse raced. "Did the kids eat them?"

"No way. We weren't gonna share with them. They had their own snacks."

A laugh rolled from her throat. She couldn't help it. "I meant to throw them away a long time ago."

"I knew it. So they were bad?"

Or laced with laxative.

"Something like that." She kissed his cheek, swinging his hand in hers. "I'll explain that later. Not tonight."

"Um. Okay." He laughed along with her.

Whitleigh held the journal over her heart. "Collier this is the best gift you could've ever given me."

"You taught me a lot about love."

"I can say the same."

"I know what it is now. What it looks like, feels like, how it acts."

"Me too." Love was a verb. It acts in the best interest of the other. It never fails. It always trusts. Hopes. Endures. Whitleigh traced his brow line with the tip of her finger.

He stepped closer, lifting her arms around his shoulders. His lips melted against hers.

She swayed in his arms, dancing to the music drifting from the center. "I didn't think it was possible."

"What?"

"Any of this." She patted the journal against his shoulder blades. "We were broken."

"And now?"

A soft breeze lifted her hair, tossing it about her neck. She blotted at a tear. "I know we've got a road ahead of us, but I see it."

"See what?" His eyes focused, never leaving hers.

"That we're going to be better than before." It was true. Truer than most things she knew.

Whitleigh tugged Collier, nudging him toward the door. Battles in life would come and go. They would fight them together, but tonight, they would dance.

The End

SUGGESTED questions for a discussion group surrounding *The Wounded Warrior's Wife*.

While the characters and situations in *The Wounded Warrior's Wife* are fictional, I pray that their story parallels the truth of God's love, forgiveness, and His ability to restore in a way that sticks with the reader for a lifetime. Please search God's Word (The Bible) and prayerfully consider the questions below as you draw conclusions.

1: Whitleigh and Collier created a Forever List including things they wanted to accomplish throughout their marriage. Would you consider creating a similar list? Feel free to share what your list would include.

2: Conflicts happen in relationships. Whitleigh and Collier experienced their share of frustrations with each other. Can you remember your first argument with your spouse or loved one? How was it resolved?

3: Whitleigh and Collier find their faith tested when troubles come their way. Why is it easy to believe God has our best interest at heart when life is going our way?

4: We experience loss and grief throughout life. Many of the characters in The Wounded Warrior's Wife struggle with painful circumstances. How do you support, encourage, and comfort those who are grieving?

5: How would you define love after reading The Wounded Warrior's Wife? How does love shown in this novel compare to the world's view of love regarding relationships?

6: Communication is vital to a relationship. Discuss the delicate balance Whitleigh and Collier faced of knowing what sort of information to share with each other while Collier was deployed.

7: If not protected and maintained, marriages can fall apart fast. How do you defend your marriage and do you discuss these things with your spouse?

8: Several characters experience moments in which they feel there is no hope. Have you had a similar experience in your life? How did your faith get you through?

9: Forgiveness and restoration show up throughout this novel. When a friend or loved one hurts or betrays us, are we quick to dismiss them or do we work to mend the relationship?

10: Just like in this novel, bad things happen in real life to good people. Would you agree or disagree with the following statement: It doesn't matter why bad things happen, but how you handle them.

ABOUT THE AUTHOR

HANNAH CONWAY is an Army wife of more than ten years, mother of two, writer, and speaker. She is active with American Christian Fiction Writers (ACFW) and My BookTherapy. A Kentucky native, she and her family reside in Clarksville, TN near Fort Campbell where they are currently stationed.

Hannah holds a BA in History from the University of Colorado at Colorado Springs and has spent many years in ministry working with both youth and women's groups. In her time in ministry, she served two years as a Youth Director and one year as a Co-Coordinator of a Mothers of Preschoolers (MOPS) group.

When she isn't writing, you'll find Hannah volunteering for community service projects, jogging (slowly), neck deep in Pinterest crafts, or browsing thrift stores. A good book, a piece of chocolate, Chai tea latte, and an outdoor setting take her captive on more occasions that she likes to admit.

The most important thing about Hannah, is that she's a follower of Christ. It's her prayer that you will come to know how much God loves you through her writings.

Author Website: www.hannahrconway.com

Facebook: www.facebook.com/authorhannahconway

Newsletter: http://tiny.cc/hannahconwaynews

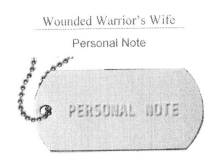

A Personal Note from Author Hannah Conway ...

Dear Reader,

I love you and it doesn't matter that I've never met you. You will now, and forevermore, be on the top of my prayer list. Consider yourself covered in prayer.

Thank you for taking the time to read *The Wounded Warrior's Wife*. I pray that it has blessed you in some way, shape, or form and, if it has, please pass this book on to someone else.

My ultimate goal in writing this book is for you to know that God loves you no matter what, always and forever.

Please connect with me online. I want to hear from you, your thoughts on *The Wounded Warrior's Wife*, and how I can pray for you.

Love,

MORE INSPIRING
CHRISTIAN
FICTION

Wedding a Warrior

By Hannah Conway

The inspiring Prequel to ***The Wounded Warrior's Wife.***

Before they married, Whitleigh and Collier were college sweethearts. Then we became a nation at war and Collier answered his nation's call. Please enjoy this special excerpt from the novella that reveals the details that led to ***The Wounded Warrior's Wife.***

COLLIER slouched against the inside of a phone booth, one hand over his heart, his eyes wide in astonishment. The bright Fort Benning, Georgia morning sun rays bore down on the glass walls allowing intensifying heat to pass through. Sweat and water dripped from the tip of his nose, splattering against the toe of his muddy boots. Slick perspiration soaked him to the core from grueling training, but Whit's response tore at his being more than the demands of any Drill Sergeant.

Soldiers looking as worn as he did stood in a long procession, quarters in hand, waiting their turn for the pay phone. Collier squinted, tears stinging at his eyes. His dry throat cracked as he struggled for words.

"Whit." The only audible word he managed.

"Collier ... I ... what about school? My scholarship? What will my mom and dad say? And what about the mission trip this summer I've been saving — "

"Please, just listen before you say anything else." Collier scratched at his head. "I've been praying about when to propose and I keep hearing now. I know it's crazy."

"Beyond."

"Tell me you don't want to marry me."

"It's not that. You know I do."

"I can take care of you, be a good husband." Collier swiped a hand over his forehead, eyebrows drawn tight. "I drew out a few pie graphs and charts. From the looks of it, I'm pretty sure I can provide a nice life for you, Whit." Collier bit his bottom lip, scratching his thumbnail over a crack in the glass.

"Pie graphs?"

"I even sent a copy of the charts to your dad. He should've gotten them by now."

"Oh, Collier."

"I wish I would've had a chance to ask your dad for your hand in marriage the proper way, but a letter is the best I can do right now. There's just no more time." The line remained silent. Collier wrung the metal phone cord around his wrist. "Whit, it looks like I'm going to be stationed in Colorado for a while and not Fort Campbell like we hoped."

He noted her gulp and twisted his lips to the side. She usually said more.

"Whit, you're the only one I want at my side. I don't know how often I'll be able to come see you when I'm out west for a few years, and well, long distant relationships …." he let the sentence end. "Please say something, anything."

"I want to say yes, Collier. I do … but …."

"Then say yes, Whit." Did his voice sound too pleading? "I know this isn't a proper proposal. I'm sorry about that — I am. Whit, I love you, and I know you love me. Let's take a leap of faith and do this. Be my wife Whitleigh Haynes, and make me the happiest man in the world."

"Collier."

"Whit, what's holding you back? You love me, right?"

"That's not even a question." She made a clicking noise with her mouth. "You make it sound so easy to say yes."

"It is."

Whitleigh's laugh sounded exhausted. "This isn't what we planned."

"Plans work out in a perfect world, not this one." He rested an arm on top of the black metal phone box. "I'm positive there are excellent universities out in Colorado, and other scholarships. I'll make sure we have the means so you can finish and become a teacher. I want to help make that dream come true for you. Help make my dream come true and marry me."

"You're asking me to marry you in a few months, drop my summer plans, move to Colorado, and leave everything I've ever known."

"I'm asking you to take a leap of faith with me." Collier closed his eyes, sending up a prayer. *Please say yes.*

The ebook version of **Wedding a Warrior** is also available from Olivia Kimbrell Press™ wherever fine books are sold. Download a copy from your favorite online bookseller today.

More Great Reads From Olivia Kimbrell Press

SEVEN women from different backgrounds and social classes come together on the common ground of a shared faith during the second World War. Each will earn a code name of a heavenly virtue. Each will risk discovery and persevere in the face of terrible odds. One will be called upon to make the ultimate sacrifice.

Best-selling, award winning Christian author, **Hallee Bridgeman,** presents a labor of love years in the making. Each story is inspired by actual events and based on genuine unsung heavenly heroines who risked everything for the Allied cause during the second World War.

Part 1	Temperance's Trial
Part 2	Homeland's Hope
Part 3	Charity's Code
Part 4	A Parcel for Prudence
Part 5	Grace's Ground War
Part 6	Mission of Mercy
Part 7	Flight of Faith

INSPIRED by real events, these are stories of Virtues and Valor.

Find out more at www.oliviakimbrellpress.com